Praise for Annelise Ryan and her Mattie Winston series

"The funniest deputy coroner to cut up a corpse since, well, ever!"
—Laura Levine, author of *Killer Cruise*

"A puzzler of a mystery. Annelise Ryan has created a smart and saucy heroine in Mattie Winston . . . What a thrill ride!"
—*New York Times* bestselling author Jenn McKinlay

"Has it all: suspense, laughter, a spicy dash of romance."
—*New York Times* bestselling author Tess Gerritsen

"Entertaining . . . Another winning mystery."
—*New York Times* bestselling author Leann Sweeney

"Sassy, sexy, and suspenseful."
—*New York Times* bestselling author Carolyn Hart

"[Ryan] smoothly blends humor, distinctive characters, and authentic forensic detail."
—*Publishers Weekly*

"The forensic details will interest Patricia Cornwell readers . . . while the often slapstick humor and the blossoming romance between Mattie and Hurley will draw Evanovich fans."

**Books by Annelise Ryan (who also writes
as Allyson K. Abbott):**

Working Stiff
Scared Stiff
Frozen Stiff
Lucky Stiff
Board Stiff
Stiff Penalty
Stiff Competition
Dead in the Water
Dead Calm

**Books by Allyson K. Abbott (who also writes
as Annelise Ryan):**

A Mack's Bar Mystery:

Murder on the Rocks
Murder with a Twist
In the Drink
Shots in the Dark
A Toast to Murder

DEAD IN THE WATER

Annelise
Ryan

KENSINGTON BOOKS
http://www.kensingtonbooks.com

KENSINGTON BOOKS are published by

Kensington Publishing Corp.
119 West 40th Street
New York, NY 10018

All Kensington titles, imprints and distributed lines are available at special quantity discounts for bulk purchases for sales promotion, premiums, fund-raising, educational or institutional use. Special book excerpts or customized printings can also be created to fit specific needs. For details, write or phone the office of the Kensington Special Sales Manager: Kensington Publishing Corp., 119 West 40th Street, New York, NY, 10018. Attn. Special Sales Department. Phone: 1-800-221-2647.

Kensington and the K logo Reg. U.S. Pat. & TM Off.

ISBN-13: 978-1-4967-0666-9
ISBN-10: 1-4967-0666-8
First Kensington Hardcover Edition: March 2017
First Kensington Mass Market Edition: January 2018

eISBN-13: 978-1-4967-0667-6
eISBN-10: 1-4967-0667-6
First Kensington Electronic Edition: March 2017

10 9 8 7 6 5 4 3 2 1   33614080495905

Printed in the United States of America

For Peter . . . thanks for your faith in me.

ACKNOWLEDGMENTS

So many people are involved in the writing of my books. There are the friends and coworkers who brainstorm with me, and let me steal their witty bon mots, and tell their friends about the books, and provide me with endless observations and traits that I then roll into my characters. Have fun finding bits of yourselves in the text! There is my editor, Peter Senftleben, who is insightful, smart, and a delight to work with. There is my agent, Adam Chromy, who believes in me more than I believe in myself at times. There is Morgan Elwell, whose ongoing efforts to publicize and market my books are appreciated more than she knows. And there are all those folks behind the scenes at Kensington Books whose hard work goes into making my books a success. It is a pleasure and an honor to work with all of you. Thank you.

Of course the most important people are the readers. Without you, none of this would be possible. So thank you from the bottom of my heart and happy reading!

CHAPTER 1

Death is the ultimate equalizer. It knows no boundaries and visits everyone eventually: the rich, the poor, the young, the old, the beautiful, and the ugly. Sometimes it arrives with relentless predictability; at other times it comes with stealth and surprise. Its arrival may be peaceful, quiet, and well ordered, or it may be agonizing, brash, and messy. The only reliable predictor is that someday it will come. I think knowing this is what gives us humans drive and motivation. It forces us to make the most—or at least the best—of the time we have, because we don't really know when our clocks might stop ticking.

Determining where, when, and how death arrived for someone is the basis of my job. My name is Mattie Winston and I work part-time for the medical examiner's office as a medico-legal death investigator. That's a big fancy term for someone who assists with autopsies and the investigative part of death. Sometimes the investigative part is a slam dunk, like the drunken driver who dies wrapping his car around a tree, or the terminal cancer patient who passes on peacefully in her home. Other times the investigative part can be an annoying, vague, and troubling puzzle of circumstances that may require days, weeks, months, or even years to figure out. When a death is the result of a homicide, it's the job of my office to assist the police in figuring out who, what, when, where, why, and how. The combined efforts of our scientific procedures and law enforcement's investigative work will often provide the necessary answers. But not always. Sometimes we end up with an unsolved case. And sometimes—as is the case with the homicide I'm focused on today—it's a combination of our hard work and a bit of dumb luck. Unfortunately for me, the dumb luck in this case was mine and it might provide enough of a legal loophole for the killer to get off.

Also unfortunate for me is today I have to testify for the first time in the three years I've been doing this job. Since investigation is a key part of what I do, I often get involved in the finding and seizing of evidence and I've been subpoenaed before to testify. I've been coached on the process over the past two years by my boss, Izthak Rybarceski (Izzy to those of us who know and love him), the medical examiner here in Sorenson, Wisconsin. But up until now, I've never had to testify because the cases settled before going to trial, or the evidence I was involved with collecting was either determined irrelevant or simply accepted by both parties.

The investigative process in this current case took a different path than most, however, and the discovery of some key evidence is being contested by the defendant. I'm not going to be able to escape the courtroom this time, and the prosecuting attorney on the case, a thirtysomething man named Roger Beckwith, tried to ease my nervousness by walking me through the planned questions, reminding me to answer only what is asked, and cautioning me not to let my nerves rattle me to the point that I start babbling. Roger

Beckwith, though, is only half of the equation. There's the defense attorney for me to reckon with as well.

I'm sitting outside the courtroom, watching the occasional person walk by and waiting for my summons. There are no other people sitting out here with me, and I've been waiting for over half an hour. The murmur of whatever is going on behind the closed courtroom doors is indistinct yet intimidating. At least three times I've caught myself chewing on my lower lip, and twice I've had to force my left leg to stop bouncing up and down with nervous tension. It's a little after nine in the morning and I've just finished my third cup of coffee, but I still feel logy, thanks to a sleepless night marked by nervous anxiety and a kid who didn't want to sleep. I thought the coffee might get and keep me alert, but now I'm worried I'll have to pee really bad just about the time I'm delivering my key testimony, and I'll either have to ask to be excused or wet my pants. The bathroom isn't too far away, but I'm afraid if I go, they'll call me to testify and think I've flown the coop. I make a mental note to buy and wear a pair of Depends if I have to do this again. I've never wet myself before, but I figure testifying in a criminal court case might be enough to scare the piss out of me.

I'm about to get up from my seat and pace, figuring it will at least work off some of my nervous energy, when the courtroom door opens and the court officer says, "Ms. Winston, they're ready for you."

It's not my first time inside a courtroom, but it is my first time doing anything other than observing. At least I'm here as a witness, not as a defendant or claimant, so I don't have to worry about my future, but it's nerve-wracking walking down the aisle and feeling the stares of everyone on me. I'm afraid of stumbling before I get to the witness-box, or doing something stupid and embarrassing when I do get there, like stuttering, or stammering, or laughing at an inappropriate moment . . . something I do a lot. My nerves tend to express themselves through laughter, and I'm not talking about some tittering, sniggering, cover-your-mouth-and-hide-it kind of giggle. I'm talking about all-out, belly-shaking guffaws. This quirk has kept me from attending a lot of funerals. People don't take kindly to having this ceremonious ritual marked by the sound of a sitcom laugh track. Oddly enough, the only nerve-wracking events that make me cry are weddings. Though perhaps it's not so odd in my case, given my marital history.

As I approach the witness stand, I glance at the defendant, a thirty-three-year-old man named Tomas "Please just call me 'Tommy'" Wyzinski, who is on trial for killing his girlfriend. He is dressed much better today than any other time I've seen him, but his skin is the pasty color of someone who hasn't seen the sun in a while, and his longish hair is slicked back from his face with so much product it looks like the plastic hair on a Ken doll. He doesn't look at me, which is just as well. His eyes creep me out.

I shift my focus to the woman standing in front of the witness stand. I know she's there to swear me in, but suddenly I can't remember for the life of me if I'm supposed to stop before I get into the witness-box or climb straight into it. Then I see her offer the Bible on one extended hand and I stop in front of the witness-box.

"Please place your left hand on the Bible and raise your right hand," the woman instructs. For a moment, my brain is so frozen with nervous tension I can't remember which hand is which. I make a couple of tentative jabs, take a deep breath to center myself, and then do as she instructed.

"Do you solemnly swear that the testimony you shall give in this matter shall be the truth, the whole truth and nothing but the truth, so help you God?"

"I do." Two of the scariest words in the English language. As the woman turns away, I climb the step into the witness-box and take a seat. Roger Beckwith gets up and walks to a lectern centered between his table and the defense's.

"Good morning, Ms. Winston," he says with a warm smile. I return the greeting after making a funny movement with my lips because they're sticking to my dry teeth. "Can you please state for the court your occupation and where you work?"

"Sure. I'm a medico-legal death investigator working out of the medical examiner's office in Sorenson, Wisconsin. I work under the auspices of Dr. Izthak Rybarceski and in conjunction with the Sorenson police when necessary."

"How long have you had this position?"

"For three years."

"And what exactly is it you do in the course of your job?"

"I assist Dr. Rybarceski with autopsies and I investigate the means, locations, situations, and circumstances surrounding any suspicious deaths."

Beckwith makes a somber face that he aims at the jury. "Sounds like difficult, complicated work. It must be hard dealing with death and dying all the time like that, day in and day out."

My nerves relax a little. So far, everything is going the way Beckwith said it would, right down to his comment about my job, which is to provide me with an opening to pontificate on how much I love my work and how dedicated I am to it. I'm supposed to do this in a way that makes me seem friendly and approachable, yet professional. Beckwith's exact words to me were "try to come across to the jury as professional and dedicated, but not macabre or weird." So I practiced in front of my mirror all week, stating how much I enjoyed my work, how satisfying it was, and how those of us in the medical examiner's office have to step in and be the voices of the dead . . . all of it done with various vocal tones and facial expressions that made me seem maniacal and scary one minute and Valiumed to the gills the next. After three days of practice, I felt I had achieved the perfect mix of professionalism and normalcy so that my fascination and daily work with the dead didn't sound like I was someone who kept their mummified mother in a closet somewhere.

I prepare to deliver my well-rehearsed lines, but before I can, the defense attorney—a petite, blond woman named Joan Mackey, who bears a striking resemblance to the murder victim in this case—interrupts.

"Objection," she says in a rote tone of voice as if she's bored. "There is no question there. And the defense is willing to stipulate to Ms. Winston's current job title and experience."

The judge says, "Sustained," sounding as bored as Joan Mackey, an unusually tame response for him.

I'm a little perturbed—after all my practice, I'm going to be bummed if I can't recite my job-loving mantra—but one look at Judge Wesley Kupper makes me swallow my own objection.

Judge Kupper would be an intimidating man even without his position of authority and his wood-cracking hammer. He's six-and-a-half feet tall, weighs in the neighborhood of three-fifty, has no neck, and speaks in a deep, rumbling voice that sounds like thunder. When he walks into the courtroom with his massive black robe billowing out around him, it's hard not to compare him to Darth Vader. His blue eyes are pale and icy—when he looks at you, it's as if he can see right through you—and his head is as bald—and as big—as a bowling ball. Whenever he shifts his position, his large leather chair groans beneath his weight like a house about to be ripped off its moorings.

"Is there a question in there somewhere, Mr. Beckwith?" Judge Kupper asks in a tired tone. "If not, please move on."

"Very well," Beckwith says. He gives the jury members a

tolerant smile and then looks back at me. "Ms. Winston, what did you do before taking your current job?"

"Objection!" says Mackey with much more enthusiasm than before. "Relevance?"

"It's very relevant to the issue in question," Beckwith says. "Ms. Winston's background and prior employment directly impacted her actions on the day in question."

Mackey shakes her head and rolls her eyes.

"Overruled," Judge Kupper says.

"Thank you, Your Honor," Beckwith says, and then he shifts his attention back to me. "Ms. Winston, please tell the court what job you held prior to your position in the medical examiner's office."

"I was . . . technically I still am an RN, a registered nurse. I was employed at the hospital in Sorenson for thirteen years—six in the emergency department and seven in the surgical department."

"Thank you," Beckwith says, scanning the jury members' faces. Per his pretrial counseling, pointing out that I'm a nurse one of the most trusted occupations out there not only helps to make me seem less "creepy," it also gives my testimony more veracity. In this particular case, it will play another, more significant role as well, one Beckwith is about to get to. "Let's move on to August fourteenth of last year, the day in question, the day you and Detective Bob Richmond arrived at the home of the defendant, Tommy Wyzinski. Can you tell me why the two of you went to his house?"

"It started when Detective Richmond and I were called to the scene of a suspicious death that—"

"Objection!" Mackey hollers. "The characterization of the death as suspicious is inflammatory."

Judge Kupper narrows his eyes at Mackey and in a tight-lipped voice says, "Overruled."

Beckwith nods and looks back at me. "Just to satisfy everyone's curiosity here, can you state why this death was determined to be suspicious?"

"Sure. To begin with, the body was wrapped in plastic sheeting and it was found in some woods about a hundred feet from County Road A. We, Detective Richmond and I, felt pretty confident the victim didn't get there under her own power or wrap herself up prior to dying, because the body had no head, hands, or feet."

I'm surprised none of the jury or audience members gasp at this revelation, but there is a lot of uncomfortable stirring and shifting going on.

"Oh, my," Beckwith says with an overwrought grimace he makes sure the jury members can see. Then, with a pointed look at the defense table, he adds, "I think we can all agree that qualifies as suspicious."

There is a snort from the jury box, whether out of humor or derision I can't tell. I look over at them and try to determine who the culprit might have been, but everyone is straight-faced and somber looking.

"Please continue, Ms. Winston."

"In examining the remains and other evidence at the scene, we readily determined the victim was a woman. While surveying the scene and the surrounding area, we found a piece of paper in a parking lot that was approximately one hundred feet away from the wooded area where the body was found. It was a prescription for insulin."

"And was there a name on that prescription?" Beckwith asks.

"There was. It was written out to a Tomas Wyzinski."

"Was there an address on this prescription?"

I shake my head. "No, just the name. But fortunately the name is unusual enough that it was easy to do a computer search and find out where Mr. Wyzinski lived."

"And that's how you ended up in Pardeeville, at the defendant's home?"

"Yes."

"What time of day was it when you arrived at Mr. Wyzinski's house?"

"It was a little after ten in the morning."

"Why did you go to the defendant's house?"

"Given the proximity of the prescription to the scene where the body was found, Mr. Wyzinski was considered a potential witness. The police wanted to find out when he was there and determine if he had seen anything that might be relevant."

"So was Mr. Wyzinski a suspect at this time?"

"He was considered a person of interest," I say, using the term the police use until something more can be determined.

"And can you tell me what happened when you arrived at the defendant's house?"

I nod, sorting my thoughts out to make sure I say everything I need to say. "We . . . Detective Richmond and I walked up to the front door and Detective Richmond knocked. We waited, but there was no answer. After a minute or so, Detective Richmond knocked again. And again there was no answer."

"Did you leave at this point?"

"We did not. There was a car parked in front of the house and Detective Richmond determined it belonged to Mr. Wyzinski. Since the address was out in the country and the closest house was two miles down the road, we figured Wyzinski was probably around, maybe somewhere else on the property. So we headed for the back of the house."

"What did you see at the back of the house?"

"There was another entrance, a back door, and there was also an old barn about fifty feet behind the house."

"What did you and Detective Richmond do next?"

"We climbed the steps to the back door and knocked on it."

"Did anyone answer?"

"No, but this door had glass in the upper half and Detective Richmond looked inside."

"What did he see?"

"Objection!"

Beckwith raises his hand in a conciliatory gesture before Mackey can voice the reason behind her objection and rewords the question. "Did you also look through the window in the back door?"

"I did."

"What did you see?"

"A man prostrate . . ." I hear Beckwith's voice in my head reminding me to keep my terms simple and aimed at the layperson, and amend my answer. "There was a man lying face down on the kitchen floor."

"And what did you do next?"

"I reached down and tried the knob to see if the door was unlocked."

"Was it?"

I nod.

"Please state your answer for the record," Beckwith prompts.

"Sorry. Yes, it was unlocked."

"What happened next?"

"I opened the door, went inside, and knelt down next to the man on the floor. I felt along his neck for a pulse."

"Did you find one?"

I nod, then quickly say, "Yes, I did. But it was very faint, thready, and irregular. I shook him then, and he mumbled, but it wasn't anything intelligible."

"What was Detective Richmond doing at this point?"

"He was calling for an ambulance and checking to see if anyone else was in the house."

"Were there other things you noticed about the man on the floor?"

"Yes, his skin was very cool to the touch, and he was

diaph—" I catch myself and do a quick mental conversion. "He was very sweaty."

"Is the man you saw on the kitchen floor that day here in the courtroom today?"

"Yes, it was the defendant." I point. "Mr. Tomas Wyzinski."

"Objection!" Mackey says, shooting out of her seat, her tone one of impatient disbelief. "The witness had no way of knowing at the time if the man on the floor was my client or someone else."

"Actually, I did have a way," I say before anyone else can respond. "Detective Richmond showed me a DMV picture of Mr. Wyzinski prior to our arrival. The man on the floor fit that picture. Though to be honest, knowing who he was wouldn't have changed what I did in any way."

"Your Honor . . . ," Mackey says in a strained tone.

"Overruled," Judge Kupper thunders.

Mackey drops back into her seat with a pout, and after watching her do this, Beckwith turns to me with a little smile. "Ms. Winston, would you please share with the court some of the thoughts going through your mind when you found this man on the floor and how those thoughts led to what happened next?"

"Of course," I say. "The prescription we found at the body dump site was for insulin and the man on the floor was displaying classic signs of insulin shock—decreased alertness, sweating, and cold, clammy skin. When I rolled him onto his back, his shirt hiked up, and I could see tiny pinpoint bruises on his abdomen. I knew from my years of nursing that those were injection marks. The abdomen is the preferred site for insulin shots in most diabetics. Given all of that, it was a pretty safe assumption the man on the floor was the same one whose name was on that prescription, particularly since he was the owner of record for the house we were in."

Mackey looks apoplectic, like she wants to object, but she doesn't. I don't know if it's because I'm talking as fast as I can to get it all out, or because what I'm saying isn't objectionable—at least from a legal standpoint. Maybe it's both.

Beckwith nods solemnly and then says, "Just to clarify things, did you at any point verify the identity of the man on the floor in any other way?"

"We did. Detective Richmond removed a wallet from the man's pants pocket and the ID inside belonged to Tomas Wyzinski. But as I said before, his identity wasn't an issue at the time and wouldn't have changed what I did next."

Mackey is frowning now, her forehead heavily creased, her mouth turned down at the corners.

Beckwith has the barest hint of a smile on his face as he asks his next question. "What did you do next?"

"Well, the treatment for insulin shock is sugar in some form. If a diabetic is completely unconscious and unresponsive, some form of injectable sugar is preferred to ensure they don't choke. But if they have some level of alertness and appear to be able to swallow, then some juice, like orange juice, preferably with a spoonful of sugar thrown in, is a good option. Hard candies can work, too, but they are slower acting and more likely to be a choking hazard. Mr. Wyzinski wasn't alert enough to walk, or talk sensibly, but he was mumbling and he wasn't drooling, meaning he was able to swallow his own secretions. So I got up and went to the refrigerator in search of some juice to give to him."

"And what did you find in the refrigerator?" Beckwith asks, and I swear the corners of his mouth are twitching in an effort not to smile.

This time my answer garners plenty of gasps, both from the jury and the others in the courtroom. "I found a woman's head."

CHAPTER 2

"A woman's head?" Beckwith says with mild revulsion once the gasps have died down. He glances at the jury members with a horrified expression. "Was this an actual human head?"

"Yes, it was."

"And it was in the refrigerator?"

"Objection," Mackey says, sounding a little defeated. "Asked and answered."

"Sustained," Judge Kupper says. "Move along, Mr. Beckwith."

"Sorry, Your Honor," Beckwith says, looking genuinely apologetic even though I'm certain he's not. "Ms. Winston, was this head you saw in the refrigerator in plain sight?"

"Yes. It was on a shelf at eye level, right in the front. There was plastic wrap around it, but it was clear and I could easily see the facial features through the plastic."

"And what did you do once you found the head?"

"I called Detective Richmond over to the refrigerator and

showed it to him. We both donned gloves, and after shooting some pictures of the inside of the refrigerator, we removed the head so we could get a better look at it."

Beckwith walks over to his table, picks up a picture, and shows it to me. It's a shot of the head, wrapped up like some forgotten leftover, lying sideways on the refrigerator shelf. "Is this one of the pictures you took?"

"It is." He then parades it in front of the jury members, all of whom look aghast. "Ms. Winston, can you walk us through the process you went through to retain this head as evidence?"

I do so, citing all the steps in the process of bagging the head at the scene, transporting it to the medical examiner's office with it always in my presence in order to assure the chain of evidence, and then processing it into the department.

"Was the head eventually identified as belonging to someone?" Beckwith asks when I'm done.

"Yes. Initially Izzy . . . Dr. Rybarceski confirmed through photographs and dental records, and later with DNA, that the head belonged to the body we found, that of Marla Weber."

"Thank you. I have no further questions at this time."

I swallow hard, preparing myself for Ms. Mackey's onslaught. Beckwith had warned me the cross-examination could be brutal, and that the attorneys often try to rattle opposing witnesses by obfuscating the facts until the witness either becomes confused or sounds as if they are contradicting themselves.

"Ms. Winston," Mackey says, approaching me with the fakest-looking smile I've seen in a long time. She is wearing a formfitting, tailored suit with sensible pumps, and her hair and makeup are impeccable. Her resemblance to the victim, Marla Weber, is striking and a bit unsettling, making me wonder if she was chosen to defend Wyzinski precisely for this reason. The firm she works for is a big, high-powered one out of Milwaukee—Wyzinski's very well-to-do family is from there—and there are plenty of other, more seasoned attorneys who could have done the job. But I can see how the subliminal message delivered by having a woman who looks like the victim working with, smiling with, consulting with, and acting unafraid with the suspected killer might prove valuable.

Mackey walks up to the podium, studying the lined tablet she has in her hands. "Ms. Winston, you told the court this man you saw on the kitchen floor of the house appeared to be in insulin shock." At this point, she looks up at me, pinning me with her steely gaze. "Are you a doctor?"

"No."

"Then how is it you're able to diagnose this condition?"

"Insulin shock is a common problem for diabetics and I saw it dozens of times when I worked in the ER. It's something we are trained to respond to quickly, with or without a physician present."

"I see," Mackey says, sounding like she doesn't see at all. "Isn't it standard, however, to first check the blood sugar on the patient using a finger prick and a blood glucose meter before treating them?"

"Yes, if the meter is available."

"Was there a meter at Mr. Wyzinski's house?"

"Not that we saw in the kitchen."

"Did you look for one?"

"I did not."

"Did you ask Detective Richmond to look for one?"

"I did not." I'm tempted to try to explain my rationale, but I hold back. Beckwith told me to stick to basic "yes" and "no" answers whenever possible and to resist the urge to pontificate or expound further.

"I see," Mackey says. She gives the jury a pointed look while I work at keeping my face impassive. "So you came to this diagnosis of insulin shock based on the man's physical condition, is that right?"

"Yes."

"So his cool, clammy skin and his altered mental state were the symptoms you based your decision on?"

"In part, yes. He also—"

"Yes, yes, you said the prescription you found near, not at, but near the body dump site was for insulin, so you assumed the man on the floor was the person the prescription was written for, is that right?"

"Yes," I say, a bit hesitantly, trying to parse out her every word to make sure she isn't tricking me into saying something I don't mean.

"So with no proof whatsoever of who the man on the floor was, you immediately jumped to the conclusion that he was Tomas Wyzinski and therefore a diabetic in insulin shock."

"Objection," Beckwith says. "Is there a question in there?" He states this in a smug tone, I suspect, to point out to Mackey that he's using her prior objection against her.

Before Judge Kupper can respond, Mackey holds up her hand and says, "Ms. Winston, are there other conditions that present with the same symptoms you observed in this man you found on the floor?"

"Yes."

"Can you give me some examples?"

"Well, essentially any condition that causes a drop in the blood pressure or heart rate, or any sort of shock, can cause those symptoms."

"I see. And would the treatment for any of those other conditions lead to you looking in the refrigerator?"

I don't answer immediately. My brain runs through several shock scenarios and I try to determine what actions I might take. "No," I admit eventually, "but—"

"And these bruises you say you saw on the abdomen of the man on the floor, the bruises you said were injection sites, are there any other drugs besides insulin that might be injected into someone's abdomen that would cause the same sort of bruises?"

"Yes, but—"

"Couldn't the man on the floor have been a relative of Mr. Wyzinski's? A father, or brother, or cousin? Or perhaps even an acquaintance of some type who happened to resemble Mr. Wyzinski?"

"Yes, I suppose so. But as I said before, Detective Richmond had shown me the DMV photo of Tomas Wyzinski prior to our arrival, and the man on the floor looked like that picture."

"Yes, except you said he was pale, and clammy, and appeared to be in shock . . . all of which would alter one's appearance, wouldn't you agree?"

"A little bit, I suppose."

"So the man on the floor could have been a relative of some sort with a strong family resemblance?"

"Objection," Beckwith says. "Asked and answered. And relevance."

"Sustained," Judge Kupper says. "Ms. Mackey, I think it's clear Ms. Winston would have responded in the manner she did regardless of who the person on the floor was."

Mackey looks perturbed, but she hardly misses a beat. "Ms. Winston, you said Detective Richmond had already called for emergency responders to come to the house. Couldn't you have waited until they arrived to treat this man on the floor?"

I have to bite back a smile. Mackey's stubborn refusal to refer to the man on the floor as Tomas Wyzinski is laughable. "No, ma'am," I say. "Insulin shock can kill someone in a matter of minutes when it gets to the point it was in this case, and we were out in the country. That area is served by volunteer EMTs, and the response time could have proven fatal."

"So because of your previous job as a nurse, you felt you needed to do something for the man on the floor right away in order to save his life, is that right?"

"Yes."

"And that was the only reason for opening the refrigerator?"

"Yes."

Mackey walks over and picks up the picture Beckwith had shown earlier. "Permission to approach the witness," she says.

"Permission granted," Judge Kupper says.

She walks up to me and shows me the picture, tapping one part of it. "And when you found this head in there, did you go ahead and reach past it to grab this bottle of orange juice that was behind it?"

"No."

"I see. Well, then, what did you take from the refrigerator to treat Mr. Wyzinski's life-threatening, time-sensitive condition?"

"I didn't remove anything from the fridge," I admit. "I didn't want to risk disturbing the evidence."

"Really?" Mackey says in a tone of disbelief. "So you entered my client's house without an invitation and opened his refrigerator—also without an invitation—all supposedly so you could play nurse and treat this life-threatening condition you thought he had, but then you did nothing for him. Is that right?"

"Well, the—"

"Yes or no, please, Ms. Winston. Did you at any point do anything to treat the man on the floor?"

"No."

Mackey shakes her head in dismay and lets out a *"tsk"* for the benefit of the jury. She takes a long moment before asking her next question and I'm not sure if the pause is so she can gather her wits, or rattle mine. But I learned long ago how to play the silence-is-awkward game. You can cue the crickets all day long and I'm content just to sit back and listen to them.

"Ms. Winston," Mackey says finally, "you stated to Mr. Beckwith here that you and Detective Richmond took pictures of the head you say you found in the refrigerator. Don't you normally shoot video in these situations?"

"We use video for some things," I tell her. "In this case, we weren't approaching Mr. Wyzinski as a suspect, but rather as a person of interest. Had he answered his door and agreed to sit down and chat with us, then we would have used a video camera."

"I see," Mackey says. Clearly this is her standard phrase. "Did you take any pictures before you opened the refrigerator?" I start to answer, but she goes on before I can. "For instance, did you take a picture of the man on the floor from outside the door before you entered the house? Or did you take a picture of him after you entered the house?"

"No, and no."

"Did you take any pictures of the kitchen before you opened the refrigerator?"

"No."

"And these pinpoint bruises you said you saw on the man's abdomen, did you take any pictures of those?"

"No."

"So basically, we only have your word that the head you took back to your office was found in the refrigerator of Mr. Wyzinski's house?"

I hesitate, giving a little sideways nod of my head before answering. "My word and Detective Richmond's."

"No further questions," Mackey says, spinning on one of her sensible pumps in a quick, dismissive manner and heading back to her table.

"Redirect, Your Honor?" Beckwith says, rising from his chair.

The judge grants him permission to ask more questions. "Ms. Winston, why didn't you treat Mr. Wyzinski?"

"To be honest, I was thrown a little by the discovery of the head and less than a minute later one of the EMTs who was on call arrived at the house. I found out later this particular EMT lives just down the road from the Wyzinski house and on that day he arrived on the scene in his private vehicle. This EMT happens to be a diabetic also, and he had some glucagon—an injectable form of sugar—with him. So he treated Mr. Wyzinski with that."

Beckwith turns and looks at the defendant. "Obviously, the treatment worked," he says. "Did you see an improvement in Mr. Wyzinski's condition while you were there?"

"I did. Insulin shock can be reversed very easily and quickly if you treat it in time. Within two or three minutes of receiving that glucagon injection, Mr. Wyzinski was alert, his pulse was stronger and steadier, and he was no longer sweating or clammy."

"Is it safe to say that if not for you and Detective Richmond arriving at Mr. Wyzinski's house when you did and taking the actions you did, Mr. Wyzinski would have died?"

"Almost certainly," I say quickly because I see Mackey is about to object. She does, but not before my answer is heard.

"Objection! Relevance?"

"Withdrawn," Beckwith says, and then he follows it with "No further questions, Your Honor."

To me, Mackey's objection is painfully ironic. It's as if she is objecting to the fact that I saved her client's life, something I'm inclined to object to myself. After seeing what he did to Marla Weber, and looking into his cold, emotionless eyes, I'm not sure saving his life was the right thing to do.

I am dismissed and leave the courtroom feeling like a huge weight has been lifted off my shoulders. I exit the courthouse into a beautifully sunny, cloudless June morning, and while I know I need to head to my office, the thought of being cooped up inside anywhere seems stifling. As soon as I get into my car—a midnight-blue, slightly used hearse with so many body reinforcements the POTUS could safely ride in it—I take out my cell phone, turn the ringer back on, and check for missed calls, chagrined to see three from my office. Two years ago, when I was pregnant with my son, Matthew, there was a crazy man trying to kill me. He almost succeeded, and after the first attempt, Detective Steve Hurley, the love of my life, the father of my child, and, for lack of a better term, my current cohabitation partner, had my car done up like the Popemobile. It now has steel-reinforced side panels, bulletproof glass, and run-flat tires. While the irony of bulletproofing a car intended for transporting dead people isn't lost on me, I have to admit I feel very safe inside my hearse. It has a few other perks, too.

I start the engine, which purrs like a kitten, and as I shift into reverse and start backing out of my parking place, I tell my phone to call the office. Cass, our receptionist/file clerk/secretary, answers on the first ring; and thanks to caller ID, she forgoes any greeting niceties.

"Mattie, are you done testifying?" she says right off.

"I am. What's up?"

"Izzy called in—he's sick with some sort of stomach bug. I made some calls and found someone to cover for him, but he can't get here for another hour or so. And we just got a call for a body here in town. I would have tried Hal, but he's in Chicago for the day."

"I'll take the call," I tell her. "Text me the address."

"Already did."

I smile at her efficiency, and after disconnecting the call, I give one last, wistful look at the brilliantly blue June sky. My beautiful summer morning is about to get ugly.

CHAPTER 3

For the young woman on the floor at my feet, I think it's safe to say death came with stealth and surprise, and while it may have been well ordered initially, it's definitely messy now. She has been dead for several days, lying on her kitchen floor, waiting for someone to find her. There is an oft-repeated saying in the *Book of Common Prayer* about death and committing one's body to the ground: earth to earth, ashes to ashes, dust to dust. This makes the whole process sound orderly and tidy . . . almost sterile. And in today's supposedly civilized society, the only aspects of death most people are typically exposed to are just that. But death can be—and often is—very messy.

I'm wearing a Tyvek bodysuit with a plastic face shield, booties, and a mask. The mask is not to hide the smell—those nasty odiferous molecules have a way of seeping into every crack and crevice—but because we don't yet know what killed the woman. On the chance it might be some airborne disease or other type of infectious agent, I don't want to breathe the death-infested air. The rest of my protective gear serves two purposes. One is to protect me from the detritus of death and decomposition; the other is to protect our scene from contamination.

I've grown used to the sights and smells that accompany my job, but today's miasma is particularly bad timing. I know from past experience that while my gear may keep most of the nasty stuff off me, the cloying, sickly-sweet smell of death and decay will cling and linger despite my best efforts.

For the past ten minutes or so, I've been snapping pictures of the scene, sidestepping the body as I try to get a shot of it from every possible angle. There are two uniformed cops standing in the room with me: Brenda Joiner and Patrick Devonshire. Brenda seems immune to the smells and sights, but Patrick is having a harder time of it. He keeps putting his hand over his mask—whether to keep outside stuff out, or his inside stuff in, I'm not sure—and the color of his skin is a mix of pasty whiteness with a touch of green around his gills.

"Patrick, you can leave if you want," I tell him, snapping a close-up picture of the jewelry on the woman's right hand: a simple gold-colored bracelet and three rings, none of which look expensive. Her fingertips are nearly gone, I notice, most likely a combination of decay and insect activity, but out of sync with the condition of the rest of her body.

Patrick eyes the corpse with trepidation and for a second I think he's going to take me up on my offer to leave. However, his machismo kicks in and he shakes his head, which is then followed by a barely suppressed gag.

"If you puke on my crime scene, I'm going to be pissed." This statement comes from Hurley, the primary homicide detective here in Sorenson. At the moment, he is sifting through a stack of envelopes on the counter. "This mail is all addressed to a Carolyn Abernathy," he says.

"That's who the neighbors said lives here," Patrick offers.

"Does she live here alone?"

"No, she has a roommate, but she's out of town. A couple of the neighbors mentioned a recent boyfriend who spent the night a time or two, but they're pretty sure he wasn't living here."

This triggers one of my pet peeves. "Speaking of living together," I say to no one in particular, though I'm hoping a different topic might distract Patrick, who is looking greener every minute, "why hasn't anyone come up with a good term for heterosexuals who live together?"

"What do you mean?" Brenda says.

"Well, how do you describe a relationship with someone you live with? Take Hurley and me. We've been living together for nearly a year now, but whenever I try to explain our relationship to someone who doesn't know us, I can't come up with a term that doesn't sound confusing, contrived, or immature. He's not my husband . . ."

"Not yet," Hurley tosses out with a wink.

". . . and it sounds silly to use terms like 'girlfriend' and 'boyfriend' when you're past a certain age, not to mention the parents of a child together. Gays have kind of stolen the whole 'partner' and 'life partner' thing, so that doesn't work."

"I disagree," Patrick says, and I'm happy to see his color is moving a little more toward the red end of the spectrum.

"Trust me, they have," I tell him. "When I went to a forensic conference a few months ago, I told the woman sitting next to me that I shared a house with my life partner. A short time later, she hit on me, and when I explained to her that I was straight, she was ticked off that I'd led her on. Apparently, the term 'life partner' implies things I didn't realize."

"Apparently, it implies impermanence to her," Brenda

scoffs. "Hitting on you when you've just told her you're in a committed relationship makes her a skank."

"Maybe you give off a strong lesbian vibe," Patrick says, his eyes narrowing in thought. I can't tell from his expression—what little of it I can see above his mask—if this idea intrigues or disappoints him. Since this new line of thinking has brought some color back into his face, I continue with the thread.

"So if you eliminate the terms 'partner' or 'life partner,' all you're left with are stupid, cumbersome things, like 'significant other,' or 'cohabitation partner,' or 'housemate,' all of which still leave both the nature of the relationship and the gender ambiguous."

"It's something you won't have to worry about much longer," Hurley says. "As soon as we're married, you can resort to the tried-and-true husband-and-wife descriptors."

"There you go," Brenda says. "You can refer to Hurley as your fiancé."

"Technically, yes," I say, glancing at the naked third finger on my left hand. "But what if we weren't planning on getting married?" Hurley frowns at this. "What if we were just living together?" I go on, ignoring him. The subject of an official engagement, complete with ring, had come up between me and Hurley a number of times over the past year or two, but I kept insisting on not having a ring. I knew from past experience with the engagement ring my ex-husband, David, had given me that those faceted stones are a nightmare when you're donning and doffing latex gloves all day long. The ring tears the glove nearly every time, so I was forced to take the ring off whenever I worked. Unfortunately, I wasn't very ritualistic about where and when I removed it and the end result was a lost diamond ring. I no longer work in the hospital, but I still have to don and doff gloves on a regular basis and in a greater variety of places, and I don't want to risk losing another engagement ring. Besides, I'm not real big on jewelry. Other than earrings for my pierced ears and the occasional necklace I might put on if I'm getting dressed up, I don't wear any. "Lots of people live together these days without any plans to marry," I go on. "So what term can they use?"

"There's always the old-fashioned, but ever so reliable, terms like 'old man' and 'old lady,' or the 'old ball and chain,'" Patrick quips.

"Right," I say, giving him a withering look. "I'm just saying that in this enlightened age where the types and structures of relationships are morphing almost daily, it seems odd that no one has come up with a good, catchy term to describe cohabitating people."

"Let's think of one," Brenda says. "What about 'cohab'? Like a shortening of 'cohabitation.'"

I shrug. "It's not bad, but it still leaves gender and the nature of the relationship in question. That can lead to confusion, like I experienced with the woman at the conference."

"Can't you just refer to Hurley as your roommate?" asks Jonas Kriedeman. Jonas is an evidence tech for the police department, and the two of us are working the room together. I and my camera are following behind him as he places plastic numbered tents next to anything of evidentiary value and logs each tent number and its corresponding item or area in a notebook.

"Not really," I tell Jonas. "It doesn't imply the bonded nature of our relationship, nor does it indicate gender."

"I've got an idea," Patrick says. "What about 'he-mate' and 'she-mate'?"

Silence falls over the room as we all contemplate his suggestion. "I like it," I say after a moment, snapping a picture of the double-sided kitchen sink. Inside the right half of the sink is a full dish rack. On the left side is a half-scrubbed pan with the burnt residue of something inside it, and a pair of yellow dishwashing gloves. I've gotten ahead of Jonas at this point, so I nod toward the gloves and pan and wait for Jonas to set down some tents before I aim and shoot.

"She-mate," Hurley says slowly, like it's something he's taste-testing. "It's not bad."

"It could work," Brenda agrees.

"Nice job, Patrick," I say. "Now all we have to do is convince the rest of society to start using it."

"I'll take out an ad in the paper first thing tomorrow," Patrick jokes. His gaze has gone back to the woman on the floor and I see his Adam's apple bounce up and down as he swallows hard several times.

"I have some Vicks in my bag there, Patrick, if you want to dab a little under your nose. I always carry it for those of you who have weak constitutions."

"I'll be fine," he says, though his appearance belies his words. He drags his eyes from the corpse and looks at me. "Doesn't it ever get to you?"

"It did a few times when I was pregnant, but otherwise I seem to manage. Besides, I've spent the last few weeks dealing with potty-training attempts on a kid who poops toxic waste. This is nothing."

Hurley scoffs. "Boy, you aren't kidding! What the hell are you feeding our kid when I'm not watching? Even Hoover won't go near Matthew's dirty diapers, and that dog rolls in rotting garbage and decaying animal guts every chance he gets."

I wince, though no one can see it behind my mask, thinking the mention of decaying anything isn't wise. My suspicion is confirmed when I look over at Patrick and see the Grinch color returning. Hurley sees it, too. He steps in front of Patrick, blocking his view of the victim, and says, "Okay, give me the bullets on our victim, everything you've found out so far."

Patrick swallows several more times as he takes out his

notebook and flips the pages. "Carolyn Abernathy, age twenty-eight," he starts, his voice only a little shaky. "She lives here with a female roommate, works in the business office at the health clinic next to the hospital, and attends school at the Madison Area Technical College at the east Madison campus. She has a sister, Christine Abernathy, who lives in Ohio. The sister tried several times over the weekend to reach Carolyn and left several messages. She never got a call back, so she called the clinic this morning and they told her Carolyn called in sick on Friday and didn't show up for her scheduled shift this morning. So the sister called and asked us to do a welfare check."

"Was the house locked when you arrived?" Hurley asks.

"It was. Brenda and I scouted around the place and found a bedroom window open partway. We could smell . . . well . . . that," he says, glancing toward the body and then quickly looking away. "So we figured we better get inside. We pushed out the screen, and then I gave Brenda a boost in."

"No signs of any forced entry?"

Both Brenda and Patrick shake their heads. "No sign of anything being out of place in the house, either," Brenda adds. "The TV was on when I came in and I turned it off, but everything else is exactly how we found it."

A trickle of sweat runs down my back, creating an itch I won't be able to scratch. The inside of the house is quite warm. While the temperatures today are only going to hit the high seventies, over the weekend we had a mini heat wave with temps in the low nineties. "Does this place not have air-conditioning, or was it not turned on?" I ask.

Brenda shrugs and walks into the living room, presumably in search of a thermostat.

"Did the clinic say if Carolyn told them what was wrong with her when she called in on Friday?" I ask Patrick.

He nods. "She said she had a migraine headache and vomiting." The mention of the word "vomiting" seems to divert his attention back to the body, and after a quick glance, he swallows hard and squeezes his eyes shut.

I log the headache complaint in my brain, thinking it might give us a clue about what caused her death. It's too soon to tell if there is any type of lethal trauma to the body, such as stab wounds or bullet holes, but I doubt we'll find any. There is some liquid on the floor that has come from her body, but none of it is blood.

"The house has central air, but it wasn't turned on," Brenda announces, returning to the kitchen. "I flipped it on long enough to hear something kick on in the basement, so I'm guessing it works, but I turned it back off again so it wouldn't affect anything with our scene."

I nod and do some mental calculations. "Based on the level of decomposition, I'm going to say our victim has been dead on the floor since sometime Friday morning or late afternoon. We might be able to be more precise as to time, once the insect activity is analyzed. Although . . ." I look around at the floor near the body. There are dozens of dead flies and maggots surrounding the body, particularly near the hands.

"What?" Hurley asks.

"It's odd that all these insects are dead. It makes me think they ingested something that killed them. I think there's a possibility our victim was poisoned. It would explain the lack of trauma."

Hurley nods and scribbles something down in his notebook.

"Of course we won't know for sure until we do the autopsy," I add. "Some sort of disease or contagion is also a possibility."

This comment makes everyone, except Jonas and me, take a step back away from the body. I notice Patrick is looking bug-eyed and green again.

"What was she going to school for?" I ask. It's probably

not relevant to anything, but I want to keep Patrick talking and distracted as much as possible.

"She was in nursing school," Patrick says. "Just finished her first year, according to her sister."

This fact makes the likelihood of disease a little more likely and I make a mental note of the fact.

Charlotte "Charlie" Finnegan enters the kitchen, returning from her filming duties in the rest of the house. As our official videographer, she arrived on the scene when Hurley and I did, and videotaped the kitchen before going through the rest of the house. The combination of her videography and my photos will provide a detailed depiction of the scene that anyone can consult later if needed.

"All done," Charlie announces. "The only thing I saw that looked askew was a bedroom window that was open with the screen knocked out."

"That was us," Patrick says. His eyes haven't left Charlie since she walked in; as a result, his color is once again much improved. As distractions go, Charlie is a major one. She's a stunningly beautiful redhead in her late twenties. Ever since her initial arrival at the police department, she's been turning heads, Hurley's included. I'd love to hate her, but she's also smart, friendly, and funny—just the kind of woman I'd like to have as a friend. It's created quite the conundrum for me.

"Where's Izzy?" Charlie asks.

"He's sick," I tell her. "He called in this morning and said he had some kind of stomach bug. Unfortunate timing for me. I was hoping to get off a little early today, but with a sub coming in, I don't think I'll be able."

"What about the new guy?" Brenda asks. "Can't he cover for you?"

The new guy Brenda is referring to is Harold "Hal" Dawson, a transplant to our office who came here from Eau Claire. He was hired last year when I moved in with Hurley and made the decision to cut back to part-time. Both of these decisions were so I could spend more time with Matthew, and also with Emily, Hurley's teenage daughter from a previous marriage. Hurley didn't know Emily even existed until two years ago when she and her mother showed up out of the blue. A short time later, Emily's mother died, leaving Hurley to care for his newly discovered daughter. Emily didn't adapt well at first, in part because of her grief over her mother's death, in part because her mother had lied to her all her life, telling her that her father was dead, and in part because her newly found father was in the process of building a family of his own with me and my yet-unborn son at the time. Poor Emily felt abandoned, unwanted, and like the proverbial fifth wheel. This led to some acting-out behaviors that worried and frightened Hurley and me. But after Emily underwent a near-death experience, things began to turn around. With time and a lot of counseling, her behavior and her relationship with me slowly improved.

In truth, my decision to move in with Hurley was only partly motivated by the situation with Emily. Izzy's mother, Sylvie, took a turn healthwise, requiring her to return to the cottage Izzy had built for her a few years back, a cottage that sits on Izzy's property. Sylvie had lived in it originally, right after it was built, but she moved out less than a year later when her health improved. Her timing was prophetic for me, since my then-husband and I lived next door to Izzy, and my marriage blew up and crashed with all the speed and ferocity of the *Hindenburg* only weeks after Sylvie moved out. I settled into the cottage for what I thought would be a temporary stay, and ended up calling it home for nearly two years.

When I decided to cut back my hours, Izzy hired Hal Dawson, a divorced, childless man in his mid-forties. It took a while to get to know Hal because he tends to be shy and reserved around people he doesn't know well. Some people find his looks a bit off-putting, too. He resembles Ichabod Crane: tall and thin, to the point of being gaunt, with long arms and legs, large feet, and a very prominent nose. He quickly proved himself to be a great addition to our staff: smart, funny, and dedicated to his job. He's constantly reading up on all the latest advances in forensic science and he's shown Izzy up a time or two with his knowledge of some of the latest techniques and processes. His main redeeming quality in my opinion, other than his smarts and dedication, is his wry, often dark sense of humor, a quality that also won over most of the police department, Brenda Joiner in particular.

"Quit being coy, Brenda," I say, arching a brow at her. "I know you know Hal's name. You've had the hots for the guy since he first got here, which was a year ago, by the way, so I think you can stop calling him 'the new guy.' And to answer your question, I told him I'd cover for him today because he had something he had to do out of town somewhere. Chicago, I think he said. He's supposed to be back around five to take call."

Brenda's cheeks, what little of them we can see above her mask, redden. She shakes her head in denial, making Patrick snigger. "Seriously, Joiner," he says. "You couldn't be more obvious."

Brenda's color deepens and spreads down her neck. "Not that he would notice," she says with a scowl. "Besides, he's seeing someone."

"You should ask him out anyway," Patrick says. "All he can do is say no, and who knows? He might say yes."

"I'm not desperate enough to try to break up another couple," Brenda says.

Patrick scoffs. "Hell, even I can hear your biological clock ticking, Joiner. You should go for it. Life is too short to play those kinds of games."

With the reminder of just how short life can be, we all turn our attention back to the woman on the floor, and Patrick's color starts to turn again.

CHAPTER 4

After taking a few seconds to remind ourselves that none of us escape alive from "this thing called life," Brenda, who I suspect is eager to change the subject, says, "Bummer that you're going to have to change your plans, Mattie. What were you going to do?"

"Desi, Emily, and I were going to drive into Madison to go shopping for a wedding dress this afternoon."

"Wedding dress?" Patrick says. "You two are finally going to do it? For real?" He looks over at Hurley and gives him a playful punch in the shoulder. "It's about damned time." This earns Patrick the evil eye from Hurley. I'm not sure if Hurley's annoyance is because of the punch or the comment, but this is clarified a moment later.

"It wasn't from a lack of trying," Hurley grumbles. "I've been proposing to this woman for two years, ever since I found out she was pregnant."

Patrick looks over at me and raises his eyebrows in question. "Playing hard to get, eh?"

"No, things were . . . complicated."

This is an understatement of astounding proportions. My relationship with Hurley has been a teeter-totter ride of emotional ups and downs, career ups and downs, financial ups and downs, and family wonkiness. We hurdled so many obstacles during the first year and a half, we should have a wall filled with gold medals. What we have instead are walls covered with crayon scribbles, teenage heartthrob posters, and a sampling of all the foods Matthew doesn't like. Turns out our kid is a spitter.

The inauspicious circumstances under which we first met should have been a clue that the road ahead would be a rocky one. It happened over the dead body of the woman I had just discovered was having an affair with my husband at the time, a doctor named David Winston. David and I met at the hospital in town where he worked as a surgeon and I worked as an ER nurse. I switched to the OR when David and I started getting serious, thinking it would bring us closer together. He proposed soon after and the first six years of our marriage were good ones. But during the clichéd seven-year itch, David's eye began to wander. I discovered this when I happened upon him and his ill-fated paramour alone together in an otherwise-abandoned surgical suite one evening. David was performing exploratory surgery on her using his penis as the only surgical instrument.

Running from both him and my job—small towns are rife with gossip and a small-town hospital is a pivotal hub for hot news—I ended up working for Izzy and living in his backyard cottage. It was the perfect hideaway for me. Not only did the cottage suit me financially—I left with little more than the shirt on my back, since all of our assets other than the house were in David's name—it was located next door to the house I had shared with David, providing ample spying opportunities.

My new job with Izzy helped me get over my marital

woes in several ways. It gave me something to do other than sulk and feel sorry for myself all day. It gave me a degree of financial independence. And it gave me Hurley.

My attraction to Hurley was swift, powerful, and mutual, though that didn't make the relationship an easy one. After muddling through several crises, we settled into the beginning stages of what appeared to be a promising relationship. That's when Hurley discovered he had a fourteen-year-old daughter he never knew existed, and a wife he thought he'd divorced fifteen years before, except she never filed the papers.

Needless to say, discovering he had a wife and child he didn't know about threw a big wrench into the works of Hurley's relationship with me. And as if one unexpected family arriving on his doorstep wasn't enough, I discovered I was pregnant around the same time.

My pregnancy wasn't planned; it was the hapless result of some inattention on my part, and a course of antibiotics that interfered with my birth control pills. I was happy to discover I was carrying Hurley's child, but the timing couldn't have been worse.

Given how my relationship with Hurley began and evolved, it feels as if the Fates are trying to tell us something. And the obstacles haven't stopped. Though I've finally agreed to marry Hurley, my attempts to plan the wedding have been an unmitigated disaster thus far. It started with my efforts to secure a venue. To date, I've made reservations at three different spots, only to have all three fall through the cracks—in one case, literally. The most recent place I tried to book was a small park with a gazebo, a nice backup to have in case it rains. The park setting seemed perfect, given that we were planning a small ceremony with a date in early June, a glorious time of year here in Wisconsin. But the original date came and went last week because in April, after ten days of torrential downpours, a giant sinkhole opened up under the park, swallowing the gazebo and most of the parking lot. It's a miracle no one was injured or hurt, though there were some kids playing at the park at the time who will probably have nightmares for years to come. The other two places I tried to book fell through because of a scheduling error in one case, and a fire in the other. It's hard not to take this stuff personally.

Now, finding a wedding dress, which will likely be a nightmare all its own, is proving to be a problem, too. Shopping for clothes is not one of my favorite pastimes. Finding anything that doesn't resemble a gunnysack or a bedsheet, that will fit my six-foot-tall, well-rounded body seems impossible. Sleeves are never long enough, the busts are always too tight, and if length is involved, it's never enough. Then we have the shoes to deal with. I have size-twelve feet—though ever since having Matthew, they seem to be more like a twelve and a half—and I feel like I'd have better luck finding a fit in a kayak store. Turns out size does matter.

Hurley has gone on record as saying it makes no difference what I have on, as long as we get the deed done. He's planning to wear some nice slacks—though he hasn't given up on the idea of jeans yet—and a plain dress shirt. He might wear a tie if I insist, but he doesn't want to. We're keeping it casual, after all. But as much as I'd love to buy into his it-doesn't-matter philosophy, I can't help but feel like I should have something special to wear to mark the occasion.

I was supposed to go shopping with Emily and my sister, Desi, this afternoon. Dress shopping will have to wait, however. Not only will I be pressed for time at this point, I don't want to do it smelling like death. I suppose Desi and Emily could still go and find dresses for themselves. Desi is standing up for me as my matron of honor—a title she hates—and Emily is going to be a bridesmaid. We won't have a flower girl, but in an effort to keep everyone involved, the plan is for Matthew to be our ring bearer, though at just shy of two years old he tends to be unpredictable. I have my dog, Hoover, in line as a backup.

I look down at what's left of Carolyn Abernathy and realize my grumbles are petty. At least I'll have the opportunity to reschedule my plans for the day. Whatever plans Carolyn had on her agenda for last Friday and beyond are forever canceled.

"Any final thoughts on cause of death?" Hurley says, bringing me back to focus.

"Hard to say, given the level of decomp," I say. "I don't see any obvious outward signs of trauma, and it looks as if she went down quickly and unexpectedly. And the dead insects are bothering me. So I'm still leaning toward poison at this point, though I suppose a medical condition of some sort is also within the realm of possibilities, particularly since she was a nursing student. I don't see any signs of a catastrophic disease process, however, and I can't think of one that would take her down in such a quick, unexpected way. Based on what I see here, I'd guess she was doing dishes at the sink when something made her stop, take her gloves off, and sit down in that chair beside her. She probably felt ill, I'm thinking. Then she either passed out or died, falling onto the floor. It could be something like a ruptured brain aneurysm, or a lethal heart arrhythmia, though that doesn't explain the insects. It will be relatively easy to rule the medical problems in or out, once we get her opened up."

"Sounds reasonable," Hurley says. "We'll do a quick walk-through of the house to be thorough, notify her family, and then start hunting down friends and more of the neighbors for a chat."

"Check the medicine cabinet and her bedroom for any prescription drugs," I say.

Hurley nods at Patrick, who looks relieved to leave the room.

"It may take some time to get a definitive ID," I say. "Obviously, any sort of temporary photo ID is out of the question, and her fingertips are gone so I can't just print her and run them. We'll probably have to use dental records and DNA, and that's beyond my scope. I can hunt for a dentist and request the records, but then the docs have to take over. I don't know who will be filling in for Izzy, or how quickly he or she will be able to jump in. Some of these subs have no problem picking up the scalpel and getting right to it, but others need some adjustment time. So there's a good chance Carolyn won't get autopsied until tomorrow morning."

"Understood." He nods toward the body. "Can you manage this on your own?"

"With the help of the Morticia twins I can," I tell him. "You guys go ahead and do what you need to do. I'll see to it that Carolyn gets to the morgue."

All of the remaining cops leave the room and they're none too slow about doing it. Can't say I blame them.

I take out my cell phone and call the Johnson Funeral Home, a family-owned business going back four generations. They are the official transporters of bodies going to our morgue. The latest generation in the business, identical twin daughters who are named Katerina and Cassiopeia, which has resulted in the ironic nicknames of Cass and Kit, have pale complexions, long, straight black hair, and an affinity for tight-fitting black attire. Their appearance and attire earned them the additional nickname of "the Morticia twins." They are a little creepy, both in their appearances and their demeanors, but because of their slender but buxom builds and the fit of their clothes, they are often ogled by any man they run into, creep factor aside. It's always entertaining to watch what my sister, Desi, refers to as the "Battle of the Heads": men whose brains are telling them to run even as their penises are urging them to move in and conquer.

Once I have the Johnson twins on the way, I place a call

to my younger half-sister, Desi. While we share the same mother, Desi was the progeny of my mother's second marriage. We look nothing alike. I favor my mother in terms of general looks with my fair complexion, blonde hair, and blue eyes, though my body build clearly came from my father. Not that I know what my father looked like. He abandoned my mother and me when I was a toddler, and all I have are some vague, misty memories of a large man with dark hair who smoked a pipe. My mother is tiny and petite, and Desi inherited her build, but with the dark hair and complexion of her father.

"Guess what?" I say when Desi answers.

She sighs her disappointment. "Someone died."

"You got it."

"You don't think Izzy will let you out early?"

"He called in sick with some kind of stomach bug, so we have a sub coming. And Hal is out of town for the day. I don't feel comfortable taking an early day with a temporary ME coming in."

"Your sense of duty is both admirable and annoying," Desi says. "However, all is not lost. I found a dress online I think will be perfect for you. In fact, I found two of them."

"Desi, you know how hard I am to fit."

"No worries. If they don't work, I'll return them and we can keep on looking. I can have them here in a day or two if I order them now."

"No long sleeves?"

"One is sleeveless and the other one has capped short sleeves."

"Overall length?"

"They're both tea length, so they should be fine."

"What about the bust?"

"The sleeveless one—the skirt of which has a silver underlining with a sheer, mesh overlay in a pale blue that will look fantastic with your eyes—has a crisscross bodice with a V-neck in the same blue color. And it's made of polyester and spandex. The one with the capped sleeves, which is peach colored, has a popover top made of polyester."

"Popover?" I ask, envisioning a breakfast treat.

"You know, like a peplum, except this one doesn't stick out below the waist and has a scalloped hem. The bodice is beaded and sequined, and the skirt is solid peach."

"What about my hips and tummy? They're bigger than ever since I had Matthew."

"Both dresses have flowing, A-line skirts with lots of slinky, billowy material."

"They sound like parachutes."

Desi laughs and then clucks at me. "Trust me, okay? The lines on both of them will be very flattering on you. They won't cling, and they'll hide your hips and thighs."

She'd covered all of my negatives rather well except for one. "What sizes do they come in?"

"Up to a twenty in both. I figured I'd order you a sixteen and an eighteen, to see which size fits best."

"Okay," I say, giving in. "Let me know when they arrive. Do you want my credit card number to pay for them?"

"Nope, I'm fine. If one of them works for you, I'll buy it. You can consider it your gift from me."

"I don't want you to do that, Desi. The dress should be my expense. Plus, you and Lucien are just getting back on your feet financially and Erika is going to be heading off to college in another three years. Save your money."

"We're doing fine," she insists. "Please let me do this for you. You and Hurley already have everything you need householdwise. I don't have anything else I can get for you."

"We'll talk about it later," I say, knowing once my sister has made up her mind, she's nothing if not determined. It's a family trait. "Thanks for your help."

"Happy to do it."

After saying good-bye, I make one final call to my office.

I expect our receptionist, Cass, to answer again, but instead I get Laura Kingston, one of our lab techs. She's a relatively new addition to our staff, someone who came on during my pregnancy. She and our other lab tech, Arnie Toffer, have an on-again, off-again relationship that is making Arnie crazy . . . or rather crazier. Arnie is both paranoid and a fervent conspiracy theorist, traits that apparently carry over into his personal life. The latest machination he's been spouting off about has something to do with a top secret group of scientists somehow using the Hadron Collider to hijack the missing Malaysia flight so they can send all the passengers and crew to Mars to establish a colony there.

I think Laura likes Arnie a lot, but she also works with the police department, splitting her time between the two entities as a way of meeting budgets. And Jonas Kriedeman, her other coworker, has shown an interest in her as well. Whenever Arnie gets too clingy and needy, Laura gives him the brush-off and starts spending time with Jonas.

As far as I'm concerned, both men have the patience of a saint to spend any amount of time with Laura. She's a nice person and very good at her job, but she has no off button when it comes to talking. She spews words the way a volcano spews lava—an often rambling, yet amazingly coherent, stream of every thought that goes through her head.

"Hey, Laura, it's Mattie." Before she has a chance to start talking, I quickly add, "I have a body I'm bringing in. Do we know yet who our covering ME is going to be?"

"Yep, it's Doc Morton . . . Otto Morton. He arrived about twenty minutes ago. I was showing him around. Do you know him? He's been doing this stuff for years now, like thirty-some. He was one of the first ME's in Madison. A super nice guy and very smart. Remember that case of the coed who was found dead a couple of years ago, the one they thought—"

"Laura! Please!" I've learned that the only way to stop

Laura's verbal stream of consciousness is to yell at her. Fortunately, she responds well. She may be annoying at times, but at least she's self-aware when it comes to her faults. "I don't have much time. Would you please let Dr. Morton know to expect me in a half hour or so?"

"Sorry," she says in a sheepish tone. I wonder if Dr. Morton is with her at this moment, and if he is, what he thinks of her verbal diarrhea. "I'll tell him. See you soon."

I don't bother to say good-bye, knowing even that could lead to another bout of loquaciousness. Instead, I simply disconnect the call. Rude, perhaps, but like Patrick said earlier, life is too short. It certainly was for Carolyn Abernathy.

CHAPTER 5

The Johnson twins arrive in good time, and to their credit their cute little noses don't register so much as a wrinkle as they set about helping me with my task. Half an hour later, we have Carolyn Abernathy's body bagged, and we have stripped out of our protective gear and bagged that, too.

On the way out of the house, I stop and tell Hurley I'll see him later, either at the morgue or at home. "If I don't see you at the morgue, I'll pick Matthew up when I'm done," I tell him. "Hal is supposed to be back after five, so I don't think I'll have to stay on duty any later than that."

"I'm not sure when I'll be home. Depends on what you find during the autopsy. And by the way, we found no medications anywhere in the house except for a generic bottle of acetaminophen that's nearly full."

That makes me frown. The likelihood that Carolyn had some sort of disease or disorder that led to her death has just diminished considerably.

"What do you want to do about dinner?" Hurley asks.

I make a face. "Hard for me to think about food at the moment." The smells are stuck inside my nostrils, tiny molecules of stench I know from past experience will linger for hours, even after I've showered several times. "I'll think of something," I tell him. I always seem to find the time, energy, and stamina to eat regardless of how nasty life gets.

With the household details taken care of, I head outside and watch as the Johnson twins load the body cart into their hearse. It makes for an interesting scene given that my day-to-day car is also a hearse, bought three years ago when my other car was totaled. It was the only car I could afford at the time, since I was only months out from abandoning my marriage and all the comforts that went with it. And my car, like most everything else from that marriage, was in David's name. I've since managed to improve my bank account substantially, thanks to work, a tidy divorce settlement, and sharing household costs with Hurley (though feeding and clothing two kids has certainly put several significant dents in our checkbooks).

Once the body is loaded, I get behind the wheel of my hearse and follow the Johnson sisters to the morgue. We've done this two-hearse caravan a number of times and it always seems to cause a few traffic snafus as people try to figure out if we're part of a funeral procession. We pull into the underground garage area five minutes and several curious looks later, and by the time I'm out of my car and to the elevator, the girls have the body out and are mere steps behind me. On the main level, they wheel the cart into our intake area, where they then help me slide the body bag onto one of our morgue carts. After signing some paperwork, their job is done, and with a somewhat inappropriately cheerful "See you later," they depart.

I weigh the body on a special scale that automatically deducts the weight of the cart, enter info into a computer to create a record for the remains, and then wheel the body into the X-ray room and shoot pics of it from head to toe. From there, I wheel our victim, still inside the body bag, into the morgue. A man I presume is Dr. Morton is there waiting for me, seated at a small table near the entrance.

He looks to be around Izzy's age, in his early to mid-fifties, but then I remember Laura telling me he has been doing this work for thirty years and realize he's probably in his sixties. He's a big man, standing around six-two and weighing between two-fifty and three hundred pounds. With his white hair, white beard, lively blue eyes, and rosy red cheeks, he looks like a scrub-suited Santa Claus.

"You must be Mattie Winston," he says, getting up and extending his hand. "I'm Otto Morton."

"Nice to meet you," I say, "but I'm going to pass on the handshake for now." I hold up my gloved hands.

"Right," he says with a grim nod. It doesn't take him long to get the gist of what sort of autopsy we'll be doing. Seconds after we've finished the introductions, he wrinkles his nose and says, "Guess I better get out the Vicks."

Vicks VapoRub is sometimes used by morgue workers and police alike to help deal with the nasty odors that sometimes accompany the job. A small dab in the little cleft beneath the nose, topped off with a mask, is supposed to help abolish the smells. I tried it once, but found the combination of the menthol and decomp smells worse than decomp alone. Not everyone uses the stuff, and its use is considered among the cops to be a sign of weakness and a reason for some lighthearted ribbing from one's coworkers that typically includes a word synonymous with "kitty." Most cops don't "Vape" more than once, deciding the smell is easier to deal with than the ribbing and loss of prestige. I'm surprised Otto uses it. Not many people I've encountered who do this line of work do. The smells are something you get used to, horrible as they can be.

While Otto goes off to get suited up, I wheel Carolyn's

cart over and park it alongside the autopsy table. Then I head for the locker room and don my own gear. By the time I get back to the suite, Otto is there, wearing his biohazard apparatus and eyeing the body bag with a contemplative expression. The exhaust fans are on and running full blast.

"Tell me what we have," Otto says.

"Assuming it's the resident of the house we were in, it's a deceased female, age twenty-eight, whose last-known proof of life was Friday morning. There is significant decomposition with bloating and slippage—the house didn't have the air-conditioning on—and insect activity. Though oddly, a lot of the insects near the body were dead. I've sent them to Arnie to analyze. Her fingertips seem to have more tissue loss than the rest of the body. From what I observed, there are no outward, obvious signs of trauma, so at this point I'm leaning toward a poison of some sort as a cause of death, though I suppose an aneurysm or lethal arrhythmia is also an option. Based on what I saw at the scene, I think she was standing at the sink, washing dishes, and felt ill. Then she went over and sat down at the table, where she then either died or passed out, falling to the floor."

Otto nods, with his eyebrows knitted in contemplation. "Help me move her over?"

I do so, and then wheel the morgue cart away. "I'm going to go get the X-rays. I'll be right back."

Otto nods again; then after taking in a deep breath, he unzips the body bag.

Over the next hour and a half, we examine the body, but it's slow going. The skin is loose and falls away easily, the organs are misshapen and partly dissolved, and there are insects present, all of which contribute to making the job difficult and disgusting. I leave the majority of the initial slicing and dicing to Otto while I busy myself collecting more maggots and flies, dropping them into containers for Arnie.

"Too bad my nephew isn't here," I say before realizing

how crazy that sounds. I hold up a maggot between my forceps and explain further. "My nephew, Ethan, is a bug fanatic. He has a collection of bugs at home that would impress any entomologist. He'd be in seventh heaven doing what I'm doing right now. Well, if he could do it without the corpse," I amend. "Although, I don't know that the body would bother him. He's kind of a . . . different kid."

Otto chuckles. "Yeah, there's one of them kids in almost every family."

As we continue, Otto helps make the grim process a bit less onerous. From the professional and methodical way he handles his scalpel and the other tools of the trade, he clearly knows what he's doing. And as we work, each body part we come to seems to trigger a relevant anecdote about some mysterious or puzzling case he's had in the past. Doing an autopsy with him is like attending a class, except more entertaining. I know this because I've attended a lot of classes over the past year and a half in an effort to learn more about forensic science and crime scene investigation. Most of them were great, but a few classes were so boring they could've been listed on a death certificate as a cause of death.

Hurley shows up about an hour into our process. After introductions he informs us he has spoken to several neighbors, and one was able to tell Hurley what dentist Carolyn used. The dental records and X-rays arrive shortly thereafter, and by the time we have finished our autopsy, we know for sure the body is that of Carolyn Abernathy.

"I've located the next of kin," Hurley says. "There's the sister in Ohio, and her parents live in Minnesota. I'll get some guys there to do the notifications right away."

It's always a bit of a relief when family members live far enough away that we don't have to do the notification ourselves. It's the most dreaded and difficult part of the job.

"Have you got a cause of death for me?" Hurley asks.

Otto stands back with his messy hands laced together and

resting on his ample belly. "I do not," he says with a frown. "There's no evidence of any trauma, and I don't see any pathological processes going on. At this point, we're going to have to wait on the toxicology reports to come back."

"Damn," Hurley mutters. "I was hoping this case would be an easy wrap-up. I guess I'll get some guys to help me pound the pavement some more and see what we can find out about her."

"Did you find any evidence of drug use in her house?" Otto asks.

"None," Hurley says. "The diciest behavior we know of is a new boyfriend she sometimes let stay over. Her neighbors say she was a quiet, studious young lady. No wild parties, and she was home every night."

"Nursing school will do that to you," I tell the men. "It sucks all the party right out of you, at least until graduation. Then it's no-holds-barred."

Hurley shoots me a curious look. "I sense a story in there somewhere."

I shrug and give him my best Mona Lisa smile. "Some secrets need to stay secret," I say.

"Even after we're married?"

"Yes, even then."

Otto has watched this exchange with curiosity. "You two are an item?" he says.

"We're something," I tell him, giving Hurley a wink.

"When's the big day?" Otto asks.

"That's a bit up in the air," I say with a grimace. "Our first date has come and gone. We need to find a place to have it and, so far, I'm O for three on site reservations."

"Well, I might be able to help you out with that, depending on how many people you have coming. I live on Lake Mendota in Madison, and if you want, you can use my backyard. You could do fifty people comfortably, seventy-five if you want to be a little cozy, and the lake makes a nice backdrop. We have an under-the-deck patio area, too, in case it rains."

"Wow, Otto, that's very generous of you," I say. "Thank you."

Hurley frowns. "We're not going to have fifty people, are we?"

"Not if I can help it," I say. "I think we're around twenty with family and close friends."

"Well, you let me know," Otto says. "My wife loves to entertain. She'd jump at the chance to host a reception for you."

"But she doesn't even know us," I say, worried Otto may be volunteering his wife for something he—and she—will later regret.

"And you don't know my wife. She lives for that kind of stuff. She ran a party-organizing and catering business for a few years, but it grew so fast it got overwhelming. She sold it for a nice little profit and nowadays she does the occasional side job, picking and choosing what she wants. Weddings were always her favorite thing to do."

"We'll let you know," I say. I'm leery of the offer, both because of the distance and the fact that we just met Otto and I wouldn't know his wife if she was standing right next to me, but I'm not going to say no until I know if we have another venue lined up. A bird in the hand, and all that.

Hurley says, "Thanks, Dr. Morton. I'd shake your hand, but under the circumstances . . ."

"Yeah," Otto says with a smile, looking down at his mucky, gloved hands. "Another time, perhaps."

I glance at my watch and see it's just past three-thirty. "I'll finish this up if you want, Otto. Izzy taught me how to suture and he lets me close most of the time. This one will be good practice for me. A bit of a challenge, I imagine."

"That would be great," he says. "Don't worry about the

aesthetics. Use big sutures and find the most intact skin you can. It will help if you wire the rib cage together."

I nod, eyeing Carolyn's body dubiously. Intact skin is in short supply. "When I'm done with this, I'm going to call it a day, if that's okay. Hal Dawson is our other morgue assistant. He should be back in town by five and he's on call tonight if anything comes up."

"Got it," Otto says. "I'm going to do some paperwork and then call it a night as well. I'm staying at the Sorenson Motel if anyone needs me. The girl at the front desk has my cell number."

With that, Otto strips off his gloves and carefully removes the large protective gown he was wearing. Then he washes his hands and removes his mask. "Have a great evening, you two," he says over his shoulder as he leaves.

Hurley eyes Carolyn Abernathy's body with distaste. "I'd say you have your work cut out for you."

"Yeah," I say with a sigh. Then I give him a sly smile. "Was that autopsy humor you just threw out there? You know, work *cut out* for me?"

"I *do* like to cut to the heart of the matter," he says, winking.

"Ah, very clever. I should have this sewn up in an hour or so." This is what passes for witty repartee when you're part of a couple that deals with death on a regular basis. "When I'm done, I'm going to shower at least twice, and then go pick up Matthew and check on Izzy. What time do you think you'll be home?"

"Sevenish?" he says, and I know it's an estimate. By now, we're both used to odd hours and having to drop everything at a moment's notice when we're on call. We've adapted. Fortunately, both my sister and Izzy's partner, Dom, are flexible when it comes to being available for last-minute babysitting. I use Emily, too, at times, but more often than not these days, she's out doing something with her friends.

"I'll order a pizza," I say to Hurley. "I'll plan on having it delivered around seven, but if you're held up, you can always nuke it later."

"Sounds good. Pepperoni, sausage, and mushroom?"

"Works for me, but Emily doesn't like mushrooms, remember?"

"Right. How about onion then?"

"That will work. See you later."

He blows me a kiss, not wanting to get any closer to me than he has to. I make kissing sounds back at him. So goes the romance in our lives on many a day.

As soon as Hurley is gone, so are any thoughts of romance I might have had. It takes me a little over an hour and a half to put Humpty Dumpty Abernathy back together again. There will be no open coffin for Carolyn; that's a given.

I pulled up her DMV photo when I checked her into the morgue, and there were several photos in the house of her and others—presumably family members. Carolyn Abernathy was a pretty girl with a longish brown bob, bright blue eyes, and deep dimples in both of her cheeks. Seeing what she looks like now and knowing what she looked like before leaves me feeling sad and angry—sad that this beautiful young woman had to be seen by anyone looking like this, and angry she died so young. And since it appears that her death might have been caused by someone else, my anger will soon turn to dogged determination. There aren't many avenues for positive intrinsic feedback in this line of work, but seeing justice done is one of them.

CHAPTER 6

Even though I'm running later than planned, I spend a long time in the shower, trying to wash off the smell of death. Once I'm as scrubbed as I can get and dressed in fresh, clean clothes, I head to the front desk. Our receptionist, Cass, is there—at least I think it's her—preparing to leave for the day. The fact that I don't recognize the woman standing by the desk is my first clue it's Cass. She's a dedicated thespian who believes in embracing her roles in every way possible. She embodies her characters day in and day out, dressing as them, speaking as them, wearing whatever makeup she needs to look like them. I've seen her in getups that range from a young boy to an elderly woman, and from a young girl to a sassy French whore. Today she is dressed in a man's pinstripe suit, replete with a tie and a creased white shirt. She has a mustache and full beard, and her hair is cut short in a style that would work on either a man or a woman. It is currently styled with some sort of pomade and has a side part that looks like it was made with a cleaver.

"Oh, good," she says when I walk in. Her voice is low and husky and she's speaking with some sort of accent. "I was just about to come and find you. Dr. Morton said to be sure you got his phone number."

She hands me a slip of paper with the number on it and I promptly enter it into my cell. "Have you heard from Hal yet?" I ask her.

She nods. "He called in about twenty minutes ago and said he was at home. So you should be good to go."

"Great, thanks." I turn to leave, but can't resist asking, "What character are you supposed to be?"

"Sigmund Freud," she says. "Can't you tell?"

"Oh, okay. Now I see it. Are you performing tonight?"

"Dress rehearsal," she says, shaking her head. "We have them all week and then our first performances are this weekend. You and Hurley should come."

"We just might do that." This is a lie. I know I'd have to kill Hurley before I'd be able to drag him to a play, but I might try to hit up one of the performances on my own. I love local theater productions and Dom is a part of the same group Cass is, so he's often got a role in whatever play is being done at the time. It just so happens he isn't in this one, mainly because he has new duties at home. He and Izzy adopted a three-month-old baby girl in March.

I bid good night to Cass/Sigmund and head down to the garage, where my hearse is parked. Ten minutes later, I'm standing in the living room of Izzy's house, though the room looks more like a makeshift nursery. In addition to the couch, chairs, and TV that have always been here, the room now contains a playpen, two toy boxes—both of which are typically filled to capacity when the contents aren't in use—a bassinet, and a large, colorful rug with big letters on it.

"Mama!" says the tiny voice I love, and my son, Matthew, hops off the couch, where he was sitting next to Dom, the two of them reading a Dr. Seuss book. Juliana, Izzy and Dom's new daughter, is asleep in the bassinet.

Matthew runs into my arms and I scoop him up and give him kisses all over his face. This makes him giggle hysterically, which then makes Juliana awaken. She starts to cry and I give Dom an apologetic look. "Sorry," I say. "Matthew forgot to use his inside giggle."

Dom smiles. "I've been wanting her to wake up anyway," he says, and judging from the beaming expression on his face, I believe him. "It's time for her to eat."

Matthew sandwiches my face between his palms and turns it so that he and I are nose to nose. "Eat, Mama," he says, and I have to laugh. His eyes are big, his expression eager. Clearly, my son has inherited my love affair with food.

"What would you like for dinner, Matthew?"

"Macka-kee."

"He said that to me earlier," Dom said. "It's a new one to me. What does he mean?"

I smile and wink at Dom. "Macaroni and cheese. Clearly, he takes after me." I have yet to meet a cheese I don't like.

"Ah," Dom says, nodding knowingly as he gets up from the couch and heads for the bassinet. "His verbal skills are really coming along. And we played a little game of find the match today, where I hid items in pairs around the room. He caught on super quick and finished the game in no time." Dom hoists Juliana into his arms and she immediately stops crying.

"How is Izzy?"

Dom frowns. "Not good. He's been sick to his stomach all day, and when I checked on him a little while ago to see if he wanted some broth or toast, he looked pale and kind of sweaty." His frown deepens and he shoots me a concerned look. "He's going to be okay, isn't he? He's never sick. I'm not used to seeing him like this."

"Some of these GI bugs can be quite vicious. I'll go check on him if it will make you feel better."

"It would," he says with a grateful smile. "Give me Matthew and I'll go fix a little snack for him while I feed Juliana."

I put my son down on the floor and he immediately raises his arms, opens and closes his little hands, and says, "Me up," with an imploring face.

"Give me a minute, Matthew," I say, rustling his hair. "I need to go check on Uncle Izzy, okay? You go with Uncle Dom."

Dom holds a hand out and says, "Come on, Matthew. I've got peanut butter and crackers."

"Cacas!" Matthew says, his attention fully diverted for the moment. He takes Dom's hand and the three of them head for the kitchen.

I make my way upstairs to Izzy and Dom's bedroom. The door is closed, so I knock. I listen for an answer, but don't hear one. I debate simply walking away—if Izzy is sleeping, I don't want to disturb him—but I promised Dom I would check on him. So as quietly as I can, I open the door and step into the bedroom. The bedclothes on the king-sized bed are heaped up on one side and I make my way to that side of the bed. Near the pillow, I see Izzy's dark hair—what little of it he has—protruding out from the covers. The rest of him is hidden.

"Izzy?" I call out.

He stirs; an arm comes out and pushes the covers down partway. He is lying on his side, but he rolls onto his back and hoists himself up on his pillow. Dom was right; Izzy doesn't look good. His color is ashen; his hair is damp; there is a sheen of wetness on his face.

"Mattie," he says. His voice is weak, tenuous, very unlike Izzy. I feel a burn of worry start in my chest.

"How are you doing?" I ask, walking closer.

He shakes his head. "I've been better. This damned bug has really taken me down a notch." He makes a fist of his left hand and rubs it over the center of his chest. "I've only vomited once, but I have a terrible case of reflux."

My worry burn starts to flame. "You have pain in your chest?"

He senses where I'm heading right away and the hand massaging his chest waves away my concern. "It's just some heartburn."

I'm at his side now, and I reach down and take hold of his right arm, my fingers palpating his radial pulse. His arm is cool and clammy; his pulse is rapid and irregular. My eyes take in his overall appearance, not missing the fact that he grimaces and hunches forward—that fist massaging his chest again.

"Izzy, you need to go to the ER."

"Don't be . . . ridiculous." He grunts in between the words. Not a good sign.

"Don't argue with me," I tell him in my sternest ER nurse voice. "You look like you're having a heart attack." He starts to protest again. However, before he can get a word out, I continue. "And even if you're not, you'll feel a lot better with some IV fluids to perk you up and some medication for the nausea." I take out my cell phone, preparing to call 911.

"Damn it, Mattie, I'll be fine," Izzy grumbles.

"Shut up and listen to me for once, would you?" He sighs as I punch in the numbers for 911 and an operator comes on the line a moment later. I explain what I want, alarmed by the fact that Izzy has capitulated so easily. He's worried, too, I realize.

I walk out of the room and over to the top of the stairs, where I yell down to Dom. "Dom? I've just called an ambulance to take Izzy to the hospital."

There is a moment of silence and then Dom dashes up the

stairs, his normally pale face whiter than I've ever seen it. With one arm wrapped around Juliana, he runs a hand anxiously through his strawberry blond hair and stops at the top of the stairs. "Matthew's in his high chair," he says quickly, lest I think he's abandoned my boy to run amok downstairs. "What's wrong?" His eyes are wide with worry.

With anyone else, I might take a few seconds to try to reassure them, but I know Dom can handle the truth and function in a crisis, as long as he doesn't see any blood. When he witnessed me giving birth to Matthew in my bathtub, he passed out cold. Knowing there will be a lot of hubbub going on when the EMTs arrive, and if we start an IV on Izzy here—and I suspect we will—there will also be blood, I stop him with a firm hand to his chest just the other side of Juliana.

"I don't like the way Izzy looks and he's having some chest pain," I tell him. "I think we need to play it safe and get him checked out. I'm going to stay here with him. You go downstairs and stay with the kids. Send the EMTs up here when they arrive. Go!"

I see tears well in Dom's eyes, but to his credit he nods, turns around, and heads back downstairs. I return to Izzy's bedside.

"Got any aspirin?" I ask him.

He nods toward the bathroom that's attached to the bedroom and I head in there and open the medicine cabinet. Inside I find a bottle of baby aspirin and shake four of them out into my hand. As I go to put the bottle back I see a few other prescription bottles, and one small brown bottle. I shut the medicine cabinet door and hurry back to the bedside.

"Here, chew these up," I tell him, handing him the baby aspirin.

He does so without argument and that stokes my worry flame.

"This isn't the first time you've had chest pain, is it?"

He doesn't answer me, but his sheepish look tells me all I need to know. "Damn it, Izzy, how long have you been having chest pains?"

"It only happened once," he grumbles. "A couple of months ago. I went to my doctor when it happened and my EKG looked fine."

"Did he prescribe you the nitro?"

Izzy looks guilty again and shakes his head. "No, they're my mother's."

Belatedly I remember Sylvie, who is now living in the small cottage behind Izzy's house, where I used to live. I can hear sirens approaching, and when they pull up in the drive, she's going to wonder what the hell is going on. I walk over and push aside the drapes on the window overlooking the shared driveway out back. Dom is out there, holding Juliana in one arm, his other hand with a firm grip on Matthew. Sylvie is standing next to them with her walker, listening as Dom talks to her.

A cop car whips into the driveway and Patrick Devonshire gets out. I watch as Dom says something to him and gestures toward the house. Patrick goes around to the trunk of his car, opens it, and removes an automated external defibrillator. Then he hightails it toward the house. More sirens close in on us, and as Patrick enters the bedroom half a minute later, his face flushed from his exertions, I see the ambulance pull up.

"Need this?" Patrick says, proffering the AED.

I shake my head. "Not yet, but stand by, okay?"

A moment later, an EMT comes rushing up the stairs carrying a large case in one hand. His name is Joshua and I know him from when I worked in the ER.

"He's having chest pain, and he's diaphoretic and clammy. Give me the stuff to get an IV started. Get him on a monitor and check his blood pressure."

Joshua nods, sets down his kit, and opens it. By the time

I have a tourniquet on Izzy's arm and I'm ready to poke him, the other EMTs arrive in the bedroom with a stretcher. Joshua finishes taking Izzy's blood pressure.

"It's eighty over fifty," he says, the worry clear both on his face and in his voice.

Things move quickly after that. A little over ten minutes later, we have Izzy downstairs in the back of the ambulance, an IV in his arm. The EKG machine is being attached as Sylvie and Dom, with the children, stand off to one side at the back of the rig, both adults looking terrified. Another car pulls into the drive and I'm relieved to see it's Hurley. He parks off to one side, leaving a clear path for the ambulance when it's ready to go.

"What's going on?" he says, hurrying over to where I'm standing by the rear ambulance doors. I've been keeping one eye on Izzy the entire time, the fact that he hasn't protested or uttered a single word throughout all of this is very worrisome to me.

The EKG machine is now hooked up and it spits out a strip of paper. Joshua rips it off and hands it to me. The flame in my chest grows into a conflagration.

"He's having an MI," I say to Joshua. "You need to go, now!"

Sylvie has walkered her way closer to us. Her thin white hair is standing up in tufts on her head, and her dark eyes are red-rimmed and watery. The skin on her arms is so thin I can see tendons and veins beneath it, and her hands are opening and closing, opening and closing, around the handles on her walker in an effort to control their shaking.

"Oy vey," she says in a quivery voice. "What's an MI? What's happening?"

I walk over to her and put an arm over her shoulders. "Izzy is having a myocardial infarction, a heart attack," I tell her, trying to keep my own voice calm. "He needs to get to the hospital right away."

"Heart attack?" Sylvie says, her voice rising to near hysteria. "My boy's having a heart attack? Oy vey!" She lifts the walker and tries to squirm out from under my arm, heading for the back of the ambulance. I grab her arm in a tight grip, and as I try to reel her back in, the walker whirls around and hits me in the shin. "Sylvie!" I say with a wince. "Get a grip! You need to be strong right now, okay?"

Her eyes are wild-looking, and for a few seconds, she tugs against my grip, the rubber feet on the walker scraping across the concrete surface of the driveway. Then she stops and her shoulders sag. Her head hangs as the ambulance doors slam shut and the rig starts to turn around. With the sound of the backup alarm, something seems to click with Sylvie and she straightens up, squares her shoulders, and turns to me, setting the walker down firmly in front of her.

"We go to the hospital," she says, suddenly all business.

"I'll take you," I tell her. I look over at Hurley. "Can you take Matthew?"

"Sure." He walks over to Dom, scoops our son up in his arms, and heads back to his car.

The ambulance has reached the bottom of the driveway and the driver turns on the siren. Matthew startles for a second, staring at me over Hurley's shoulder, and then he smiles. *"Woot, woot,"* he sings, mimicking the siren sound. "Mama, *woot, woot!"*

He is still *woot-woot*-ing as Hurley fastens him into the child seat in the backseat of his car and shuts the door.

"I'm going to take him home," Hurley says. "Call me as soon as you know anything."

I nod, and as he gets in behind the wheel, I turn my attention back to Dom, Sylvie, and Juliana.

Dom is surprisingly calm at the moment, perhaps putting on a front for Sylvie's sake, or perhaps not wanting to rile up Juliana. Maybe it's both, but whatever the reason, I'm grateful for it. "I need to grab a diaper bag," he says.

"Do you want me to wait and drive you to the hospital?"

He shakes his head. "No, I'll be fine. I can drive myself." I take a moment to gauge the truth of his statement. He looks concerned but calm, and I'm inclined to believe him.

I nod and turn my attention back to Sylvie. "How about if I drive you to the hospital? Dom can follow along behind us."

Sylvie shoots a disapproving look at my hearse and shakes her head. Then she looks at Dom and shakes it even harder. "Oy vey," she mutters. "Not much of a choice here, eh? I ride in the car of death, or I ride with the sinner and my granddaughter." She juts her chin defiantly. "I think maybe I can walk." With this, she lifts the walker, sets it down, and steps up to it. She repeats this three more times while Dom rolls his eyes and I let out a sigh of exasperation. Sylvie doesn't approve of her son's lifestyle and she almost never passes up a chance to let anyone who will listen know how she feels.

"I told him," Sylvie says, lifting the walker again. "I told my boy that his sinning would catch up to him." She halts her progress long enough to gesture wildly with her tiny, stick arms in the general direction of the ambulance. "Now look what happens!" She flails her fists at the air a few times and then grips the walker again, ready to continue her painfully slow march.

Under normal circumstances, I might take the time to try to reason with the woman, or to cajole her, but these aren't normal circumstances and I don't have the patience. "Sylvie, knock it off," I say irritably, walking up and positioning myself in front of her walker. "Are you really going to stand here and get all pious and preachy? Your son could die at any moment." I hear Dom utter a little gasp and hate that I'm upsetting him as well, but I know Sylvie well enough to know that if I'm not blunt and firm with her, she'll continue her stubborn rant. "I don't want to hear one more word of your opinionating. Now turn around, get into my car, and let me drive you to the hospital. Do it now on your own, or I'll pick you up and put you in the back. Your choice." I take one more step toward her, my feet coming to a stop between the front legs of her walker, my body looming over hers. I stand with my hands on my hips, my lips clamped firm, and look her right in the eye, which is almost like looking at my feet. Sylvie is just under five feet tall. If I step any closer to her, I won't be able to see her because my boobs will be in the way.

Her eyes look fierce, her expression defiant, and for a second I think I'm actually going to have to haul her into my car. But a loud *crack* emanates from her neck as she tips her head back to look up at me and it seems to suck all the wind from her sails.

"Fine," she says, letting her head fall into a more normal position. She hauls her walker around with surprising agility and heads for my hearse. "Put me in the damned death car. I'm halfway there already." She makes it to the car, opens the door, and settles in on the passenger side. Then she sits there, her walker keeping her from shutting the door and too big for her to manhandle into the car. She folds her arms over her chest and glares at me.

I take the walker, collapse it, and load it into the back of the hearse. By the time I'm done, Sylvie has shut her door and she's seated facing front, arms again folded over her chest. Dom is heading inside, and after one more look to make sure he still appears to be coping okay, I settle in behind the wheel.

"Put your seat belt on, Sylvie," I say, pulling my own over and latching it in place.

"Seat belt, *schmeat belt,*" Sylvie grumbles. "So what if I die? I'm in the perfect place, yes?"

I start the engine but before I shift it into gear, I turn and glare at her. "Either you put your seat belt on or I'm going to come over there, pick you up out of your seat, carry you over to my seat, and put you behind the wheel. Then I'm going to sit on you, put my seat belt on, and drive us to the hospital."

She stares me down, her defiance and anger glaring. Our eyes lock for an interminable number of seconds in a game of chicken. "Fine. Have it your way," I say, undoing my seat belt, my eyes still locked on hers.

She blinks . . . and then her face crumples and she looks away. With one sticklike arm, she reaches for the belt. "You big girls," she snarls. "You t'ink you can boss people around." She snaps the belt into place with a vicious jab and then folds her hands in her lap and stares out the front window.

She looks so frail and frightened all of a sudden that all my anger dissipates. I realize she's scared, and I feel myself softening toward her. I shift the car into gear and turn it around, heading down the driveway. "He's going to be okay, Sylvie," I say as I pull out onto the road.

I pray to God I'm right.

CHAPTER 7

The hospital is only five minutes away. I pull up into the circular drive in front of the ER entrance and stop to let Sylvie out. An elderly male volunteer is manning the door; normally, he would scurry out to my car and offer me valet parking service. But the sight of the hearse throws him and he stands in the doorway, gaping at us.

I get out and walk around to open the back and take out Sylvie's walker. After unfolding it, I set it by the passenger-side door. Sylvie has her door open already and she's struggling to haul herself out of the car. The volunteer finally snaps to attention and walks over to assist us.

"Her son is in the emergency room," I tell the volunteer. "Will you please escort her there while I park?"

He appears relieved to discover he won't have to be parking the hearse and a walker is the only thing I dragged out of the back of it. With a smile and a little nod, he says, "Right this way, ma'am," and walks over to hold the entrance door for Sylvie.

I hop back in the hearse and head for the parking lot, my thoughts at this point fully focused on Izzy. I snag the closest space I can find, and then jog into the hospital. By the time I reach the ER waiting area, Sylvie is just arriving there, too, her volunteer escort beside her.

The girl behind the registration desk is someone new, someone I don't know. I curse, knowing things would go much easier if there was someone here I knew.

"Hi," I say. "I'm Mattie Winston. I used to work here as a nurse. This lady's son was just brought in by ambulance with a heart attack. It's Dr. Rybarceski."

The girl nods, consults her computer, and says, "Hold on a minute." She picks up her phone and punches in a number. "I have Dr. Rybarceski's mother here to see him," she says to whoever answered on the other end. After listening for a few seconds, she says, "Okay," and hangs up.

"If you'll take a seat, someone will come out and let you know when you can go back. They're working on him right now."

The term "working on him" strikes fear in my heart. It's a term I know ER staff sometimes use when they're coding someone who has gone into cardiac arrest. I'm about to object to our instructions to take a seat when I hear a familiar voice behind me.

"Mattie? Is that you?"

I whirl around, breathing a sigh of relief. It's one of the ER nurses—Phyllis, nicknamed "Syph" by those of us who used to work with her—a fifteen-year veteran in the ER.

"Syph!" I say. "Thank goodness. Izzy is in the ER. He's having an MI. This is his mother, Sylvie," I add, pointing to her. "Can you get us in the back?"

"Of course," she says, and I see the receptionist make a face. Her authority has been usurped and she doesn't like it.

We follow Syph around a corner and through a badge-controlled door into the main ER area. She stops at the desk, tells me to wait a minute, and asks the clerk seated behind the desk what room Izzy is in.

"Room two," she says. "But they're pretty busy in there right now. The helicopter is on the way."

Knowing a helicopter is en route both frightens and reassures me. It frightens me because it symbolizes how serious Izzy's condition is. It reassures me because I know it's the fastest way to get him to a cath lab, something our hospital doesn't have. In cases like this, patients are routinely med-flighted to one of the bigger hospitals in Madison or Milwaukee.

"Helicopter?" Sylvie says, looking confused.

Syph says, "Let me go poke my head in. I'll be right back."

As she heads for Izzy's room, I explain the need for the helicopter to Sylvie.

Her only response is "Izzy always wanted to ride in a helicopter."

It's a bizarre segue, but probably the only one her mind can handle at the moment.

Syph returns and says, "He's stable for the moment. They have a couple of IVs going, he's had some meds, and they're getting him ready for transport. His pain is under control right now, so that's a good sign."

"Blood pressure?" I ask, recalling how low it was earlier.

Syph grimaces. It's quick, fleeting, but I see it. I know her too well. "It's on the low side, but for now he's holding his own."

"Can we go in and see him?"

"Sure." She leads us into the room and Sylvie moves faster than usual with her walker. As she approaches the bedside, Izzy looks over at her and makes a face.

"You should be resting, Mom," he says. "I'm fine." He looks at me then and adds, "Mattie, can you please take her home?"

"I'm not going anywhere," Sylvie says in a tone that brooks no objections. "At least not until you leave." She looks up at the other nurse in the room, someone I don't know. Her name tag reads PENNY. "Where are you sending him?"

Penny gives us the name of a hospital in Madison; then Sylvie turns around and looks at me. "Are they good?"

"They are," I say. "They have some of the best stats in the country for their heart catheterization lab. Izzy will be in good hands."

"Will you take me up there?" Sylvie asks.

"Of course, but you're going to have to ride in the death car."

She clucks at this and shakes her head. Then she turns her attention back to her son. "I'm not surprised this happened," she says. "I told you our sins come back to bite us in the ass."

"Sylvie!" I say. "Really? This is *so not* the time for this." I hear the distant percussion of the helicopter blades and know our time with Izzy is running short.

Penny has heard it, too, and she says, "I'm going to have to send you back out to the waiting room for now. The helicopter crew will be here in a minute and things are going to get tight in this room. I'll come and get you right before they wheel him out, okay?"

Sylvie looks like she wants to protest, so I lean over and whisper in her ear. "Don't be the cause of any delays, Sylvie. Time is of the essence right now."

With a sigh, she steps forward, pushes the walker to one side, and clutches the bed rail. Then she bends down and kisses Izzy on his forehead. "You better not die on me," she says. Then she grabs her walker and clip-clops out of the room.

I walk up to the head of the bed and give Izzy a smile. "You doing okay?"

"I'll be fine," he says, but there is a hint of hesitancy in his voice that tells me he's a little scared.

"You best listen to your mother," I tell him. "Dom will never survive her without you to run defense."

Izzy starts to smile, but it fades quickly. "Speaking of which, where is Dom?"

I frown, realizing he should have been here by now. "He was coming right behind us. He said he had to go inside and grab a diaper bag for Juliana, but then he was going to come straight away."

Izzy's brow furrows with worry, making me curse to myself. The last thing he needs right now is more stress.

"Let me see if I can find him." I lean over and kiss him on the forehead the same way Sylvie did, and then hurry back to the waiting room, passing the helicopter crew along the way. It won't be long now before Izzy is in the air, but there's no sign of Dom. I walk to the front entrance and scan what I can see of the parking lot. Nothing. I take out my cell phone and dial his number. When it flips over to voice mail, my heart lurches in my chest. Has something happened to Dom? Has he been in an accident?

By the time I get back to the waiting area, Penny has come to fetch Sylvie for one last good-bye. I tell her to go ahead and I'll catch up with her later. Then I go back to the front entrance, praying Dom will appear at the last second and have a chance to see Izzy before he goes.

Time ticks by as I mentally urge Dom to hurry. But the next thing I know, Sylvie is at my side and Dom is nowhere to be seen.

"You're looking for . . . *him*," she says, spitting out the last word with obvious distaste. "I told Izzy he was making a big mistake hooking up with that boy. He should settle down with a nice lady, someone a little younger maybe, so she won't mind taking care of Juliana."

I give Sylvie a look of impatience and almost start to argue the point with her, but realize it will be a waste of time and breath. "Come on," I tell her. "I need to go back to the house and see where Dom is, make sure he and Juliana are all right."

We walk outside and I tell Sylvie to wait while I get the car. Our ride back is made in total silence and I tell Sylvie to sit tight while I go inside to see if Dom is there. I see her shiver, so I leave the engine running and turn the heat on low, aiming the vents at her. I enter through the garage, using a punch code to get in. When I see both Dom's and Izzy's cars inside, my fear and worry turn to confusion. When I enter the kitchen, I'm stunned. Dom is sitting at the table with Juliana in a seat on top of it, and he's calmly feeding her from a jar of baby food fruit.

"Dom? What the hell? Why are you still here?" He doesn't look at me, nor does he answer, but I see tears welling in his eyes. I walk over and put a hand on his shoulder. "Dom, what's going on?"

"Is Izzy okay?" He freezes as he asks this, the spoon halfway between the bowl and Juliana. He is as still as a statue as he waits on my answer.

"For the moment. They med-flighted him up to Madison. He needs a cardiac catheterization."

Dom drops the spoon into the bowl with a clatter and buries his face in his hands. "This is all my fault," he sobs. "I did this to him."

"That's crazy talk. You are not responsible for Izzy's heart attack."

He drops his hands and looks up at me with a pathetic, tearstained expression. "Yes, I am. You told me, he told me, everybody told me it was crazy to adopt a kid, that the stress of raising a child would be too much on him at his age. But I kept pushing for it until Izzy caved. And now look what's happened."

"Dom, trust me. If Izzy felt that strongly about the kid thing, he never would have caved. You know that."

He shakes his head and sobs some more.

"He asked for you at the hospital. He was hurt you weren't there."

"I couldn't do it," Dom answers, sobbing. "I can't face him. He knows this is my fault. And what if he doesn't . . . what if he . . ." He can't complete the thought.

"I don't know for sure how this is going to turn out," I say. "But I do know one thing. If things go badly and Izzy dies without knowing the man he loves was there for him, it would be a damned shame. How are you going to live with that?"

Dom sniffs back a sob, but says nothing.

"Plus, you're giving Sylvie more fuel for her fire. For heaven's sake, Dom, do you love Izzy?"

"More than anything." He chokes back another sob.

"Then prove it. Get your ass to that hospital in Madison and let your face be the first one he sees when he comes out of that cath lab. If you want, I'll keep Juliana for the night so you can stay there."

I see Dom's mental wheels turning, so I toss out one last gambit. "And just so you know, Izzy told me a couple of weeks ago that bringing Juliana into his life has given him more joy than he ever imagined was possible."

Dom eyes me with skepticism. "Did he really say that? Or are you just telling me what I want to hear?"

Izzy did say it, more or less, just not exactly the way I said it to Dom. What Izzy actually said was that Juliana brought a lot of chaos and change into their lives initially, and he felt disconnected from her at first. But with each passing day, he could see more and more of her personality emerging and he was surprised by how much joy each revelation brought him. I figure my interpretation is close enough. "Yes, he really said that. Now go pack a bag and get your butt to the hospital. I'll take care of Juliana."

Dom nods slowly, his eyes looking distant momentarily. Then he pushes back his chair and stands. "Okay," he says, heading for the stairs. "Thanks."

Crisis One averted. Now all I have to do is figure out what to do with Crisis Two: Sylvie.

CHAPTER 8

I take Juliana from her infant seat and carry her outside. Sylvie is where I left her and I breathe a sigh of relief. The thought had crossed my mind that she might slide behind the wheel and take the "death car" off to Madison on her own. Sylvie doesn't drive anymore, but it wasn't a privilege she gave up easily. I empathized with her, knowing I wouldn't want to give up the freedom and independence a set of wheels provides, either. But safety had to rule over independence and Sylvie caved only after Izzy insisted, which he did after her fourth accident in as many months. The accidents were all minor ones—she sideswiped a car in the grocery store parking lot, took out a postal box while trying to parallel park downtown, backed over the flower bed in her previous neighbor's yard, and hit a stop sign while trying to make a right turn. At first, Izzy was worried Sylvie's mind was going, but the woman is sharp as a tack and misses nothing—in every sense of the word when it comes to her driving. It turns out her problem is her eyesight. It's so bad she can't read the large-print books and magazines anymore, and her depth perception is almost nonexistent.

A visit to the eye doctor and some new specs helped some, but she was unable to pass the eye test at the DMV, so her license was revoked. The lenses in her new eyeglasses are so thick they make her eyes look three times bigger than they are. Her thinning hair, which is currently a shade of whitish yellow, has been the same ever since I've known her. She favors a short little bob that probably looked chic back in the day, but now looks like tufts of silk on an ear of corn. With the vents in the car blowing on her face, two little strands of hair are standing almost straight up from her forehead, one on either side. This, combined with the giant eyes, makes her look like a bug. The irritated expression on her face doesn't help, but then a minor miracle happens. When she sees I'm carrying Juliana, her expression morphs into one of sheer delight.

I walk over to the passenger window and wait for Sylvie to open it.

"Dom is going to Madison to be with Izzy," I tell her. "They need some time alone." I stare at her, daring her to object or make one of her typical judgmental comments. "I'm going to take care of Juliana for now. I'm heading to my house so I can take care of my son as well. Would you like to come along?"

I can tell from the various muscle twitches in her face as she weighs my offer that she really doesn't want to go with me. I understand. More than anything, I want to be in Madison right now and I'm betting she feels the same way. But Dom is the one who needs to be there, and the last thing Izzy needs is more stress. As Sylvie sits there, weighing her options, the garage door opens and Dom backs his car out. With a little maneuvering, he backs up beside my hearse and rolls his window down.

"Give Izzy a kiss and a hug for me," I say, and I hear

Sylvie cluck behind me. "And please call as soon as you have any kind of update." I glance at my watch. "Izzy should be in the cath lab by now, so by the time you get there, you should be able to find out how everything went."

"I'll let you know as soon as I hear anything," Dom says. He looks past me to Sylvie. "Are you going to be with Mattie or here? I want to make sure you stay informed."

If Sylvie is impressed by Dom's deference to her, it doesn't show. "I haven't made up my mind yet," she says, punctuating it with a little *harrumph*.

Juliana, who is awake, has so far been content to be held. But she begins to squirm and fuss a little, and a telling smell informs me her diaper is in need of changing. Tiring of Sylvie's games, I look at Dom and say, "I'll take Juliana to my house and wait there until I hear something from you. Sylvie will be with me." Another *harrumph* emanates from the hearse, but she voices no objection.

"Let me give Juliana a kiss," Dom says, leaning out the window. I hold his daughter out for him and he gives her a big *swack* on the cheek. This makes her smile and kick her legs about, which makes Dom beam. "Love you, baby girl," he says. He gives me one last look and then pulls himself back inside the car and continues backing around. A moment later, he's gone.

"I need to change Juliana's diaper and grab some supplies from the house," I tell Sylvie. "Is there anything you want from your place?"

Sylvie is sulking, her pout creating an aura of wrinkles around her mouth. She shakes her head and sighs.

"Wait here, then. I'll be right back."

It takes me fifteen minutes to get Juliana's diaper changed, her bag packed, and remove the infant seat from Izzy's car and install it in the backseat of mine. My phone rings just as I get behind the wheel, and I hope it's information about Izzy. But when I look at the caller ID, I see it's Hurley.

"Hey," I say, answering the call. "I'm heading for the house now. I've got Juliana and Sylvie with me."

"Any word yet on Izzy?"

"No. They've flown him to Madison and they'll take him straight to the cath lab. He was stable when he left, but it's very serious. Dom just left to head to Madison. His number is the emergency contact and he promised he would call as soon as he heard anything."

"I've got Matthew here and he's acting hungry. I really need to go back to the station to get some things done. Emily's here for the moment, but she has a volleyball game she needs to get to by seven-thirty. Are you going to be able to stay here?"

"I'm good for the rest of the night," I tell him. "Hal is back in town and he's the one on call, so the evening is mine."

"I'm going to head out then," he says. "Call me as soon as you hear anything."

"I will."

It takes me all of ten minutes to drive to the house—our house, I force myself to think, though in my mind it has always been Hurley's house—and Juliana falls asleep in the back. Sylvie stays quiet, too, and I'm tempted just to keep driving around for a while so I can enjoy the silence.

Unloading everyone from the car is a bit of an ordeal between hauling Juliana and all of the stuff I brought for her into the house and helping Sylvie with her walker. As we enter the living room, I look beyond it into the kitchen and see Emily seated at the table with Matthew, coloring. Hoover, the seventy-pound retriever mix I rescued from a grocery store parking lot three years ago—though he was only half his current size back then—is at Matthew's feet, his favorite spot to be since Matthew drops a lot of food.

"Hey," Emily says, looking up at us. "Hi, Sylvie."

Matthew stops his scribbling, drops his crayon, clambers

down from his chair, and runs into the living room. "Mama!" he says with a happy smile that makes my heart melt. He wraps his arms around one of my legs and clings for a few seconds; then he lets one arm loose so he can plug a thumb into his mouth.

"Let go, Matthew," I say. "Let's move into the kitchen."

Matthew shakes his head and says the first word he ever spoke and the one he seems to use most these days. "No." Then he unplugs his thumb long enough to raise his hand and open and close his fist. "Me up."

"I have Juliana right now. Let's go into the kitchen and then you can come up when I put Juliana down, okay?"

Matthew again shakes his head. "No." Then his free arm joins the other one, wrapping around my leg. I try to shake him off, but he tightens his grip and starts to cry. Emily walks over and tries to pry him loose. Matthew adores his big sister—a feeling that is mutual, and normally he's more than content to substitute her for me—but he's having none of it at the moment.

"It's okay," I say with a sigh. I walk into the kitchen with Matthew clinging to my leg so tightly that with every other step he's lifted off the floor. I'm forced to move slowly enough that Sylvie manages to beat me. I set Juliana on the table in her seat, and then I bend down and scoop my son up, giving him a big hug. He wraps his tiny arms around my neck, a feeling I can never get enough of, and I hold him tight and close for as long as he'll tolerate it. It isn't long. After a few seconds, he lets me go, leans back in my arms, and looks at my face. Before I realize what he's doing, he sticks a finger up my nose. "Mama nose," he says with a big smile.

Emily bursts out laughing. "Sorry," she says between guffaws. "That's my fault. I was teaching him body parts right before we started coloring."

Sylvie drops heavily into a chair at the table and I give

her a worried look. She's no spring chicken and her list of ailments would make a good primer for a medical intern. "Are you okay, Sylvie?"

"I could use something to drink," she grumbles.

Emily says, "I'll get it. Would you like a soda, or some juice, or some water?"

Sylvie shoots me a sly look and says, "Actually, I was hoping for something a little stronger."

I'm about to caution her and remind her of how alcohol can interfere with a lot of different medications—and I've seen Sylvie's pill bottles lined up like soldiers on the kitchen counter of her cottage, so I know she's on a lot of them—but I stop myself. She's been through a lot today, and she may have to go through a lot more before the day is done. What's one little tipple going to hurt?

"What's your poison?" I ask her.

"I wouldn't mind a shot of vodka."

"Do you want anything in it, or just straight?"

"Straight is good."

I walk over to the fridge and take a small bottle of vodka out of the freezer. Hurley likes it this way, and, apparently, Sylvie does, too. *"Ooh, ya!"* she says, clapping her hands. "This is the best way."

I pour her two fingers of vodka, and as I'm about to recap the bottle, she reaches out and grabs my arm, nodding toward the glass. "You can have seconds if you want," I tell her. "Let's start with this." She looks like she's about to protest, but my cell phone rings. I set down the vodka bottle and take out my phone. When I look at the caller ID, my announcement shuts her up. "It's Dom."

Still holding Matthew in one arm, I answer the call with my free hand and listen as Dom fills me in. "The doctor just called. I'm not at the hospital yet, but I should be in about twenty minutes. They said Izzy is out of the cath lab and stable, and should be back in his room in half an hour or so."

"That's great," I say, giving Sylvie a thumbs-up with the hand I have cradled around Matthew's bottom. Matthew is pulling at the ear I don't have to the phone and saying, "Ear . . . ear."

"The doctor said they had to do a stint in two of his arteries," Dom says, sounding a little puzzled.

"It's a 'stent,'" I say, correcting him as Matthew jabs a finger in my ear. "It's a tiny mesh tube they insert in the artery and then expand to keep the artery open and reestablish the blood flow."

"Oh, okay. I was wondering what it meant." He laughs, a small nervous titter. "I had this image in my head of some tiny little man inside Izzy's artery scraping away stuff on the sides of it and then going home to his tiny wife and telling her he had to do a stint inside someone's heart."

Poor Dom. I can tell he's a bundle of nerves, and anxious about facing Izzy now that we know he's okay. "Well, you were partly right," I say. "Tell Izzy we're all thinking about him. And when he feels up to it, maybe he can give his mom a call. I have her here at my house."

Sylvie narrows her eyes at me and then slugs back half her vodka.

"Will do," Dom says. "Thanks for everything, Mattie."

"You're more than welcome. Spend the night there if you want. I have things covered here."

When I disconnect the call, I fill Sylvie in on what Dom said as best I can because Matthew has moved on to my mouth and he keeps poking a finger into it, a finger that tastes like earwax. I expect Sylvie to be happy or relieved by the news, but instead she looks annoyed. As soon as I'm done with my update—delivered in between Matthew's repeated "mouf . . . mouf," comments, I discover why.

"You don't need anyone to tell my boy to call me," she grumbles. "Izthak is a good son. He knows to call his mom."

"I'm sure he does, Sylvie, but he's going to be under the influence of some sedating drugs for a while, so he might not be thinking straight."

Sylvie *harrumphs,* finishes off her vodka, grabs the bottle, and pours herself another shot.

I hand Matthew off to Emily and he starts trying to pick her nose while I drag out the menu from a pizza delivery place in town and prepare to order dinner. "What do you like on a pizza?" I ask Sylvie.

She makes a face. "I cannot eat da pizza," she says. "My digestion!" She waves a hand around her chest and grimaces. "I get the agita."

"Okay, then, what would you like?"

"A nice home-cooked meal," she says, giving me a Captain Obvious look.

I'm about to tell her I don't have the time, but decide instead to give her most of what she's asking for. I'll cook, but I doubt it's the meal she's hoping for.

Juliana seems content for the moment, so I ask Emily to keep an eye on Matthew for a bit while I fix us all something to eat.

"I'm happy to watch him for a little while, but I have to be at my volleyball game in forty-five minutes," she says.

I had forgotten about her game. Emily is old enough to drive now, but she only recently got her learner's permit and she can't drive by herself yet. That means I have to take her. Unless . . .

"I don't suppose you'd be willing to ride your bike to the gym," I say. "Either your father or I will come pick you up when you're done."

"I can do that," she says, shrugging. Then she scoops Matthew up and hauls him into the living room.

Sylvie sits at the table, watching me as I prepare our meal. When she sees what I'm making, she *harrumphs* her displeasure; by the time I set the table and serve up the food—macaroni and cheese from a box, hot dogs, and corn—she looks apoplectic.

"Eat it or starve," I tell her, giving her a look to let her know I'm not in the mood for any more kibitzing. "It's what Matthew will eat, it's home-cooked, and it's all bland enough to agree with your digestion."

We gather around the table and everyone, including Sylvie, eats. Hoover, who hasn't budged from his spot beneath the table, waits patiently for Matthew to drop some tidbits, which he inevitably does. Emily scarfs her food down because she has to leave, and after telling me when her game will finish, she heads out to the garage and her bike.

"Be careful," I tell her.

"I will."

"And wear your helmet."

"Do I have to? It messes up my hair so much."

"Brains spilling out of your skull messes your hair up, too. Wear the helmet."

She rolls her eyes but gives me no more argument. I'm almost certain she'll put the helmet on long enough to ride out of eyesight of the house, at which point she'll take it off.

Izzy calls a little before seven-thirty. He sounds groggy, but relaxed. His chat with his mother is a brief one, and either it was enough to placate her, or her constant clucking, *harrumphing,* and eye-rolling at me has worn her out because she remains pleasant, cooperative, and nonjudgmental for the rest of the evening. I call Hurley to update him on Izzy's status and he tells me he'll be home late because of the time he lost picking up Matthew and taking him home, probably after eleven, and not to worry about dinner for him. "I'll grab a sandwich or something on the road."

At nine-thirty, I get everyone into the hearse and drive to the school gym to pick up Emily, who is flush with success after her team won all three games. I load her bike into the back of the hearse, and as we drive Sylvie home, Emily treats us to some of her personal highlights from the games, including a game-winning spike at the net and three ace serves.

Entering Sylvie's cottage fills me with a momentary sense of nostalgia as I remember the time I spent here. So many momentous events in my life happened here, including Matthew's birth. We stay awhile and I let Sylvie hold and feed Juliana a bottle, an act that transforms her into a doting, happy grandmother for half an hour. As she's burping Juliana over her shoulder, Matthew walks up to Sylvie, lifts her blouse, jabs a finger into her navel, and proudly says, "Tummy!"

Sylvie lets out a loud "Oy!" and just then Juliana spits up on her shoulder. I take it as my cue that it's time to go home.

With Sylvie safely tucked in for the night, I drive the rest of us home. Matthew falls asleep during the ride and stays asleep as I carry him into the house, change him into his jammies, and put him to bed. His bedroom at one time was Hurley's office, but there are only three bedrooms in the house, so Hurley's current office space is a laptop he sets up on the kitchen table when he has work to do.

Matthew recently graduated to a big-boy bed, right after Hurley and I awoke one morning to find him nestled between us in our bed. In our early-morning fog, we spent a little time trying to figure out which one of us had gotten up, fetched him, and brought him into our bed while sleepwalking, but we eventually figured out the little monkey had managed to climb out of his crib on his own. This was confirmed later that night when I put him to bed and went to the bathroom, only to have him open the door and join me moments later. After five more attempts to put him to bed, all of which were accompanied by toddler tantrum meltdowns, he finally fell asleep. The next day, I went out and bought him a big-boy bed.

I haven't taken down his crib yet and I settle Juliana into

it. I let Hoover out to do his business, check the food and water bowls for him and our two cats, Tux and Rubbish, neither of which has put in an appearance yet this evening. After cleaning up the kitchen and doing a load of laundry, I inform Emily—who's watching a rerun on TV of *America's Next Top Model*—that I'm heading up to bed. Upstairs in the bed I share with Hurley, I finally find the cats, both of them stretched out on our bedspread. I take another quick shower—one more attempt to wash away the lingering death molecules—and sink into bed exhausted.

I take a moment to call my sister, update her on what's going on, and ask her if she can take care of both Matthew and Juliana tomorrow. She readily agrees, saying she'll watch the kids for as long as we need.

As I disconnect the call and set the phone on the table next to my bed, I say a silent prayer of thanks for my sister. Then I'm on to other thoughts. It's been a busy, emotional day and my mind is spinning, whirling with thoughts of Izzy, Carolyn Abernathy, and my crazy, exhausting life. I half expect to lie awake for hours, but both my mind and my body manage to shut down in short order. I enjoy a dreamless, heavy sleep—"the sleep of the dead," my mother used to call it, though the term seems cruelly inappropriate to me now.

CHAPTER 9

I awake the next morning to find Hurley snoring beside me, Rubbish curled up behind his knees. This is a hard-won position for the cat because Hurley not only doesn't like cats, he's afraid of them, though getting him to admit that is like pulling teeth. Over time Tux and Rubbish have won him over—not that he likes cats, or even likes these particular cats, but rather he has learned to tolerate them. The cats are drawn to him, of course. That seems to be a curious quirk of cats: wanting to be with the people who don't want to be with them. I'm not sure if the attention Tux and Rubbish give Hurley is meant to make him feel loved and appreciated, or to torture him. Anyone who's ever seen a cat toy with a live rodent knows they have a mean streak in them, so it could be either.

I feared my cats might end up being a deal breaker when it came to Hurley and me moving in together. The first few weeks were touch and go: Hurley acting like the cats were deadly criminals who were stalking him night and day, while the cats strolled around acting as if they didn't have a care in the world. Tux handled the move better than Rubbish did, probably because he's been moved before. I inherited him from a murder victim, because Tux had nowhere else to go. Rubbish, as his name implies, was rescued from a garbage Dumpster when he was a kitten. Understandably, he tends to be the clingier of the two and I think he suffers from abandonment issues. When I moved him into Hurley's house, he hunkered down under our bed for three days straight, refusing to come out. I put his food and a litter box under there with him, and Hurley slept on the couch for three nights, convinced the cat would surface in the middle of the night and try to rip his throat out. Eventually Rubbish came out of hiding, and he and Hurley reached a détente of sorts. Both cats sneak up onto our bed, but only if Hurley isn't in the bed, or after he's sound asleep. If he comes into the room when they're there, they run. And if they're sleeping on the bed when Hurley wakes up, they hightail it out of the room.

I glance at the clock, see it's just after five, and wonder if Juliana awakened at some point during the night and I slept through it. I throw back the sheet, grab my cell phone from the nightstand, climb out of bed, and put on my robe, dropping my phone into the pocket. I tiptoe out of the room, stepping over Hoover, who is lying across the threshold. Hoover wags his tail a few times, creating a loud *thump, thump, thump.* I bend down and give him a scratch behind his ears, followed by a pat on his rump to silence the tail.

When I get to Matthew's room, I see he's sound asleep, lying sideways in his bed with his feet through the safety railing. Juliana, however, is awake, lying on her back, contentedly playing with her toes. When she sees me, her face breaks into a smile and she thrashes her arms and legs with glee. I whisper, "Good morning, pretty girl," and go about changing her diaper. Once I have that done, I pick her up and tiptoe out of the room, hoping Matthew will sleep a little longer.

Just as I step out into the hallway, my cell rings. I fumble to switch Juliana to my other arm and take the phone out of my pocket, hoping to answer it before the sound wakens everyone, but my efforts are wasted. Matthew stirs, stretches, and opens his eyes just as I answer the call.

"Dom?" I say, seeing his name on the screen a second before I answer. "Is everything okay?"

"Everything here is fine," he says, and I breathe a sigh of relief. "I'm calling because I know Juliana typically wakes around this time every morning and I figured you'd be up."

"You figured right."

Down the hall in the master bedroom, I hear the sound of bedsprings creaking and Tux and Rubbish come flying out of the room, dashing past my feet and down the stairs. I hear Hurley's familiar shuffling footsteps and know he is up, at least long enough to go to the bathroom. Whether he stays up or goes back to bed is anyone's guess. I look over at Matthew, who is now on his knees, his hands on the side rail of his bed.

"How's my girl doing?" Dom asks. From the wistful, longing tone in his voice, it's obvious to me how much he misses Juliana.

"She's doing fine. I'm just about to go downstairs and feed her breakfast."

"Can you put the phone up to her ear so I can say good morning to her?"

I roll my eyes and suck in a deep breath. I don't want to hold the phone up for Dom, not because I think his request is silly, or unnecessary, or even a hassle, but rather because I see Matthew squirming the way he does when he has to go to the bathroom, and one hand is grabbing through his pajama pants at his crotch. I've had some success at getting him to use his potty chair for peeing, though the number twos aren't going quite so well.

"Sure," I say to Dom. "Hold on a sec. I need to get Matthew into the bathroom." I place the phone against my chest, hoping to muffle things, and tell Matthew, "Let's go potty, okay?"

He clambers down to the bottom of the bed and onto the floor, and then follows me down the hall to the bathroom. Without further ado, he pulls down his pajamas and his nighttime pull-up and sits on his potty chair.

"Good job," I tell him with a big smile. A second later a stream of urine squirts out past the potty chair and up into the air, hitting the side of the tub and splashing onto the floor. Belatedly I notice Matthew has a tiny erection, and it's pointed at the corner of the ceiling across the room. Matthew starts to giggle. With a weary sigh, I put the phone to my ear and tell Dom, "Here's Juliana."

As I switch the phone to Juliana's ear, Matthew looks over at me. "Tock," he says, his word for talk. He stretches his arm toward the phone in my hand and opens and closes his fist in a gimme gesture. I nod at him and smile as I hear the slightly distant sound of Dom greeting his daughter through the phone. Then Matthew says, "Me tock."

"In a minute," I tell him.

Matthew pushes himself up from the potty chair, his pajamas and pull-up down around his ankles, and shuffles toward me. He has both arms extended, his hands doing the gimme thing. "Tock, tock, tock," he pleads, his voice growing more urgent and a smidge whiny. I realize then that he's still peeing, his stream marking the trail ahead of him until he is standing at my feet, his pleas growing ever more desperate, urine squirting onto my feet and legs.

"Matthew!" I grumble, louder and more stringently than I mean to. This startles Juliana, who starts to cry. It doesn't startle Matthew, but it does make him mad, so he also starts to cry. I put the phone to my ear. "Dom, I have to go. I'll call you back later, okay?"

The "okay?" is an automatic response, triggered by some subliminal vestige of politeness left in me, but it's nothing more than a gesture. I don't give him a chance to respond or agree before I disconnect the call and drop the phone into my pocket. Juliana is screaming in my left ear; my son is screaming at my feet, where we are both standing in a puddle of urine; then I see a sleepy-eyed Hurley shuffling his way down the hall toward me. I half expect Hurley to grumble something about the noise and his need for sleep, but instead he bestows me with a meager smile.

"Good morning, sunshine," he says in a loud voice so I'll hear it over the clamor.

I hold up my hand like a traffic cop. "You best stop there," I tell him. "Your son didn't quite get it all in the potty this morning."

That's enough to make Hurley's smile fade as he takes in the urine on the floor, on my legs, on Matthew's crumpled pajama bottoms and feet, and on the side of the tub.

Matthew stops crying long enough to release his death grip on my legs and try to waddle over to his father. The wet stuff around his ankles is too much of an impediment so he drops down into a crawl. Hurley bends down and picks him up, holding him out at arm's length. The soggy pajama pants and pull-up slide off Matthew's feet onto the floor.

"How about I take care of this one and the bathroom," Hurley says to me, "and you can take care of Juliana and yourself."

"Deal."

We pass each other, sharing a brief morning-breath kiss along the way. I head downstairs—urine-sprinkled pajamas and all—to the kitchen, knowing that feeding Juliana is my first priority. I turn on the coffeepot, which someone—I assume it was Hurley, though Emily has recently taken to having a cup in the mornings—thankfully had the foresight to set up the night before, and while the java is dripping, I put Juliana in her seat and start fixing her breakfast.

By the time Hurley has a chance to join me with our son in tow, I have Juliana fed and drinking a bottle, half a cup of coffee in my body, and Matthew's breakfast ready to go.

"Here you go, Matthew," I say, patting the chair with his booster seat on it. Hurley sets Matthew into the chair and scoots it up to the table. Hoover promptly trots into the kitchen and positions himself beneath the table at Matthew's feet. In front of Matthew is a cereal bowl with some dry Cheerios topped with slices of bananas and strawberries. There is a glass of milk on the side. Matthew doesn't like milk in his "co-cos" as he calls them, a point he drives home by tipping his bowl upside down onto his head every time we add milk to his cereal. So now he gets them dry with his milk on the side.

Through a combination of saintly patience, taking turns, and solid teamwork, Hurley and I manage to feed, clean, and dress both children, as well as ourselves, over the next hour and a half. Then I get everything ready for hauling them off to Desi's.

I've considered letting Emily watch Matthew during the day, but haven't done it yet. After the issues we had with her during the first few months of Matthew's life—issues that have since been resolved, but were serious enough that my trust of her had to be built in stages—we've been slowly, but steadily, building our new family dynamic. My role in helping Emily through the incident a couple of years ago was instrumental in getting our relationship turned around and back on track. I feared my moving in with Hurley might upset the fragile détente we'd established, but if anything it helped, that and regular counseling sessions—for all of us in group and alone sessions—with our psychiatrist, Dr. Maggie Baldwin.

Things are much better now . . . great, in fact. But Emily *is* a teenage girl, and as such there have been some disagreements, arguments, and a tantrum or two. We have engaged in talks and negotiating sessions that would impress heads of state, debating things such as curfews, acceptable clothing, and time spent on cell phones and computers. Oddly enough, one of the stabilizing forces in Emily's life is her boyfriend, Johnny Chester, a local boy whose family tree tends to branch into correctional institutions with each generation. Somehow Johnny, thus far, has managed to avoid his legacy. Though I remained skeptical for a long time, I have to admit Johnny is a bright, friendly kid with good ambitions and a clean record. I don't know if he and Emily will last throughout high school or beyond, but they seem quite committed to one another so far.

The other reason I'm reluctant to have Emily sit for Matthew during the day is I don't want her to feel like she's built-in slave labor. She sits for us in the evenings quite a bit—a huge help for those nights when Hurley and I get called out in the evening or the middle of the night—and we've started up a fund we pay into for every time she does it. She taps into the fund now and again for spending money—she calls it her "funny money"—but she's trying to save most of it so she can buy a car.

By the time Hurley and I leave the house, Emily is still asleep upstairs, blessed with that depth of slumber only teenagers seem able to achieve. It's her summer break and she has nowhere she needs to be for the day, so we let her sleep. I agree to play chauffeur this morning, since Juliana's seat is already in my hearse. After giving Hurley a longer, fresher kiss in the driveway, we part ways.

My sister was born to be a mother, so much so that I sometimes fear Matthew won't want to come home with me after spending a day with Aunt Desi. My thirteen-year-old nephew, Ethan, who adores and collects all things six- or eight-legged, is at some bug camp for the week. But my fifteen-year-old niece, Erika, is home for the day and thrilled about having both kids to play with.

By the time I drop the kids off and head for my office, I'm exhausted and my day hasn't really begun. Yet I'm jazzed and energized about going to work. I love my job. I adore my son and my state of motherhood, but I don't think I'd make a very good stay-at-home mom. Part of me thinks it sounds wonderful, fulfilling, and rewarding. But there is another, far more realistic part of me that knows I'd be crazier than Arnie at a Men in Black Convention if I was stuck with a two-year-old kid all day, every day, even if Matthew is the smartest, handsomest, funniest, most amazing kid in the universe.

I park in the underground garage and head up to the main floor. As soon as I step out into the hallway, I see a group of people congregated in the library, the room that also happens to serve as office space for both Hal and me. In the beginning, he and I shared a desk and a computer, but eventually we each got our own. I still have to share my space with Laura Kingston, the part-time evidence tech who splits her hours between us and the police department.

Hal is seated at his desk and the rest of the group, which includes Arnie, Cass, Laura, Hal, and Dr. Morton, are assembled around him.

"Mattie, thank goodness," Hal says. "We're all anxious to hear about Izzy. How's he doing? Nobody here has heard anything since last evening. Do you have an update?"

"I do," I say with a smile. "He's stable and doing well."

"Are they sure it was a heart attack?" Arnie asks, looking worried. Given his tendency to turn everything into a conspiracy, I'm not sure if his concern is for Izzy's health, or his ongoing fear that we missed some horrible contagion present in one of our bodies. Arnie isn't usually a hypochondriac—

my mother planted her flag on that territory long ago, giving her a firm claim—but his paranoia does run deep.

"It was a heart attack," I assure him. "I saw the EKG myself. They took him straight to the cath lab last night and put stents in two of his arteries. Dom has been with him all night. I talked to him early this morning and he said Izzy was doing fine, complaining about the food and the bed."

"Classic Izzy," Arnie says, looking a bit relieved.

"The cardiologist told Dom if all goes well today, Izzy will probably be discharged tomorrow morning. But I imagine he's going to be off work for quite a while." I look over at Otto. "How long can you stay with us?"

Otto cocks his head and shrugs. "As long as you need me. I'm semiretired at this point, so I choose the hours I want to work. I can fill in as needed."

"Good," I say. "I'm sure Izzy will be relieved to know everything is covered for now." I'm relieved, too. So far, Otto Morton has proven to be an easy person to work with, and having one person fill in all the time, as opposed to a series of temporary fill-ins, makes transitioning easier. Not to mention that some of the temporary docs I've worked with over the past two years have been difficult, picky, or just plain strange, like the guy from up north who was obsessed with the idea of a zombie apocalypse and insisted that all of our corpses have their ankles zip-tied together.

Now that the drama about Izzy has been dealt with, the group drifts away from Hal's desk toward something more important: a box of fresh donuts sitting at the end of the library's conference table.

"Do we have any autopsies pending this morning?" I ask Hal, eager to get things back on track.

He shakes his head. "We had two calls during the night, but they were both expected deaths with known medical problems."

"Who brought the donuts?"

"Doc Morton."

"Hunh. Good to know he's not above ingratiating himself to the staff."

"And does it well," Hal adds with a smile. "I like the guy."

"Me too. I'm glad he can stay to cover for Izzy."

Hal pushes back his chair, stands, and stretches. "Thanks for covering for me yesterday," he says, pushing his chair back into place.

"No problem. Did you get everything you needed done?"

"Mostly," he says with a furrowed brow. He pats his hand on his pants pocket as if checking to see if something is there, smiles, and says, "I heard you pulled a nasty one yesterday."

"It wasn't pretty," I say with a grimace. "And sad, too. She was young, only twenty-eight."

"What took her?"

"We don't know yet. There was no evidence of any trauma or any obvious medical conditions. We're waiting on the tox screen to come back."

"Her medical records were faxed over last night. I gave the original to Morton and left a copy on your desk."

"Thanks."

He turns to leave, but then snaps his fingers and turns back. "I almost forgot to ask. How did your first time testifying go?"

"Nerve-wracking," I say, rolling my eyes. "But I got through it. I haven't heard from Beckwith yet about how the case is going, but I can't imagine the guy won't be convicted."

"Let's hope so. And on that happy note, I think I'll head home."

"Got any plans for your days off?"

"Tina and I are going out in the boat today," he says, stifling a yawn.

"Maybe you should go home and sleep," I suggest.

Hal shakes his head. "I'll be fine. Got some fun stuff planned for the day."

Tina is Hal's girlfriend. She's in her mid-forties, with glasses and long, straight blond hair. Like Hal, she's tall, thin, and lanky. To me, she looks like a stereotypical spinster. I've met her twice, both times at social gatherings, and she is a quiet, socially awkward, bookish type who works as a librarian and seems content to hide in a corner and be a wallflower. Since Hal is more or less the same way, I've found myself wondering on these occasions why they bother to attend at all. They don't engage with anyone else unless they're cornered and forced to. Hell, they hardly engage with one another.

"Does Tina like to fish?"

"Not at all," he says with a wry grin. For a moment, I think he's going to leave it at that, but then he adds, "She likes going out in the boat, though. She reads while I fish."

I envision the two of them together at opposite ends of the boat: Hal with his rod and reel cast off one end; Tina, with a floppy sunhat I've seen her wear and some hefty tome in her lap, seated at the other, bobbing on the waves, each in their own little world.

"Well, have fun," I tell him. "I'll give you a call Friday evening to report off for your weekend call."

"Sounds like a plan." With that, Hal finally leaves. I watch, amazed, as he walks right past the donut box without a hint of hesitation. I find this both admirable and puzzling because I know I could never do it. After a moment of internal debate and self-loathing, I walk over and survey what's left in the box, helping myself to a glazed apple fritter, the first bite of which makes me forget everything else for a while.

CHAPTER 10

I spend the next few hours wading through the stacks of paperwork I have on my desk, starting with the oldest files and working my way up to the most recent addition: Carolyn Abernathy. Ms. Abernathy was young and healthy, and her medical file is a correspondingly small one. The only health issue I see mentioned is a type of psoriatic condition that makes her skin dry up and crack open when exposed to certain agents, like dish soap, which explains the rubber gloves we found in her kitchen sink. It might also explain why her fingertips showed more decomposition than the rest of her body did. If she had cracked, bleeding sores on her hands, the insects would have attacked those fingers the way I attack the all-you-can-eat ice-cream sundae buffet one of our local restaurants holds twice a year. Psoriasis aside, there is nothing else in Abernathy's medical record to suggest she might have had any undiagnosed, catastrophic medical conditions. For now, her cause of death remains a puzzle.

Curious, I give Hurley a call to see if he's dug up anything on the girl that might be helpful. His phone flips over to voice mail, so I leave a message asking him to call me back. He does, a few minutes later.

"Sorry I missed your call," he says. "I was in the john, and unlike some people, I refuse to talk on a phone when I'm doing my business."

"That's okay. It's probably the only private time you get all day long. I know it is for me, at least when I'm here. Home is another story. My workday bathroom breaks have become very important to me."

Hurley chuckles. "This morning *was* a bit chaotic."

"You think? Mornings like this help reinforce my decision to stop with Matthew and not have any more children."

"I'm still keeping an open mind," Hurley counters.

"Well, you might have to call Rent-A-Womb then, because my mind snapped closed on the idea this morning."

"Tomorrow's another day."

I shake my head and smile. We've danced around this particular topic several times lately, trying to decide if we want to have another child. On the days when my son is sweet and adorable and does everything I tell him to do, I think it might not be a bad idea to have another one. And if we decide to do the deed, it would be nice to do it soon so Matthew can have a sibling close to his own age. But on days like today, or days like the one where Matthew started screaming, kicking, and thrashing around in the grocery cart because I bought the milk with the red top as opposed to the yellow one, the idea of another child is out of the question.

Hurley has pro days and con days, though the vast majority of the time he's on the pro side of the fence. I'm surprised today was a pro day, given how the morning went.

I steer the conversation back to work. "What have you come up with on Carolyn Abernathy?"

"I talked to her roommate, a young woman named Barb Holden. She left last Thursday right after her work shift at a grocery store and drove to Minnesota to spend the week with family. She said she texted Carolyn on Friday to let her know she arrived okay and Carolyn sent a text back, telling her to have fun. That was around eight-thirty in the morning. As far as we know, that's the last time anyone saw or communicated with Carolyn. I've since verified that the roomie was and still is in Minnesota. She gave us enough verifiable locations for Friday and Saturday to rule her out."

"What about the boyfriend?"

"Ah, yes, he's an interesting specimen. I found his number written down in Carolyn's address book. His name is Keith Lundberg, thirty-three, and he's an auto mechanic at the local Ford dealership. Apparently, he and Carolyn have only been dating for about a month. I talked to him on the phone last evening and he said he hadn't seen Carolyn since spending the night at her place last Thursday. He said he left Friday morning around seven to go to work. He claimed he tried to call and text Carolyn several times over the weekend, but she never answered. He gave us permission to look at his phone records, so once we get them we'll see if that's true."

"What about her cell phone?" I ask. "We bagged it as evidence."

"I haven't had a chance to talk to Jonas yet to see if he's looked at it. It's on my agenda for later today. There was an interesting tidbit we got from one of Carolyn's neighbors who said she heard yelling coming from the house on Friday morning. She said when Keith left, he slammed the door and looked mad as he walked to his car."

"What does Keith say about that?"

"Haven't asked him yet. I didn't get the info about what the neighbor saw until just a bit ago. I did ask Keith if it was unusual for Carolyn not to answer his calls or texts, and he said she sometimes turned her phone off when she had studying to do."

"What studying did she have to do at this time of year? Isn't she on summer break?"

"Sort of. Apparently, she was taking a summer class."

"What about her other neighbors? Did any of them see or hear anything?"

"Nope. We talked to everyone within a two-block radius and no one saw Carolyn or anyone else go in or out of the house on Friday, Saturday, or Sunday, with the exception of the boyfriend early Friday morning. Several of the neighbors did say it wasn't unusual for Carolyn to stay shut in for days at a time, and since the closest neighbors knew the roommate was out of town, no one got worried until Monday when they started picking up on the odd smell coming from the house. We also talked to her coworkers, some of her fellow students, and one of her teachers. They all seemed genuinely shocked to learn about her death, and none of them can think of anyone who would want to hurt her."

"Man, this case is nothing but dead ends," I say, grimacing at my unintended pun.

"An apt and accurate description," Hurley says with a chuckle. "However inappropriate. Maybe something will pan out when I have my next chat with Keith."

"When are you planning to do that?"

"I was thinking of heading over there now. Want to come along?"

"Sure." I glance at my watch. "Maybe we can sneak in a lunch along the way?"

"Sounds good. Want to try out that new sandwich shop over on the east end of town?"

"Yeah, we better hit it up before it tanks."

New restaurants pop up all the time in Sorenson, but most of them don't last out a year. It's not because their food is bad, or their service sucks, it's because we have several established restaurants that are reliably good and Sorenson's population will only support a certain number of eating establishments. Every time a new place opens up, many of the residents—myself included—will flock to it in the beginning to try out the menu. We do this knowing it may well be our one and only chance at it. Eventually the newness wears off and business slows until the doors close for good.

"I'll pick you up out front in ten," Hurley says.

"Got it."

I check in with Otto to let him know where I'm going and what I'm doing, and to see if he needs help with anything. He seems to have things well under control—paperwork is tedious, but not that complicated—so I head out front to meet Hurley.

The Ford dealership where Keith Lundberg works is located near the edge of town and the assortment of new and used cars parked on the lot are all sparkling in the warm June sun.

"Thinking it's time to consider doing a trade-in?" Hurley says as I eye one of the new SUVs on the lot.

"Nope, I love that stupid hearse. I'll drive it until it dies. I'm just looking to see what's out there for Emily. She's going to need a set of wheels pretty soon."

Hurley sighs and runs a hand through his hair. "Yeah, don't remind me. When I took her driving the other day, she was distracted by all kinds of stuff—people walking, stores we passed, a house she likes. Then her cell phone dinged with a text message, and before I knew what she was doing, she had reached into her purse and grabbed the thing. I made her pull over immediately, took the phone away, and gave her the standard lecture. But I'm worried that it went in one ear and out the other. She gets distracted so easily. I think she may have a mild case of ADD, or ADHD, or whatever that alphabet soup is."

I shake my head. "She has a not-so-mild case of being a teenage girl," I say. "Make her put her phone in the trunk when she's driving. Then there's no way for her to look at it."

"Not a bad idea," Hurley says with a begrudging nod. "I was thinking along the lines of giving her an extra-safe car to drive."

"Extra-safe?" I say, turning and heading for the service counter inside.

"You know, something with reinforced side panels?"

I shoot him a look of disbelief. "You want to give Emily my hearse?"

He shrugs and flashes me a guilty smile. "You have to admit, even if she did wreck it, she's safer than she could possibly be in any other car."

I stop, turn, and gape at him. "What about me and Matthew? What about our safety?"

"Of course I care about that, too," he says. "But you're a good driver. I'm not sure Emily is or ever will be."

"I'm not falling for your flattery diversion," I tell Hurley, giving him a chastising look. "If you're that worried about Emily, we should buy her a new car with side and front air bags, Bluetooth, hands-free phone and messaging capabilities, and a good crash safety record. The hearse may be reinforced, but it doesn't have side air bags or Bluetooth capabilities. And while we can tell Emily to put her phone in the trunk until we're blue in the face, you know there are going to be times when she won't do it, either because she forgets or decides that this one time won't matter."

"I can't afford a new car for her," Hurley says.

"But *we* can," I say. "Let's remember we're a team now."

"But with you working only part-time, we're just scraping by every month as it is. I'm not sure we can handle a new car without tapping into your savings."

"I don't have a car payment and you have only six months left on yours. We can handle two car payments for a few months if we have to."

We arrive at the service desk and table the discussion for now. Hurley presents his badge to a balding, red-faced fireplug of a man behind the desk and asks to speak to Keith Lundberg.

"Can't help you," says Mr. Fireplug, whose first name, according to what's stitched on his gray shirt, is BRADLEY. "He didn't show up for work today."

"Really?" Hurley says, and I can tell his radar has just come on. "Did he call in or just not show?"

"Just didn't show," Bradley says with a hint of irritation. "Bummer too, because he seemed like a good hire. Knew his stuff, showed up on time, and worked fast."

"How long has he worked here?" I ask.

"Only a few weeks," Bradley says. "He moved here from somewhere in Texas. Don't think he was from there originally, though," he adds, squinting his eyes in thought. "His accent was more like one of them Boston types, you know? He said 'ka,' instead of car, that kind of thing."

"Can you give me a home address for Mr. Lundberg?" Hurley asks.

"Sure." Bradley hops off the stool he's on and wanders off into the back area. After a minute or so, he returns with a slip of paper in his hand. "Here you go."

Hurley takes it, thanks him, and we leave. When we're back in Hurley's car, he shows me the slip of paper and says, "This address look familiar to you?"

I read it and recognize it. "It's the Sorenson Motel."

He nods solemnly. "And that's not the address Lundberg had on file with the DMV." He takes out his cell phone and starts jabbing at the screen. "Damn. According to Google maps, the address on file with the DMV is a business." He starts the car, shifts it angrily into gear, and pulls out.

"Where are we going?"

"To the Sorenson Motel. I have a feeling we may have let a killer get away."

A visit to the Sorenson Motel is never high on my list of things to do, in part because I was forced to live there for a week while my cottage was being held hostage in an investigation, and in part because Joseph Wagner, the owner, is a crusty old curmudgeon who could try the patience of a saint.

It takes less than five minutes for us to drive there, and based on Joseph's reaction when we enter his office, I'm guessing he's about as happy to see us as I am to be here.

"You two," he says, making a face like he just tasted something sour. He's wearing overalls with a T-shirt that has a large arrow front and center pointing downward. Above the arrow is printed VACANCY. Given that Joseph is twice my age and looks like Larry Fine from the Three Stooges, I'm guessing that vacancy will be there for a long time.

"What sort of havoc do you want to try to wreak on my place this week?" Joseph asks.

"We'd like to know if this man is staying here," Hurley says, showing him Keith Lundberg's DMV photo.

"He was, but he turned in his key early this morning," Joseph says. "He'd paid through to the end of the month, but didn't ask for a refund. Good thing, 'cause I don't give 'em." Joseph's stingy ways are probably the only thing that's kept him in business all these years, since he hasn't done any upgrades to the motel since the eighties and there isn't much in the way of entertainment close by.

"Can I take a look at the room he was staying in?" Hurley asks.

"Sure," Joseph says, shrugging. He slides off the stool he's sitting on and walks over to a locked cabinet. He opens it, removes a key hanging under the number five, and hands it to us. "My housekeeping girl already cleaned the place, so I hope you aren't looking for any of that forensic evidence kind of stuff."

Hurley frowns at this. It would be better if the room hadn't been cleaned, but there's no guarantee of finding anything useful even if that were the case.

"How long was he here?" I ask.

"Since the start of the month. Said he wanted to pay by the week, but gave me a month's worth to start out. Then he left after only two weeks."

"Did he say where he was going? Or why he was leaving?" Hurley asks.

"He didn't offer and I didn't ask," Joseph says.

"I don't suppose he left a forwarding address of any kind?" I ask.

Joseph snorts a laugh.

We walk down to unit five and Hurley unlocks the door. The room is your standard motel fare: a queen-sized bed, basic bathroom with a shower/tub combo, a small table with two chairs in the corner by the door, and a credenza with a TV on top. It's not a smart TV or even a flat screen, but a placard next to it does boast basic cable and rentable movies, including a few whose ratings could "mark the spot."

Hurley and I do a basic tour of the room and bathroom, but there's nothing of interest. The maid has done an excellent job. The place may not be modern or fancy, but it's clean. As we shut the door behind us, Hurley stands there a moment, looking across the parking lot. Then he takes out his phone and makes a call.

"Bob," he says, letting me know who the call was to. Bob Richmond is one of the other detectives with the police department, the same detective I was with when we entered the Wyzinski house. He was semiretired not long ago, but one stray bullet and a couple hundred lost pounds later, he's back working full-time. "I need a favor," Hurley says. "Can you meet me at the Sorenson Motel right away?" He listens for a few seconds, says, "Thanks, and bring Jonas," and then hangs up.

"What are you going to have Jonas do?" I ask him. "That room looks like it's been scrubbed clean."

"It has," Hurley says. "But that garbage Dumpster hasn't

been. Look at it. It's full. That means it's due to be emptied soon. I'll bet there's a week's worth of trash in it. And who knows what we might find in there?"

I realize what a smart idea this is, and thank my lucky stars I'm not Jonas. Wading through a week's worth of motel trash can't be anyone's idea of a fun time.

CHAPTER 11

We hang around the motel long enough for Bob Richmond and Jonas to get there and take charge of the trash.

"I want all of it," Hurley says. "Haul it all back to the evidence room. We need to go through it and look for any clues as to who this Keith Lundberg character is and where he might have gone."

Jonas eyes the Dumpster wearily; to his credit, he says, "I'm on it," and then gets down to the task.

Hurley and I climb back in his car and head for the sandwich shop. It has a drive-through, and after a brief discussion, we decide to use it and take our sandwiches back to the station.

"What plans do you have for after lunch?" I ask Hurley as we wait for our food.

"After we eat, it's garbage-sifting time," he says.

"Oh, joy," I say without any. My cell phone rings then, and I find myself hoping it's a death call so I can get out of garbage duty. A second later, when I see it's Otto calling and realize it might very well be a death call, I'm overcome with guilt. Hurley's phone rings then, too, an ominous sign.

"Hey, Otto," I say, hoping my assumption about the nature of the calls is incorrect.

"Hi, Mattie. I hope you got your lunch, because we just got a call." I give Hurley a grim, questioning look and he nods back at me, looking resigned.

Our sandwiches are ready and Hurley props his phone between his ear and his shoulder as the food is handed to him. He drops the bag on the seat between us and drives on through, pulling into a nearby parking slot.

"Where?" I ask Otto at the same time Hurley asks his caller the same thing.

"They found a body trapped up against the dam downtown. So we need to go there first, but then we might need to go to the lake. The sheriff's office got a call half an hour ago for an abandoned boat on the lake, and it has blood in it, apparently a lot of blood. Don't know yet if the two are connected, but for now we're going to work with both the local cops and the county guys until we figure it out."

"Okay," I say. "I'll be at the dam in ten."

I disconnect my call and Hurley says a moment later, "Got it. I'll be right there." Then he disconnects his.

"The dam?" I say. He nods. "And the lake?" He nods again. "I guess lunch is going to have to wait."

Hurley gives me a disappointed look. "Damn the dam," he grumbles. "I'm starving. I'm going to eat mine anyway."

I need no further convincing. "Me too."

Hurley pulls out of the parking space and turns back onto the street, heading through town toward the dam. He has the steering wheel in one hand and his sandwich in the other, and all I can think of is how we need to make sure Emily does what we say and not what we do. While a sandwich might be a smidge better than a cell phone, it's a gooey, cheesy, saucy thing that provides plenty of distraction. We make a quick stop in the underground parking lot beneath my office so I can grab my camera and scene kit from the hearse. We are only blocks from the dam at this point and through some unspoken agreement we stay parked until our sandwiches have been fully inhaled.

We arrive at the site a few minutes later and park on a bridge that spans the river. Parked in front of us are a couple of marked cop cars and an unmarked sedan, which I recognize as Junior Feller's. Junior has been with the Sorenson PD for twelve years and he's a Sorenson lifer, like me. He was promoted to detective a couple of years ago, and mostly handles vice issues. But he also gets pulled in to help on any homicides. It's a small-town police department, so crossovers are common and necessary. Junior is standing several feet away, talking to Brenda Joiner. When he sees us, he comes trotting over. I hear sirens closing in and give Junior a questioning look.

"I thought we had a dead body," I say, thinking the sirens are ambulances.

"We do. That's the fire department," he explains. "We're going to need their help retrieving the body. It's over there." He points across a grassy expanse on the far side of the bridge toward the dam, which is located in the town's small park area.

The river that flows through town runs into a lake two miles or so below the dam, and it's fed from above us by another lake, which is about a mile upriver. While the width of the river for most of its run through town is roughly two to three hundred feet, here in front of the dam it pools out into a wide, shallow area creating a mini lake of sorts with a grassy, tree-studded park area all around it. It's Sorenson's equivalent to a town square, and it serves as the site of the annual fireworks on the Fourth of July, and any number of other town functions. It's a peaceful, bucolic setting located just outside the center of town, and the townsfolk come down here all the time during the summer months for picnics, games, fishing, or the occasional lover's tryst on a blanket beneath one of the many towering oaks bordering the river's edge. So it's no surprise to see there are dozens of lookie-loos hovering around the taped perimeter Junior and the uniformed officers have already set up.

"Mattie? What's going on?" says a female voice behind me.

I turn and see Alison Miller, the Sorenson newspaper's ace photographer and reporter. "I heard something on my police scanner about a drowning."

"I don't know yet," I tell Alison. "We just got here and all I know so far is that there's a body in the water by the dam."

Alison nods and looks around. "I'll go talk to some of the rubberneckers and see what I can find out." She heads off for the largest group of spectators, a dozen or so people gathered along the shore on the north end of the dam, about fifty feet from the body. I can see several of them holding up cell phones, no doubt snapping pictures of the floating, bobbing corpse.

Alison Miller used to be a huge nemesis to Hurley and me, and to the police in general. She was always so eager to get a scoop on whatever was going on that she often published stories containing information we didn't want released. At one point, right after I first started my job with Izzy, she was also a competitor for Hurley's attentions, which put her at the top of my fecal roster. But things have changed a lot in the past two years. A case we had involving a famous, wealthy family bickering over who would inherit the estate's millions put Sorenson on the map of every news agency across the country and Alison at stage center. It got her a bigger, better job offer out of town, but just as she was about to take it, her mother was diagnosed with ALS. Alison was forced to give up her dream job so she could stay home and care for her mother. This humbling life event changed her, and an agreeable détente was achieved. Now Alison works with us rather than against us in exchange for any scoops we can provide her. Her mother passed away several months ago, and because I helped Alison care for the woman in her final days, we forged a solid friendship.

With Alison off to query the lookie-loos, Hurley and I follow Junior down a path toward the dam, ducking under the police tape and climbing up onto one of two matching embankments bordering the structure. There, facedown in the water, is a body—a man, I think, judging from the build and the bald spot on the back of his head—one side of his body bobbing up against the wall of the dam. He is wearing knee-length shorts, and a Hawaiian-patterned shirt is billowing out around his torso. One of his feet is bare; the other is outfitted in what looks like a deck type of shoe.

"How deep is the water here?" I ask.

Hurley shrugs. Junior says, "The guys at the fire department said they think it's around eight feet deep at the wall."

I set down my scene kit, take out my camera, and start snapping pictures of everything I can see: the body, the dam, the park, the people in the park, the ground at our feet.

I hear footsteps behind us and turn to see Otto trudging toward us.

"Bummer," he says, with a bleak expression, staring at the floating corpse. "Do we know yet if he went in here?"

"He didn't," Junior says, shaking his head. "Some of the folks here in the park said they saw his body drifting downriver toward the dam. And a couple of kids who were fishing on the Main Street Bridge saw him go floating by about twenty minutes ago. So he went in somewhere upriver."

The fire department has arrived with their water rescue boat. They are hauling their equipment through the park when Otto turns to me and says, "One of us should be in the boat. Ideally, I'd prefer to have a diver in the water to take a look at the body before it's hauled out, but I don't suppose that's possible."

I chew on my lip, thinking. "I could do it," I tell him. "I received my PADI certification nine years ago when my ex and I were on a vacation in the Florida Keys. And I've done a half-dozen scuba dives in other places since then. If someone has the tanks and other equipment for me to borrow, I can go in and take a look."

Hurley looks at me like I'm crazy. "There's no way you're going in there."

"Why not? I know what I'm doing and if we want to maintain the best evidentiary chain, it should be someone from our office who goes in."

Otto looks at Hurley and shrugs. "She's right."

"It's too dangerous," Hurley insists.

"I can go in with a safety line, and another diver if need be."

Hurley rakes a hand through his hair, frowning at me. I know he can tell I've got my mind made up, and I also know he knows me well enough to know he won't be changing it. "We can get a police diver down here," he says, making one last attempt to dissuade me.

"I suppose you can, but how long will it take?" I say. "We don't have anyone local and it will take an hour or more to get someone here from Madison. I'm here, ready to go. And I have the necessary experience."

Hurley throws his head back and stares up at the sky, as if he's appealing to the gods. He lets out a weighty sigh and I know he's caving.

I look over at Junior. "Can you send someone over to the drugstore on Main to buy a couple of waterproof cameras? That way, I can take some pictures once I'm down there."

He nods, takes out his cell phone, and makes a call. The fire department folks are standing on the shoreline, eyeing the water and the body, calculating their best approach. I push past Hurley, who grumbles something unintelligible, and walk over to them. They all know me and there are some nods of acknowledgment, along with a couple of "Hey, Mattie" mumbles.

"Who's in charge?" I ask.

A guy named Dennis Andruss raises his hand.

"Do you guys have diving equipment? Tanks, masks, BCDs?"

Dennis nods. "We do, but at the moment I'm the only one here who's certified to use it. Our other local diver is out of town." He looks over at the body. "I don't think we need divers, though. We can take the Zodiac out there to the body and haul it in on an attached sled."

"I'd like to get a look at the site and the body before you move it," I tell him. "There's another site up at the lake that might be related. Any chance you can loan me the necessary equipment and go in with me?"

Dennis considers this and eventually nods. "Don't see why not."

"I don't have a bathing suit with me. Do you have a wet suit I can borrow?"

Dennis nods and waves for me to follow him. We head back to a locked trailer hitched onto the back of a pickup truck and Dennis unlocks the padlock. Inside is a ton of diving and water rescue equipment. Dennis climbs in and after a few minutes he has rounded up all the necessary equipment to get suited up.

"We'll have to rig both of us with a safety line," he says. "We'll be on the upriver side so we won't have the hydraulics to worry about, but the water at the base of the dam can still churn pretty hard."

The trailer has a light in it, so Dennis kindly allows me to undress inside with the doors closed. Taking my clothes off is easy, but getting into the wet suit, which is a smidge on the small side for me, is a bit of a challenge and every lump, bump, and extra bit of padding on my body is on full display. My scarfed-down sandwich is sitting in my stomach like a lead balloon and I swear I look like I'm pregnant again. I try to suck it in, but it's a futile effort. By the time I finish, I'm sweating like a pig. Stepping out into the warm summer air doesn't help the situation much, and I'm desperate to get into the water.

We haul the rest of our equipment back over toward the dam, but instead of climbing the bordering embankment, we head for a nearby shore area. I put on a weight belt that I suspect wouldn't be heavy enough if I wanted to descend any deeper than I need to today—fat is very buoyant. An officer hands me one of the waterproof cameras that were purchased, and I attach it to my wrist with its strap. Then Dennis and Hurley help me don my buoyancy vest and tanks, and I test the vest and the respirator. Finally I put on my snorkel and mask, and with some help from Hurley, my flippers. As I stand there bearing some ninety pounds of weight, and feeling my knees and back complain, the firefighters attach my safety line.

Feeling like a beached seal, I turn my back to the water and wade in backward. It's awkward going—the wet suit is so tight on me that my knees won't bend all the way— and Hurley takes off his shoes, rolls his pants legs up, and walks with me partway in. When he gets knee deep, I tell him I have it and part his company. After a few more steps, I'm in waist-deep water and the weight of the tanks eases some. I pause and look over at Dennis, who is shorter than I am, so the water is midway up his chest.

"Ready?" he asks me.

"Ready," I tell him, and then we both put our regulators in our mouths. We turn and aim ourselves toward the dam and the body, and then dive under the water. In an instant, I feel buoyant and wonderfully free of gravity and the weight I'm carrying. I kick my way over toward the dam, following Dennis, who has an underwater light. It's a good thing because the water is murky and green and our visibility is only about six to eight feet.

With frightening suddenness, the wall of the dam becomes visible and the body looms above us. I reel backward, afraid I'm going to bump into it. There is a lot of debris up against the dam wall, and I snap several pictures of it before doing anything else, knowing that some of that debris might be evidence. With those shots done, I turn my attention to the floater. I ease my way up closer to him, camera at the ready, and then stop in shock. My heart begins to race and I instinctively backpedal in the water. My eyes are fixed on that face, and Dennis, sensing something is wrong, swims up to me and tugs on my arm.

I look over at him, my eyes filled with fear, sadness, and disbelief. I want to tell him what the problem is, but, of course, I can't talk. Instead, I take a moment to collect myself and then give Dennis an okay sign with my hand.

But I'm not okay, far from it, in fact. The man in the river, the man whose body is floating above me, is my coworker Hal Dawson.

CHAPTER 12

After giving myself a few more seconds to calm my pounding heart and slow my breathing, I start snapping pictures of Hal. His eyes are colorless and opaque; his skin is so white it looks like alabaster. I can see a gaping wound on one side of his neck, and as I force myself closer, I see that it's deep—deep enough that both his jugular and carotid were likely severed. Hal probably bled out in a matter of a minute or two, which explains his coloring, but the bigger question is what caused the wound. I wonder if it might have been made postmortem— bodies in the water are sometimes hit by boat propellers, and fish and turtles tend to feed on the flesh—but the lines of the wound are clean and straight, not jagged like a propeller tear, not ragged or gnawed on as it would be if animals had fed on it. Someone cut Hal's neck intentionally.

I examine the rest of his body with my eyes, noting a gash on the palm of his right hand. It has the same clean edges as the neck wound and looks like a defensive wound. I snap pictures of it, and after I scan the rest of Hal's body, I motion to Dennis. I point upward and we break the surface a moment later.

"What happened down there?" Dennis asks me after he spits out his regulator.

I swim closer to him and talk right up next to his ear. I know sound carries well over water and I don't want the rubberneckers to hear what I have to say. "I know him," I tell Dennis. "It's my coworker Hal Dawson."

"Oh, geez," Dennis says, grimacing. "Sorry."

Hurley and Junior are standing on the embankment, straining to hear what we're saying. I tell Dennis, "We can go ahead and get the sled in the water." Dennis nods and swims over to where the rest of the water rescue group is on the shore. I swim up to the embankment and beckon Hurley down to my level with a finger.

"It's Hal Dawson," I tell him when he's on his knees.

"You're kidding," Hurley says, louder than I like, and I put a finger to my lips to shush him. "Are you sure?" he asks me just above a whisper, his face grim.

"I'm sure. And I'm also sure he didn't drown. He has a huge gash in his throat and his body is exsanguinated."

Hurley's brows draw down in confusion. "Ex-what?"

"Exsanguinated," I repeat. "His body is drained of blood. I also saw a gash on his hand that looks like a defensive wound. I don't know how he ended up in the water, but his death is anything but accidental."

I flash on my last conversation with Hal and remember something. "When I saw Hal this morning, he told me he had plans to go out in his boat today. Have the sheriffs traced the owner of the boat they found in the lake?"

"Good question," Hurley says, and he takes out his cell phone. I wait, watching Dennis swim the water sled—basically a rectangular surfboard with raised edges on three sides—over to where we are. By the time he reaches us, Hurley has finished his call. "Looks like we're going to be heading for the lake after this," he says. "The boat they found is registered to Hal."

"He said he was taking his girlfriend, Tina, with him. Was she on the boat?"

Hurley shrugs. "Don't know. Let me call them back and see what details I can find out."

As Hurley gets back on his phone, I swim back toward Hal. Over the next hour, Dennis and I retrieve Hal's body from the water, rolling it onto the sled so that he ends up facing the sky, and then pushing it over to the shore, where Otto takes charge with the help of Hurley and the rest of the fire department.

Once the body is secure, I go back down to snap pictures of and search among the debris on the river bottom and up against the dam. There are plenty of sticks, some soda and beer cans, a couple of beer bottles, a half-buried tire, and part of an old rubber boot. Then, about three feet back from the dam, I see something shiny on the bottom, nearly buried in silt. After snapping a picture, I carefully dig around and pull out a cell phone. It's dead, of course, so there is no way to know if it's Hal's or not, but I bring it to the surface and hand it off to Junior for bagging. After I feel I've searched the area thoroughly, I resurface and head for shore.

"Any news about Tina?" I ask after I've removed my flippers. Hurley helps me wade the last few feet out of the water and I toss the flippers aside. Then I turn around to let him help me out of my vest and tanks.

"Nope," he says in a low voice over my shoulder. "She wasn't on the boat. I've got some guys trying to track her down. The sheriff's office is sitting on the boat, watching it until we can get there."

I walk over to Hal's body, which is still on the sled covered with a sheet. Hurley shows me a set of keys, a wallet, and a small cloth-covered box—the kind that would hold a ring—items removed from Hal's shorts pockets. "It's Hal's wallet," he says unnecessarily. I have no doubt about the identity of our victim. As I head for the trailer to change back into my clothes, I can't tell if the wetness on my face is drips from my hair or tears for Hal.

It takes me half an hour to get out of my gear and dress, once again making use of the fire department's trailer. Otto has already called for a transport of Hal's body and, accompanied by Otto, it is on its way to the morgue by the time I emerge. I call Otto to check in.

"Hurley and I were planning to head up to the lake and take a look at the boat," I tell him. "Are you okay with that?"

"Absolutely. Keep an eye out for any evidence. From what I hear, there was a lot of blood on the boat, so I'm guessing that's our crime scene."

"There's something else," I say, giving Hurley a bleak, worried look. "I don't know if Hurley told you or not, but when Hal said he was going out on his boat today, he said he was planning on taking his girlfriend, Tina, with him."

Otto is silent for a few seconds. "Do you think she might have done this?"

"I've only met her a couple of times and they were both brief. She isn't the chatty type, and neither is Hal, so I don't know her or the nature of their relationship well enough to say. All I know is they've been dating for about a year. Hurley has some guys working on trying to find her now. I'll let you know as soon as I hear anything."

"Please do. In the meantime, I'll call around to see if I can get someone to come and assist with the autopsy. I imagine it will be difficult for you to do it."

"I'm on board with that," I say, feeling relieved. Autopsying anyone can be a grim process. Doing one on someone you know well is beyond the pale—though I'm not sure any of us could truly say we knew Hal well, because he was a quiet, keep-to-himself kind of guy.

I disconnect the call and look at Hurley. "This sucks."

"I'm sorry," he says. "Are you sure you're okay with coming along to look at Hal's boat?"

I nod. I can do it, but it will be hard.

The drive to the lake area takes us twenty minutes, and when we arrive, there is a taped-off area on the shore and an inflatable Zodiac at the water's edge. There are several sheriff's deputies milling about. As soon as we get out of the car, one of them, a woman named Greta Zorski, approaches us.

"Hey, Steve, Mattie," she says. "Hell of a day, eh?"

We know Greta because our police force and my office have worked closely with the sheriff's office in the past. Both forces are small enough and the county area covered is large enough that help is often needed from neighboring cops for cases. Hurley and I worked with Greta just a few months ago.

"Is that the boat?" Hurley says, shading his eyes with his hand and gazing out over the water. About two hundred feet from shore, we can see another Zodiac and a smaller, motorized jon boat moored up next to a larger, sleek-looking cruiser.

"It is," Greta says. "My guys are going over it now. I'll take you out to it if you want."

"We want," Hurley says.

The sound of a car approaching diverts our attention and I see Alison Miller drive up. She hops out of the vehicle and comes at us at a half-run, ducking beneath the police tape Greta's men have strung up around the area.

"Hold up there!" Greta says, moving toward Alison with her hand held out.

"It's okay," I say. "She's with the local paper. Let her through. She can be trusted."

"I know who she is," Greta grumbles, making me suspect Alison has ticked her off at some point in the past.

"She'll work with us," I say. "Trust me."

Greta doesn't look happy, but she lets Alison through.

"You guys left me," Alison says with a pout, slowing to a walk as she approaches. "If I hadn't heard one of the firemen say something about another search up this way, I wouldn't have known what was going on."

"Sorry, Alison," I say. "We were a bit distracted."

"That was Hal you found down at the dam, wasn't it?"

I don't know how she figured this out, but I see little sense in lying to her at this point. "It was."

"I thought so. One of the bystanders had one of those drone things with a camera and he got a good shot of the face."

That answered one question. These days, nothing could be kept secret.

"It looked like his throat had been slashed," Alison goes on, her eyes big. "Was he killed?"

"It appears that way," I say, "but it's not official yet. You can't—"

"I know, I know," Alison says, holding up a hand to stop me. "I won't print anything unless you guys okay it."

"Did you get anything out of the bystanders you talked to?" Hurley asks.

"Only the image of Hal's body. I offered the guy money for the shot, but he refused."

Greta clucks her disapproval at this and Alison shoots her a look. "I didn't want the picture so I could print it," she says irritably. "The paper wouldn't put anything that gruesome out anyway. I wanted it so the guy couldn't sell it to some other news outlet."

Greta rolls her eyes in disbelief.

"Is that Hal's boat?" Alison asks, nodding toward the bobbing flotilla out on the lake and dismissing Greta's blatant disapproval.

"It is," I say. "We're about to go out and have a look at it."

"Mind if I hang here and wait for you to come back?"

"That's fine," I say. "But don't pass on anything you know about this case until we give you the okay, got it?"

It's Alison who rolls her eyes this time. "I think I have the rules of the game down pat at this point," she says with a hint of impatience. She then steps aside, settling in at the base of a nearby tree.

After donning gloves and loading our scene kits into the Zodiac, a grumpy Greta takes us out to the boat. The sound of the Zodiac's motor and the roar of the wind make conversation difficult without yelling. If not for that, I'm sure Greta would be expressing her displeasure over our tolerance of Alison.

There are two techs and another sheriff on the boat already. It's a twenty-four-foot outboard with two seats and a bench going around the back. It could easily seat eight people, but with all of us standing and trying not to contaminate the evidence—a large pool of mostly dried blood just behind the driver's seat—it's a bit awkward. The sloshing of the boat in the waves makes for unsteady footing and doesn't help us any.

I shoot pictures of it all, my heart heavy as I imagine Hal seated behind the wheel, the wind blowing his thinning hair back, a big smile on his face. What the hell happened? There is a fishing pole on the deck, fully rigged with a hook, weight, bobber, and a dead minnow on the end. A second pole is lying over the bench seat on the starboard side, its line in the water. The pole is at an odd angle, the reel resting on the boat deck, and it looks like it was dropped rather than positioned there intentionally. On the bench on the port side is a tackle box, open, its trays scissored up, exposing all the contents. On the floor behind the passenger seat is a cooler, the lid of which is closed.

"Have you guys moved anything?" I ask the men on board.

The sheriff nods. "We opened the cooler to have a look, but we didn't touch or move anything inside it. Then we closed it again. It's just some beer and soda on ice, though there was some kind of oily substance on the lid. It's probably some kind of fish lure scent, but we went ahead and swabbed it. Other than that, all we've done is dust the handles on the rods for prints and obtain a bunch of swab samples from the blood."

I look at the blood pool again. There is a lot of it, and my nursing eye makes a rough estimate of about three pints. The perimeter of the pool is irregular, tentacles of blood running out from the main splotch, presumably a result of the boat's bobbing motion. There is also blood that has run down both sides of the back of the captain's chair. Along the top rim of the chair back, the blood is smeared on one side with what looks like the faint impression of a palm print. Along the starboard side of the boat and on the driver's control panel, I see several spray patterns of blood, some of which looks like castoff from whatever was used to cut Hal's throat, and some that looks like arterial spray. I wince, angry and sad over what happened to Hal, but also a smidge grateful knowing that, at least, his end came quickly.

"We need to find out Hal's blood type," I say aloud, snapping a picture of the palm print. "And we need to know if Tina was out here with Hal, try to find her, and get her blood type, too."

The sheriff who was on the boat frowns. "Are you saying there might have been two people on this boat originally?"

"It's possible. We know the victim. He works with me in the medical examiner's office. He said he and his girlfriend were planning to go out in the boat today."

I remember the ring box we found in Hal's pants and his comment this morning about how he had some fun stuff planned for the day. Had he proposed to Tina out here on the boat?

"Do you think she might have killed him?" Greta asks.

I give her an equivocal shrug. "It's possible, I suppose, but I doubt it." Then I tell her about the ring box.

Greta snorts a laugh. "I've been married and divorced three times already. A proposal would be enough to make me want to kill someone."

The other cops on the boat let out a few polite sniggers.

I manage a wan smile, but it's hard. This one is too personal for me and the typical morgue humor that tends to surface at scenes like this is lost on me today. To get everyone back to serious, I say, "If we go with the idea that Tina did kill him, how did she leave the boat?"

One of the techs, a short pudgy guy dressed in a bodysuit, mask, gloves, and booties, says, "There are some scratch marks and paint smears on the port side of the boat. Looks like they might have been made by a second boat coming alongside this one."

"Show me."

He does so, the two of us attempting to lean out over the side of the boat and peer down. It's awkward because neither of us wants to touch the edge of the boat or the bench seat in case there might be evidence there. By bending as far as I can, I just make out several scratches and what looks like smears of silver paint running about two feet along the side. I try to shoot some pictures of it, but the angle makes it difficult.

I look back at Greta. "Can you take me around to this side of the boat in the Zodiac?"

"Sure." We get back into the smaller boat and a minute later we are bobbing a few feet away from the port side of Hal's boat. I'm able to get some good pictures from this angle, and after I snap them, I ask Greta to circle the entire boat slowly so I can examine the rest of the exterior. There are no other marks we can see, but I notice something along the back of the boat, just to the right of the outboard motor.

"Look there," I say to Hurley. "It looks like hair."

He peers at where I'm pointing and nods. There are two long blond hairs caught between the edge of the motor and the boat body.

"Hal's hair is reddish brown and not that long," I say.

The implication is obvious. "You think those might be Tina's hairs," Hurley says.

We sit in the Zodiac, bobbing about on the waves, the three of us lost in thought. Finally I look at Hurley and say, "I need to dive down under the boat and take a look. Can you call Dennis and get him and his diving gear out here? And we're going to need some more of those waterproof cameras."

Hurley nods and makes the call. In the meantime, Greta eases the Zodiac up closer to the back of Hal's boat and we go about collecting the strands of hair. With that done, we tell the guys on the boat to stay put until our return, and Greta takes us back to shore.

"What did you find?" Alison asks as soon as we step ashore.

I defer to Hurley, letting him decide how much to reveal. "It's definitely the scene of the crime," he says. He purses his lips and frowns, and I know he's debating whether or not to tell her about Tina. "It's possible more than one person was on Hal's boat," he says finally.

Alison looks confused for a moment. "Are you saying someone who might have killed him was out on the boat with him?"

"Possibly," Hurley says, hedging.

It doesn't take Alison long to make the connection. She's shrewd, intelligent, and good at digging out the truth. "You think there might be another victim," she says. "I heard you talking on your phone and asking for the dive equipment to be brought out here."

"You heard that?" Hurley says, looking irritated.

"Sound travels quite well over water," Alison says, shrugging. "Is it his girlfriend, you think?"

"Do you know her?" I ask.

"A little," Alison says. "I've seen them out and about together in the past. They seemed like a solid couple."

"I don't want to speculate anymore," Hurley says, shutting down the information flow. "Let's wait until we're done here and see what we find."

While we wait for Dennis to arrive, Hurley makes some more calls to see if anyone has found out anything about Tina's whereabouts. "She's not at her house," he reports when he's done. "At least she's not answering the door, but her car is there. That suggests Hal might have picked her up. We need to check the marinas and see if we can find his car." With that, he's back on his phone, assigning more duties.

Dennis arrives and he and I are once again suited up and ready to go a short time later. As Alison settles in by her tree again, we climb into the Zodiac and put our flippers on as Greta runs us back out to the boat. She stops about ten feet away, and after doing a final safety check, Dennis counts down from three with his fingers. Holding our masks and regulators in place, we simultaneously roll ourselves backward, out opposite sides of the Zodiac. As soon as I'm situated in the water, I give the diving okay sign, which isn't an actual okay sign. I raise one arm up and curl it over my head. Dennis does the same, and then we release the air in our buoyancy vests and begin to descend.

The depth of the lake here is twenty to twenty-five feet, not deep enough for us to have to worry about the bends, and shallow enough to make an emergency ascent if we have to. After the dive in the river, I had Dennis add a little more weight to my belt, and I can feel the difference. My body's fat content makes me too good a floater and that makes it hard to achieve the neutral buoyancy needed to dive. But this time we seem to have hit on the right mix.

The water is green—a product of the runoff from all the neighboring, fertilized fields—and murky with a visibility of twelve to fifteen feet. It's enough for me to be able to make out Dennis's shape on the other side of the Zodiac. When we're about four feet below the surface, we start swimming toward Hal's boat. In a matter of seconds, the boat's bottom comes into view, and Dennis and I stop just beneath the hull and take a few moments to examine the underside of the boat. We find nothing of interest on the bottom of the boat after doing the full circuit, so I look over at Dennis and point along a line running from the back of the boat down to the lake bottom—presumably the anchor. He nods, and we deflate our vests and descend some more.

I see something that looks like seaweed, or a weird type of grass emerging from beneath me. Seconds later, I grab my regulator to keep from spitting it out.

Floating in front of me, her feet tied around an anchor, is the lifeless face of a blond-haired woman.

CHAPTER 13

Dennis sees her, too, and the two of us float, suspended in the water just above the lake bottom, staring into her dead eyes. I've only met Tina a couple of times before, but I can tell it's her. After recovering from my initial shock, I gather my wits enough to snap some pictures. It's a grim tableau, her eyes wide open, her hair billowing out around her head in a corona of wavering death, her mouth gaping open in a final, terrifying scream for air. The sound of my own ragged, frightened breaths makes me aware that I'm on the verge of panic. I tear my gaze away from her face and focus on her feet.

I stare at the anchor sitting on the lake bottom and focus on slowing my breathing. There is two feet or so of yellow nylon rope extending up from the anchor to Tina's feet. It's intertwined around her ankles with several knots, tied so tight it has caused indentations and abrasions on her skin. I snap a few close-up pictures of the anchor, the rope, and her lower legs. When that's done, I take a moment to survey the

Annelise Ryan

lake bottom, looking for anything else that might have gone over with her. I find a pair of eyeglasses and place them in a mesh bag I have attached to my waist. Tina wore glasses, and I remember Hal telling me how she didn't like to fish, but she did like going out on the boat to sit and read. I try to recall if there was a book anywhere on the boat and don't remember seeing one, but it might have been collected and bagged already by the sheriff's evidence techs. I move up higher on Tina's body, noting her hands are also bound, this time with fishing line. A bright glint of light catches my eye and I zero in on the diamond ring on her left hand: an engagement ring.

A wave of sadness washes over me. Given the ring box we found in Hal's pocket and the shiny bauble on Tina's hand, it seems obvious Hal chose today's boat ride as an opportunity to pop the question. I think about Tina planning for her wedding, her first wedding at the age of fortysomething. How excited she must have been for whatever brief amount of time they had before their happiness turned to tragedy. The thought makes me feel a sense of urgency about finalizing the plans Hurley and I are making. For a moment, I'm distracted by my mental list of things to do. I recognize my brain's attempts to escape the horror before me by dwelling instead on something more mundane and task oriented. I give myself a mental slap and refocus my brain on the job at hand, though the list remains a nagging reminder in the back of my mind.

When I'm done taking pictures, I give Dennis the sign for us to surface. We slowly inflate our vests and let the buoyancy bring us up. When we break the surface, I see the Zodiac that we came in floating some ten feet away, and the hull of Hal's boat a few feet from my face. I remove my regulator from my mouth and look at Dennis.

"How should we bring her up?" he asks.

"Let's head back to the Zodiac and let Hurley and Greta

know what we found. Then we can brainstorm on the best way to get her out while preserving as much evidence as we can."

He nods, and I stick my snorkel in my mouth and proceed to kick my way back to the Zodiac. When we get there, I take my face out of the water, spit out my snorkel, and give Hurley a grim look.

"Tina is down there, tied to an anchor. I didn't see any obvious wounds on her, so my guess at this point is she was tossed in and drowned."

Hurley and Greta both grimace with anger, disgust, and horror.

"How do you want us to bring her up?" I ask.

We discuss the options for a few minutes while Dennis and I float in the water. A shiver shakes me, and I'm not sure if the temperature or the situation caused it. Eventually we decide to cut the nylon rope somewhere between the anchor and Tina's legs, and then Dennis and I will bring up the body and place it on the same sled device we used on Hal. The anchor can then be winched up onto Hal's boat.

One hour and some extra manpower later, we have Tina's body on the sled being towed to shore, and the anchor with all the rope attached to it is safely ensconced in an evidence bag. A helicopter has been flying low overhead for the past half hour, and there is a TV news van with a satellite on top parked behind Alison's car, just beyond the scene perimeter. A reporter and cameraman are hovering at the edges of the police tape, chatting with the sheriffs assigned to maintain the scene. Alison has remained on the sidelines on our side of the tape, watching and listening, and occasionally glancing back at the other reporter with a smug expression. I have no doubt the story will be on the evening news, but I don't know how much the other agencies know at this point.

I place a call to the Johnson Funeral Home to arrange a pickup and get them on their way. Then I call Otto and give him an update on what we found, letting him know there will be another autopsy to perform.

"This is a horrible mess," he says when I'm done. "How are you holding up?"

"I'm doing okay," I say, wondering if I am. I can't shake off the image of Hal's and Tina's bodies floating pale and lifeless in the water. "Have you started on Hal's autopsy yet?"

"Not yet. There's been a delay in getting someone here to help. I had someone coming from Milwaukee, but there was a big smashup on the interstate, apparently involving a truck carrying some sort of chemical, and they have it shut down in both directions. My help is sitting in the middle of it, so I might have to call someone else to come in. Or maybe I'll just wait until the morning."

"What do you want me to do once I get Tina's body back to the morgue?"

"Check her in and then leave the rest up to me. Why don't you focus on helping the cops with their investigation? You knew Hal, so you might be able to provide some insight into the case. I don't want you or anyone else in your office involved in the autopsies. You're all too close."

"Understood. I should be there within the hour."

I feel waterlogged and creeped out, and I can't wait to get into some dry clothes. I change in the trailer and getting out of the diving gear helps some, but my fingers are wrinkled and white, and I can't get the smell of the lake water out of my nose or hair—but, I remind myself, it's still a better state than I was in last evening after sewing Ms. Abernathy back together.

When I emerge from the trailer, I see the news van has left. Alison approaches me, with a look of concern on her face. "Do you think this is a random thing, or do you think it might have something to do with Hal's job?"

"I don't know," I say honestly. "I hope it's the former."

"How much can I reveal in the paper?" she asks. "An edition comes out tomorrow."

I sigh, frowning. "I don't know if the connection between Hal and this scene has been made by the other agencies," I tell her. "And we don't have official IDs on either victim yet."

Alison cocks her head to the side and gives me an exasperated look. "Come on, Mattie. You and I both know who the victims are."

"But until the official IDs are made, the families won't be notified," I remind her. "Let's not cause too much emotional chaos."

Alison sighs and rolls her eyes at me. "Can I at least mention there might be a connection between the two deaths?"

"Check with Hurley. He might be willing to let you say the police are investigating a possible connection between the two." It's not an answer, but it's enough to make Alison's expression brighten, and she hurries over to Hurley. Judging from the happy look she has when she leaves him and heads back to her car, I'm guessing he agreed.

After helping to unload Tina's body from the sled into a hearse provided by the CassKit sisters, Hurley and I follow it back to the morgue. Hurley helps me check the body in and wheel it into the giant cooled storage room. Then we go looking for Otto. We find him in the dissection room, standing next to a table where Hal's body is already laid out. Hal is still fully clothed, his opaque eyes staring up at the ceiling, his skin the pale white of a fish's belly.

I glance at my watch and see it's already after five. I need to call Desi and tell her I'm going to be late. Then I realize I haven't heard anything from Dom or Izzy all day. I check my phone to see if I missed a call—the phone spent a lot of time hanging in my pants pocket in the trailer—but there's nothing. I think about Matthew, and then about Juliana, and I have an overwhelming urge to hug and hold those tiny, warm bodies, so full of blood and life and simple, smiling, innocent happiness.

"What's the status?" I ask Otto.

"Someone should be here in about thirty minutes. I called Madison and asked them to send someone, since the Milwaukee people are still tied up on the interstate and likely will be for hours."

"I put Tina's body in the fridge. I checked her in and did the necessary paperwork, but I didn't print her, get any vitreous fluid, or X-ray her at all."

"That's fine. You go on home. You look like you could use a meal and a hot shower."

"That I could," I admitted. "Have you heard any word on Izzy?"

"Oh, yes," Otto said, giving himself a slap on the forehead. "I'm glad you asked. I almost forgot. Dom called and said he's doing great and they are going to discharge him first thing in the morning. He asked if you could bring his daughter by the house sometime after six. He'll be home by then and he said he plans to head back to Madison in the morning to bring Izzy home."

"Can do," I say. While I adore Juliana, just thinking about caring for two kids for the rest of the evening leaves me feeling exhausted. No doubt the reality of it would have been much worse.

As Hurley and I bid Otto a good night and leave the morgue, I take out my phone and call my sister. "Hey, Desi. How are the kids doing?"

"They're fine. You can leave them here anytime you want. We've had a fun day."

"Wish I could say the same."

"Uh-oh, a rough one?"

"Very."

"It's not Izzy, is it?"

"No, he's fine. Apparently, he's going to be discharged in the morning."

"Oh, good. So it's something to do with a case, then?"

"It is. I don't want to go into detail over the phone. I'm getting ready to leave the office and should be there in ten minutes."

"Take your time. You can leave both kids here all night if you want."

"It's very kind and a little insane of you to offer, but I think Dom wants to have Juliana home with him. And I miss my little guy."

"He's missed you, too. He's pointed to the door and said 'Mama come,' at least ten times today."

"Aw, how sweet," I say, fighting a sudden, inexplicable urge to cry.

"Don't let it go to your head," Desi cautions. "He asked about Dada as many times as he did Mama, maybe more."

I look over at Hurley and smile. "Yeah, the kid's a bit of a daddy's boy," I say with a wink. "See you soon."

I disconnect the call and tell Hurley what Desi told me. He looks pleased, but also sad. "What's wrong?" I ask him.

"I want nothing more than to go home and spend some time with my kids, both of them," he says. "But I'm going to be at it all night long."

Such are the vagaries of both of our jobs. There is no nine-to-five standard. People die whenever and wherever.

"I can help you out, once I get Matthew fed and to bed. Emily can stay home with him tonight. I can't do much in the office right now anyway."

"Speaking of which," Hurley says with a frown, "we're going to have to look into Hal's desk space, and any cases he was working on."

I nod slowly, the full implications of Hal's death dawning on me. Had some case we'd worked in our office led to his murder? I wrack my brain thinking back on the cases we've handled since Hal joined us. He and I often shared cases and duties, so if something he worked was connected to his death, then I might be connected to it as well.

I look at Hurley and say, "You have to eat at some point, even if you work all night. Why don't I get Matthew home, figure something out for dinner, and then call you when we're ready to sit down. That way, you can come and join us."

"I can manage that," Hurley says with a grateful smile. But the smile fades quickly. "You aren't going to cook, are you?"

My cooking skills, or rather the lack thereof, are well known to all who know me. It's not that I *can't* cook; I just don't have the patience for doing it well and right. I've made an effort since Matthew's birth, and in the past year and a half, I've cooked more meals than I had in all of my thirty-five years before that. But even Matthew, whose appetite is as healthy and undiscriminating as my own, has been known to turn his nose up at my offerings. Worse yet, my dog, Hoover, named for his ability to suck up food, has even passed on some of my offerings. Last night's boxed mac and cheese with hot dogs is one of the few things I've mastered. It's my signature meal. I'm the kind of cook that would make Gordon Ramsay pop an aneurysm.

"No," I assure Hurley. "I'm thinking I'll get some takeout from Pesto Change-o. Do you want your usual?"

"Sounds good." He gives me a kiss—a quick peck on the lips—and without another word, he turns and leaves. I watch him walk away, admiring the sight of his retreating backside.

I make my way down to the underground garage, hop in my hearse, and arrive at my sister's house in just under ten minutes. Matthew is in the living room with his cousin Erika, the two of them reclining on a beanbag chair. Erika is reading Dr. Seuss's *One Fish, Two Fish, Red Fish, Blue*

Fish. It's Matthew's all-time favorite, so much so that I have the entire book memorized from reading it to him so often. As much as he loves the book, he loves his mama more. As soon as he sees me, he scrambles out of the beanbag chair and runs over to me.

"Me up," he pleads, extending his arms, and I oblige him, giving him a tight hug.

"Hi, Aunt Mattie," Erika says. "Mom's in the kitchen with Juliana. How was your day?"

"It was okay," I say, a bold-faced lie. Erika senses this and scrunches her face at me. "My bullshit detector is going off," she says, cocking her head to the side. "Want to talk about it?"

"Can't, at least not yet," I say. "And are you allowed to say 'bullshit'?"

"Absolutely not," she says with an evil smile. "You won't tell on me, will you?"

"Not if you promise to keep your language clean when you're around the little guy here."

"Oh, right." She claps a hand over her mouth and utters a muffled "Sorry."

I carry Matthew out to the kitchen, where I find my sister feeding turkey and rice baby food to Juliana, who is propped up in a baby seat on top of the counter.

"Almost done here," Desi says. She spoons some more of the concoction into Juliana's eager mouth and eyes me with a sidelong glance. "Anything you can tell me?"

"I can tell you some basics, because I'm sure it's going to be on the evening news. My coworker Hal Dawson was killed today."

Desi's mouth falls open and she drops the spoon into the bowl. "Oh, no," she says, giving me a sympathetic look. "What happened? Was he in an accident of some sort?"

I shake my head, debating how much to reveal. I don't know yet how much information will be released on the news, but plenty of people saw Hal's body come out of the water today. Despite our best efforts to keep the crowd at a distance and keep the body covered, given the prevalence of phone cameras these days—not to mention the drone Alison told us about—I have no doubt someone, somewhere, recognized Hal and saw that his throat was injured. What they won't know is how that injury occurred.

My sister is one of those rare birds that can actually keep a secret, an uncommon trait in a small town where gossip and insider knowledge is a highly valued commodity. However, her husband, Lucien, is a local attorney who specializes in defense. On the off chance he might end up representing whoever killed Hal, I don't want him to be privy to any insider knowledge ahead of time. And I don't want to put my sister in the position of having to keep secrets from her husband. Their marriage has gone through a rough patch in the not-so-distant past, and I don't want to complicate whatever repairs are in place.

"I can't say any more, at least not yet," I tell her.

She accepts this with an indifferent shrug. "You'll tell me when you can," she says, understanding my position.

"How have the kids been?" I ask, eager to change the subject.

"Good as gold." She picks up her dropped spoon, scoops some more of the baby food mixture onto it, and offers it to Juliana, who makes a face and turns her head.

"Looks like the princess here is done," she says, setting the spoon back down and wiping Juliana's messy face with a washcloth. Juliana clearly hates this; she squirms and fusses and then begins to cry. Desi scoops her out of the seat, holds her over her shoulder, and starts bouncing her. Juliana is instantly consoled, making me, not for the first time, marvel at my sister's mothering instincts and abilities. Desi was born to mothering, whereas there are days when I feel like I was dragged into it, kicking and screaming.

It takes me half an hour to package up the kids and all the paraphernalia that goes with them, and then load everything and everyone into the hearse. Lucien drives up just as I'm giving my sister a hug good-bye; to avoid any questioning from him, I hastily climb behind the wheel, give him a little wave of acknowledgment, and drive away.

CHAPTER 14

My next stop is Izzy and Dom's house and I'm glad to see Dom is home. He comes outside to the concrete area between their house and the cottage to help me unload Juliana and her stuff. Sylvie wanders out, too, pushing her walker ahead of her.

"There's my girl," Dom says, taking Juliana from my arms and kissing her on the cheek. Juliana coos and smiles at him, making Dom beam.

"About time my granddaughter came home," Sylvie grumbles with a telling glance at her watch.

"Sorry, I had a long day," I say. "How's Izzy doing?"

"He's cranky and complaining about the care, the food, the accommodations . . . all of it," Dom says with a roll of his eyes. But he's also smiling.

"Ah, so he's definitely on the mend," I say, returning the smile. A grumpy, complaining Izzy sounds like the good old Izzy we both know and love as opposed to the quiet, frightened Izzy I saw the other day. "I hear he's being released in the morning. Did you two have a chance to talk things over?"

Dom nods. "We have a ways to go yet, but we made some definite progress."

Sylvie lets out one of her *harrumphs* and clucks her tongue.

I'm tempted to give Sylvie a chastising look, but I know it would be a wasted use of my facial muscles. The woman can't be shamed or embarrassed, and she has no interest in political correctness or social politeness.

"Desi is watching Matthew for me again tomorrow and she said she'd be happy to keep Juliana, too," I say to Dom.

"That's okay. I'm going to bring her with me to the hospital. But thanks for taking her last night."

"Anytime. She's an angel."

"Yes, she is," he says, giving her another big kiss on the cheek.

I grab the diaper bag from the car and hand it to Dom. Then I take Juliana's car seat out and set it in the garage. "Desi just finished feeding Juliana, but she didn't give her a bottle yet."

"Got it. Thanks."

"If it's okay, I'll give you a call tomorrow afternoon after you get Izzy home and settled."

"That will be fine. Thanks again, Mattie." Dom turns and heads inside, and after a moment of hesitation, Sylvie toddles along behind him.

I get in my car and call Emily to make sure she's home and ask her what she wants to eat. Then I call Pesto Change-o—a number I have on speed dial—and order dinner before heading home to drop Matthew off.

As soon as we enter the house, Matthew releases my hand and runs toward the kitchen, where his sister is sitting at the table, doing something on her laptop.

"Memmy!" Matthew yells doing his funny waddle run.

As he approaches the doorway between the kitchen and living room, I see Rubbish hunkered down on the back of the couch by the doorway. I know what's about to happen, but I'm a split second too slow in trying to warn Matthew or distract Rubbish. The cat leaps off the back of the couch just as Matthew runs past, hitting him in the side of the head. Matthew staggers sideways, a look of surprise on his face, and then tumbles to the floor. The cat dashes between my legs, does a sliding turn at the base of the stairs, and runs up the steps.

Emily and I both burst out laughing. Matthew, who is still stunned and not sure what happened, pouts. He picks himself up from the floor and continues his journey, arriving at Emily with his arms extended, doing his standard "Me up." Emily, still laughing, scoops him into her arms, gives him a big kiss on the cheek, and says, "How's my favorite brother doing today?"

Cat attack already forgotten, Matthew smiles up at his sister and says, "Cookie." That's a word he learned very early on—not surprising, given who his mother is.

"Not until after dinner," I admonish, and Matthew sticks out his lower lip, points his finger at my face, and says, "Mama bad."

This makes both Emily and me laugh. "I have to go pick up dinner," I tell her as Matthew squirms out of her arms and crawls under the table to give Hoover a hug. "Are you planning on staying home tonight?"

"Yeah, why? Need me to babysit?"

"If you don't mind. Your dad and I picked up a big case today and there's a lot of stuff to do. He'll be home for dinner, but after that, he'll probably be working until very late. I thought I'd give him a hand if you can stay home with Matthew for a few hours."

"No problem."

Matthew, still under the table, his head resting on Hoover's belly, says, "Hooba cookie."

"Aw, he wants a cookie for Hoover," Emily says, getting up from the table.

"Don't fall for it," I tell her, giving my son a sly look. "Matthew will eat a dog cookie, just like he eats a human one."

I leave Matthew in Emily's hands and head for Pesto Change-o to pick up our meal. I call Hurley on the way back, to let him know the food is ready. By the time I get home, Emily has the kitchen table—which seems to be a gathering place for all kinds of paraphernalia, such as mail, purses, laptops, diaper bags, dog treats, and the occasional dirty dish—cleared and ready to go. Hurley arrives a few minutes later and we manage to pretend for the next half hour that we're a normal family sitting down to dinner. Though I'm dying to ask Hurley about the investigation, the two of us steer the conversation in other directions in deference to the kids. It turns out to be for naught.

"When are you going to tell me about your coworker?" Emily asks.

I nearly choke on a piece of sausage I've just stuffed in my mouth, and I take the time to chew and think about my answer.

"I saw it on the news," Emily says as I'm stalling. "They said someone was found dead in the river, and there was a picture of the dead man taken by someone with a drone camera. They tentatively identified the victim as Hal. And then they said there was another body found in the lake near a boat. They showed footage from some flyover news copter and from the shore, though the shore footage just showed a bunch of police tape and the boat off in the distance. But the overhead pictures made it clear something bad happened, because there were cops everywhere and blood on the boat.

They said the second victim appeared to be a woman, but they didn't identify her. And they said the two bodies might be connected, because the registration number on the boat identified it as belonging to Harold Dawson."

So much for keeping things under wraps. I imagine Alison will be annoyed that the TV news people were able to dig up that much information, but it should help ease any doubts Hurley might have had about letting Alison print the same information in tomorrow's paper.

I shoot Hurley a look and say, "What you heard is true. But I'd rather not discuss it in front of Matthew."

At the sound of his name, Matthew looks up from his plate of spaghetti, half of which he is wearing, and smiles. "Me," he says.

"That's right," I say with a return smile. "You are Matthew."

Hurley reaches over and picks several strands of spaghetti off Matthew's shirt and then plucks one hanging from his hair. Then he chucks Matthew beneath his chin with a finger.

"Dada," Matthew says, flinging out his fork-holding hand and pointing it at Hurley. Unfortunately, the fork is full of spaghetti, half of which is now on Hurley's shirt. Matthew laughs hysterically, and this makes Hurley chuckle.

"Don't laugh, you'll just encourage him," I say, struggling to refrain from doing so myself. Emily is biting back a smile, too, and Matthew, seeing he has a rapt and appreciative audience, promptly scoops more spaghetti onto his fork and flings it at his father.

"Matthew!" Hurley says, trying to sound stern, but our kid isn't buying it.

Matthew laughs so hard he drops his fork on the floor. Hoover makes quick work of the lingering spaghetti on the utensil—one nice thing about Hoover is I rarely have to clean food off the floor—and Matthew giggles for a moment and then points to his dropped fork. "Up," he says. When no

one responds quickly enough, he turns and gives me a pleading look. "Up!" he says more adamantly.

I shake my head at him, get up and grab a clean fork—
though the kid is using his hands more than anything else to
eat the spaghetti—and hand it to him. Matthew promptly
throws the clean fork aside, points to the one on the floor,
and repeats his demand.

"Use this one, Matthew," I say, handing him the clean fork
again. Not only does he refuse to take it, he starts kicking and
screaming. "Up!" he cries, pointing to the floor. "UP!"

It amazes me how the kid can go from laughing hysterically to a complete meltdown in less than thirty seconds. We
all stare at him as his tantrum builds. His arms and legs flail,
and he's crying so hard you'd think someone was torturing
him.

I give Hurley a tired smile. "I think he's done. Do you
want to take him upstairs or should I?"

"Let me," Hurley says, setting down his fork. "I need to
clean up and change anyway."

Hurley drags Matthew, kicking and screaming, out of his
chair. Then he tucks him under one arm like a football and
hauls him upstairs. I look at Emily with a wan smile. "Are
you sure you're up for this? I think we're seeing the start of
the terrible twos."

"He'll be fine," she says. "I'll be fine. He doesn't seem to
throw his tantrums with me."

This is true. I've noticed Matthew will do anything for
his big sister, Memmy. It's ironic when I remember how I
once thought his presence was the source of all of Emily's
problems. It turned out I was the bigger problem.

"How are the wedding plans going?" Emily asks.

"I think we may have to put things on hold for a bit. With
what happened to Hal, I'm going to have to work full-time
for a while. And with Izzy's heart attack, things are bound to
be more hectic than usual in the office."

As if my words could be heard miles and miles away, my cell phone rings and I see from the caller ID that it's Izzy.

"Speak of the devil," I say, showing Emily the caller ID. As I answer the call, she gets up from the table and heads upstairs to help her father. It's probably a good thing, because I can hear Matthew still screaming.

"Izzy, how are you?"

"I'm fine," he grumbles. "Or at least I will be when I can get out of this place. I just heard about Hal on the news. What the hell is going on?"

I fill him in on the details of Hal's and Tina's deaths. "Otto had someone come in from Madison to assist with the autopsies, and Hurley and I are going to be looking into the case tonight."

"I should be there," Izzy says.

"No, you should be home with your feet up, letting Dom wait on you. Did he tell you he blames himself for your heart attack?"

"Yeah, he said something along those lines last night when he got here. It's a bunch of bull, and I told him so. He seems to think Juliana's presence has added too much stress to my life."

"Has it?"

"Hell no. That little girl is what kept me going the past twenty-four hours. Has her presence in our lives complicated things? Yeah, I can't deny that. But she's wormed her way into my heart and I can't imagine life without her."

I smile, wondering if I should warn him now about the terrible twos or wait and let him find out on his own. I decide to wait. Chances are, he'll get to see a display of what's in store for him one of these days when I drop by for a visit with Matthew.

"We have things under control at the office," I tell him. "Otto seems quite capable and he said he can stay on as long as we need him. You rest, get better, and spend some time with that little girl of yours. And with Dom. That man loves you so much, Izzy. You're lucky to have him, you know."

"Yeah, yeah, I know. I could say the same thing about you with Hurley."

"Yeah, yeah, I know," I repeat. And then, with a laugh, I add, "He's lucky to have me."

The sound of Izzy's chuckle does my heart good.

"You scared the crap out of me, Izzy," I say, sobering. "I was so afraid I was going to lose you."

"I'm tougher than you think."

"Oh, I know you are. That's part of the problem. You need to learn to let stuff out more often, not hold it in."

"If I do that, I'll turn into my mother."

"Well, she's what . . . eighty-six? And still going strong. Maybe she's onto something."

"I think she's just too ornery to die."

I'm inclined to agree with him, but don't want to accede my point, so I change the subject. "You're going to have to make some dietary changes, too, you know. Start eating healthy stuff."

"Yeah, yeah, yeah. Next you'll be trying to drag me off to the gym with you and Richmond."

"I haven't been to the gym in months," I admit.

"Uh-oh," Izzy says. "Nurse Ratched just came into the room. I need to go so I can fend her off."

"Okay, good night, Izzy."

"Good night, Mattie."

As I disconnect the call, I say a silent prayer of thanks to whatever deities are keeping Izzy safe and alive. He's the closest thing to a father I've had for the past decade. My real father deserted my mother and me when I was four, and though I suspect he may soon resurface, it will most likely be behind bars.

CHAPTER 15

With Matthew once again returned to the sweet, loving child I know he can be, now that he's in Emily's care, Hurley and I head out for the police station.

"I've got some guys going through Hal's house," Hurley tells me when we're settled in the car. "And I'm working on trying to get into Tina's house, but we haven't found any trace of a purse or keys on her person or on the boat."

"Have you notified any next of kin yet?"

"I called the state patrol in Illinois and had some guys notify Hal's parents right before I came home for dinner. I don't want to notify any of Tina's family until we have a definite ID. Doc Morton was able to get her fingerprints, but they're not in AFIS. So he has to try to get the dental records. He said he isn't going to do her autopsy until the morning."

It's probably smart to wait, I think, though I wonder if it is. The worst thing would be for the family to hear about

Tina's death on the news before any official notification is made.

"Tina had no keys?" I say to Hurley. "That seems odd. Have you checked in Hal's truck?"

Hurley shakes his head. "Not yet. We only just found it. We scoured all the marinas, starting with the ones closest to where Hal lives, but struck out. Then we got a phone call an hour ago from some guy named Ted Washburn, because a friend of his who stores his boat at his house went out earlier today and hasn't returned. Washburn heard there were cops out on the lake swarming over a boat, so he called the state patrol. They called us when Washburn told them his friend was Harold Dawson. We arranged to have the truck towed to the police garage, but I don't know if Jonas has had a chance to look it over yet."

As soon as we arrive at the station, we head straight down to the basement, where the evidence locker, police garage, and Jonas's work area are located. We find Jonas in the garage standing alongside a blue Chevy pickup, which I recognize as Hal's. The driver's-side door is ajar and Jonas is standing next to it, jotting something down on a clipboard. I see several small evidence packages laid out on a nearby table, each one sealed and labeled. Also on the table is a woman's purse.

"Hey, guys," Jonas says when he hears us enter. "Good timing. I was just about to go through that purse over there." He nods toward the table. "I found it tucked under the front passenger seat, so I'm guessing it belonged to Hal's lady friend."

"Find anything else of interest in the truck?" Hurley asks.

"Maybe," Jonas says. "But before I get into that, I wanted to let you know I finished going through Carolyn Abernathy's cell phone. That Lundberg guy did text and call her several times over the weekend, but there was no response from her. I looked into his phone number and it belongs to a pay-as-you-go burner phone, a pretty basic one."

"So nothing of much help," Hurley says. "Any luck with that trash from the motel?"

"Haven't finished with it yet," he says. "I got pulled into this thing with Hal."

Hurley nods. "I understand making Hal a priority," he says. "But let's not forget the other case. If you need some help, get some of the uniformed guys to come in and sift through that trash. With three deaths to investigate, I'm certain the chief will okay the overtime."

"Got it," Jonas says. "On to Hal's case." He waves a hand over the items on the table. "This is the stuff I found in his truck. Ordinary for the most part, but there are a couple of interesting things. The lip balm might prove helpful if we can get DNA from someone other than Hal or Tina off it, but given where I found it in the center console, I'd be surprised if that happens."

He then points to a clear plastic evidence bag containing a necklace. It's a thick gold chain with a round gold disc on it. Engraved on the disc is the profile of a woman, similar to what one might see on a cameo. I pick up the bag and stare at the necklace. Something about it seems very familiar, giving me a strong sense of déjà vu.

"This is an interesting find," Jonas says. "It appears to be a piece of old Gypsy jewelry. I dated a girl years ago who collected old jewelry, and I did some research on it. The Gypsies always used real gold in their jewelry, and the profile on this pendant is a typical engraving you might see on a Gypsy piece. It's probably close to a century old, a family heirloom most likely. I found it underneath the passenger seat, so it might have belonged to someone other than Harold, probably Tina, though I've never seen her wear jewelry of any kind. On the off chance that it's not hers, I swabbed the chain. With any luck, we might be able to find some skin cells in it and get a DNA profile."

I keep staring at the piece, wracking my brain, certain I've seen it somewhere before. A flash of memory comes to me—a vision of a dark, hairy chest—and for a split second, I think I can smell pipe tobacco. I raise the bag to my nose and sniff it.

Hurley gives me an amused look. "What are you doing?"

"I thought I smelled something." I look over at Jonas. "Did you notice any smells on it when you bagged it?"

He shakes his head.

I shake mine, too, more to rid myself of a growing suspicion than anything, and set the bag down. Then I take out my phone and snap a picture of it. "Any smells you noticed inside the truck?"

Jonas shrugs. "There's a pine-tree-scented thing hanging from the rearview mirror, and the seats are leather. Other than that, not really."

"What's with the smell fixation?" Hurley asks, looking at me strangely.

"I don't know. I thought I smelled something on the bag with the pendant, but it must have been some weird brain trick."

"What was it you think you smelled?"

"I don't know," I lie. "It was there and gone, kind of vague. I think it must have been a figment of my imagination, or some kind of subconscious memory association." I shrug and smile. "Maybe it will come to me later."

Jonas moves on to some other items on the table: some receipts, a metal travel mug, with its inside stained from coffee, some coins, some maps, and a USB stick. Other than the thumb drive, none of these items seem of any great interest. After Hurley tells Jonas to have a look at what's on the USB drive as soon as possible, we move on to the purse that is, presumably, Tina's.

Our presumption is verified when we find a wallet inside containing Tina's driver's license, a set of keys including one to a Toyota, and a variety of other miscellany: makeup, loose change, a tampon, a checkbook, some pens, some lip balm, a small bottle of ibuprofen, and an older-model flip-type cell phone.

Jonas opens the phone and starts pressing buttons. "No voice mails, no texts," he says. "There are several calls from Hal Dawson—that's no surprise. And there are some other calls here, one identified as the library, one from and one to . . ." He drifts off, his brow furrowed. "That's weird," he says. "Those calls are to a Lech Wyzinski."

"Wyzinski?" I say. I look over at Hurley. "Tomas Wyzinski is the guy I testified against earlier this week. And he has a brother named Lech."

"Why would Tina be talking to Tomas's brother?" Hurley asks.

"I have no idea," I say. "But I'm going to find out."

Hurley fingers the keys from the purse with his gloved hand and says to Jonas, "Tina Carson owns a Toyota, so these must be hers. Hopefully, one of these other keys will get us into her house. Can you dust them for prints, so I can take them?"

"Can do," Jonas says. He takes the key ring from Hurley and carries it over to another table in the far corner. There, Jonas has a variety of powders, brushes, tape, and other paraphernalia used to recover fingerprints, including several small bottles of superglue and a plastic box with a small heating pan inside it used for cyanoacrylate fuming, a process used to obtain latent fingerprints. He spreads the keys out, selects a red-colored powder and a brush, and starts dusting the keys.

While Jonas is busy with the keys, Hurley and I walk over to the truck and take a look. The inside of the cab is quite clean, not a surprise since I know Hal was a very meticulous person. I take a whiff of the inside air, doing so in a way I hope Hurley won't notice. If there is any lingering scent of pipe tobacco in the cab, I can't smell it, and I chalk up the earlier experience to a weird memory hiccup.

We move on to the bed of the truck, which has a black liner in it. It, too, is quite clean. There is a spare tire on one side, and an empty gas can on the other. The floor has a few small areas of dark staining, which could be anything from spilled oil or gasoline to fish guts.

"Can you swab these stains in the bed of the truck?" Hurley says over his shoulder to Jonas. "I don't expect they'll be anything significant, but we should check them out anyway."

"Will do," Jonas says. "I'll have to get Arnie to run them on his mass spec, but that likely won't happen until tomorrow sometime."

The mass spectrometer, an expensive piece of machinery that analyzes substances by their chemical makeup, is housed in Arnie's laboratory. We prefer to do as much of the evidence processing as we can here in town rather than send it to the lab in Madison. The local duties are shared by Jonas and Arnie, who work closely together to avoid duplication and keep communication channels open. Arnie and Jonas also share Laura, perhaps in ways I don't want to imagine. Personal issues aside, her hours are split between the two entities, a budget-managing tactic that helps us get the job done. Jonas does all of the large-item processing, things like vehicles and boats, and Arnie has most of the delicate scientific equipment for analyzing small stuff. They both collect and process evidence in their respective work areas.

All findings related to a case get uploaded into a computer file for that specific case and a paper copy is kept as a backup. Anything significant is verbally communicated to the lead detective as well.

"That's fine," Hurley says. "No rush. I doubt you'll find

anything relevant to the case in the truck. Everything seems to have taken place in the boat."

"It's due to arrive here in the next hour or so," Jonas says. "I'll get on it as soon as it does. And Laura is going to work all night tonight to help."

I wander back to the evidence table and study the pendant. A cold feeling settles over me. In a flash, I know where that necklace came from.

Jonas finishes his job on the keys and hands them over to Hurley. "I got several prints, mostly partials," he says. "Odds are, they'll be Tina's."

"Get them over to Arnie first thing in the morning and he can do a comparison for us," I say.

"Will do," Jonas says with a snappy salute.

"Sorry," I say with an apologetic smile. "I didn't mean to sound like a drill sergeant."

Jonas waves away my concern. "Just messing with you," he says with a smile. Then his expression turns somber. "This case has special meaning to all of us and that's bound to set everyone's nerves on edge a little more than usual. I was just trying to lighten things up a little. Sorry."

"Don't worry about it," I say. "You're right. This case won't be easy for any of us. Let's just make sure we do our very best to get some justice for Hal and Tina."

"Let's work on that with a visit to Tina's house," Hurley says to me, pocketing Tina's keys. "Keep up the good work, Jonas."

Hurley and I leave the station and get into his car. Both of us are silent during the drive and I assume his thoughts, like mine, are focused on Hal, Tina, and the tragedy that befell them. But it turns out I'm wrong, at least partially.

"What was the deal with that pendant you were looking at?"

"Nothing special," I say with a halfhearted shrug. "For a moment, I thought it looked familiar to me, but it wasn't."

"You're lying to me, Winston." He frowns and makes a noise like he's trying to clear his throat. "I've got to quit calling you that. You're not going to be Mattie Winston much longer."

"Well, if I take your name, it will just get confusing because we'll both be calling one another Hurley," I say, glad the subject has been changed. "I suppose you could call me by my first name like everyone else does."

He shakes his head. "Nah, I need something unique, something that is just mine."

"How sweet," I say with a smile.

"I could call you 'Matterhorn,' since that's technically your real first name."

"You could," I respond, my smile fading in a flash, "but then I'd want to kill you."

"Ouch. Okay, how about something along the lines of 'wifey' or 'old lady'?"

I give him a sly smile, knowing he's yanking my chain.

"Or to get back to my original question, how about 'liar'? I know you're not telling me the truth about that pendant."

"Yeah," I say very slowly. "Okay, I have a hunch about the pendant, but it's a long shot and I'm not sure it will pan out. I need to think about it a little more before I commit." This is my attempt at a stalling tactic, and I hope it will work, but Hurley can be as determined as a dog on the scent when it comes to things like this.

"If it's relevant to the case, or even may be relevant, you should tell me. Talk it out with me. Two heads are better than one."

"Not yet. Give me a day, okay?"

Another frown, and for a second, I think I've won. But then, to my shock and surprise, he pulls over to the side of the street and stops the car. He turns toward me, his arm on the edge of my seatback. "Sometimes I feel like you're keeping things from me," he says. "Important things. And if we're going to go through with this marriage thing, we need to get things out on the table."

I sigh and let my head loll back. His hand drops down from the seatback and massages the top of my head.

"Look, if you don't want to go through with the marriage thing, I'll understand," he says.

"That's not it, Hurley."

"Then why are you waffling on setting a date?"

"Because it's complicated. And if you remember, I did agree to a date, but things fell apart—literally—in the case of the park. So we still need to find a venue, and there are a million other things to plan and do. I have to find a dress for me, and a dress for Emily, and figure out if we're going to have a reception, and who to invite to what . . . it's an endless list. And my life has been a bit busy lately, in case you hadn't noticed. Not to mention it's going to get a lot busier now that Hal's . . . with Hal and Izzy . . . you know."

"I know. We're both busy. But we don't need to do anything fancy. Let's keep it simple . . . go before a justice of the peace, or take Otto up on the offer of his backyard. The ceremony location doesn't matter. What matters is our commitment to one another and to our family, right?"

"Of course," I say, rolling my eyes at him. "But I want it to be something meaningful and memorable. I don't mind casual, but I'd like to have something special to wear for the occasion. And you don't know how hard it is for me to find nice clothes that fit. I'm too tall, too round, and have arms like a baboon. Finding an outfit of any kind is a challenge. And don't even get me started on the shoes. I've got feet like the Abominable Snowman and they don't make pretty, girly shoes in Sasquatch sizes."

"That's it!" he says, taking his hand from my head and snapping his fingers. "I'm going to call you 'Squatch' from now on."

I roll my head to the side and give him a look of disbelief. "You're kidding, right?"

"It's something uniquely you," he says, leaning over and giving me a kiss on my nose.

He's right about that, and for some odd reason, though I should probably be offended by the name, I kind of like it. "Fine," I say. "Squatch it is."

"Okay, Squatch," he says, checking his side mirror and shifting the car back into gear. He pulls out onto the street and continues our drive. "If you're being honest about your willingness to go ahead with it, then let's firm up the date and the place. We're getting married in two weeks, in the early evening on the Fourth of July. We'll do it at our house and it will be a small group of just family. That includes Izzy and Dom, of course. I've already talked to a judge here in town who's willing to officiate. We'll make it very informal. Hell, you can wear your jammies and slippers if you want. After that, we'll host a small dinner party at Pesto Change-o to celebrate. I've talked to Georgio and he said he'd be glad to let us use his banquet room."

"I don't know what to say," I tell him. It's the truth. I'm speechless. I can't believe Hurley has been planning this all along, some of it behind my back.

"You can say it's okay. You've done the big fancy wedding stuff before, so there's no need to do it again, right?"

"Right." I have no qualms about the level of simplicity he's suggesting, but the rapidly approaching date has me nervous, not because I'm unsure about marrying him. I've never felt more certain about anything in my entire life. But there's a small catch. Hurley is absolutely right to suspect I'm keeping secrets from him . . . one secret anyway, and it's a big one. His intuition is on target: it has to do with that pendant.

"So let's do it, Squatch," Hurley says as we arrive at Tina Carson's house. He pulls to the curb and turns off the engine. Once again he turns to look at me, his big blue eyes searching my face, his expression hopeful yet guarded. He reaches over and brushes a strand of hair away from my face, his gaze roaming over my head. "I do love you, Squatch," he says, his voice low and tender. I feel something in my gut go all soft and squishy. "You know that, right?"

I nod. "I love you, too, Hurley, so much it scares me."

"Then what's the problem?"

I realize the time has come. I need to tell him the truth, the truth about my father, my background, his background, and how they all tie together. I'm not sure how he'll take it, but the truth needs to come out.

"Before I agree to your plans, I need to tell you something," I say, bracing myself. "If you still want to marry me once you hear what I have to say, then I'm more than happy to go ahead with your plans."

He leans away from me, effectively bracing himself. He looks wary, a little frightened even, and I wonder what possibilities are racing through his mind.

With a steadying breath, I turn in my seat to face him and begin.

CHAPTER 16

"It's about my father," I tell Hurley. But before I can utter another word, a pounding sound comes from behind me, making me jump. I whip around, banging my knee on the glove box. A face is staring at me through the window and it takes me a second to recognize it. It takes me several more seconds to slow my heart.

For once, I'm glad to have Alison Miller show up at an inopportune time, though I can't say the same for Hurley. He looks thoroughly annoyed as he lets out a perturbed breath.

Alison waves, staring back at me with a smile bordering on maniacal. I lift my handle, my warning to her to step back, and she does so. "What are you doing here, Alison?" I ask as I open the door. I spin around and put my feet on the ground, taking a moment to massage my aching knee.

"I figured you guys would be showing up here sooner or later. I tried to get someone over at Hal's house to tell me something . . . anything . . . but none of them will talk to me."

Hurley has gotten out of the car and walked around to my side. "What makes you think we're going to be any different?" he grumbles.

"Aw, come on, Hurley. Give a girl a break."

Considering all Alison has been through over the past year, it's hard to ignore her plea, especially since she's also helped me out a time or two by digging up information. Hurley has been a lot more trusting of Alison lately—a trust she had to earn—and I think his reticence now is because he's so annoyed by her untimely interruption of our conversation.

I give Hurley a pleading look and his stern expression goes slack. Not that it makes any difference. "We'll keep you in the loop, Alison," I tell her. "But to be honest, we don't have anything new to tell you yet."

Hurley stares at the house impatiently.

I look around at the neighboring houses. It's still light out, but the sun is low in the west, casting shadows over the lawns and street. In another hour, it will be dark. I see curtains twitching in windows in nearby houses as curious neighbors spy on us, eager to know what's going on.

And then the front door opens in the house immediately to the right of Tina's. An elderly woman with steel-gray hair, a full, wrinkled face, and a plodding, cane-assisted gait emerges and heads for us. She is dressed in a ratty-looking housecoat worn over a pair of overalls and an old, faded Grateful Dead T-shirt.

"You the cops?" she asks, a bit breathless from her exertions.

Hurley nods and flashes his badge. I show my badge, too, but don't offer any explanation as to what office I'm from. Alison says and does nothing.

"Was Tina the one killed in that boating incident?" the woman asks.

"Why would you think that?" Hurley counters, handily avoiding an answer.

"I talked to her yesterday and she said she was going out on the boat with that boyfriend of hers today." The woman shrugs. "She sometimes spends the night at his place, but I noticed when he picked her up this morning that she didn't have any kind of overnight bag. Usually, she's home by now if it's just a day trip."

"We haven't officially identified the woman involved yet," Hurley says. "But if it was your neighbor, are you aware of anyone who might want to harm her?"

"Harm Tina?" She makes a little *pfft* sound and shakes her head. "Can't imagine it," she adds. "Tina is one of the nicest people you'll ever meet. Kind of a quiet loner, though, other than the time she spends with that fella." She pauses and cocks her head to the side, narrowing her fleshy eyes at Hurley. "I may be old and slow, but I'm not stupid. If you haven't identified the victim yet, what are you doing here at Tina's house?" She nods toward his hand. "I'm pretty sure those are her house keys you're holding."

I look over at Hurley and raise my eyebrows, giving him a "gotcha" smile. I'm curious to see how he's going to field this one.

"Okay, we're fairly certain the victim was Tina," Hurley says, "but until we make an official identification and notify her family, I don't want that information getting out. I'm sure you can imagine how devastating it would be to learn about a loved one's death via gossip or the TV news."

"Of course," she says, sounding a tad annoyed. "Like I said, I'm not stupid. I'm also not one of them gossipy types. I like my privacy and I try to respect other people's, too."

"I'm glad you understand, Ms. . . . ."

"It's *Miss,*" she says impatiently. "But please just call me Gloria, Gloria Needham."

"Thank you, Miss Needham," Hurley says with his most charming smile. "Please don't share any information with your neighbors until you hear the identity announced officially on the news." He turns to head for Tina Carson's front door, but Gloria stops him in his tracks.

"So, does that mean you aren't interested in the man who was snooping around Tina's house earlier today?"

"Who?" Alison asks, jumping on it as Hurley whirls back around with a frown.

"Hell if I know," Gloria says. "Never seen the guy before. And he's the type I would remember. Distinctive-looking, you know?"

Hurley opens his mouth to ask her something, but Alison beats him to it.

"How so?"

"He was a real big guy, like six and a half feet or so. I could tell because he was able to look into Tina's kitchen window around back without standing on his toes or anything. He was big the other way, too. Broad, you know. Kind of resembled a block of cement with legs."

"What time was this?" I ask, beating Alison to the punch.

"It was this morning, around eleven or so," Gloria says. "Tina wasn't home, of course. She left around nine when her boyfriend came to pick her up."

Hurley finally gets a question in. "Did he knock on the front door at all, or was he only in the back?"

Gloria shrugs. "Can't say for sure. My kitchen window looks out on the back of the house, so he might have gone to the front first. If he did, I wouldn't have been able to see it. You could ask Elsie. She lives in that yellow house across the street and she's usually watching out her living-room window every day. Elsie's got the dropsy, you know, so she spends most of her day in a recliner right by her front window. She doesn't get around so well, but she doesn't miss much that goes on in the neighborhood."

I glance across the street and, sure enough, I can see the vague shape of someone on the other side of the sheer curtains in the picture window of the house Gloria indicated.

"Can you describe this man more for me?" Hurley says, taking out his notebook and pen. "What about his hair? Did he have any distinctive facial or body features? And what was he wearing?"

Gloria scrunches up her face, creating even more wrinkles. "His hair was dark and thin on top. He had one of those comb-over things, you know, the way men do when they try to hide the fact they're going bald? The breeze caught it once and made it stand up on his head like a Mohawk."

Hurley nods and scribbles down the details as Gloria continues. I see Alison is taking notes, too, and I make a mental note to remind her she can't print the info in the paper.

"As for his clothes, he wasn't much of a dresser. Had on them chino kind of shorts, and he wore them low beneath his gut. His shirt was just a big old tee, gray I think. I remember his shoes well, though," she adds after a momentary pause. "They were sneakers, all white. Didn't go with the rest of his outfit at all. And his feet were huge." She pauses again and glances down at my feet. "Kind of like your lady friend here."

Hurley bites back a grin and shoots me a sly side glance.

"That's about it," Gloria concludes.

"This is very helpful," Hurley says, still scribbling. After a moment, he finishes and tucks the notebook back into his jeans pocket. "Again, I'm going to ask you to keep this information to yourself," he adds, giving Gloria a stern look. "This man might be dangerous and it might not bode well for you if it got out that you saw him."

Gloria waves away his concern. "*Pshaw*. I can take care of myself," she says. "I got Bessie to protect me."

"Bessie?" I echo. "Is that a dog?"

"Hell no," Gloria says, looking at me like she thinks I'm dumb as a box of rocks. "Bessie is my Luger." She pats one of the side pockets of her housecoat. "I keep her loaded and ready to work all the time. Take her with me everywhere I go."

We all stare at Gloria with newfound fear and respect. I half expect Hurley to give her a lecture on carrying a concealed weapon, or, at the least, a warning to be careful with old Bessie, but he, perhaps wisely, says nothing.

"Thanks for the information, Gloria," I say. "If we have any other questions, is it all right if we call you?"

She nods and gives us her phone number, forcing Hurley to take out his notebook again so he can write it down. With that done, Gloria wishes us good night and waddles back home.

"Alison," I say, "you can't print any of the stuff she told us until we say so, understand?"

She nods. "I promise to play fair as long as you promise to keep me in the loop and give me first dibs on anything you come up with."

"We can do that," Hurley says.

"Can I come inside with you guys?"

Hurley shakes his head. "You know I can't allow that."

Alison shrugs. "Had to ask." She glances across the street. "Mind if I go talk to this Elsie woman?"

"Yes, I mind," Hurley says with an impatient sigh.

"Does that mean you're going to be mad when I tell you I already did?"

"What?" Hurley moans. "How? When?"

Alison shoots him an apologetic look. "I've been parked here for hours, waiting for you guys to show up. I saw her over there and figured it couldn't hurt to ask her a few questions about Tina."

"And?" Hurley says in an irritated tone. He rakes a hand through his hair and grimaces, squeezing his eyes closed.

"I asked her if she'd seen Tina today." She hesitates, looking abashed. "I told her I was hoping to chat with her about an article I wanted to do on Tina."

Given that Tina is a local librarian, it's hard for me to

imagine what there might be about her that would be article-worthy.

"I didn't really have an article to write about her," Alison explains, looking embarrassed. "But she does work at the library and she's very well-read, so I told Elsie I was hoping to get Tina to write some book reviews for the paper, but needed a reference."

"And what did this neighbor lady tell you?" Hurley asks, massaging his left temple with two fingers.

"She said she saw Tina leave this morning with her boyfriend and hadn't seen any activity over there since. No one in or out. I told her I was going to wait around for a bit to see if Tina showed up, hoping it would keep her from calling in a complaint about me. She seems like the type who would do that."

"And rightly so," I say. "If more neighbors were as attentive as Elsie and Gloria, we'd probably have a lot less crime in this town."

"And we'd all be out of a job," Alison quips.

She has a point.

"Look, Alison," Hurley says, "I appreciate the info you've obtained, but I can't involve you anymore at this point without compromising my investigation. You already know what we know anyway, and I promise you'll be the first to know as soon as we have anything new."

"I'm going to hold you to it," she says, her shoulders slumping as she turns and heads back to her car.

Hurley and I watch her go, and as soon as she pulls away and drives down the street, we grab some gloves and equipment from the car and head for Tina's front door. As Hurley tries keys, I turn on a video camera. I have a digital in my scene kit for stills, but these days we try to use video for any formal searches or questioning—lest we end up with another Tomas Wyzinski case. Hurley strikes gold with the third key he tries and we enter the small ranch-style home. While Hurley opens a scene kit and takes out some powder and a brush so he can dust the doorknob for prints, I shoot video of the living-room area off to my left. Hurley finds a couple of prints on the knob and I capture them with the camera before he lifts them. With that done, we shut the front door and I prepare to continue with my video documentation until Hurley stops me with a hand to my shoulder.

"Hold on," he says. "Before we do anything else here, you and I need to finish our conversation."

CHAPTER 17

Not for the first time, I curse Hurley's elephant-like memory and laser-sharp focus, traits that make him a top-notch detective, but an annoying partner at times. I swallow hard and think fast.

"Look, Hurley, it's getting late and we need to get a move on here. I promise you we'll continue this conversation, but let's put it off until later tonight, okay? Let's do it at home, not in some dead woman's house."

Judging from the look he gives me, he's not pleased with my manipulation—no big surprise. He closes his eyes, takes in a deep breath, and says, "Fine. But we *are* having this discussion tonight."

"I promise."

"I'm holding you to it."

"I said I promise," I repeat a bit irritably.

Seemingly satisfied for now, he drops the matter and starts looking around Tina Carson's living room.

It's always a sad thing to explore people's homes when

they've died unexpectedly. Things are left lying about in a manner that suggests the owners might return at any moment, and the knowledge they never will imbues the places with a tragic sense of loneliness and finality. Such is the case with Tina's house. In the living room we find a half-finished cup of coffee, now cold, on the table in front of the couch. Next to it is a laptop, its lid open, the screen dark, either from a lack of power or, more likely I think, sleep. Hurley taps the space bar and proves my hunch right. The screen comes alive and reveals a library website featuring new books scheduled for release.

Hurley runs his gloved finger over the touchpad and a toolbar pops up at the bottom of the screen revealing other open programs: e-mail and word processing. Hurley opens the e-mail program and we read several recent ones: two from Hal detailing their plans for today, one from a lady named Edith thanking Tina for a book recommendation, and a couple of spam e-mails. Hurley looks in the deleted mail file, but all we find are more spam e-mails and some work-related stuff.

Next he looks at some of the word-processing files. The one that is open appears to be some sort of novel Tina was working on. A quick peek at several other files shows more of the same. It seems Tina was an aspiring author, and, ironically, a mystery writer, judging from the titles she's given the works. I doubt she ever imagined she'd end up the victim in her own story.

Hurley closes the laptop, unplugs it, and bags it. Just to be safe, we collect the unfinished coffee in a container and bag both it and the mug, too. The obvious assumption is that it was Tina who was drinking the coffee, but to *assume* in a murder case risks more than just making an *ass* out of *u* and *me*.

A large-screen TV is hung over the fireplace and its remote is sitting on the table. Out of curiosity, I pick up the remote and turn on the TV. The last thing Tina was watching was the Weather Channel. She doesn't have a DVR, so there aren't any saved shows to view, but there is a DVD player on one of two overflowing bookcases in the room. I click the TV off and bag the remote. Then I wander over to the bookcases and peruse the titles. Not surprisingly, given her job, Tina's reading tastes are eclectic. She has every genre of fiction imaginable, and several shelves are filled with nonfiction titles ranging from self-help and cookbooks to stuff written by Carl Sagan. The fireplace itself is clean and empty, and there's a basket of knitting supplies and yarn on the hearth.

Little here appears to be of any evidentiary value, but I shoot video of it all anyway. Tina's life may have been a largely solitary one for most of her years, but I get the sense she was content with it and had built a peaceful, cozy hideaway for herself.

Once we are done in the living room, we move into the adjacent dining room—a formal table and chairs that look like they haven't been used in forever, and a china cabinet in one corner that holds some fancy champagne flutes and wineglasses—and from there into the kitchen.

A large window over the sink looks out into the backyard, which is beautifully landscaped. A small stone patio extends off from a door at the far end of the kitchen, and a small mosaic-topped table with two chairs sits on it. Off to the side of the patio is a small barbecue grill, utensils hanging from one end. Tina's yard isn't fenced, but the backyard of the house behind it is, creating a convenient border. All along the length of the fence is a huge flower bed bookended by a Japanese maple tree on one end and two large lilacs on the other. A colorful riot of flowers is in bloom: irises, wild phlox, forsythias, red and purple monardas, and several others I don't recognize or know the names of. At the center of the yard is a majestic old oak tree, which will turn the yard into a roller-skating rink once the acorns start to fall. Walking in a yard filled with downed acorns is like walking on hundreds of ball bearings. But for now it provides a lovely shaded area Tina obviously enjoyed. A white wooden rocker sits near the trunk, a tiny, white, wicker-topped table beside it. On top of the table is an open book, pages down, waiting for Tina to pick it up and continue her read. It tears at my heart knowing she'll never finish that book or see this beautiful yard again. It makes me wonder what Hal's place is like, and which house—if either—they planned to live in after they were married.

The kitchen is spotless, like the rest of the house, and there is nothing of interest in the trash, the fridge, or the sink, though we grab the trash so we can go through it more thoroughly later. We move on to a bathroom off the main hall, which appears to be a guest bath. There are some generic bottles of over-the-counter allergy and pain medications in the medicine cabinet, but no personal items. The master bedroom at the end of the hall has its own bathroom and here we find some of Tina's stuff. Based on the brands of shampoo and bath soap, Tina was a sale shopper, not a brand devotee. In the medicine cabinet, I find a prescription for an antibiotic, which is only half gone, and birth control pills. The one thing I don't find is the usual stash of makeup most women have. There is one tube of lipstick on the counter and a compact with some blush, but nothing else.

In the bedroom, I find a stack of books next to the neatly made bed, all of them current fiction. Tina's closet is as neat and organized as the rest of the place, her shoes lined up and paired on the floor, her hanging clothes arranged according to color. The color spectrum doesn't vary much—it's almost all browns, blues, blacks, and grays—and the styles are basic. Jonas was right about Tina and jewelry. The only baubles we find are two pairs of clip-on earrings sitting on top of a dresser. For all intents and purposes, Tina Carson was a plain and simple woman.

Hurley and I spend an hour and a half searching through the rest of the place, bagging some items, but finding little that looks to be of interest. When we're done, we check to make sure all the windows are locked—particularly the one over the sink where the man was seen peering in from out-side—secure the house, and move on to search Tina's car. It's as tidy and neat as the house was, and we don't find any-thing that appears to be useful. From there, we go out to the backyard and, using our flashlights now that dark has settled in, we search for footprints. We find two of them—one full and one partial—in some soft dirt beneath the kitchen window. Gloria was right: whoever was peeking in through Tina's win-dow had huge feet.

"These look to be a fifteen or sixteen," Hurley says as we shoot video and take pictures. Once we have photo docu-mentation, we set the cameras down and go about making casts of both prints. While waiting for the casting material to dry, Hurley dusts the ledge beneath the window for prints.

"Who do you think was the target here, Hurley?" I ask while he dusts. "Tina or Hal?"

"It's hard to know," he says. "Maybe it was both of them. Maybe it was a modern-day pirate type of thing where someone went to rob them and then got mad because they didn't have anything of value."

"They had the boat," I point out. "And Tina was wearing a diamond ring. Granted, the stone in it wasn't huge, but it's still worth some money. And if you're going to kill the peo-ple on the boat, why not just hijack the boat?"

Hurley shakes his head and doesn't answer.

"I think one of them had to have been the target and the other one was in the wrong place at the wrong time."

"Maybe," Hurley says. "Probably. But so far we have no reason to think either of them would have been targeted. We need to find a motive." He shines his flashlight on the window ledge and sighs. "Though I would have settled for a fingerprint or two."

"We have those two phone calls on Tina's phone to Tomas Wyzinski's brother," I point out. "That seems like an odd coincidence."

"True, but I suspect it may have been nothing more than research for one of her writing projects," Hurley points out. "I think for once we might have a real coincidence. Let's see if anything else pans out first."

We leave Tina's house around nine-thirty and head back to the station. I'm hungry again—not an unusual state for me—and even though I know it's likely useless, not to mention dangerous, I sneak a peek in the station's breakroom fridge. On the bottom shelf is a large plastic jug half filled with an amber-colored liquid. The bottle's original label says it's apple juice, but a second label taped over it says URINE—DO NOT DRINK. I wonder if the second label is accurate or simply an attempt to get other people to quit drinking it. On the shelf above the questionable liquid is a plastic take-out container with a clear lid that appears to be some sort of science experiment. Green, blue, and black fuzzies decorate the remains of whatever food is inside it, and the plastic top bulges threateningly. I'm tempted to remove it and toss it out, but I'm afraid if I touch or jostle it, it will explode.

The only other items in the fridge are a box of bullets, an open half pint of 2 percent milk, with an expiration date from six months ago, and a Baggie holding two pairs of folded men's underwear—tighty-whities. I spend a moment or two trying to come up with a logical reason why a man would want his undies chilled in the fridge, but decide it's the stuff of nightmares and move on. With a sigh, I close the door and head for the vending machine down the hall, where I pay five times the normal price for a bottled iced tea and a tiny bag of chips.

I head for Hurley's office and see Bob Richmond is there, seated at a desk just in front of Hurley's. They used to share a desk, but when Richmond returned to full-time work, he inherited a desk vacated by another detective who moved away.

"Hey, Mattie," Richmond says as I walk in.

"Hi, Richmond."

"Bob has been in charge of the search at Hal's house," Hurley says. "He was just about to fill me in on the results."

"Anything of interest?" I settle into a chair and rip open my bag of chips, tearing it down the side and laying it open-face style on Hurley's desk.

"We bagged a laptop and a bunch of home office files," Richmond says. "Dropped them off to Jonas a bit ago and he said he'll probably get to them in the morning, unless Laura has time tonight. Jonas said he already talked to you two about what he found in Hal's truck."

"He did," Hurley says, shooting me a pointed look, a subtle reminder of the conversation we still need to have. "We found Tina's purse and keys in the truck and just finished going through her place. There wasn't much there, but we took her laptop, just in case it has anything to offer. One of the neighbors said she saw a guy peeking in Tina's window earlier today and we did find some shoe prints, but no fingerprints."

"Interesting," Richmond says. "One of Hal's neighbors said he saw some guy poking around Hal's house earlier this afternoon."

Hurley perks up at this. "What kind of description did you get?"

"Big guy," Richmond says. "Taller than any of us and quite big in the chest and gut, but with thin legs. The neighbor who saw him said he was built like SpongeBob SquarePants. Mid-to-late fifties, dark hair but balding, with one of those comb-over jobs."

"That same guy was seen at Tina's house," Hurley says. "We need to find out who he is. Anyone see him get into or out of a car?"

Richmond shakes his head. "The neighbor who saw him said he appeared from the backyard of the house behind Hal's and then left the same way. So if he had a car, it was parked on the next block over. We canvassed those homes, but no one recalls seeing anything."

"What time was he there?"

"Around ten-thirty, according to the neighbor," Richmond says, reaching over and swiping a couple of my chips.

"He must have gone to Hal's place first," Hurley says, "and when he didn't find him there, he went to Tina's house."

"What about Hal's office?" Richmond asks. "Have you gone through his desk yet?"

"Not yet. That's next on our agenda. After that I think I'm going to call it a night and start again early in the morning. Hopefully, we'll have some information by then from those laptops or that USB drive Jonas found in Hal's truck."

"We should hit up the library tomorrow and talk to Tina's coworkers," I say. "Since we don't know who the primary target was, we should consider motives and suspects for both of them. Maybe they know something about why Tina was talking to Tomas Wyzinski's brother."

"Agreed," Hurley says. "Though based on what we know about Hal and Tina, I'd be surprised if she turns out to be the primary target."

"Anything new on the Abernathy case?" Richmond asks, shifting subjects. "Figure out a cause of death yet?"

Hurley frowns and scratches his head. "Nope," he grumbles. "Got the report on her initial tox screen this morning and it was negative, so I've got Arnie looking into some of the more obscure poisons and testing for what he can. If it wasn't for the fact that the boyfriend has flown the coop, I'd be inclined to say she died of some natural cause we can't identify and call it good. But there is the issue of the dead insects, and the boyfriend seems a little off to me. I feel like I need to keep plugging away at it, do what we can, though obviously Hal's case is the priority for now."

The three of us sit in silence for a minute until Richmond says, "Do you think this thing with Hal could have been a random attack of some sort?"

"It's possible," Hurley says, "but I doubt it. The way they were killed seems a little too personal to me. Not to mention the fact that they left Hal with a wallet full of cash. And Tina was wearing a diamond ring." Hurley pauses and looks at me with a sad expression of sudden dawning. "Oh, jeez," he says. "I just realized . . . diamond ring . . . that ring box in Hal's pocket . . ."

I nod, fighting back tears.

"What am I missing here?" Richmond asks, looking back and forth between the two of us.

"I'm pretty sure Hal proposed to Tina while they were on the boat this morning," I tell him. "He told me he had something fun planned for the day, and I'm guessing that's what it was."

"Damn," Richmond mutters with a frown. "That sucks."

It does indeed and I spend a moment contemplating the unfortunate series of events that turned one of the happiest days in Hal and Tina's lives into their last one on earth.

CHAPTER 18

Hurley tells Richmond to head home for the night so we can all start fresh again in the morning.

Richmond agrees—he's got a hot date with Rose Carpenter, a divorcée he's been seeing for the past two years.

Hurley and I walk over to my office and use my key fob to get in. There are a few basic night-lights on, but the place is eerily quiet and dark. Being here at night when there's no one else around should be scary, but most of the time I find it soothing. I don't believe in ghosts—at least not the malevolent spirits that want to harm the living kind of ghosts—so I'm not bothered knowing there are dead people in the cooler downstairs. Those people are why I'm here and why I do what I do. I work to find out what killed them, hopefully so the same fate won't befall someone else.

It's the living that frighten me, but here in my office, with all the doors locked and the security alarms in place, I feel safe. Hurley, on the other hand, looks a little creeped out, so

I flip on a couple of extra lights for his benefit as we make our way to the library.

The top of Hal's desk is neat and orderly, like everything else in Hal's life, and the only item of interest is his computer.

I settle into Hal's chair and turn the computer on. "You realize with everything that's happened, I'm going to have to pick up a lot of extra shifts," I say as we wait for the computer to boot up.

Hurley nods. "Hopefully, it will only be temporary."

"Hard to know. With Izzy out for who knows how long, I have no idea when we'll find a replacement for Hal. I'm not sure Otto will want to take on the hiring process."

"Whatever happens, we'll make it work."

The computer is up and I click on Hal's e-mail program first, but it's password protected. "Dang it," I mutter. I think for a moment and then try various iterations of some obvious guesses: the word "password," some number strings, Hal's birthday, and after a phone call to Jonas to get it from Tina's driver's license, her birthday. None of them work. I'm not surprised. Hal was too professional to use anything so simple for a password.

"Any other ideas?" I ask Hurley.

He takes out his notebook and consults it. "Try his mother's name, Carlotta."

I do so, with no success. "What's his father's name?"

"George," Hurley tells me.

It seems an unlikely one and, sure enough, it doesn't work, either. I try both names again with some numbers tacked on, and change the case on the first letters, but all to no avail. We stare at the password prompt and the taunt of the blinking cursor, both of us frowning in frustration. Then I snap my fingers, type something, and, just like that, I'm in.

"What was it?" Hurley asks.

"It was *Persephone,* the name of his boat. Kind of apt in a way. In Greek mythology, Persephone became goddess of the underworld after being kidnapped by Hades. I suspect that was Hal's little inside joke about what he does . . . did for a living."

"Clever girl," Hurley says, bending down and giving me a kiss on the cheek. He then makes a phone call to Jonas, passing along the password we figured out in case the USB drive or the laptop requires one.

Over the next thirty minutes, we wade through Hal's e-mails: current ones, deleted ones, and those he sent out. The vast majority of them are related to work, though there are a few from people in Eau Claire and Illinois who appear to be friends. None of the e-mails appear incriminating or point to any potential adversaries, motives, or dealings that might have gotten Hal into trouble. I move on to his documents file and wade through those, but they all appear to be innocuous work-related things as well.

"I don't see anything helpful here," I say, shutting down the computer. "Maybe his personal laptop or that USB drive will have something."

Next we go through Hal's desk drawers, a process made easier by the man's obsessive neatness and need for organization. There is a drawer filled with hanging files and Hurley pulls them out and puts them in a box. "Let's take these home and you can go through them there," he says. "It's getting late."

By the time we get home, Matthew is in bed asleep and Emily is curled up on the couch watching one of the *CSI* shows. She has shown a keen interest in what Hurley and I do for a living, and she's also shown an amazing talent when it comes to drawing. She once drew a face using a skeleton hanging in our office library as her basis for the sketch. That skeleton belonged to the wife of a prior medical examiner and her picture hangs in one of our office hallways. Emily's drawing, despite the fact that she didn't know the woman in question and hadn't seen the picture, was a near-perfect rendition of the woman's face.

"How was Matthew?" I ask her.

"He was fine," Emily says, grabbing the remote and pausing the show. "He peed in the potty . . . well . . . mostly in the potty right before he went to bed."

"Aw, that's great. Thanks for watching him and be sure to add the hours to your account."

"Oh, I won't forget," she says with a smirk and a wink. "Johnny wants me to go with him to some kind of outdoor-theater thing in the Dells on Friday night. Is it okay if I go?"

"Sure. Write down the specifics on the kitchen white-board," Hurley says. "Remember to be smart and be safe, and make sure you take your phone. If you need—"

"—anything at any time, no matter the hour or distance, call," she finishes for him with a wry smile. "I got it, Dad."

Hurley's lips curl into a smile and his posture relaxes. He visibly softens whenever Emily calls him "Dad." It took her the better part of a year before she used the term for the first time. Prior to that, she always referred to him by his name. Then one night on her way to bed, she walked over, kissed Hurley on top of his head, and said, "Good night, Dad." That was it and he's been Dad ever since. There was no big event, no emotional moment, no celebration or ceremony that triggered the transition.

"Any news about Hal?" Emily asks, deftly changing the subject.

"Nothing solid yet," Hurley says. "But we've got lots of evidence to wade through. Hopefully, something will break soon."

"Was the woman on the boat his girlfriend?"

Hurley and I exchange a look. I let Hurley handle it. "She was," he says, "but that's not official yet, so you can't tell anyone."

Emily mimes locking her lips with a key, which she then tosses over her shoulder. Then she looks at me and her brow furrows with worry. "Do you think what happened to Hal has anything to do with a case you've worked on?"

I start to give her a reassuring platitude, but I stop myself. Emily is not only sharp, but she's good at reading people. "We don't know yet," I tell her. "But we're looking into it." I nod toward the box of files Hurley is holding. "Those are the files Hal had in his desk. We're going to take them upstairs and go through them. And we have a busy day ahead of us tomorrow, so we probably won't be back down tonight."

"So the remote is all mine," Emily says, wiggling her eyebrows, something I've seen her father do dozens of times. It's intriguing to see the bits and pieces of Hurley that emerge in Emily and wonder how many of them will also show up in Matthew.

"Yep, it's all yours," I say. "Thanks again for watching Matthew."

"My pleasure."

We say our good nights and head upstairs. Hurley carries the file box into the bedroom while I detour into Matthew's room to peek in on him. He's asleep on his side, his dark hair sticking out everywhere, his thumb firmly planted in his mouth, his down-covered cheeks fluttering as he sucks in his sleep. Knowing I'm responsible for this tiny little boy sleeping in his big-boy bed both exhilarates and frightens me. I stand there and watch him for a time, my heart swollen with feelings of love and tenderness. But deep down in my gut, there's also a cold spot, an icy ball of fear. I'm too aware of all the things that can go wrong, all the ways life gets cut short with little to no notice.

A hand on my shoulder makes me jump.

"Sorry," Hurley whispers, his head alongside mine, his front side along my back side. He stares at Matthew with me, and after a moment he says, "He's growing up so fast."

"I know."

"I kind of want to make another one," Hurley whispers, nibbling on my neck.

"Let's get through the wedding stuff first. Then I promise to think about it."

"We could practice," Hurley says, his nibbles getting a little more urgent.

And so we do.

An hour or so later, Hurley is lying on his side in our bed, his head propped up on his hand, staring at me.

"What?" I say.

"You know what. You promised me a chat once we were home. Something about your father, I believe? I think it's time."

I grimace, knowing I have to do it, but not wanting to, especially on the heels of the glorious time we just spent together. But it has to be done. I sit up and scoot back to lean against the headboard, tucking the covers around me like some metaphorical protection from the anger I'm anticipating. Apparently taking a cue from me, Hurley does the same.

"Okay, here goes," I start. I brace myself with a deep breath, exhaling it slowly. "I've told you before that my father left when I was four. And according to my mother, he left because he was a wandering Gypsy, who didn't want to settle down. I always figured my mother was exaggerating and that she drove him away with all her idiosyncrasies and craziness. But it turns out there was a whole lot more to the story my mother never told me about, and a whole lot more she didn't know about. At least I don't think she knew."

"Okay," Hurley says slowly, "but what does that have to do with us getting married?"

"Hang in there and I'll get to it. Remember when you came back to town after Kate died and I was being investigated for killing that guy who shot at me?" I don't give him a chance to answer. I'm not asking because I question his remembrance of those events, but rather to ground him in the proper setting for what I'm about to tell him. "We had all those state troopers milling about down at the station and looking into my background. It turns out they delved pretty deep, going back to when I was a kid. And they came up with some interesting facts."

"About you?"

"No, about my father. It turns out he hasn't always been on the right side of the law."

Hurley shrugs this off. "So he broke some laws. That shouldn't impact our getting married. Unless you've broken some laws I don't know about."

"None that I'm aware of," I say with a smile. "But my father apparently broke some serious laws, or at least the cops think so. They think he killed someone."

"Well, technically, so did you. Apparently, it runs in the family."

I give him a light punch in the arm and roll my eyes at him. I know he's trying to lighten things up by making a joke, but he has no idea just how serious the matter is going to get.

"Okay, what were the circumstances?" he asks in a more sobering tone, realizing I'm not buying into his attempt at humor.

My heart is pounding so hard I swear Hurley must be able to hear it. "They think he killed an undercover cop, Hurley," I say. I hold my breath, biting my lip, listening for his reaction. I expect a sharp intake of breath, or a muttered curse, but his breathing stays even and regular. "A cop named Roy Gilligan."

This time I get a reaction. Hurley's breath catches as he turns sharply toward me, his face a mask of confusion. "My ex-partner, Roy? That Roy Gilligan?"

I nod. "One and the same."

"He and I used to run patrols together down in Chicago. I heard he was killed during an undercover sting looking into a mailbox store scheme that Quinton Dilles was suspected of running. That's one of the reasons I went after Dilles as hard as I did when he killed his wife. I figured he had something to do with Roy's death as well."

"He may have, but only tangentially," I say. "Trooper Grimes told me the suspected hit man in Roy's death was a man named Cedric Novak."

It doesn't take Hurley long to make the connection. "This Cedric guy, he's your father?"

I give him a slow, tentative nod, watching him warily as he digests what I've just told him.

He reaches up and scratches at his scalp, though I doubt anything itches. It's something I've seen him do before when he's puzzling through something. His eyes stare down at the bedspread, though there is a distant, almost vacant look in them that tells me all he sees are the connections forming in his mind. "Okay, why?" he says after several long seconds of silence. "Why did this Cedric guy, your father, kill Roy?"

"Apparently, Cedric worked at the mailbox store. In fact, he was the manager, and as such, the cops believe he was Dilles's right-hand man."

There it was . . . all the awful truths laid out on the table. Not only was my father suspected of killing a cop who at one time was Hurley's partner, he was also suspected of working with Hurley's archenemy, the man he hates more than any other, the man that caused Hurley to lose his job in Chicago: Quinton Dilles.

Dilles was suspected of killing his wealthy wife five years ago. As the lead detective on the case, Hurley pursued the man with a vengeance—for reasons I now understand— and Dilles complained about the harassment. Hurley ended up losing his job over the matter, only to have Dilles eventually arrested and convicted of the crime. Hurley's exoneration came too late to save his job, and to add to his resentment, Dilles managed to coordinate a frame-up of Hurley from prison a few years ago. He almost succeeded in costing Hurley not just another job, but his freedom.

Ironically, though I got caught up in the Dilles doings as well, and nearly ended up unemployed and dead as a result, I owed a small debt of gratitude to the man. Had Dilles not gotten Hurley fired from his job in Chicago, Hurley never would have come to work in Sorenson. That meant I never would have met him, and the sleeping angel in the other room wouldn't exist.

"What evidence did they have against this Cedric guy?" Hurley asks. He folds his arms over his chest, his body language telling me he's having an understandably hard time with this new revelation.

"I don't know the specifics. All I know is they didn't have enough to arrest him for it, and even if they had the evidence, they couldn't find him. You could talk to Trooper Grimes to find out, or ask Richmond."

"Richmond knows about it?" Hurley said, shooting me a wounded look.

"He does," I say, wincing. "I made him swear he wouldn't tell you."

"Son of a bitch," Hurley mutters, staring off across the room and scowling. He shakes his head, his brows furrowed in anger . . . and betrayal.

"Don't get mad at Richmond," I say. "It wasn't relevant to anything we were investigating at the time, and I was so afraid that knowing about it would turn you against me. I badgered him into his silence on the matter. If you want to get mad at someone, get mad at me."

Hurley looks at me, letting out a long, slow sigh. "Is that why you kept telling me no when I asked you to marry me?"

"That was part of the reason," I admit. "But I also didn't want you to feel obligated to marry me because of the pregnancy. The combination of the two made it hard for me to accept in good conscience. This thing with my father still does."

Hurley leans his head back against the headboard and stares at the ceiling. I want to ask him what he's thinking, what he's feeling, but I'm too scared to do it. Instead, I sit, chewing on my lip, waiting anxiously. Time ticks by with an almost audible heaviness.

Hurley finally straightens up and shifts himself in the bed so that he's looking me right in the eye. I can barely breathe. "Regardless of what your father may or may not have done, I love you, Squatch. You are *not* him. You are the mother of my child, the woman I love, and the person I want to marry." He reaches up and sandwiches my face between his hands. Then he kisses me, lightly, but full on the lips. It's a tender, loving kiss that makes my relief and love for the man burst out of me in sobs.

"Oh, God, Hurley," I sniffle when his lips leave mine. "You don't know . . . how worried . . . how scared I . . ."

He shushes me with his thumbs on my mouth, his eyes looking so deep into mine that I swear he can see my soul.

"I wuv you," I mumble from behind his fingers. And then I fall into him.

We embrace, and I take a moment to enjoy the warmth, the closeness, the security I feel in his arms. Eventually he lets me go and he resettles onto his side of the bed, leaning back against the headboard again. And then he reaches over and takes my hand in his, holding it.

"That gold necklace," he says after a while, "how does it fit in? Because it has something to do with all of this, doesn't it?"

I nod. "I've seen that pendant before. I'm pretty sure it belonged to my father. And that means my father might somehow be involved in Hal and Tina's deaths, too."

"I think we need to sit down with your mother and have a long chat."

"Good luck with that," I scoff with a healthy dose of sarcasm. "She won't tell me a thing other than the fact that she doesn't believe my father capable of killing anyone."

"Maybe she's right."

His expression of doubt, his momentary belief in my father's possible innocence—however misguided—stirs a burst of hope in my chest. I've spent the past two years vacillating between pondering all the ways my father could be innocent and harboring a strong conviction that he's a cold-hearted killer. I want so badly to believe he didn't do these awful things, but the simple fact that he abandoned me when I was so young makes me think he's capable of all kinds of horrific acts.

My curiosity and my longing to know my father have always been there. And that need is stronger than ever lately because I have reason to believe he's come back into my life, albeit sporadically and on the sly. I don't know yet if I'll welcome him into my life, should his appearances become more permanent, but I'd like to have the option. Though if he really is guilty of the murder he's suspected of committing, that option will be gone.

"I suppose if we're going to get to the truth of this matter, we need to figure out who killed Hal and Tina," Hurley says, climbing out of bed. He walks over by the door and picks up the box he'd dropped there earlier, the one containing Hal's office files. He carries it over and plops it on the bed, climbing back in and pulling it up between us.

"I imagine this is as good a place as any to start," he says. Then he digs into the box and hands me a stack of files.

CHAPTER 19

I wake to the morning sun prying open my eyes. Then I realize it isn't the sun doing the prying, it's Matthew.

"Mama eye," he says, beaming a big smile at me.

I pull back before he can jab a finger into my eyeball. "Good morning, Matthew," I say. I steal a glance at the alarm clock and see it's just past five-thirty. Given that we were up until almost one going through Hal's office files, I'm hoping I can convince Matthew to crawl into bed with us and sleep a little longer. One more hour would be heaven. I reach out an arm and wrap it around him, giving him a hoist up. I hear Hurley mumble something behind me, and Matthew's smile broadens.

"Dada," he says, and he scrambles up into the bed, crawling over my hips and settling down between Hurley and me. I roll over to give Matthew a kiss and tell him to go back to sleep, though I know the odds of that happening are small at best. Some distant part of my mind registers the fact that the cats aren't on the bed or making a mad scamper out of the room, but I don't give it much thought. Until the smell hits me.

I sit up, wiping more of the sleep from my eyes and realize my son is stark naked from the waist down. He has removed his nighttime pull-up and the reason he has done so becomes glaringly apparent. His butt and legs are covered with poop, some of it dry, most of it not.

"Oh, no, Matthew," I say, snatching him up, though my efforts are for naught. There are already smears of poo all over the bedspread and sheets. Hurley props himself up on his elbows and squeezes his eyes closed before trying to focus. Hence the smell hits him before the sight does.

"Oh, crap," he says, scooting his body away from us.

I burst out laughing. "A very apt remark," I say, hauling Matthew out of the bed. I carry Matthew down the hall and into the bathroom, holding him at arm's length. He reaches out with a poop-covered finger and points at my face.

"Mama nose," he observes, and I thank my lucky stars he hasn't inherited my freakishly long arms, at least not yet. Otherwise I'd have a poopy finger up my nose.

I set Matthew on the floor and grab some washcloths from the linen closet. Then I plug the sink, squirt in some body soap, and fill it with warm water. Matthew makes a mad dash out of the bathroom and I curse under my breath as I turn to chase him. I don't have to; a second later, Hurley walks in, carrying him in the same extended, biohazard hold I'd used moments before.

"I caught this prisoner trying to make an escape," Hurley says as Matthew giggles hysterically and wriggles in his father's hands.

Fifteen minutes later, we have our son clean, dressed, and ready for breakfast.

"I'll feed him," Hurley says. "You get yourself ready and then we can switch off."

"Thanks." I head back to our bedroom, strip off the bedspread and the sheets, and toss them into a laundry basket. Then I go into the master bathroom, strip myself down, and hop in the shower.

Half an hour later, I'm dressed and ready for the day, carrying an overflowing laundry basket downstairs, since the washer and dryer are in the basement. I poke my head into the kitchen and find Hurley and Matthew seated at the table eating scrambled eggs and toast. Hoover, as usual, is parked under the table and he thumps his tail loudly when he sees me. However, he doesn't move.

"Want me to fix some for you?" Hurley offers.

"Sure, thanks," I say, opening the basement door as the warm, buttery smell of the toast makes my stomach gurgle. "I'll be right back. I need to go throw these bed linens into the washer."

The laundry pile on the floor in front of the washer reminds me of how far behind I am on the laundry duties. I decide to leave a note for Emily, offering her additional credits for her funny-money fund if she'll run a load or two for me today. I toss the sheets and bedspread in, set the cycle for sanitize, and head back upstairs.

Hurley has finished my eggs and he scoops them onto a plate that already has two pieces of buttered toast on it. "Here you go, my love," he says, setting the plate on the table next to a cup of hot, steaming coffee topped off with a dollop of heavy cream—just the way I like it.

"You're a keeper," I say, giving him a kiss before I settle in.

"That's what I'm hoping."

The rest of our morning time at home is relatively uneventful, and Matthew and I are out the door headed for my sister's house a little before seven-thirty. Desi looks surprisingly awake for the hour—her eyes bright, her skin smooth—though her hair has a major case of bedhead.

"Good morning, cutie pie," Desi says, taking Matthew from my arms. My son goes readily, shoving a finger in

Desi's ear and saying "ear." Matthew has never shown much in the way of separation anxiety. He likes everyone he meets—a trait that scares me a little—and is typically on his best behavior around others. His meltdowns are kept in reserve for his father and me.

I follow Desi into the kitchen with Matthew's diaper bag and carrier. Lucien is there, briefcase in one hand, cup of coffee in the other.

"Morning, Mattiekins," he says, waving his coffee mug at me. "Gotta run." He gives me a quick kiss on the cheek and disappears.

"He seems busy," I say to Desi.

She smiles. "He is. Business has been picking up for him. Things are turning around."

"Good. It's been a while since I've asked how things are going with the two of you. Is everything still okay?"

"We're making slow and steady progress."

"Great," I say, but with little enthusiasm. "Glad to hear it."

Desi doesn't miss the dullness in my voice. "What's up?" she says, narrowing her eyes at me. "Is it this thing with Hal?"

"That's part of it, plus last night I told Hurley about my father." I shared the news of my father with Desi a year ago, making her swear she'd keep it to herself. As far as I know, she has.

"Oh. How did it go?"

"Better than I could have hoped. Hurley is fine with it . . . well, not fine with it, but fine with me."

"Of course he is. That man loves you."

"I know."

There is a moment of silence before Desi says, "Why the glum tone?"

I take a long, slow breath. "It's my father. I feel . . . I don't know . . ."

"Torn?" Desi suggests, and I nod. "Understandable.

You're curious about him and at the same time you're afraid of what he might be. You want him in your life as a father and you're mad as hell at him for not being in your life as a father."

Tears well in my eyes and I blink them away, staring at my sister in awe. "You nailed it," I tell her. "If he really did kill someone, a cop no less, how can I possibly let him into my life? And yet . . ."

"You want to."

I nod, slowly, miserably. I feel so conflicted. "Hurley wants to talk with Mom about him, see what she knows, what she's been hiding all these years."

Desi frowns, shakes her head, and then gives me a sardonic half-smile. "You don't think she'll actually tell you anything, do you?"

"I don't, but I know Hurley won't be happy until we try."

"You know," Desi says, assuming the same expression she had twenty years ago when she suggested we sneak out to Misty Scallon's party by climbing out our bedroom windows, "there might be another way to get some information."

I arch an eyebrow at her. "Spill."

"Remember when you and David went to the Keys the year Mom moved into her current house? It was the year you got married, I think. Anyway, Lucien and I helped her with the move, and she had this old chest up in the attic, which she had us put in the basement of the new place. I asked her what was in it because it looked like it had been kicking around for years—the lock and hinges were rusted, the wood was worn, and it had some leather trim on it that was torn, faded, and missing in spots. Mom said it was just some old memories, personal stuff she might want to look at one day. I tried to push the issue to get her to be more specific, but she wouldn't tell me anything more."

She pauses, flashes me a guilty smile, and then focuses

her attention on Matthew. "My curiosity got the better of me so I decided to sneak a peek," she says, smiling at Matthew and bouncing him up and down on her hip.

I know the reason she won't look at me is because she's about to confess to something she's ashamed about. Unlike me, Desi is a basically good and honest person who suffers immense guilt over the tiniest of crimes, though it doesn't stop her from committing them. And she's a horrible liar, something I used to my advantage a lot when we were growing up.

"It had a padlock on it," she continues, "but it was rusted and kind of small, so I thought maybe I could pick it with a bent bobby pin or paper clip, the way I used to do with your diary." She still isn't looking at me, but I roll my eyes at her anyway. "So I went up into the attic and tried, but all I managed to do was break off part of a paper clip inside the lock. And then I couldn't get the piece of paper clip out. For all I know, it's still stuck in there because I've never heard anything from Mom about the lock being screwed up or tampered with, and I know I asked enough questions about that chest for her to suspect me if she discovered the lock was messed up."

"Interesting," I tell her, my mind already calculating what it will take to get a peek inside that chest. "I'll look into it." I glance at my watch. "I have to get going. It's going to be a busy day."

I thank Desi again for her willingness to watch my son at a moment's notice, drive to my office, park in the underground garage, and head upstairs. I carry the box with Hal's office files into the library and set it on my desk. Then I go in search of Otto. He's in Izzy's office, sitting behind Izzy's desk, writing on a pad with Izzy's pen. Though I'm glad Otto is not only able to step in on short notice, but stay for a while to fill the gap, seeing him here in a spot that's always been Izzy's, using Izzy's things, saddens me. I feel a funny twinge in my chest, a reminder of just how fragile life can be and how it can change in the blink of an eye.

"Good morning, Otto. I see you're at it bright and early."

"Felt it was best," he says, setting down the pen and putting aside whatever form he was working on. The paperwork in this job, even in our current computer age, is never-ending and often daunting. It piles up faster than the dust bunnies under Hurley's and my bed, and with a dog and two cats, it only takes a day or two for me to have an entire bunny ranch under there.

"Are you planning to do Tina Carson's autopsy this morning?"

He nods and glances at his watch. "I am, just as soon as my traveling assistant gets here. He's not as punctual as you are, apparently. What have you got planned for the day?"

"Hurley and I are going to check in with the evidence techs regarding Tina and Hal's laptops, to see if they found anything of interest there. I went through Hal's desk last night, including a bunch of files he had in his drawer. I didn't find anything that looked helpful, but I still have a few more to go through. There's also a thumb drive the PD's evidence tech found in Hal's car. After that, Hurley mentioned hitting up some of the lake marinas to see if we can figure out who else might have been on the lake yesterday, to see if anyone saw or heard anything. And there's a mysterious man some of the neighbors saw lurking around both victims' houses. Not sure what follow-up Hurley has in mind for that, but I know it's on his list."

"Sounds like a busy day."

"I heard Carolyn Abernathy's initial tox report came back negative." Otto nods. "Any ideas about what killed her? We're concerned we might have missed something because the boyfriend's history is suspicious and he has skipped town."

"I've already got Arnie looking into other, less-common

toxins, but I don't know how much time he'll have to devote to it now that we have Hal and Tina's case. You know, it's possible our Ms. Abernathy had an arrhythmia of some sort that simply stopped her heart. It's rare, but it happens. If that's the case, we may not find anything that points to a clear-cut cause of death."

I accede his point with a nod and a frown. "Except there were all those dead bugs," I remind him. And then I change the subject. "Did you find anything of interest in Hal's autopsy?"

"He had water in his lungs, but I'm not sure yet if it got there pre- or postmortem. I've got Arnie looking for diatoms to see if he can tell where Hal was when the water got in there. It's possible he was still breathing when he went into the water. The neck wound was deep enough to hit both his carotid and his jugular, but the trachea was intact. The wound follows an odd, downward trajectory, making me think two things: there was a significant height difference between Hal and his attacker, and Hal tried to turn away at the last minute."

I wince and swallow hard, envisioning Hal's terrifying last moments, his desperate attempts to stave off the rapidly pumping blood spurting from his neck, his attacker no doubt coming at him again, and Tina . . . Was Tina still on board and alive when all this happened?

Otto looks at my face and says, "Damn, sorry about that. I shouldn't have gone into so much detail. I forgot this isn't just another case for you guys."

"It's okay," I say. "Let me know if you find anything with Tina's autopsy that might help. I'll have my cell on me if you have any other autopsies come in." I turn to leave, but Otto calls me back.

"Mattie?"

"Yes?"

"About Hal, I'm really sorry."

"Thanks."

"There are some things about his death we should discuss."

"Such as?"

"For one thing, the possibility his death has something to do with this office. We don't have any evidence of that yet, but be aware it's one of the possibilities. Stay safe and be watchful."

I nod solemnly. "You may be right," I say. Then I tell him about the Tomas Wyzinski case, and the calls to and from his brother Lech that we found on Tina's phone. I end by sharing Hurley's theory about the calls being research related to Tina's attempts to write mystery novels.

"The other thing is Hal's workload." Otto makes an apologetic face. "I'll have the temp who's coming work on the paperwork and other stuff related to Hal and Tina, but the regular workaday duties still need to be done."

"I've already thought about that," I tell him. "I told Hurley last night I expect I'll have to be working full-time for a while until we can find a replacement for Hal." The last part of this statement makes me wince. Here I stand, discussing the horrific death of a coworker in a detached, clinical tone that leaves me feeling like a traitor, or a callous, coldhearted human being.

Otto gives me a sympathetic look and again says, "I'm sorry."

"Me too," I say, and then I leave before I start to cry.

I head back to my office and settle in at my desk, tackling the remaining files from Hal's desk drawer. The rest of the files prove as uninteresting as the first ones, until I get to the last one. This one, unlike the others, is labeled with a number only, most likely a case number. All the other files had both numbers and names. When I open it, goose bumps rise on my arms. It's a file on Tomas Wyzinski.

The top page of the file is a letter from Lech Wyzinski to

Roger Beckwith, the prosecuting attorney in the case. The letter, which is handwritten in scrawling, printed letters, and peppered with spelling and grammatical errors, states that Tomas didn't kill the woman, and that he was intentionally given an overdose of insulin and left to die.

It's a common theme among criminals, the whole I've-been-framed excuse. I doubt Roger Beckwith gave the letter much credence, particularly since it doesn't name the culprit responsible for the supposed frame-up. But why did Hal have a copy of it?

I look behind the letter and see a page of scribbled notes in what I recognize as Hal's handwriting.

There is a phone number and beneath that the phrase *Tomas drug screen after arrest?* On another line, Hal has written, *Find out results of lie detector test.* There is one more scribbled note: *Prints at Wyzinski house?*

Curious, I place a call to Roger Beckwith's office and his secretary answers. "Hold on, Ms. Winston," she says. "He's just about to leave for court." She puts the call on hold, and after half a minute or so, Beckwith comes on the line.

"Hey, Mattie. Great job the other day."

"Thanks."

"The judge denied the defense's attempts to exclude the head discovery. The defense is putting on their case now and I expect they'll be done by day's end. Not much there for them to defend. It should go to the jury by this evening or to-morrow morning at the latest."

"That's great," I say, "but it's not why I'm calling. Do you know Harold Dawson from my office?"

"Sure. I know of him. Can't say we're close friends or anything, though. Why?"

"Did you hear on the news that he's dead?"

"*Dead?* God, no! What happened?"

"He was murdered yesterday. He and his girlfriend, though we haven't released the girl's name yet."

"That's horrible," Beckwith says. "I've been so focused on this case I haven't paid much attention to the news. Any idea who did it?"

"Not yet. That's why I'm calling. I was going through Hal's files in his desk and I found one on Tomas Wyzinski. It contains a letter from Tomas's brother, Lech, claiming his brother was framed."

"Oh, yeah, that," Beckwith says with a dismissive tone. "Standard stuff. I didn't put much stock in it. More than half the criminals we prosecute try to claim they were framed."

"How did Hal get a copy of this letter?"

"He called me and asked for it. So I made a copy and had it sent to him."

"Did he say why he wanted it?"

"He said it might have something to do with another case he was investigating. He claimed he wanted it to show a pattern of behavior, or something like that."

"Did the defense get a copy of the letter?"

"Oh, yeah. Lech sent one to me, to Tomas's attorney, to the judge . . . probably sent one to the governor, too, for all I know. All the letters are identical except for the salutation. No one has done anything with them. There isn't any useful information about who supposedly framed Tomas. And then there's Lech."

"What do you mean?"

"Have you met the man?"

"No."

"He's not the sharpest tool in the shed," Beckwith says with a sneer. "Apparently, he was injured when he was a kid and it resulted in some permanent brain damage. Tomas has been his caretaker for several years. The two of them lived together in that house."

"So where is Lech now?" I ask.

"Still at the house. The Wyzinskis hired a caretaker of

some sort who stops by several times a week to clean, do the shopping, and make sure Lech is managing okay."

"His parents aren't involved?"

"They sign the checks, but they don't want the responsibility for the day-to-day stuff. They travel a lot, spend half the year overseas."

"So Tomas was your basic trust-fund kid and paid babysitter to his brother."

"Not totally. Tomas has a college degree in chemistry and at one time held down a job with a pharmaceutical company. He made decent money, from what I understand. But he quit a few years ago when his brother came to live with him."

"Interesting," I say. I recall the pasty, wild-eyed look Tomas always had. "I wouldn't have pegged Tomas as a softie."

"Only with regard to his brother," Beckwith says.

"Hal made a note in this file about a lie detector test. Was one ever administered to Tomas?"

Beckwith lets out a weighty sigh. "How the hell did he find out about that?"

"So there was one?"

"There was. Tomas claimed he didn't remember anything and didn't kill the girl."

"And the results of the test?"

"Look, I don't know why you're so focused on this, Mattie. Tomas is guilty as hell. And he's probably a sociopath, so the lie detector test is meaningless. It's not usable as evidence."

"Are you saying he passed it?"

"Yeah, he passed it," Beckwith admits irritably. "But like I said, these sociopathic types can beat those tests. Listen, I'd love to chat some more, but I need to be in court. Let this go, Mattie."

I think about mentioning the phone calls between Tina and Lech Wyzinski, but I sense that Beckwith is both in a hurry and anxious to end this topic of conversation. "Okay," I say. "Thanks for talking to me. And good luck."

"Thanks, and sorry about your friend." With that, he disconnects the call.

I sit for a moment, staring at the letter and Hal's notes. After a moment, I scribble down the phone number Hal had written down, tuck the slip of paper into my pocket, and put the Wyzinski file in my desk drawer, locking it. Then I head over to the police station, which is only a couple of blocks away.

The walk does me some good, giving me time to get my thoughts and emotions reined in. I enter through the front door and greet Heidi, the day dispatcher on duty.

"Mattie!" Heidi says. She greets me with a smile, but it evaporates and her expression turns morose. "Awful thing about Hal and his girlfriend."

I nod, noting the identity of our second victim, while not yet official, is common knowledge among some folks. "Is Hurley in his office?" I ask as she buzzes me through.

"He is. Alison Miller is in there with him. She was here bright and early this morning."

I head back to Hurley's office, curious as to why Alison is here. Had she dug up some new info? Judging from the excited look on Hurley's face, I guess yes. He's sitting at his desk, typing on his computer; Alison is standing over his right shoulder, watching.

"Mattie," Hurley says, looking up and waving me in. "Alison has done some of our legwork for us. She went around last night and canvassed a bunch of the neighbors who live on the streets behind Tina and Hal. She found someone who wasn't home when our guys canvassed Hal's neighbors. This guy not only saw our mystery man from yesterday, he wrote down a make and model for the car he was driving, and a license plate number. I'm just about to run it."

I walk over to the desk, stand next to Alison—who is wearing a broad beam of a smile—and peer over Hurley's shoulder at the computer.

"The man I talked to is Norman Chevelle, a retired ex–military cop, and he saw our mystery man go around to the back of the house behind Hal's," Alison explains. "He had a feeling the guy might be up to something, so he waited and watched until he saw the guy reemerge onto the street. Then he watched to see where he went and saw him get into a gray Chevy sedan. He's a bird-watcher and had some binoculars handy, so he used them to get the license plate number. After the mystery man left, Norman went over to Hal's house and scouted around the place to see if it looked like it had been broken into or vandalized in some way, but nothing seemed amiss. Just to be safe, he told his neighbor about it when she got home later, and the two of them walked around the place, checking everything. Nothing was amiss, so they dismissed it. Fortunately, Norman still had the info when I came knocking last night. He'd tossed it into a drawer, just in case anything came up later."

"Way to go, Norman," I say.

"Remind me to find out what the old guy likes to drink so I can get him a little thank-you gift," Hurley says. "And there we are," he adds, pointing to the screen. "That car is registered to one Peter Carmichael, twenty-nine, lives over on Garfield Street."

The DMV photo of Peter Carmichael pops up and it's clearly not our mystery man. The picture shows a heavyset young man with blond hair, blue eyes, and a full beard and mustache. His stats, according to his DMV data, say he is five-six and 230 pounds.

"That's not the guy," I say.

Hurley prints the sheet off and goes to push his chair back, forcing Alison and me to step back. "No, it's not," he says. "But maybe he knows who our mystery man is and can explain why the guy was driving his car." He looks at me, his car keys hanging on one finger. "Want to come along?"

"Sure."

"What about me?" Alison says, making a pouty face. "I'm the one who came up with the lead."

Hurley hesitates, chewing on the inside of his cheek. I know he doesn't want Alison to come with us and could easily tell her so, citing official police business, or some other such nonsense. But the simple truth of the matter is Alison can—and knowing her the way I do, I feel certain she will—follow us anyway. Short of arresting her for interference, there isn't much Hurley can do to stop her. It seems we are in need of a compromise.

"Alison," I say, "there's a good chance this Carmichael guy might know something and there's an equally good chance he won't tell us anything, either because he's on the side of the bad guys, or because he's afraid he'll get someone he knows into trouble."

Sensing I'm about to quash her hopes of riding along, Alison starts to say something, but I hold up a hand and continue before she can.

"And if that happens, there's a good chance Mr. Carmichael will try to contact someone he knows, perhaps our very mystery man. He's probably smart enough not to do it by phone, so he'll try to do it in person. If so, he needs to be followed. He'll recognize Hurley and me in a heartbeat, but you? He won't think twice about you. So how about this? Why don't you come with us, park down the street, and stay in your car. Let Hurley and me go in and see what we can find out from this Mr. Carmichael. We'll call you when we come out, and if it doesn't look like he knows anything, we'll let you know and you haven't missed out. But if it looks like he does know something and he's holding back, we'll let you know that. Then you can sit and wait and watch to see where he goes."

Alison wrinkles her brow in thought. She's clearly intrigued by the idea of playing spy for us, but I can tell her base curiosity is also clamoring for attention. Plus, I think she's a little suspicious, wondering if I'm trying to put one over on her.

She looks at Hurley, her eyes questioning, and he shrugs. "It's not a bad plan," he says. "But it might put you in some danger." At this, Alison's eyes grow brighter. She's drawn to danger. "You'd have to promise me you won't do anything stupid like try to confront this guy, or anyone he might meet up with."

"I promise," she says, sounding breathlessly eager, and I exhale a sigh of relief, knowing we've swayed her.

"Okay," Hurley says. "Let's do it."

Alison exits out the front of the police station because her car is parked in the public lot. Hurley and I head out the back door to the police lot behind the building.

"That was some quick thinking, Squatch," Hurley says. "I was stymied there for a moment, trying to figure out a way to tell her to buzz off without pissing her off."

"We need to throw her a bone now and then. She's been playing fair lately, sticking to the rules we set down for her. And she did get this lead for you."

"We would have gotten to the guy eventually," he says as we get into his car. I shoot him a look of exasperation. "Okay," he admits in a conciliatory tone. "She did me a favor, so we'll let her pretend to play spy for us. But if the scenario you suggested does come to fruition, I'm going to have to put an unmarked out there, too. And whoever it is will have to watch both Carmichael and Alison."

"Let's deal with that *if* and *when* it happens," I say. "For now, let's focus on getting what we can out of Mr. Carmichael and hope he not only knows something, but is willing to share."

Hurley nods grudgingly and pulls out. Alison is waiting for us at the entrance to the front parking lot and she pulls in behind us as we drive by. As we negotiate the streets of downtown and head for Mr. Carmichael's neighborhood, I switch gears and fill Hurley in on what Desi told me this morning about the locked chest my mother has in her basement.

"I suppose we could try to talk to her first," I conclude, "but based on my past experience with her, I doubt she's going to give us much."

Hurley frowns. "If it comes to that, I might have to leave it up to you. I'm not that comfortable stealing or breaking into something that belongs to your mother on a wild guess about what might or might not be in it. Besides, we don't know for sure yet if your father is involved in this."

"Even if he's not involved in this case somehow, I want to get a look inside that chest. I'm tired of half-truths and innuendos. I want to know who and what my father is. And I want to find him and talk to him, ask him why he deserted us all those years ago."

A crusty silence fills the car as Hurley opens and closes his fingers around the steering wheel and I pick at a cuticle hard enough to make my finger bleed.

"Are you sure you want to do that?" Hurley says finally. "There's a certain level of comfort to be had in plausible deniability."

"I'm sure," I say with absolute conviction, though a funny little niggle in my chest tells me I'm not 100 percent on this. There is a fear there, a fear I'll discover my father is a total lowlife, a person unworthy of my time and effort. And if I'm completely honest with myself, I'd have to admit there is a part of me—bigger on some days than on others—

that hopes to exonerate him on at least some of the suspicions and accusations. Still, regardless of the outcome, I have to know. The not knowing is driving me crazy.

Or maybe, I think, my crazy is something I come by honestly, something I inherited from my murderous deadbeat of a father.

CHAPTER 20

During the final leg of the journey, I fill Hurley in on the Wyzinski file I found in Hal's stuff and my conversation with Beckwith regarding the letter. Hurley shrugs it off the same way Beckwith did.

"I doubt it's significant. Criminals use that I've-been-framed excuse all the time. It's almost never true."

"Almost," I echo. "But do we accept that it's a coincidence Hal had a file on Wyzinski, and Tina apparently conversed with his brother?" I know what Hurley thinks about coincidences, and, sure enough, he frowns and lets out a conceding sigh.

"Yeah, okay, we should look into it," he allows. "But I think it's likely that Hal had that file because he was helping Tina with the research for a book."

This scenario is plausible enough, and our conversation ends because we have arrived at our destination. We pull up in front of Peter Carmichael's house and Alison drives past us and parks half a block away. As Hurley and I get out of the

car and approach Carmichael's front door, Hurley nudges
my arm and points toward the back of the house, down
Carmichael's driveway. There, sitting in front of a one-car-
sized, ramshackle garage, which looks like the Big Bad
Wolf could blow it down with a good sneeze, is a gray
Chevy sedan.

"That's the car," Hurley says. "And the plate number."

Carmichael's house is in better shape than the garage, but
not much. The roof is missing a number of shingles; the
paint is peeling; the lawn—what few patches of it there are
amidst what is essentially a dirt front yard—is brown and
dead-looking. The west-facing front porch is small, has several broken boards in the floor, and is badly in need of cleaning and some paint. The wooden front door has been bleached
to a pale yellow along the bottom half by the baking rays of
the late-afternoon sun sneaking in under Carmichael's porch
roof. At one time, there was a screen door to protect the
main one, but it is now propped off to the side, hanging on
one hinge, though it looks as if it's held in place by a hu-
mongous spiderweb, the strands of which are as thick as
licorice whips. The screen door is to the right, so I shift to
Hurley's left as we climb the rickety steps of the porch.

There is no doorbell, just a hole in the wood siding to the
left of the door where one used to be. So Hurley knocks
firmly and we wait. I survey the neighboring houses and
guess Carmichael isn't much appreciated by his neighbors.
These older neighborhoods in town are a mish-mash of
house styles, eclectic collections of Victorians, fifties-style
ranch homes, Cape Cods, Colonials, and Craftsman homes.
The streets are lined with stately old trees—oaks and maples
that have been there for decades—though a couple have
been taken down or fallen due to rot and disease. It's a gentri-
fied neighborhood with homeowners that maintain their
houses, landscape their yards, and take pride in their home
ownership. Amid all of this tender loving care is Carmichael's

house, a definite eyesore—a pustular red zit on an otherwise unblemished neighborhood complexion.

Hurley raises his hand to knock a second time when the door suddenly creaks open. Standing on the other side is Peter Carmichael. He looks just like his DMV photo, except his hair is longer and looks like it needs a good shampooing. He is dressed in a stained, baggy T-shirt, a pair of cutoff sweatpants, and flip-flops. His feet are filthy.

"Can I help you?" he asks, and I see that his teeth haven't been cared for any better than his house. I wonder if he's renting or owns the place.

Hurley and I both flash our badges, and as Hurley starts talking, I watch Carmichael's reaction closely.

"Mr. Carmichael, I'm Detective Hurley with the Sorenson Police Department and this is Mattie Winston with the medical examiner's office. We'd like to have a chat with you for a moment about a case we're investigating."

Carmichael doesn't look worried or particularly interested. He looks annoyed. "I'm kind of in the middle of something right now," he says. "Can you come back at a later time?"

"This won't take long," Hurley says, neatly avoiding an answer to the question. "We just have a couple of questions about your car."

"My car?" Carmichael says, now looking a smidge wary. "What about it?"

"It was seen in a neighborhood where a homicide occurred yesterday," Hurley says. This isn't technically correct, since the deaths occurred elsewhere, but Hurley likes to unsettle people with a tiny dose of shock factor. "A witness saw a man who was snooping around the victim's residence get into your car and drive away."

Carmichael strokes his beard, his brows making a V over the bridge of his nose. He says nothing for half a minute or so, and we both wait him out. Carmichael finally says, "It wasn't me."

"I know that," Hurley says with an easy smile. "The description doesn't fit you at all. But it was definitely your car." The smile disappears. "And that makes you a potential suspect. Aiding and abetting someone else in the commission of a felony is punishable the same as if you'd committed the crime yourself."

Carmichael doesn't like this. He frowns, shifts his weight from one foot to the other, and strokes his beard more furiously. "If he committed some kind of crime while using my car, I know nothing about it," he says, his voice quavery.

"He who?" Hurley says. He takes a step forward across the threshold, forcing Carmichael to back up. "Let's sit down and talk about this, shall we?" Hurley steps past Carmichael, who does nothing to stop him. I follow and we pause several feet inside the door, looking back at Carmichael expectantly. We're in a hallway with a staircase to the second floor. To our left is a living room and I see what Carmichael was doing when we arrived. There's a gaming system on a coffee table set up in front of a couch. The middle cushion of the couch is half the height of the two surrounding cushions—not hard to tell where Carmichael sits most of the time. On the opposite wall is a giant TV atop a credenza. Some kind of military shoot-'em-up game is displayed on the screen, momentarily frozen. All the window shades in the room are down, and neither of the lamps at the ends of the couch have been turned on, leaving the TV screen as the only source of light. It's enough light, however, for me to see the heavy layer of dust in the room, though the coffee table's dust is broken up by the occasional glass or bottle ring. There are several soda cans on the right side of the gaming console—this makes me think Carmichael is right-handed, an interesting but unhelpful observation at this point—and the couch has a half-empty bag of chips, a box of donuts, and a closed Styrofoam take-out container sitting on the end cushion farthest from us.

There are no other seats in the room, so Carmichael heads down the hall toward the back of the house and the kitchen. Here things are a bit tidier, but I suspect it's because Carmichael hardly ever uses the room. A trash bin near the sink is overflowing with take-out and microwavable food containers. Immediately to our left as we enter is a small table pushed up against the wall with four folding chairs—two on either side—tucked in around it. Carmichael waves a hand toward it, and Hurley and I settle in on the two chairs closest to the doorway while Carmichael takes a chair on the opposite side.

"Tell me who this 'he' is you referred to," Hurley says as soon as Carmichael has sat down.

"He's a friend. Well, more of an acquaintance, actually. He says he knew my mother back in the day."

"Did your mother verify that? Does she live here with you?" Hurley asks, and I wonder if he seriously thinks this is a possibility. To me, it's obvious this house hasn't had a woman's touch of any kind in a long time, even from a woman like me who knows how to live peaceably among dust motes, clutter, and the occasional dried-food particle.

Carmichael shakes his head, looking sad. "My mother used to live here, but she's dead now. Died six years ago from breast cancer. My father died right after I was born, and I don't have any brothers or sisters, so I inherited this house after my mom passed."

That explained the deteriorating state of the house and lot.

Hurley takes out his notebook and pen. "What is this friend's name and how did he say he knew your mother?"

"His name is Walter Scott, and he said he used to work with my mom in a canning factory thirty years ago."

This piques my interest. The canning factory is long gone, shut down nearly two decades ago, but something about Walter Scott's name niggles at my brain. "What does this guy look like?"

"He's big, like six and a half feet tall," Carmichael says, stretching an arm above his head. "He's got hazel eyes and very dark hair, though I think he colors it. It doesn't look natural. He's going bald on top, and once I saw a stain on his scalp, which I think was from hair dye."

Hurley is busy jotting all this down, but he asks another question as he writes. "So you just took this guy's word for it that he knew your mother? And you let him borrow your car?" His voice is rife with skepticism and it makes Carmichael bristle.

"No, I'm not stupid," he says irritably. "It's not like I just met the guy and let him take my car. I've known him for two years and I talked to some other people who knew him to make sure he was okay."

"How did you meet?" Hurley asks.

Carmichael hesitates, looking back and forth between Hurley and me before he sighs, cocking his head in resignation. Clearly, whatever his answer is, he expects us to judge him by it.

"I met him through an online gaming forum," he says. "And before you go warning me about all the hazards of the Internet, and how trolls are lurking around every corner, I'm well aware of that. Like I said, I spent some time getting to know the guy." He pauses and shrugs. "To be honest, he's been super nice to me and I enjoy his company. I suppose he's been kind of a father figure to me."

I shake my head in disgust. Assuming the man we're discussing is Cedric Novak, it irritates me to think of him being a father figure to some stranger when he can't be bothered to do the same for me, his own kid. Yet another check mark in my mental disappointment column. So far, my mental chart is heavily one-sided, weighted toward the negative.

"How can we get a hold of Mr. Scott?" Hurley asks.

"He doesn't have a phone," Carmichael says, looking a tad sheepish. He blinks real fast a few times and leans back away from us in a mini flinch, like he's expecting us to slap him upside the head or something. Based on what he's told us so far, we probably should. I couldn't script a better victim for a serial killer. "I'm well aware of how it looks. But it's nothing sinister. The guy simply doesn't like cell phones, that's all. He's a little on the paranoid side and he's convinced the government tracks people through their phones— reading their texts, listening in on calls, and monitoring where they go with GPS. What's more, he's convinced the radio waves coming at the phone can cause brain tumors. So he refuses to have one."

While this sounds like something from Arnie's rhetoric, there is some evidence to support the brain tumor theory.

"He does have e-mail, though," Carmichael adds hopefully. "That's how I typically communicate with him."

Our mystery guy sounds like the perfect president for Arnie's Paranoid Ideation Club; although if it is my father, his paranoia is more justified than Arnie's. Someone probably is after Novak.

"Can you give me his current e-mail address?" Hurley asks.

Carmichael nods and rattles it off from memory. "Ivanhoe51580@gmail.com."

The use of the ID "Ivanhoe" and the numbers that follow suddenly clarify my niggling thought. Now I'm certain our mystery man is my father, and I ask Carmichael one more question. "Does Mr. Scott smoke by any chance?"

Carmichael starts to shake his head, then stops. "Not cigarettes. But he does puff on a pipe now and again."

All the puzzle pieces fit. I shoot a nervous look at Hurley, but he's still busy writing. He fires off a few more questions at Carmichael. "What time did Mr. Scott borrow your car yesterday? And when did he return it? Did he say why he wanted it?"

Carmichael hesitates before answering, parsing the questions. "He said he needed to run some errands. He picked the car up around ten yesterday morning and brought it back a little after three. And he gave me ten bucks for gas money. I can't imagine he used that much, even if he took the car out of town, but he's always been real generous about that kind of stuff."

A tiny surge of anger makes me clench my fists. Though I suppose it's easy to be generous with gas money to a stranger when you skip out on fourteen years of child support.

Hurley pockets his pen and notebook and gets up from his chair. "Mind if we take a look at your car?"

Judging from the expression on Carmichael's face, he does mind. But I can see him mentally weighing the pros and cons of refusing, and apparently the cons win out. "I suppose," he says, getting up from the table and reaching into his pocket. He hands over a key ring with four keys on it, one of which is for a car. "You can go out that way if you want," Carmichael says, pointing to a back door.

Hurley leads the way with me on his heels and Carmichael bringing up the rear. The back door is locked—both a knob lock and a dead bolt—and Hurley undoes them both. We descend three stairs from a cement stoop into the backyard, which is in worse shape than the front. A chain-link fence surrounds the yard and along the perimeter are several flower beds, which are overgrown with weeds. The yard is almost all dirt, with a few patches of dead, brown grass scattered here and there. There is a gate in the fence just to the right of us and the car is parked on the other side of it. Hurley opens the gate, which protests with a loud, tooth-chilling squeal, and unlocks the driver side door of the car.

It squeals, too—though with less vehemence—thanks to a large dent peppered with rust in the front quarter panel near the hinges. The driver's seat is cloth covered and there are several small tears in it. The dashboard, which was red when the car was new, has been sun-bleached to a weird shade of orange. Hurley pokes his head inside and I lean in over his shoulder and take a big whiff of the inside air. The smell of apple-scented pipe tobacco is unmistakable and it's like a ride in a time machine. I don't have many memories of my father, and the ones I do have are fading, but this one has persisted over time. Whenever I smell apple pipe tobacco, I can see myself curled up on his lap; I can feel the warmth of his chest against my back; I can hear the deep rumble of his voice as he reads to me. The memory makes me feel secure, loved, safe . . . and sad.

"I need to get someone out here to dust the inside of this car for prints," Hurley says, straightening up and shutting the car door.

"Do you really think Walter killed someone?" Carmichael asks, looking alarmed. "He's a nice guy, honest. I can't see him doing something like that."

Hurley looks at him, his face devoid of emotion. "We don't know if he did anything. All we know is he was seen in the area and is therefore a person of interest. I need to find him and talk to him. Do you have any future plans to see him?"

Carmichael shakes his head immediately, and if it wasn't for the blatant look of relief on his face, I'd suspect him of lying.

Hurley gets on his phone and calls Jonas, explaining what he needs. "Jonas will be here in fifteen minutes," he says once he's done and has disconnected the call.

Carmichael is standing at the base of his back stoop, staring at us with a dumbstruck expression. I imagine his mind is whirling like a tornado inside his head, trying to sort everything out.

"You can go back inside and resume your game if you want," I tell him. "We can do this without you here and we'll return your keys as soon as we're done."

He nods robotically, turns, climbs the stairs, and disappears inside his house.

"'Walter Scott' is a phony name," I tell Hurley.

He nods. "Figured as much."

"And it's one I'm betting our mystery guy picked for a reason. It's the same reason he used 'Ivanhoe' in his e-mail address."

Hurley narrows his eyes at me. "What are you saying?"

"My father's first name—his given first name—is Cedric. When Trooper Grimes told me about him, I got curious and did some research on the Internet. I didn't find him, of course, but I did find out some interesting tidbits about his name. The first time Cedric ever appeared anywhere was in the novel *Ivanhoe* by Sir Walter Scott. The original Anglo-Saxon spelling was Cerdic, but Scott transposed the letters, effectively creating a new English first name. And those numbers in the e-mail address? They're my birthday."

Hurley contemplates this for a moment. "Hunh," he says finally. "So you're convinced our mystery man is your father?"

"I am, even more so after poking my head inside the car. There's a lingering scent of apple-flavored pipe tobacco in there and I distinctly remember that smell from my childhood. My father smoked a pipe and he always used the apple-flavored tobacco."

"That was thirty years ago," Hurley says. I start to argue the point, but he stops me with a finger on my lips. "You may well be right, but you need to be careful about jumping to conclusions. If you get your mind too set on one answer, you'll be inclined to ignore any facts suggesting a different one. An open and objective mind-set is critical during an investigation."

His cautionary tone annoys me for some reason, but before I can say another word, my cell phone rings. When I take it out of my pocket, I see it's Arnie calling.

"Hey, Arnie. What's up?"

"I've got some findings I thought you and Hurley would want to know about."

"Okay, hold on a sec while I put you on speaker so Hurley can hear, too." Hurley and I both look around us to make sure no one who can overhear is nearby. Though the coast appears clear, Hurley motions me closer to the garage, which moves us farther from the house. "Okay, Arnie, go ahead."

"I looked at the water we found in Hal's lungs, water Otto said came from deep inside, so it was likely the very first water he came into contact with after his throat . . . after he . . . after the incident on the boat," he manages finally, and I wonder if he's being careful with his words for my sake, his own sake, or both. "I found the same diatoms in the lung water that I found in the section of the lake where the boat was anchored. Hal definitely went into the water there and he was still breathing at the time."

There is a moment of silence. I squeeze my eyes closed, as if this could somehow shut out the images trying to form in my brain.

Arnie says, "If it helps, Otto said Hal was probably unconscious due to blood loss when he went in the water."

"It does help," I say, opening my eyes. "Thanks."

Hurley says, "The diatoms thing is an interesting find, but I don't see how it gets us any closer to figuring out who's behind this."

"I know," Arnie says. "But at least it verifies our current version of the events. I imagine I'll find the same diatoms in Tina's lungs once Otto gets them to me."

"Thanks, Arnie," I say, disappointed. "Give us a holler back if you come up with anything else."

"But I'm not done," he says, and I detect a hint of excitement in his tone that I know well. Arnie has something juicy, something big, and my heart does a little flip-flop in anticipation.

"Bear with me," Arnie says. "We all pulled long hours through the night to work on this stuff. To start with, Laura went through that garbage from the motel. She found a bag of stuff that clearly came from Keith Lundberg's room, because there were items in it with his name on them, a pay envelope and some benefit information from the Ford place. The bag was tied with a knot and closed tight so everything in that bag would have come from Lundberg's room. And in it she found a bunch of shredded paper. So she started putting the shreds back together—fortunately, it wasn't one of those cross shredders—and she found an invoice for a large order of liquid tobacco juice, like the kind used in those e-cigs, you know?"

"Yeah, I know," I say. "So Keith vapes. How does that help us?"

"Well, for one thing, the invoice wasn't in his name. It was billed to a Jeremy Prince, but at the motel address."

Hurley says, "So Keith let someone else use his address at the motel for a delivery. That sort of thing happens more than we want to know for all kinds of contraband stuff. And tobacco juice isn't illegal."

A mental lightbulb pops on in my head and I feel a trill of excitement because I think I know where Arnie is headed. "It's not illegal, but it may be our smoking gun. Am I right, Arnie?"

"Hey, don't go ruining my reveal here," Arnie whines as Hurley looks at me with a confused expression.

"Sorry," I say. "Continue."

"Okay, so our initial tox screen on Carolyn Abernathy

came back negative and we haven't found any other causes for her death, and then it dawned on me that nicotine can be used as a poison. So I tested Carolyn's stomach contents to see if there was any in there."

"That's it?" Hurley says, sounding excited. "Somebody poisoned her food with nicotine?"

"Nope," Arnie says. "The gastric contents were negative."

Hurley scrunches his face in irritation or confusion—I can't tell which. Probably both.

"But her blood tested positive," Arnie adds. "I found levels so high in her blood it would have killed her pretty quickly. And it would have killed the bugs. In fact, it's used as a pesticide in some places."

"Was Carolyn a smoker?" Hurley asks.

"No," I tell him. "Her lungs would have shown it and they were clean."

"Then how—"

"Nicotine can also be absorbed through the skin," I say. "Lots of people use nicotine patches when they're trying to quit smoking."

"But she didn't have any patches on her anywhere," Arnie says. "I suppose it could have been injected into her. Otto said it would have been easy to miss an injection site on her body because of the level of decomposition."

"I don't think so, Arnie," I say, envisioning Carolyn Abernathy's death scene and her medical records. "I have a better idea. Do you have the rubber gloves she was wearing to do the dishes?"

"I do."

"Turn them inside out, collect any residue you find, and test it for nicotine. I'm betting it will be positive. And when you're done testing that, find the jar of skin cream she had and test it for nicotine, too."

"You are brilliant!" Arnie says.

"She is indeed," Hurley says with a smile.

"It makes sense," I tell them. "She had a bad skin condition and her hands and fingers were severely affected. According to her medical record, her fingers were often cracked open and bleeding. That's why she wore the gloves, to protect her hands. But if her skin cream was contaminated with nicotine and she put it on her hands with those open wounds, she would have absorbed the nicotine quickly and easily. She probably put the cream on right before she went to do the dishes and she started feeling the effects almost immediately. That's why she took the gloves off and sat down at the table."

"So we have our cause of death," Hurley says.

"We do," I say with a smile. "And a manner of death as well. Carolyn Abernathy was definitely murdered."

Jonas has arrived and Hurley walks over to meet him by the car. Hurley opens the driver's-side door, points to the handle, and then points to stuff inside the car. I notice the driver's seat is pushed back as far as it will go, the way it would be if my father had been behind the wheel.

"Stellar work, Arnie!" I say.

"Thanks! And if you like that, you're really going to like what I tell you next—because I'm still not done. I also ran an analysis on this oily substance the county guys collected from the lid of the cooler on Hal's boat. Basically, it was fishing lure oil, but it had one distinctive quality that was unusual. It had a high level of nicotine, not a substance you typically find in that stuff."

I take a moment to digest what Arnie just told me. Jonas and Hurley have their heads stuck inside Carmichael's car, and Jonas is already in the process of dusting the steering wheel.

"Oh, my God, Arnie," I say, making the connection. "Are you telling me these two cases are connected?" I must have said this louder than I meant to, because Hurley rears back out of the car and stares at me with a questioning look.

"Kind of looks that way," Arnie says.

"Have you told Otto yet?"

"I told him everything except for your idea about the cream. I'll get right on that and let you know what I find."

Hurley is standing in front of me, looking apoplectic, his eyes bugging out of his head, bouncing from one foot to the other.

"I have to go, Arnie, but this is great work. Keep us posted with anything new you find, okay?"

"Will do." I disconnect the call and fill Hurley in on Arnie's latest revelation. "Arnie found nicotine in some fish lure oil that was on the lid of the cooler on Hal's boat."

"Nicotine . . . Wait, which case are we talking about here?" Hurley says, scratching his head.

"They're connected somehow, Hurley. Hal, Tina, Carolyn Abernathy . . . they're all connected."

Hurley rakes a hand through his hair. "No wonder our Mr. Lundberg . . . or whoever he is, disappeared. Did he kill all three of them?"

I shrug. The truth is there's no way to know for sure. But at least we know the cases are connected and that might help us find more clues. Hurley takes out his phone and calls Bob Richmond. After filling him in on Arnie's findings, he says, "I need you to dig up anything you can find on Keith Lundberg, and Jeremy Prince. And dig deep. I'm starting to get a really bad feeling about this case."

CHAPTER 21

It takes Jonas nearly an hour to dust the interior surfaces of Carmichael's car—as well as some of the exterior surfaces and the trunk—and when he's done, he has over fifty different sets of prints.

"We need to get a set from Carmichael for comparison," Hurley says.

"No problem," Jonas says. "I have the tablet with me so it should only take a couple of minutes."

The tablet is a newfangled gadget the police department has had for a couple of years. It allows them to scan prints directly into a database simply by having a person set his or her hand on the tablet's screen. As soon as Jonas has packed up all his stuff, we climb the stoop to Carmichael's back door and Hurley knocks. It takes Carmichael a couple of minutes to answer, and as we wait, Hurley mutters, "I hope the guy didn't skip out the front on us."

Carmichael doesn't look happy about the fingerprint request, but he complies. His willingness to let us do this, along with examining and printing the inside of his car, makes me think he's not involved in anything nefarious, at least not knowingly.

When we're done, Jonas heads back to the station and his lab. Hurley and I return to his car. Just as Hurley is about to pull out, Alison Miller pulls up alongside us.

"What did you find out?" she asks when Hurley rolls down his window.

"Carmichael says he loaned the car to someone else," Hurley says.

"Who?"

"It doesn't matter since the name is almost certainly a phony."

Alison cocks her head to the side and gives him an impatient look. "Come on, Hurley. I promise I won't print anything you don't okay first. And I have a lot of resources. I might be able to help you figure out who the guy is."

"I don't want to give it out yet," Hurley says, soliciting a petulant pout from Alison. "When I'm ready, you'll be the first to know."

Alison is clearly ticked and I can't say I blame her. She did what we asked of her and now Hurley is cutting her out of the loop. Plus, knowing Alison, it's a wasted effort. I lean over and whisper into Hurley's ear.

"As soon as we leave, she's going to come back here and knock on Carmichael's door. She'll get the name out of him. So you might as well give it to her and appease her. If you make her mad, there's no telling what she might do."

Hurley frowns as he debates what I've told him; for a moment, I think he's going to stick to his guns. But then he sighs and looks back at Alison. "Mattie has convinced me to tell you."

Alison looks smugly pleased, and she gives me a little nod of thanks.

"The guy's name, at least the one he's using with Carmichael, is Walter Scott."

"Like Sir Walter Scott?" she says, and I nod. "And this Walter Scott guy fits the description of the man the neighbors saw lurking around Hal's and Tina's houses?"

"It would seem so," Hurley says, his frown deepening.

"I saw Jonas arrive. I'm guessing that was so you could search for evidence in the car?"

I have to give Alison credit. She doesn't miss much.

"Yes," Hurley says impatiently. "We didn't find anything other than some prints, and we haven't had a chance to run them yet."

"Will you let me know if you get a hit?"

Hurley looks over at me with an expression that implies, *"See what you've done?"* "I'll let you know as soon as I can," Hurley says aloud, looking back at Alison and forcing a smile onto his face.

This seems to satisfy her because she nods. After a moment's thought, she says, "Okay. And if I find anything, I'll let you know right away." With that, she drives off down the street.

Hurley shakes his head in dismay. "I feel like our arrangement with her is a deal with the devil," he says.

"Oh, come on, it's not that bad. Give her a chance. Besides, we didn't tell her about the other stuff."

"Speaking of which," Hurley says, "I'm going to have to delve into Carolyn Abernathy's life a lot deeper," he says. "If she's connected to Hal's case, we need to figure out how, and we need to do it fast."

"Where do you want to start?"

"It seems pretty clear that your father is involved with this somehow, so I think we should start there. It's time we pay a visit to your mother." His voice has softened, and I know he understands how difficult all of this is for me.

"I have an idea about that," I say. And then I share it with him.

"It's a good plan, but when it's all said and done, your mother is going to be pissed at you."

"It won't be the first time," I say with a sigh. "And if things play out the way I think they will, it probably won't be the last."

Hurley nods solemnly, pulls out of our parking spot, and drives back to the station, where we put our plan in motion. He makes the call to my mother from his car, putting his phone on speaker so I can listen in.

"Jane," he says when she answers. "It's Steve Hurley."

"Ah, my future son-in-law," she says with a distinct tone of disappointment in her voice. Marrying a cop is a definite climb down the social and financial ladder in my mother's mind; and it's a big fall, given that marrying a doctor was, in her mind, the pinnacle of my marital success. She still can't understand why I divorced David *just because* he cheated on me. To her, dalliances are a fact of life and not worth the loss of stature I sustained by leaving David. It's a moot point now, since David has remarried, tying the knot with Patty Volker, the woman who, at one time, was our insurance agent.

"I need to speak with you rather urgently on a matter involving a case I'm looking into," Hurley says. "And since it involves your ex-husband, Mattie's father, I think it would be best if we discussed it without Mattie's knowledge."

There is a long, silent pause on the other end of the line before my mother says, "I can't imagine what help I can be, given that I haven't seen or heard from the man in years."

"It's regarding a cold case, one that happened decades ago, around the time he left you, in fact. We have uncovered some evidence to suggest he was involved." This isn't true, but we need to come up with a way to get my mother to cooperate, and Hurley is about to tighten the screw. "There's also evidence to suggest you might have been involved."

"Me? That's ridiculous."

"I'm hoping it is, but the DA is talking about having you arrested. I'm hoping, given our connections, to be able to clear you. But if I can't, you may be spending some time in a jail cell in the near future."

I hear a gasp on the other end and can't help but smile. A jail cell is my mother's worst nightmare, not because she's afraid of being incarcerated, per se, but because she is a raging germophobe. In her mind, sitting in a jail cell is akin to eating out of a petri dish at the CDC.

"I suppose you can come by to talk," she says. "But I'm telling you, I don't know anything."

"Actually, I need you to come down here to the station," Hurley says. "I need to record our conversation for the record."

This elicits an even bigger sigh from my mother. In addition to her fear of germs, or perhaps because of it, she also has a touch of agoraphobia and hates to leave her house. Sensing her hesitation, Hurley ramps things up a notch. "The DA is moving ahead pretty quickly on this—so the sooner, the better."

"Fine," my mother says, the irritation clear in her voice. "I can be there in thirty minutes. Will that do?"

"It will. Just tell the front desk that you're here to talk to me and they'll bring you on back. See you in thirty." He disconnects the call and looks over at me with a tired smile. "You're on," he says.

"Wish me luck." I lean over and give him a kiss, and then we climb out of his car. Hurley heads into the station while I walk around and get back into the car on the driver's side. Doing what I need to do will be difficult with my hearse. It tends to get noticed.

Seven minutes later, I'm parked down the street from my mother's house. Her car is still in the driveway and I'm relieved to see that the car of her live-in partner, William, isn't there. It's a weekday and William (*"Not 'Bill,' "* he will stress, should you try the diminutive version of his name) is an accountant who keeps regular office hours. William met my mother after I fixed the two of them up on the heels of a disastrous blind date I had with him. He's as big a germophobe as my mother, and their mutual quirk has proven to be good relationship glue. They've been living together for over two years now, despite the twelve-year difference in their ages. I'm glad William isn't home. He's a sweet guy, but even so, I doubt he'd cooperate if he knew what I was about to do.

Several minutes into my wait, my phone rings. I think it's Hurley checking to see how things are going—if they are going—but it's Arnie.

"What's up, Arnie?"

"Just wanted you to know you're freaking brilliant," he says, making me smile. "I checked the inside of Carolyn Abernathy's gloves and her skin cream, and both tested positive for huge amounts of concentrated nicotine."

"You're the one who's freaking brilliant," I tell him. "If you hadn't discovered the whole nicotine connection, to begin with, I never would have focused on the gloves and the cream. And we might never have known the two cases were connected. I'm wondering if our Mr. Lundberg-slash-Prince is a contract killer of some sort."

"Any luck finding him?"

"Not yet. Hurley has Richmond working on it. What are you working on next?"

"I tried to get Hal's phone dried out to see if it would work, but no luck so far. However, we did get his phone records, and based on the towers he pinged off of the day before he died, he was in the Chicago suburb of Kenilworth, which just happens to be an enclave for the rich and famous. Don't know if it's relevant to anything, but figured I'd pass it along. Also, we found one incoming call to his phone from a month ago that came from Carolyn Abernathy."

"Just one call?"

"Yeah. Just to be sure, I checked Carolyn's cell and phone records, too, but it was just that one call, lasting about fifteen minutes. However, I did notice a call Carolyn made last week to a Chicago number, and when I checked to see what towers her phone pinged on, she was also in the Kenilworth area. I doubt it's a coincidence."

Even though I know Arnie could find a conspiracy in his morning box of cereal, for once, I'm inclined to agree with him. "I think you're right," I tell him. "Have you told Hurley any of this yet?"

"No, I thought he might be with you."

"Not at the moment, he's at the station. Give him a call." I see my mother emerge from her front door and get into her car. She's wearing a surgical face mask, something she rarely goes anywhere without. And I'm certain she has lathered any of her exposed, fair skin with lotion that has an SPF number in the thousands. I inherited my mother's fair skin, blue eyes, and blond hair, though the rest of me seems to be all my father.

"I gotta go, Arnie. Keep me posted." Without further ado, I hang up and watch as my mother backs out into the street and drives off in the opposite direction. I wait a couple of minutes to make sure she doesn't backtrack, and then get out of Hurley's car, locking the door behind me.

I have a key to my mother's house, so getting inside is easy. Just to be sure, I stop in the foyer and holler out William's name. The house is deathly quiet, so I make my way to the basement door, which is located in the kitchen. The house is utterly spotless, not a speck of dust to be seen anywhere. I can't help but feel a twinge of guilt when I compare it to the barely controlled disaster zone Hurley's house has become with four people—a toddler and a teenager among them—living there. Clutter has become a way of life and I can't remember the last time I actually dusted.

Most people's unfinished basements are dark, dank, cob-
webby places, but not my mother's. Her obsession with
cleanliness has made its way down here. The concrete floor
is spic-and-span clean. Neatly ordered shelves hold excess
canned, paper, and dry goods on one side, and similar shelves
on the opposite wall contain tools, partially used paint cans,
and neatly labeled boxes. In the far corner, off to my right,
are the household mechanicals: the furnace, water heater,
and water softener, all of them connected to special filtering
systems my mother had installed when she moved into the
place. In the corner to the left is a washer and dryer, an empty
laundry basket sitting in front of them. There are a few random pieces of furniture down here as well: an old wooden
rocking chair, some folding chairs, an antique sewing cabinet, and a floor lamp. As I descend the stairs and scan the
room, I feel my hopes sink because I don't see the chest Desi
described anywhere. Then I remember the space beneath the
stairs.

I make my way to the door under the stairs, open it, and
reach in for a light switch. There isn't one on the wall, so I
wave my hand around until I feel a string hanging from the
ceiling. I grab it and give it a pull.

A bunch of Christmas decorations and an artificial tree—
my mother would never allow a real one in her house—take
up most of the space. But off to the left, tucked under the
lower part of the stairs, I see the chest. I hunch over and get
a hold of it, dragging it out of the closet and into the main
part of the room. It looks exactly the way Desi described it.
The latch on the front is secured by a padlock, and when I
pick it up and look at the slot for a key, I can see the end of
the paper clip Desi broke off in there. I go back out to the
main portion of the room and walk over to the shelves containing tools. There is no hacksaw, so sawing off the padlock
isn't an option. I eye the tools a moment, thinking, before
settling on a chisel and hammer. Carrying them back to the

chest, I walk around looking for the weak spots before applying the chisel to one end of a hinge. I give the chisel a hard whack with the hammer. Nothing happens. I try again, hitting harder, but still it won't budge. Two more whacks later, I give up.

Frustrated, I return to the front of the chest and eye the metal loop that makes up the bottom part of the lock mechanism. There is a slotted, metal flange fitted over it and the padlock is run through the loop over that flange. I put the chisel up against the outer wall of the chest; I'm wedging it between it and the metal loop piece as much as I can. Two whacks of the hammer later, I see the loop start to move. Four more whacks, and it pops loose. I drop the tools on the floor, brace myself, and open the chest.

CHAPTER 22

On top of the inner contents are three photo albums. A quick scan of the first one reveals several blank pages in the front of the book, followed by pictures of me as a baby on the back pages. Some of the pictures have my mother in them; some are of me alone. There are several blank spots on the pages, and I feel certain these and the front pages contained pictures of my father at one time.

The second album contains pictures of my mother and one of my stepfathers, Desi's father. There are a number of pictures of me and Desi together, covering a span of about two years.

The third album has pictures of my mother and her third husband. After a quick flip through the pages, I set it aside with the others. Beneath the albums are some boxes. The first one contains several manila envelopes, which turn out to be marriage certificates and divorce papers. Included in these is the marriage certificate for my father. I stare at his name, slightly faded and typed a smidge above the line it

was meant to go on: Cedric Novak. At the bottom is his signature, written with tight, angular letters.

I set the marriage certificate aside and move on to the last
package of papers in the envelope: the divorce papers ending my mother's marriage to my father. It's a surprisingly
simple two-page document, dissolving the marriage for ir-
reconcilable differences, conveying full custody of me to
my mother, and divesting my father from any claims on all
of their shared property, including the house. The same
tight, angular signature appears at the bottom of the second
page, along with a witness's signature and a notary stamp.
My father's signature is a stark contrast to my mother's,
which is written in a big, loopy, rounded hand. The effective
date of the dissolution is September 2, 1984. I realize, looking at it, that Desi was a month old by then. I go back to the
marriage certificate for my mother and Desi's father and see
it's dated for September 30, 1984. Not only was Desi born
before her parents were married, she was born before my
parents were divorced. I never knew my mother had something so Jerry Springer-ish in her history and I'm betting
Desi never knew, either.

I move on to the second envelope and find birth certificates
for me and Desi, along with our childhood immunization
records. The birth certificates confirm the shady circumstances
surrounding Desi's birth. My mother had always led us to believe that she and Desi's father were married a year before
they actually were, and I had always assumed she and my
father divorced before Desi was born. Even as I think this, I
flash back on my mother carping about how my father disappeared around the time I turned four. And yet Desi was
born when I was four. It would seem my mother had moved
on to a new man either before my father left us or around the
same time, which might explain why he left. All these years,
my mother let me believe my father left simply because he

didn't care and didn't want to be tied down, when the truth was he left because my mother had an affair.

Feeling a stab of anger, I set the divorce and birth papers aside and move on to the third envelope. It contains all of the report cards Desi and I received from kindergarten through middle school. I chuckle when I look at mine because there's a definite theme to them. My scholastic subjects—math, science, English, history, reading, and penmanship—always had A's and B's, but two other subjects—posture and conduct—consistently got D's and F's, with written comments like *says inappropriate things, slouches too much,* and *interrupts all the time.* A quick glance at Desi's report cards reveal she was as good at being a student as she is at being a mother. Not hard to see which one of us was the problem child.

At the bottom of the chest are two handmade baby blankets, the top one folded so that Desi's name, sewn onto a silken square at the center, is displayed. I assume the one beneath it is mine, but if there is a name on it, it's hidden in the folds. I take the blanket out and let it fall open. There is no name, but hidden inside those folds is a packet of letters tied together with string. A quick flip through the envelopes shows me they are all addressed to my mother using the name Jane Obermeyer, her maiden name. None of them have a return address, and the postmarks are from several different cities: Chicago, Cleveland, Pittsburgh, and Norfolk, Virginia, and all are dated with the year 1984.

Curious, I slide the top envelope out from beneath the ribbon and remove the letter it contains. I recognize the tight, angular handwriting immediately and my heart speeds up to a racy trot. It's dated March 22, 1984.

My dearest Jane,
I don't know how many letters I will be able to send to you so I will try to convey as much as I can in this one.

The secret we discussed has gone horribly wrong. Unfortunately, my past has caught up to me and I need to go into hiding for a while, maybe for a very long time. I can't go into the details, and it's better if you don't know anyway. I understand your decision, but hope you will reconsider it. You are right that it wouldn't be easy, but at least we could all be together. However, if your mind is made up, I don't think Mattie or you are in any danger. If you ever have any reason to think you are, please call the following number and ask for Dan. All my love,
Cedric

At the bottom of the page, a phone number is scrawled— *312-555-7265*—and I recognize the area code as one for Chicago. I shove the page back into its envelope and grab the next letter in the stack. This one is dated April 2, 1984, and, like the first one, it's short and sweet. In the letter, my father says things are still up in the air and he doesn't know when he'll be able to come home. The closing is different in this one, however, as it reads: *Miss you.*

The third letter is dated July 8, 1984, and the tenor of this one is different from the others, less loving, angrier. He says he doesn't understand my mother's decision not to join him.

The fourth letter is dated August 15, 1984—two weeks after Desi was born—and in this one the tone is back to loving. While my father sounds hurt, he also seems resigned. There is mention of an enclosure he hopes will help, and he writes about how he wishes things could be different, but understands my mother's reasoning. He also says how not seeing me will be the hardest thing he's ever done.

As I read this, my eyes tear up. All this time, I thought my father left because he didn't love or want us. Yet here he is, saying how difficult the separation will be for him. What's more, he's expressing his love for my mother, his desire to be with her, apparently not knowing she has just given birth to another man's child. The anger and fury I feel toward my mother right now is so intense that if she was standing before me, I'd be sorely tempted to hit her.

There is one letter left, and before I open it, I take a moment to get my emotions under control. I wipe away tears with the back of my hand, blink hard several times, and remove the letter from its envelope.

> *November 25, 1984*
> *My dearest Jane,*
> *This will be the last correspondence you will get from me. As I'm sure you have already learned, that one final hope we had has fallen through. Since you seem determined in your decision, I guess there is no choice but to cut all ties. Please know that loving you has been one of the greatest things I've experienced in my life, and I don't harbor any ill feelings toward you because of your decision. Please tell my daughter I love her. Let her know my leaving wasn't by choice and I did so with her, and your, best interests in mind. Maybe someday we can be together again, but for now it looks as if it isn't meant to be.*
> *I wish you and Mattie nothing but the best in life. And please remember if you feel endangered at any time, you can contact Dan at the number I gave you before.*
> *Sadly, but with love in my heart,*
> *Cedric*

I swipe again at the tears on my cheeks and set the letters, certificates, and divorce papers aside. Then I return all the other items to the chest and put the chest back where it was.

Back upstairs I turn out lights as I go, though I do it more out of habit than any desire to have my presence go undetected. As I leave the house and lock it behind me, I wonder if my mother is still with Hurley at the station. If she is, her questioning is going to get a whole lot more interesting once I get there.

Five minutes later, I pull into the parking lot behind the police department and let myself into the station, using the punch lock code for the back door. I head for Hurley's office and see he's not there, but Bob Richmond is.

"Hey, Bob," I say. He waves at me over his shoulders, but continues doing whatever he's doing on his computers. "Is Hurley in the conference room?"

"Yeah, with your mother."

"Thanks. Any luck on finding Jeremy Prince?"

"Some, but nothing exciting. I'll tell you and Hurley when you're done with whatever it is you're doing in there." He nods in the general direction of the conference room.

What *were* we doing in there? More importantly, what was I about to do in there? My discoveries in the trunk had me feeling a mix of emotions: confusion, anger, sorrow, determination, even pity.

I turn and head for what serves as an interrogation room here, though it does double duty by also functioning as a meeting room. It doesn't look like any other interrogation room I've seen either on TV or in other police stations. It's carpeted, decorated—though badly—and has a large conference table surrounded by big, cushy chairs. It has audio-visual recording capabilities that can be triggered from the table. This, and a bolt in the floor by one of the chairs—sometimes used to cuff someone's feet to the floor—are the only indications the room is routinely used to question witnesses and suspects.

I consider knocking before entering, my hand raised, fisted, and ready to go. But when I hear a faint murmur of voices coming from beyond, I put my ear to the wood to see if I can make out what they're saying. The door is too thick, but I remember there is an observation room. I'd momentarily forgotten about it, since these days it hardly ever gets used for anything other than a secret trysting place. The door to it is only a few feet to my right, but it has no signage, no different look about it, making it easy to dismiss it as a storage closet. I have no idea if it's locked, but walk over and give it a try. The knob turns easily and after feeling around on the wall for a light switch, I flip it on and go in.

Turns out the room *is* a storage closet of sorts. There are several boxes containing extra office supplies: pens, paper, those little notebooks all the cops carry, paper clips, staples, and such. To the left of the door is the observation window—from the conference room side, it appears to be a large mirror—and I can see my mother sitting on the far side of the table, still wearing her surgical mask. She looks cool and collected, not the frazzled woman I expected to see. Maybe Hurley hasn't hit her up with the hard questions yet.

Hurley is currently the one doing the talking, but his voice is muffled. I study the panel below the window, see a knob with numbers on it, and turn it. Hurley's voice fills the room.

". . . and when you do, we can move ahead on this. But if you don't cooperate with me, I can't promise you what will happen."

"I've told you, I don't know anything. If I did, don't you think I'd tell you?"

"No," Hurley says without hesitation. "I don't."

My mother's expression is halfway hidden behind her mask, but her eyes briefly grow bigger, giving away her astonishment. Her voice, however, is cool, calm, and collected. "It appears we are at an impasse, Detective." She enunciates his title slowly, clearly, and I suspect this is an attempt on her part to rile him. I've asked her numerous times to refer to Hurley by his first name, since we have a kid together, live together, and are about to get married. But my mother has steadfastly refused, most likely too disappointed in my financial choice for a husband to bother acknowledging him in any way other than professional.

"Jane, I know you don't want to get caught up in a bunch of legal entanglements, and I'm certain you don't want to spend any time in jail. I'm equally as certain you know more about Cedric Novak than you're letting on. You do understand this is a homicide investigation? And Cedric is suspected of killing two people, possibly more?"

"Cedric didn't kill anyone," my mother says dismissively, assuredly.

"How would you know that? If what you've told me is true, you haven't had any contact with the man in over thirty years. Maybe he's changed during that time."

My mother stubbornly shakes her head. "Leopards don't change their spots," she tosses out, and I roll my eyes. She used that phrase on me all the time when I started dating, usually regarding a boy she didn't approve of. "Cedric isn't a saint, but he's no killer, either."

I catch something in what she just said and I'm about to rap on the window, or bust into the room, when I realize Hurley has picked up on it, too.

"You say that like you've seen him recently," Hurley says. "You didn't say he wasn't a saint, you said he isn't one. You've had contact with him recently, haven't you?"

My mother fusses with her mask for a moment, adjusting it slightly, stalling for time. Then she says, "I think I've had enough talk for one day, Detective. I'm tired and I want to go home. Am I under arrest?"

Hurley hesitates before he answers, "Not yet."

"Then I'm leaving."

She rises from her chair, and I know it's now or never. I make a mad dash for the interrogation room.

CHAPTER 23

I come face-to-face with my mother five seconds later. "Sit down," I tell her.

"Mattie, please, I don't have time for this."

"I think you do." I hold up the letters I have in my hand.

My mother's eyes—the only part of her face I can see because of her mask—look sleepy and bored at first, but the sight of those envelopes makes them open wide. She stares at them, blinking several times in rapid succession. Then her gaze shifts to me, her eyes narrowing down to a steely glint. I tower over her by at least six inches, and outweigh her by close to a hundred pounds. Yet that look in her eye instills fear in my heart and makes my legs tremble.

"You invaded my privacy," she says through clenched teeth.

"It's my life, too," I tell her. "I have a right to know the truth. You lied to me. All these years, you've been telling me my father left us because he didn't want to be with us. You said he was a wandering Gypsy who couldn't settle down.

You made me think he didn't love me, didn't care about me. But that wasn't the case at all, was it?"

My mother maintains her flinty glare, and even though I'm quaking a little on the inside, I force myself to meet her steely gaze with one of my own. It's a battle of wills, one that lasts a good thirty seconds before my mother finally looks away.

"Sit down," I tell her again, and she turns around and heads back toward the seat she was in before. But halfway there, she stops and settles into a chair at the end of the table instead.

"Let's discuss the content of these letters," I say, sitting in the chair closest to her. "What did my father do that came back to haunt him? Why did he have to disappear? Why didn't you go with him? And who is this Dan person he mentioned?"

"You don't know what you're getting into here, Mattie," my mother says, giving me a pleading look. "There are things you don't need to know, things it's better you don't know."

"My father is involved in the murder of my colleague and his girlfriend. He's here in the area. He's been seen. You need to tell me everything you know. *Now.*"

She ignores my plea and won't even look at me, focusing on her hands instead, twirling her thumbs.

"Mom, please." My frustration level is so high I feel like I'm about to cry. It gets her attention.

She stops twirling her thumbs and looks at me. "Your father was into some bad stuff before he met me," she says. "And he was a Gypsy, probably still is for all I know. He was part of a band of Gypsies that traveled around the Midwest pulling cons on people. Most of their victims were so embarrassed once they realized they'd been conned that they never reported the incidents. So the group would work an area for several months until they felt their reputation was spreading too much, and then they'd move on to a new town." She sighs, looks away from me, and a hint of a smile hits her eyes. I can almost see it behind her mask.

"Do you know how I met your father?" she says, but she doesn't wait for an answer. "He conned me. And then he returned the next day and admitted it to me, gave me back my money. He was a huge flirt, and I was so mad at him that at first I told him I wanted nothing to do with him. But there was something there between us, a spark, a connection . . . and he was persistent." She sighs. "He wore me down, but I told him the only way we could ever be a couple was if he gave up his old ways. No more cons, no more traveling. He was going to have to settle down. He agreed, and eventually his 'family' "—she makes little air quotes with the word "family"—"moved on without him."

The smile fades from her eyes and she sucks in a deep breath, making her mask go concave for a moment. "But somewhere in his past, he conned the wrong person. I don't know the details."

I grunt and roll my eyes at this.

"I swear, I don't," she insists. "All I know is at some point in his past he got his hands on something he shouldn't have. I don't know what it was, and I don't know whom he got it from. Apparently, it was important enough some cops in Chicago were offering him protection. But he didn't trust anyone and he went into hiding."

"He wanted you to go with him," I say.

She nods slowly, then sighs. "He did, but I refused. I couldn't live like that and I didn't want you to have to live like that."

"Plus, you'd already moved on, hadn't you? Does Desi know she was born before you married her father, and while you were still married to my father?"

My mother's eyes grow hooded. "You don't know what you're talking about, Mattie."

"The hell I don't! The dates don't lie. They're all right

here," I say, tossing the papers onto the table. "You didn't go with my father because you were already with someone else. Not only were you having an affair, you were pregnant with Desi, with someone else's child while my father was begging you to come with him."

My mother shakes her head. "You've got it wrong, Mattie."

"Stop with the lies, Mother," I snap. "If Dad was hiding from someone, weren't you worried they would come after you, after us?"

"Not really. I didn't take your father's name when we got married because he didn't want to leave a trail that . . . Well, let's just say his family didn't approve. We did it in a small, private ceremony and I kept my Obermeyer name. He told me he was giving up the Gypsy lifestyle, leaving his family, but he lied to me. He was living double lives the whole time, spending half of his time with me and the other half with them. So when it came time to make a choice between leaving with him and living life on the run or staying put, I opted to stay put. I couldn't trust him anymore because he'd been lying to me all that time. So, yes, I moved on. And on the off chance someone figured out the connection between him and me, I had an emergency number to call."

"Yes, this Dan guy Dad mentioned in his letters," I say, tapping the stack of them on the table. "Who was he?"

She shrugs. "I don't know. I never called him. Never had a reason to."

I stare at her, wondering if she's telling me the truth. Given how much she's kept hidden all these years, I have my doubts.

"Where's this number?" Hurley asks.

I slide the letter with the number over to him and my mother leans forward with a sharp intake of breath. "Those letters are private," she says, her tone strident.

I ignore her. I'm so angry with her right now I don't care how upset she gets. Hurley looks at the letter, scanning it quickly and then focusing on the number at the bottom. He takes out his cell phone and dials it.

"That number is more than thirty years old," I tell him.

"Nothing to lose by trying." We sit in silence, waiting. "Hello," he says, and my heart leaps. "Is Dan there?" He listens for a moment, and then says, "I see. Where are you located?" He listens again, and then says, "This is Detective Steve Hurley with the Sorenson, Wisconsin, Police Department. May I ask how long you've had this number?" I can vaguely hear the sound of a woman's voice on the other end, though I can't make out the words. "Okay, thank you for your time." He hangs up and looks over at me. "The number belongs to a real estate company located in downtown Chicago, and she said they've had the number for at least twelve years because that's how long she's been there."

"Is there any way to trace back and see who had it before that?" I ask.

"I don't know. I'll look into it."

My mother sits back in her chair, her arms folded over her chest. Her eyes above the mask look angry. "Can I have my letters back?"

I shake my head. "I'll give them back to you at some point, but not yet. I want to look at them a little more."

She glares at me. "You may not believe me or understand it, but I did what I did because I believed it was the best thing for you."

"Maybe you did," I say. "Maybe you honestly believed what you were doing was the best thing. But what I don't understand is why you lied to me about my father. Why let me think he didn't care? Why let me believe he abandoned me without a second thought?"

"Because I was afraid you'd try to look for him, or talk about him. . . . I didn't want your connection to him to be known. And there was Desi to think about, too."

"Ah, yes. Does Desi know the truth about her birth?"

My mother's eyes dart away momentarily. "No, and there's no need to tell her," she says. Then she looks at me again. "You won't, will you?"

Would I? I didn't know. My head was still reeling from all the revelations, all the lies, all the potential truths I was trying to uncover. What benefit would there be in telling Desi the truth? Unlike me, she knew her father, and while he lived in another state, hours away, with a new wife and two other grown kids, her relationship with him was cordial. Why sully that?

"I won't offer the information," I say finally. "But if she ever asks me, I won't lie to her."

"She'd have no reason to ask unless you hint to her that something is up."

"She knows about your chest of secrets. She's the one who told me about it. She's going to ask me what I found in it."

"Fine," my mother says, getting out of her chair in a huff and shoving it under the table. "Do what you want. But I'm telling you there is more to this than you know, so please consider the repercussions carefully before you go blabbing a bunch of half-truths. Don't upset and hurt other people simply because you've been hurt."

With that, she strides from the room, slamming the door behind her.

I look over at Hurley. "What a freaking mess."

"It will sort itself out." He reaches over and starts massaging the back of my neck. "Maybe we can get more of the story from your father, if we can find him. We can follow up on the e-mail address for this Walter Scott, and the fingerprints Jonas found in the car. Maybe something will come out of those."

And with that his phone rings.

CHAPTER 24

I'm hoping the call will be Jonas with a report on the fingerprints. Turns out I'm halfway right. It's Jonas, but what he has to report on has nothing to do with the fingerprints, nor does it move things along much.

I watch Hurley's face as he listens, frowns, and then says, "Thanks." He disconnects the call and gives me a grim look. "Jonas and Laura have finished going through Hal and Tina's computers and that USB drive they found in Hal's truck. They didn't find anything useful on the computers, and it turns out I was right about Tina's connection to Lech Wyzinski. Jonas said she has a novel in progress that mirrors the Wyzinski case. But there are some files on the thumb drive that are password protected and *Persephone* doesn't work to open them. So they're going to send the drive to Madison to have someone there take a crack at it."

"Dang it," I mutter. "This case is nothing but a bunch of stumbling blocks."

"Let me take a look at those letters of your mother's."

I slide them over to him. Then I tap the manila envelope I also have. "In here are marriage and divorce certificates for my mother and father, and my birth certificate. Maybe they'll have something to offer."

"We can run your father's Social to see if anything pops, but if he hid as well as I think he did, I doubt we'll get anything helpful. Those Gypsy families are masters at living off the grid, and I'm betting your father learned those lessons well."

We spend the next ten minutes reading—or, in my case, rereading—my father's letters to my mother and looking over the other documents. Hurley's phone rings again and this time I don't see the caller ID. "What have you got?" Hurley says; then, "That's great. I'll be there in ten."

He disconnects the call and smiles at me. "We may have gotten a break," he says. "Junior Feller was looking into who else might have been on the lake yesterday and he found someone who was in the area where Hal's boat was anchored. He says they saw another boat there, too. Let's go talk to him."

Before leaving, Hurley and I head for Richmond's desk. "Anything on Keith Lundberg or Jeremy Prince?"

"A little," he says. "Keith Lundberg has disappeared, not hard since he didn't have much of an existence in the first place. He popped up out of nowhere on the tax records two months ago, even though he supposedly died in a car accident four years ago."

Hurley gives him a grim smile. "So I take it Keith was a stolen identity?"

Richmond nods. "Now our Mr. Prince is another story. He has a military background and a degree in chemistry." He gives us a knowing look. "That would make it easy for him to figure out how to distill nicotine out of tobacco juice, which I understand is a relatively easy process. It's not that hard to get it out of ordinary cigarettes. Anyway, he left the military six years ago and these days he makes his money as"—he pauses and makes air quotes—"a 'business' consultant."

"Any idea where he is now?" Hurley asks.

"Nope. I'm watching. I traced back on the credit card he used to buy the tobacco juice, but the address for it is a mailbox store in Minneapolis. If he uses it again, I'll be on it. But for the moment, he's flying below the radar. I found another address on some bank records, but it's a mailbox store, too, this one in Milwaukee."

"Cell phone?" Hurley asks, sounding frustrated, and Richmond shakes his head. "What about a vehicle?"

"Can't find any registered to him, though he does have a driver's license tied to the bogus Milwaukee address." He turns his monitor to show us Jeremy Prince's DMV photo. It's ordinary: an oval face with brown eyes and brown hair; no moles, birthmarks, quirky-shaped features, or dimples. According to his stats, he's five feet ten inches tall and weighs 170 pounds. Jeremy Prince is your basic everyman, and that makes it easy for him to blend in and hide.

"Now check this out," Richmond says, tapping away on his keyboard. A moment later, another DMV photo pops up on the screen next to Jeremy's. It's another ordinary face with ordinary features. It's not the same man—the chin is a tad bit squarer and the nose a little longer—but the similarity is startling. "That's Keith Lundberg's DMV picture," Richmond says. "I'm guessing Prince picked it because of the resemblance and perhaps because Lundberg worked as an auto mechanic down in Texas. Given all the security measures in place for driver's licenses these days, Prince must have some good connections to get a fake one made."

"Good work, Bob," Hurley says. "I have something else I'd like you to work on while you're waiting for Prince to emerge from whatever hole he's crawled into." He hands Richmond the wedding and divorce papers, and then writes down the phone number for the mysterious Dan, who was mentioned in one of the letters. "See what you can dig up on Cedric Novak using the Social Security number and the other info in here," Hurley says. "And this phone number is from over thirty years ago. I don't know if there's any way to trace it, but can you look into it for me? It's currently assigned to a real estate company, but I'm guessing it belonged to something else back then."

"On it," Richmond says, nodding. He glances from Hurley to me. "You doing okay?"

"As well as can be expected," I say with a wan smile. "Thanks for asking."

With that, Hurley and I head out to his car, with him once again behind the wheel. "Where are we going?" I ask.

"To the park on the south side of the lake. Apparently, there's some sort of church retreat group there for the week and they spent yesterday out on the water in several boats, one of which was near Hal's."

"You know, Beckwith told me that Tomas Wyzinski has a degree in chemistry, just like our mysterious Mr. Prince. Another coincidence?" I let the question hang while Hurley dwells on it.

"Well, we know Tomas didn't kill the Abernathy woman."

"True, unless he somehow arranged a hit from jail."

"I doubt that."

So did I, but the coincidences were adding up and it was making me uncomfortable.

It takes us a little over fifteen minutes to get to the park and find our way to the area where the church group is located. We see Junior in the parking area waving us down, but since there are no open parking places Hurley pulls in behind a couple of parked cars, blocking them in, and turns off the engine.

It's a beautiful day to be at the lake. I climb out of the car and close my eyes for a moment, enjoying the warm sun on my head and the cool breeze on my face. I make a mental note to bring Matthew out here soon, maybe make a day of it with all four of us, a picnic with the entire family.

"Give me the short version," Hurley says to Junior, bringing me back to harsh reality.

Junior nods toward a wayside area. "That guy over there, with the white hair and beard, is the leader of a ministry, and apparently they're here for a weeklong retreat of some sort that involves"—he pauses and consults what he has written in his notebook—"building trust, finding inner peace, and getting in touch with your higher power." He says this with a healthy dose of skepticism and a hint of sarcasm. "Yesterday was a find-your-inner-peace exercise and it involved having them all go out on the water in boats and then float in deep water or something like that." Junior shakes his head and rolls his eyes. "Anyway, the group Cullen French— that's Mr. White Hair—had with him was moored not too far from Hal's boat at one point. They estimated they were a couple of hundred feet away, close enough to see there was a man and a woman on Hal's boat when it motored out to the spot where we found it and dropped anchor. About an hour later, another boat came up alongside Hal's and the ministry group heard some yelling going back and forth. So they decided to move to a quieter location, though trying to find a quiet section of lake this time of the year is pretty much impossible."

"Did they give you a description of this other boat?" Hurley asks.

Junior nods and consults his notebook again. "'Black-and-white ski and fish boat,'" he reads. "Probably a Chaparral brand, according to one of the participants. They said it looked to be around the same size as Hal's boat."

Hurley nods, writing all this down in his own notebook.

When he's done he looks up and says, "Where are the people who were on the boat? Are they the ones standing around Mr. White Beard over there?"

There are about thirty people milling about along the shoreline, some seated at tables, others standing in a circle, a few sitting in the grass. Junior nods and points to the standing group: six people, two men and four women, plus Cullen French, nicknamed "Mr. White Beard" and "Mr. White Hair."

Hurley and I head toward the group, and as we draw closer, I realize they're doing some sort of meditation. They are standing with their feet apart, their faces tilted back, and their eyes closed. Their arms are at their sides, bent slightly at the elbow with the palms of their hands facing the sky. I hear Cullen French telling them to visualize their goal, to create a scene in which they achieve their greatest expectations and let it play out in their minds.

As we draw closer, French opens his eyes and beams a smile at us. "Stay the way you are for a few minutes and let your scenario play out," he says, holding up a hand to stop us. "Replay it if you like, or, if you prefer, you can explore an alternative approach and run it through. Once you are done with that, I want you to imagine you are at the pinnacle of your success, with all the things, all the wealth, all the happiness you want, all around you. And then imagine the first three things you will do with it. How will you spend your wealth? Who will share in your happiness? What will your life look like? Where will you be? What will your house look like?"

French finally stops talking, steps out of the circle, and makes his way toward us just as beatific smiles start creeping over the faces of several of the participants. He motions us back toward the parking lot and puts a finger to his lips, indicating he wants us to remain quiet. As he passes us by—

clearly assuming we will meekly follow his commands and his steps—Hurley and I share a look that tells me we are both on the same trail of thought with regard to Mr. French. Still, we follow him, and when we reach the parking-lot area, Hurley wastes no time declaring his in-charge status.

"Mr. French, I don't have a lot of time and I need to speak with you and anyone else in your group who saw the two boats out on the lake yesterday."

"Ah, yes, I see you are pressed for time, which is very unfortunate. That causes stress, and stress interferes at the most basic levels with your ability to succeed in life. One must strive to achieve sublime happiness if one hopes to reach the goals they desire." His serene little smile hasn't faltered once, and for some crazy reason, I have an overwhelming desire to try to slap it away.

Hurley chuffs his impatience. "I deal with the dead on a regular basis, and I can assure you there is nothing sublime or happy about it for me, the victims, or their families."

"Ah, but those who go on living have goals, achievements, and desires. That includes you. Perhaps you should join my group and search for your bliss in an effort to help you deal with the stresses of your work."

Hurley looks like he wants to punch the bliss right off French's face, so I step in, hoping to defuse the situation. "Mr. French, the people who were on one of those boats you saw yesterday were friends of mine. One of them was a coworker. They were murdered in cold blood. One person had his throat slit; the other was tossed into the lake with a weight attached and left to drown. I'm sure bliss was the last thing they were seeking. And unless you feel comfortable knowing the cold-blooded killer who did this might come after you next or someone you love, I suggest you stop with the life-coaching rhetoric and answer our questions."

French has turned his pacific, calm face toward me and

he nods slowly, still beaming his irritatingly serene smile. "Of course," he says, with an expression that suggests he knew this all along. "Please ask away."

"Tell me about the people you saw on the boats," Hurley says.

"We weren't that close to them. Our trust exercise requires calm, quiet waters, so we try to avoid other boaters as much as possible. That's why we were in that particular spot. It tends to attract fishermen more than skiers and partiers. I was able to see that the first boat, the one I understand your friends were in, had a couple of lines in the water. And I was able to tell the occupants were a man and a woman, based on the clothing, general builds, and hair. The woman wore a floppy sunhat, the man had on a red baseball cap."

"How long were you in the same vicinity they were?" I ask.

"I'd guess about an hour, give or take," French says. "Though I can't be sure. Time is such a constraining concept. I prefer not to give it much credence."

Hurley's face is a mass of thunderclouds and I can tell he's ready to say or do things he'd most likely regret later. So I continue with the questions in an effort to keep French talking and keep Hurley quiet.

"Do you have any idea how long it was, or what time it was when the second boat showed up?"

"As a matter of fact, I do. Once the second boat arrived, it became obvious the serenity we sought wasn't going to continue. The second boat drove around in circles several times, creating big waves that disturbed our process. And when it pulled up alongside the first boat, I heard them start to argue."

"What were they saying?"

"I'm afraid I can't help you with that," he says with an apologetic smile. "My group was quite chit-chatty, and while I was able to hear raised voices, I have no idea what the argument was about. At that point, we motored out of the area and away from the two boats. We headed for shore and I remember Mason—he's the balding gentleman in my group over there—saying he was hungry. Someone else pointed out it was almost noon and a group decision was made to have lunch."

"Can you tell me how many people were in the second boat?"

"Only one, a man," French says without hesitation.

"How can you be sure?"

"He had a beard. And the voice was definitely masculine."

"Any more description you can give me?"

French frowns, and the disappearance of that annoying smile almost makes me sigh with relief. "Not much," he says. "He was white, shorter than the man on the first boat, and wearing a camouflage-colored baseball cap. His beard was brown, but I couldn't see his head hair clearly, assuming he even had any, because of the cap. Other than that . . ." He shrugs and that damned smile returns.

Hurley asks, "Did you notice anything in particular about the boat, such as markings, printed words or numbers, unusual rigs of any sort, anything like that?"

French strokes his bearded chin and gazes toward the sky. "Can't recall anything specific. Sorry." He doesn't look sorry.

"We need to speak to the other people who were on your boat," Hurley says.

"Of course." French glances back at the group, all of whom have abandoned their sun-worshipping poses. "It appears they have finished their exercise."

Indeed, the group is now milling about, chatting among themselves. Hurley and I abandon Mr. White Beard and infiltrate the group. The women are of no help at all, but the bald guy in the group, who tells us his name is Mason Chambers, provides an exciting clue.

"There was a name on the boat," he says. "I remember it because I thought it was clever. It said *Court A'Sea,* which I took to be a take on the word 'courtesy,' although I suppose it could belong to a lawyer or a judge."

Chambers spells out the name for us, and after Hurley dutifully jots it down in his notebook, we thank Mr. Chambers and head back to the car. On the way, Hurley's cell phone rings. He looks at the caller ID and frowns.

"Detective Hurley." He listens, and when we arrive back at the car, he stands outside the driver's door, still listening, uttering the occasional "Yeah," or "Uh-huh." Finally he says, "He's a key witness, maybe a potential suspect in a triple-homicide case I'm investigating." After listening some more, he says, "Yeah, I can do that." He thanks the caller, disconnects, and gets into the car. I climb in on the passenger side, staring at him, burning with curiosity.

He starts the engine, but rather than pull out right away, he sits there, staring out the windshield.

"Who was that?" I ask, wearing my impatience on my sleeve.

"A man named Greg Washington. It seems our inquiries, primarily the fingerprints we ran on Carmichael's car and your father's Social Security number, triggered an alarm at the U.S. Marshal's Office. That's because they belong to someone in the Witness Protection Program, or rather someone who *was* in the program. He has since left."

"Is it my father?" I ask, realizing this might explain his need to disappear all those years ago.

"Presumably, since it was his Social we ran," Hurley says with a shrug. "But Marshal Washington wouldn't commit to a name. He wants to meet with us. He's invited us, or me at least, to his office in Chicago."

"I'm going, too," I say, unwilling to brook any objections he might offer. "You can't shut me out of this, Hurley."

"I don't intend to. But be aware, your presence might make him less willing to reveal any information."

"I don't care. I'm going."

Hurley's face is a frowning scowl.

"You don't want me to come along?"

"It's not that." He shifts the car into gear and pulls out.

"Then why the long face?"

"If your father is guilty of killing my old partner, I'm none too happy to find out he was given federal protection. You don't kill a cop and get off scot-free."

"Maybe he didn't do it, Hurley."

He shoots me a look like the one he had this morning when our son pointed at the dog's rawhide bone, did the gimme gesture with his hand, and said, "Me eat."

"Don't be delusional, Mattie."

"I'm not." This comes out harsher then I mean it to, so I take in a deep breath and try to exhale my defensiveness. "Look, I'm painfully aware my father might be, at worst, a killer, and an irresponsible, unpleasant human being, at best. But I'm keeping an open mind until I have all the facts. Isn't that what you're always telling me to do when we're investigating a case?"

Hurley doesn't answer right away. His fingers open and close on the steering wheel. I study his face, trying to read it, and I'm relieved when I see the tension ease out of it.

"Fine, you got me," he says finally.

"I wasn't trying to *get you*."

He looks over at me and smiles. "I know. I'm saying you got me, Squatch, regardless of how this turns out, regardless of how crooked and sketchy your family line is. None of it will change how I feel about you, or my commitment to you. So erase those worries from that blackboard in your head, okay?"

"Okay," I say, feeling the wind leave my self-righteous, defensive sails. Lord, how I love this man. "And just so you know, it's a whiteboard, not a blackboard."

"That's a bit bigoted, isn't it?"

"Merely a practical choice. Chalk dust makes me sneeze and I hate the smell of slate. Trust me, I know, because I spent many an after-school hour clapping erasers and washing the boards in my sixth-grade class as punishment for letting Tommy Smithson see my test answers."

"I see," Hurley says. "Should I be worried? It sounds like you had quite a thing for this Tommy Smithson."

"Indeed, I did. He not only told me I was pretty, he always gave me the Little Debbie coffee cakes his mother packed in his lunch." I close my eyes and let out a little moan. "God, I loved those things."

"Sounds serious."

"It was, for about four months or so. But then one day, his mother started packing chocolate cupcakes in his lunch, and suddenly I wasn't good enough for Tommy anymore. He ate those himself. That was the end of it for me."

"Duly noted. I promise to let you have the biggest piece of our wedding cake. In fact, you can have the whole darn thing if you want." He pauses and then adds, "We are having cake at the wedding, aren't we?"

And just like that, the whiteboard in my head starts filling up again, listing all the little details I still need to tend to.

CHAPTER 25

As we're pulling into the parking lot at the police station, Hurley's phone rings again. "It's Arnie," he tells me before answering. He puts it on speaker so I can hear, too. "Hey, Arnie, what have you got?"

"I got an ISP on that e-mail address you got for Walter Scott, Ivanhoe51580@gmail.com. It was created on a computer at the local library and the last e-mails sent out from that address came from there, too."

"That's great, Arnie," Hurley says. "Can you tell me the exact computer used?"

"I can, but I don't think you need that. There's a bank of five of them for public use at the library and they're all located in the same general area."

"Any luck with those password-protected files on the USB drive?"

"Not yet. I sent it on to the Madison guys, but kept copies here. I might have Joey Dewhurst take a whack at them to see if he can get in. It won't be usable as evidence that way, but whatever the Madison guys come up with will be. I just think Joey might be able to access them quicker. What do you think?"

Joey Dewhurst is giant hulk of a man with the approximate IQ of a ten-year-old, but a savant ability when it comes to working on computer hardware and software. He's been able to hack into other files for us in the past. His talent—or quirk, depending on your perspective—has led to him adopting a superhero persona, which he calls "HackerMan," replete with a caped outfit he wears under his everyday clothing featuring a giant red *H* on the chest.

"As long as we have an official evidence trail with the Madison folks, I think it would be fine," Hurley says, looking over at me with a questioning expression. I nod.

"Thanks, Arnie. Keep up the good work." With that, Hurley disconnects the call. "I'm hungry," he says. "Want to grab a bite to eat?"

Asking me if I want to eat is like asking most people if they want to breathe. "Sure. What do you have in mind?"

He looks over at me and wiggles his eyebrows salaciously. "What I'd like to have for lunch is you," he says. "But with Emily at the house, we don't have anywhere private to go."

"We could always check into a motel."

"Tempting," Hurley says with a sigh. "But expensive. I can wait until we get home this evening. In the meantime, how about Chinese?"

"Works for me."

Fifteen minutes later, we are seated in a booth at the Peking Palace, our orders placed. We spend a few minutes reviewing the case, Hurley checking off the things in his notebook we have yet to follow up on. Our food arrives, and once the waitress has departed, Hurley switches topics.

"Let's talk about the wedding."

"Okay," I say, stalling for a minute by shoving a large wonton into my mouth.

"Should we take Otto up on his offer and do it in his backyard?"

I make a face, and then swallow. "It's very kind of him to make that offer, but we don't know him all that well and it might be a little awkward. I don't know how long I'm going to have to work with the guy. I don't want to start our relationship off by trading favors."

"Okay, then where else would you suggest?"

I shove another wonton in my mouth and shrug.

"We could do it at our house," Hurley suggests.

I make a face and shake my head. "No way," I say once I've swallowed. "I don't want everyone traipsing through there, seeing what an awful housekeeper I am. And then there's the minefield we call a backyard. I haven't pooper-scooped for a week and Hoover has been producing hugely and regularly."

"What about Izzy's house then?"

I shake my head again. "That might have worked at one time, but not now. I don't want to put a lot of extra stress on him with this heart attack."

Hurley narrows his eyes at me. "You're stalling again."

"I'm not," I insist. "We'll do it. Something . . . somewhere will come up."

Hurley looks skeptical.

"Give me a day or two and I'll find a suitable place."

"Promise?"

"Promise."

With that out of the way, at least for now, we chat about Matthew and Emily for the rest of our meal. When we're done, Hurley pays and we go back to the police station. Richmond is in his office; when we enter, he says he was just about to call us.

"I did a little background research on that phone number you gave me," he says. "The area codes for Chicago have changed over the years with the proliferation of phones and the need for numbers. The one from your letter is no longer in the 312 area code. Back in 1996, it was switched to 773. And I think I found out who it belonged to: a guy named Dan Kellerman, who coincidentally worked for the U.S. Marshal's Office. He's dead now, died of cancer a little over two years ago, but at one time the number was his home phone."

"That makes sense," Hurley says, and then he fills Richmond in on the phone call he received earlier from the U.S. Marshal's Office. "Mattie and I are going down to Chicago first thing in the morning to talk to them."

Richmond nods and looks at me. "That also explains your father's Social Security number on your birth certificate. I tried to trace it back in time, but it has been completely inactive for over thirty years."

"I imagine he got a new one when he went into the Witness Protection Program," I surmise. "And a new name. I wonder if Walter Scott is the name the marshal's office gave him, or if that's just a temporary alias he's using now."

Hurley scowls. "I'm tired of wondering with this case. We need to find your father and talk to him directly."

The suggestion triggers butterflies in my stomach. I've imagined talking to the man hundreds of times over the years—in different places, on different topics, and with a variety of attitudes—but no matter what scenario I create in my mind, the end result is always the same: awkward and uncomfortable. "Good luck with that," I say. "He may have left the Witness Protection Program, but he seems determined to stay hidden."

"There might be a way to flush him out," Hurley says, looking thoughtful. "Peter Carmichael says he communicates with him through e-mail. So what if we stake out the library computers and watch for him? We still need to talk to Tina's coworkers, so we could put someone there and knock two items off our list."

"We could," I say. "What I can't figure out is where my father's been staying. If he's here locally, he must be living somewhere. Have we checked the motels in the area for anyone named Walter Scott? Maybe we should hit up some of the apartment complexes and show his picture around."

"Or all of the above," Richmond wisely suggests. "Except we don't have a current picture of the guy."

"Yes, we do," I say. "We have the one Emily drew two years ago, remember? She was staying in my cottage and someone was peeking in the windows at her. We asked her to draw a picture of the man, and my mother later identified it as my father, so it must be a reasonable likeness of him."

"Maybe the U.S. Marshal's Office can get us a more current picture," Hurley says. "Let me call them back."

He places the call, and as he does so, my cell rings. I take it out of my pocket and see that it's Dom calling. "Hey, Dom, how are things going?"

"Well as can be expected," he says. "We just got home and Izzy is comfortably ensconced on the couch with the remote control. He wanted me to call and let you know."

"That's great. Is he up for visitors?"

"Sure, as long as you don't stay too long. He says he's really tired."

"I'm sure he is. Hospitals are the worst place to try to get any real sleep." Because I detect an undertone of concern and worry in Dom's voice, I add, "Wait and see. After a couple of days at home with a decent night's sleep or two, he'll look and feel tons better."

"I hope so. What time are you going to come by?"

"Hurley and I are about to 'start pounding the pavement,' as the cops say. I expect that will use up most of the afternoon, and then I'll need to pick up Matthew. So let's figure

around five or five-thirty, okay? Unless Otto Morton calls
with an autopsy. If that happens, I'll have to get back to you
with a new time."

"Okay, see you then."

"Do you need anything? Groceries? Baby supplies?"

"No, I'm good. But thanks."

"Okay. Let me know if you think of something."

By the time I'm done with my call, Hurley has finished
his, and he's standing next to his computer waiting on the arrival of an e-mail. When it comes, he opens the attached picture and prints it. I stand by the printer, watching it draw my
father's face, line by line: thinning black hair; a dark, ruddy
complexion; hooded hazel eyes; a flat, broad nose; and thick,
pale lips. When it's done, I take it from the tray and study the
whole, searching for a resemblance to my own face. I inherited
my father's height, long limbs, and thick build, but my facial
features and coloring are all my mother's. Ironically, my sister,
Desi, looks more like my father than I do, though she inherited
my mother's small build. My mother has a type, I realize, or
at least she did—William doesn't fit her usual mold. But all
of her other husbands were dark-haired and dark-com-
plected, though none were as tall or as big as my father.

"I have to confess, I don't see a strong resemblance,"
Hurley says, echoing my thoughts as he peers at the head
shot over my shoulder.

"My father's genes all manifested from the neck down.
From the neck up, I'm my mother."

Hurley massages my shoulders and I allow myself to lean
back into him and enjoy the moment.

"You two should get a room," Richmond says.

"Speaking of motels," I say, "Let's start looking."

"Let me make a few copies of this picture," Hurley says.
"We can leave one at the library and ask the staff to call if
they see him come in."

"I'll take care of that part if you want," Richmond says,

and Hurley eagerly agrees. Then, with pictures of my father in hand, Hurley and I head out to pound the pavement.

Three hours later, I have tired feet, an aching back, and a whole new level of respect for sensible shoes, but we are no closer to finding my father. I tell Hurley after hitting all three of the motels in the area—including yet another memorable encounter with Joseph—and eleven different apartment complexes that I don't think my father would stay here in town. "He wants to stay hidden and Sorenson is too small," I say. "And the risk of being identified is too great. He's probably in the county somewhere, not too far away, and he comes to town from time to time, but I'm betting he isn't staying here."

"Yeah, you're probably right," Hurley says. "But we still have to do the work. Footwork is the basis of all solid police work."

There is an upside to our endeavors, however. Some of the peeks I get into the lives of others make me feel better about the chaos in mine.

"I think it's time to call it a day," I say to Hurley, sinking gratefully into the passenger seat of the car after apartment complex number twelve. "We started early today and we're going to have to start early tomorrow."

Hurley nods, but he doesn't look convinced. "Why don't you go pick up Matthew and I'll see you at home in a bit. I've got a few things I want to look into."

My curiosity wages war with my fatigue, and the fatigue wins. "Okay. I'm going to stop by Izzy's on the way and check on him. What time do you want to have dinner?"

"Let's figure on seven or seven-thirty."

"Gotcha."

Hurley drops me off in front of my office and I go inside to check in with Otto. "Everything quiet?" I ask.

"So far," he says, knocking on his desktop.

"Anything turn up with Tina's autopsy?"

Otto shakes his head slowly, sadly.

"I've made the official ID and her family has been notified." I don't want to ask my next question, but I have to. "Was she alive when she went into the water?" I'm pretty sure I know the answer to this based on the way I found her, but there is a small glimmer of hope in me that wants my assumptions to be wrong, for Tina's sake.

Otto shifts uncomfortably in his seat and I can tell he doesn't want to look at me or answer my questions. But he does both. "Yes," he says, his eyes meeting mine as he shatters my last hope. "She drowned."

I nod slowly, picturing in my mind Tina's open eyes and mouth, and imagining the horror of her final moments. A little shudder runs through me.

"How are you holding up?" he asks.

"Okay," I say. I fill him in on the progress we've made thus far, which doesn't sound like much. I realize he probably knows most of it already, but focusing on the details gets my mind off Tina and her death mask. Then I realize he might not know the parts about my father. In the interest of keeping things up front and open, I fill him in on what we know so far with regard to Cedric Novak, though I leave out some of the personal information I gleaned from my mother's letters.

When I'm done, Otto says, "Should you recuse yourself from this investigation if your father is a suspect?"

"I considered it," I admit. "But we don't know for sure if he did anything. In fact, it's starting to look like this Keith Lundberg–Jeremy Prince guy is who we're after. But if it turns out my father is involved in anything illegal, I feel confident in my ability to see him brought to justice. I haven't seen him in over thirty years and have no emotional atttachment to him. I'll have no reservations about putting him behind bars, if that's where he belongs.

Even as I render my speech to Otto, a speech I've played over and over again in my head, a speech I truly believed at one time, I wonder if it's true. The revelations of the past day or so have created questions in my mind as to my father's guilt, and I'm not oblivious to how quickly and eagerly I've seized on any suggestion that he might be innocent. I do think I'd help lock him up if he turns out to be guilty, but I also know I'll be disappointed and sad if that happens.

"Be careful," Otto warns. "You don't want to jeopardize the case."

"I know. If Hurley or I feel I need to step back at any point, I will."

Otto nods, but I can tell he has reservations. Eager to change the subject, I say, "Regarding our staffing, I'll be on call every night and come in to work every day until we find a replacement for Hal."

"I appreciate that," Otto says. "I'll try to get that process going as soon as I can. Any news on Izzy?"

I fill him in on Dom's update, concluding with, "I'm going to stop by and see him on my way home."

"Give him my regards."

"I will."

CHAPTER 26

As I leave the office, all the coincidental connections in these cases are still nagging at me, enough so that I feel compelled to dig a little deeper. I know if I don't, they'll continue to bother me. Once I'm settled in the hearse, I make a phone call, and when someone answers, I immediately hang up. Then I place a call to both Dom and my sister to tell them I'll be a little later than previously planned. When I'm done with my calls, I start the engine, pull out of the lot, and head out of town, aiming my car toward Pardeeville.

After a bucolic journey through some of the countryside, I pull into the drive of the Wyzinski house. There is no car in sight, but I have no way of knowing if Lech Wyzinski drives, and I know that Tomas's car was impounded as evidence. A man answered the phone at the house when I called, and while I hope it was Lech Wyzinski, I can't be sure. The reason I didn't say who I was or speak when I called is because I'm not sure Lech will want to talk to me, considering that I testified against his brother.

I park and make my way to the front door. I haven't finished knocking when the door whips open and I see a chubby man of average height, with shaggy brown hair that sticks up in cowlicks on the crown of his head. He looks to be in his thirties, though there is something childlike and innocent in his expression that belies that.

"Lech Wyzinski?" I say, feeling confident in my guess.

He nods vigorously, a big smile appearing on his face. "Yep, that's me."

"My name is Mattie. I wonder if I might talk to you."

"Yep," he says, still smiling. Then he stands there, holding the door. He's fidgety, but it strikes me as a restless energy rather than a nervous one.

"Can I come in?" I ask him.

"Yep," he says, and then he turns and walks into the house, leaving me there.

I step inside and close the door behind me. Lech has headed into the kitchen, so I follow him there, memories of my last visit here encroaching on my thoughts. I grimace, remembering the head of the female victim, a thirty-two-year-old woman named Marla Weber. At one time, Marla had been dating Tomas, but the two of them split up right before her death. That breakup was the supposed motive for Tomas killing her.

Lech plops into a chair at the kitchen table, which is situated beneath a window that looks out on the side of the house. I walk over and take one of the other seats. He continues to smile at me, but then the smile suddenly fades and he pops out of his seat.

"Oh, I should get you a drink," he says. "Tomas says you should always offer a guest a drink. Would you like a drink?"

He starts for the refrigerator, which sends shudders down my spine. "Lech, no, that's okay. I don't want a drink. But thank you."

He stops halfway to the fridge and turns to look at me, an expression of confusion on his face.

"Come and sit down," I tell him.

The smile reappears, and he does so.

"I want to talk to you about your brother, Tomas."

"Tomas is my big brother," Lech says. "He takes care of me." His smile fades. "Well, he did. Now he has to stay at the jail."

"Yes, that's what I wanted to talk to you about. You wrote a letter, several letters, in fact, that said your brother didn't kill that girl, Marla."

"Tomas loved Marla," he says. Then he frowns. "But he said Marla had to go away for her own good." He punctuates this remark with a single, definitive nod.

It's an odd turn of phrase, and I puzzle over it a moment before dismissing it, at least for now.

"Miss Joan knows," Lech goes on. "She knows Tomas didn't kill Marla because he did real good when they gave him the lying test, and she said he's being framed. That means he didn't really do it but someone wants it to look like he did." He says this in a rote manner suggesting he's repeating something he heard. Then he frowns. "But Miss Joan also says Tomas keeps saying to let it go."

"Miss Joan . . . do you mean Joan Mackey, Tomas's lawyer?"

Lech beams a smile and nods. "She's pretty," he says, his smile morphing into a goofy-looking grin.

"Lech, did you talk on the phone to a lady named Tina?"

Lech's brow furrows in thought. "Is she the library lady?"

"Yes," I say with a smile. "That's her. What did she talk to you about?"

"She said she wanted to know about Tomas. She asked a lot of questions, but I don't remember what they were." He gives me an apologetic look.

"That's okay. Lech, do you remember the day the police came and took Tomas away?"

He pouts the same way my son does when he's not getting his way. Lech's childlike manner reminds me of Joey Dewhurst: they both seem to have approximately the same level of brain maturation and development.

"They took Tomas to jail," he says, looking sad. "They said he was bad and that he killed Marla. But Tomas didn't kill Marla. Tomas loved Marla." The way he says this leads me to believe it is a mantra of sorts for him.

"Where were you the day the police took Tomas away?" I ask him.

"Tomas took me to the YMCA in Portage," he says, enunciating the letters carefully. "I go there every Wednesday." Another punctuating nod.

"Did Tomas drive you there?"

Lech nods. "Tomas takes me everywhere. We like to go on rides. Sometimes we go on long rides."

"That must be fun."

"Sometimes we go to parks and have a picnic. I like picnics a lot!"

"Yes, picnics are fun."

"Tomas makes us lunch and sometimes he puts in cakes and cookies," Lech goes on. His expression shifts to one of guilty glee. "I get to eat them *all* because Tomas can't. He has the sugar in his blood and has to take insulin. He's very careful about that."

"Is he?" I say with a smile.

"Yep. I'll show you."

With that, Lech gets up from the table and walks over to a collection of cookbooks standing in one corner of the counter by the fridge. He pulls a book out from the group and carries it over to the table. It isn't a cookbook; it's a cardboard-covered spiral notebook filled with lined paper. Lech hands it to me and settles back in his seat.

I open the notebook. The pages inside are dated—one page to a day—and each page is filled with lists of food items under the headings of BREAKFAST, LUNCH, DINNER, and SNACKS. Next to each food are columns listing the calories and carbohydrates. At the bottom of each page are numbers listed after times: 8:00, 12:00, 4:00, and 8:00.

"What are these numbers here?" I ask Lech, pointing to the digits following each time entry.

"That's the sugar in the blood," he says. "Tomas checks the sugar in his blood all the time to make sure it's okay. It's very important," he concludes with a very serious look.

I flip through the book and note that halfway through, the entries end. The date of the last entry is the day we found Tomas on his kitchen floor. There is a BREAKFAST entry— pretty much the same breakfast Tomas had every other day—and an 8:00 A.M. blood sugar of 85 written in at the bottom of the page. There are no other entries for the day. I take out my cell phone and snap a picture of this page and several before it. I'm guessing the book was overlooked when Tomas was arrested and the techs searched his house. It would be easy to do, stuffed the way it was in with the cookbooks.

Judging from the book's contents, Tomas definitely was a well-controlled and conscientious diabetic. So how had he ended up on his kitchen floor in insulin shock? Had he tried to commit suicide? The running theory was that his insulin shock had been accidental, but what if it wasn't?

"Lech, was there anyone else here at the house on the day the police took Tomas away? I mean before he took you to the YMCA."

Lech furrows his brow in thought for a few seconds, and then shakes his head. He starts touching the thumb of his right hand to each of the neighboring fingertips, down to the pinky and back again. "The bad man came the day before," he says.

" 'Bad man'?"

He nods, slowly this time, and starts running the fingers on his other hand. "Tomas said I shouldn't talk to the bad man."

"What is the name of this bad man?"

Lech furrows his brow again. "I don't know."

"Did Tomas say why the man was bad?"

"He said it was a secret." Lech's eyes grow wide with this. "A big secret."

"What did the bad man say?"

Lech pouts. "I don't know. Tomas made me go out to the barn and feed the cats when the bad man came."

I ask Lech if he can remember what color the man's hair was and he says brown, like his own. When I ask what color his eyes were, and how big he was, he shrugs with each question and makes a face like he's about to cry. The fingers on both hands are flying at this point. Finally I hit on a question that makes him perk up and stop the finger play. "How did the bad man get here? Did he drive a car?"

The ardent nod returns and Lech smiles. "It was a pretty car. It was blue, and there was no top on it."

I gather this means it was a convertible, with the top down. It's not much to go on, but it's something. It's getting late and I can't think of anything else to ask Lech for now, so I get up from the table and thank him for talking to me.

"I like talking," he says. "Now that Tomas isn't here, I don't get to talk much."

"Someone is coming by to help you, right?"

He nods. "Darlene comes three times a week," he says in a robotic tone that makes me think he's memorized the phrase. "Monday, Wednesday, and Friday. She makes sure I'm okay, and helps me get my food and stuff. My parents pay for her to come."

"Do you need anything?"

He sighs. "Just Tomas," he says in a sad voice.

I reach into my purse and take out a pen and notepad. Then I write my number down on a piece of paper and rip it from the pad. "You have a phone, don't you?"

He responds with that excited, vigorous nod of his. "I have a phone and a computer. I play games."

"That's good. If you need anything, Lech, you call me, okay?" I hand him the slip of paper and he takes it, clutching it against his chest.

"Does this mean we're friends?"

"Sure," I say with a smile. "I'd be happy to be your friend."

What Lech does next takes me by surprise. He pops out of his seat, lunges at me, and wraps me in a bear hug. "Thank you, Mattie."

"Thank *you*, Lech."

As I climb back into my car, Lech stands in the doorway, waving at me with such vigor his entire body is moving, like a dog wagging its tail. He is wearing an endearing but goofy grin, and as I drive away, I find myself feeling oddly sad. I head for my sister's house to pick up Matthew, my thoughts spinning wildly. It's not hard to imagine a scenario where Tomas could have been framed. Most likely, he would have had to have been sedated somehow so someone could give him the deadly dose of insulin, but it could have happened. I log the idea away in the back of my mind once I get to my sister's house, promising myself that I'll give it more thought later on. And part of my mind wonders if I'm being a little too much like Arnie, seeing a conspiracy around every corner.

As always, the sight of my son and the sheer joy he feels at seeing me fills me with happiness. It makes the ugliness of the day recede, at least for a little while.

"He's had a great day," Desi says, "though we didn't

have much success with the toilet training. He sat on his potty chair for half an hour saying 'poo,' and then as soon as I got him up, he went in his pants."

"That seems to be his trend of late."

"He's pretty young still. Give him time," Desi says with an encouraging smile. Then she changes the subject. "Those dresses I ordered online for you came today. Want to try them on? I think the one with the blue is going to be perfect."

"Not today. I'm pooped—pun intended—and before I get too excited, or depressed as the case may be, about a dress, I need to secure a venue."

"Why don't you have your wedding here?"

"That's sweet of you, Desi, but I don't want to impose on you any more than I already do. And Hurley wants us to do it on the Fourth. That's only two weeks away."

"It's no imposition," she says, waving away my objection. "I would love to do it. Our yard is plenty big enough, and our patio has a roof over it in case it rains. Plus, I love doing stuff like that. Two weeks is plenty of time."

"Say yes, Aunt Mattie," says a voice behind me, and I turn to see my niece, Erika, standing there. "A wedding would be so much fun. I'd have to have a new dress, of course."

"Of course," Desi says with a tolerant smile.

I consider the offer. My sister is the most efficient, organized person I know and I have no doubt she could pull it off. "Okay," I say, "but only if you let me pay for everything. Just tell me what it costs and I'll give you the money."

"Only if you let me buy your dress."

"Okay, but that's assuming I wear one."

My sister claps her hands together and smiles broadly. Erika says, "I'm going to start dress shopping online," and runs from the room.

"We want to keep it simple," I tell Desi. "Don't go getting all fancy on me."

"It will be simple, but beautiful. And memorable. We'll need to talk about things like flowers, cake, pictures, and such, but there are lots of options."

"I've already talked to Alison Miller about doing the pictures," I tell her. "As for a cake, a simple two-layer one will do. We're only planning on about thirty guests. I'll trust your judgment on the decorations."

"Do you have a guest list?"

"Up here," I say, tapping my head. "I'll get it written down for you."

"What about flowers? Do you have a color theme in mind? Is blue still your favorite color?"

"It is," I say with a smile.

"You really need to try on that blue dress," she says. "Please? It will only take a few minutes."

Desi's excitement is rubbing off on me. "Okay, fine."

We grab Matthew and haul him into Desi's bedroom with us; a few minutes later, I'm standing in front of a floor-length mirror, looking at myself in the blue dress. Desi was right; it's perfect.

"Want to try on the peach one?" Desi asks.

"No need. This is the dress. You did it." I turn around, sandwich her face between my hands, and give her a big kiss. "Thank you, Desi."

"Oh, my gosh, it's my pleasure," she says, and judging from the glow on her face, I believe her. "I've got this wedding thing under control. Don't worry about a thing. All you'll have to do is show up."

My sister's quick seizing of the reins and her ability to bring this runaway wagon under control makes me feel like a load has been lifted from my shoulders.

"Oh, and your vows. You'll have to write your vows," she adds. My face must show the terror I feel. "You two are going to write your own vows, aren't you?" Desi asks. "Of course you are. It will be so much more meaningful that way."

And just like that, my shoulders feel heavy again.

CHAPTER 27

I'm excited to see Izzy, but I'm a bit taken aback by the way he looks. He's pale, and the circles he always has under his eyes are bigger and darker than usual. His arms are bruised and scarred from the IVs and blood draws he has endured. When he moves to shift his position on the couch, he winces. However, the smile on his face is the same old Izzy smile I've come to know and love.

Sylvie is sitting in a chair next to the bassinet, where Juliana is sleeping.

After handing Matthew off to Dom, I walk over to Izzy, kiss him on his forehead, and give him a quick once-over. "Don't you ever do that again," I admonish. "You scared the crap out of me."

"Smells like he scared the crap out of your son," Dom says, wrinkling his nose.

I sigh and look at Matthew, who grins adorably.

"How's the case going?" Izzy asks.

"We're making some progress."

"Give me the specifics."

Sylvie clucks her disapproval and rolls her eyes. "You aren't working," she huffs. "Must we listen to this nasty stuff?"

"You don't have to. You can leave the room, Mom," Izzy grumbles, soliciting a *harrumph* from Sylvie.

I hesitate, knowing Izzy needs his rest, but the eager look on his face—and the color that has sprung to his cheeks just from mentioning the case—makes me realize he's bored and wants to feel involved. I look over at Dom, who seems to realize the same thing because he gives me a little nod.

I settle in and spend the next ten minutes filling Izzy in on most of the specifics in Hal's case while Dom kindly takes my son into the other room to clean him up. I mention the finding of the Wyzinski file, the discovery that Tina had talked to Tomas Wyzinski's brother, and the novel-writing theory. But I leave out my visit to Lech, though I'm not sure why. Izzy comments that it's an interesting coincidence, but I can tell from his expression that he's curious all the same. Then I fill him in on the Carolyn Abernathy case and the discovery that the two cases are likely connected.

Despite her prior objections, Sylvie listens closely to everything we discuss. I suspect she's intrigued by what we do, but she won't admit to it because it would seem too unladylike.

Izzy comments on how lucky it was to pick up on the fact that the two cases are connected. "For all his paranoia, Arnie is good at what he does," he says.

"That he is," I agree. "In fact, sometimes I think it's his paranoia that makes him so good at it. He's driven to look under every rock, to consider every possible scenario, and it's that determination and drive that lead him to making findings like this."

Izzy nods and smiles, but the color has faded from his cheeks and his smile looks more wooden than it did earlier.

"I don't want to tire you out too much, and I need to get home," I say. "It's been a long day for both of us."

"Come back tomorrow?" Izzy asks, almost pleading. Sylvie rolls her eyes and crosses both her legs and her arms with exaggerated movements to communicate her annoyance.

"Sure. Rest in the meantime, okay? And call me if you need anything." I look over at Dom and then reluctantly glance at Sylvie. "Any of you."

I give Izzy another kiss, take my now-clean son, and head for home.

Hurley arrives home a little after seven and we all sit down to a dinner of hamburgers, veggie sticks, and French fries. I'd like to say I cooked, but the truth is I stopped at a local restaurant and ordered takeout. The food is good, and nobody seems to mind that it isn't home-cooked and we aren't eating off real plates. To me, the more important thing is we are all seated at the dinner table together, sharing.

Emily updates us on the status of her volleyball team, which is currently in first place in the league, and invites us to her game next week. As usual, we tell her we'll make it if work allows. I feel guilty every time I miss one of her games, but she seems to take it in stride.

I then announce that the wedding venue has been determined, garnering a pleased but surprised look from Hurley. "My sister has offered to have it at her house and she's taking charge of all the planning. She even found me the perfect dress." I look at Emily. "Erika is already shopping for a dress she can wear, so you should start looking, too. Desi can help you find one if need be. I'd love to do it with you, but I'm not sure I'm going to have the time with the caseload I have right now. And your dad wants us to do this on the Fourth of July."

"The Fourth of July," Emily says. "That's perfect! You'll

have fireworks to help you celebrate. It's also kind of ironic, if you think about it."

"How so?" I ask.

"Well, you two will be giving up your independence on Independence Day."

My shoulders are feeling heavy again. Matthew waves his fork in the air and says, "Ped is day!"

"Yep, that's right, Matthew," Emily says. "Independence Day. You'll get to see fireworks!"

"Fier-irks," Matthew says. And then he flings a handful of French fries across the table.

After dinner, I remember our bed has been stripped and the sheets laundered. I should have asked Emily to make it up while she was at home today, but I didn't think to do so. Actually, the thought did cross my mind at one point, but I didn't act on it. I'm very self-conscious when it comes to asking Emily for help with chores. I want her to feel like she's a contributing member of the household, but I don't want to cross a line to where she feels like she's slave labor. As a result, I tend to err on the side of laxity more than I probably need to. When I go downstairs to the laundry, I see that she did do several loads of wash, so I remind myself to thank her for that. I grab the sheets and, after making sure Matthew is under Emily's watchful eye, carry them upstairs. Hurley follows me.

"Want some help?" he says as I toss the sheets on a chair and dig out the fitted one.

"Sure. Thanks. It's a lot easier to make if there're two of us." I flap the sheet out and turn it the right way. Then I grab the top corner on my side and fit it over the mattress. Hurley pulls his corner toward him and does the same, making mine pop off. I grab my corner again and pull it toward me, making Hurley's corner pop off. The two of us stand there for a moment, staring at one another, and then we both burst into laughter.

"I know you're a sheet hog," I say after a moment, "but this is ridiculous."

"Hey, it could be worse," Hurley says. "We could be T. rexes. Imagine how hard this would be if we had short little arms." He tucks his arms back like chicken wings and tries to bend down and grab his corner. "Give it a whirl, Squatch," he says.

I adopt the same arm position he has and bend over, trying to grab my sheet corner. I lose my balance and tumble forward onto the bed, laughing. Hurley feigns a growl and falls down with me, pretending to bite my neck. We roll around on the bed, giggling and growling, until my phone rings, forcing us to sober up. I roll over and grab the phone, glancing at the caller ID. It's William-not-Bill.

I barely have a chance to say hello before he cuts in. "What on earth happened between you and your mother today?"

"We opened some old wounds."

"Well, I don't know what those wounds were, but it has your mother in the midst of a cleaning frenzy like I've never seen before. She was on her hands and knees with a toothbrush scrubbing the floor molding in the kitchen a little while ago, and now she's in the process of rewashing all the towels and linens in the house. I'm really worried about her."

"Don't be," I tell him. "This is part of her standard coping tactics when she's emotionally upset. She'll do the cleaning frenzy for the rest of today and all through the night. In the morning, she'll drop into bed out of sheer exhaustion, and when she wakes tomorrow afternoon, she'll announce she has some sort of terminal disease."

"You mean she's done this before?"

"Sadly, yes. Many times. She'll be fine in a day or two, William. Unless . . ."

"Unless what?" he asks, nearly screeching.

"Unless the thing that has her upset worsens and gets her more upset."

"What thing?" William says irritably. "What has her so upset?"

"I suspect it's partly me, and partly her ex-husband, my father."

"Oh."

"Yeah, oh. Listen, William, things are probably going to get messy in the days to come and I suspect Mother will have that house cleaner than it's ever been by the time it's all said and done. You can't do anything to change what will happen. All you can do is sit back and keep an eye on her. And when she tells you she has a terminal illness, don't try to logic her out of it. That woman has better medical knowledge than most doctors and she can twist all sorts of symptoms around to fit whatever disease she's adopted for the week. You'll just be wasting your breath if you try to get her to see the light. So take the advice of someone who's been down this road a few dozen times and just ride it out. Do not let her convince you to start making funeral plans because she won't really be ill and she's already got a plot and a plan anyway."

"Oh, my," William says.

"You'll be fine. It will all pass eventually. Call me if it gets to be too much for you."

"Okay. Um . . . what about your father? Is he back? Do I need to be worried about him?"

"He's around," I tell him. "I think he's keeping a low profile for now, but he could surface at any time. I don't think you need to worry about him, though."

"Okay." He sounds completely unconvinced.

"William?"

"Yeah?"

"You are one of the best things that has happened to my mother. So hang in there, okay?"

"Okay." This time he sounds relieved, or at least not panicked.

I bid him good night and disconnect the call.

"Poor William," Hurley says.

"He's a tough guy. He'll get through it." I then tell him about my visit to Lech Wyzinski.

"Why did you go see him?" he asks, scratching his head.

"The whole coincidence thing . . . it bothered me. I needed to talk to him."

"And?"

"And he doesn't remember what he and Tina talked about. But he did share something with me that gives me pause." I then explain to him about the logbook he showed me of Tomas's diet and blood sugars. "I don't think it's outside the realm of possibility that Tomas was framed," I conclude.

"I think it's more likely that he simply tried to off himself," Hurley says. "Besides, Richmond talked to Tina's coworkers at the library and they confirmed that she was constantly researching real crimes as fodder for the books she was writing. I'm sure that's all it was."

"Lech did say there was a bad man—that's how he referred to him—who came to visit Tomas. He couldn't tell me much about him other than the fact that he drove some type of blue convertible."

"Probably a drug connection of some sort," Hurley says dismissively. He kisses me on the forehead and climbs out of the bed. "I've got to get back to the station and see to some things. I'm not sure when I'll get home, so don't wait up."

Just like that, he's gone. I stay on the bed a few minutes longer, staring at the ceiling, contemplating the chaos my life has become. Then I get up and make the bed. After that, I do two more loads of laundry, pick up Matthew's room, run the dishwasher, and sweep and mop the remains of the day—and Matthew's meals—from the kitchen floor. Once all of that is done, I take Matthew upstairs, bathe him, and get him ready for bed. I read him *One Fish, Two Fish, Red Fish, Blue Fish* three times before he falls asleep.

I tiptoe out of his room and go back downstairs to find Emily watching yet another iteration of the *CSI* shows on TV. "I'm going to take Hoover for a walk," I tell her. "Be back in a bit."

Having heard me mention his name and the word "walk," Hoover is already at my feet, wagging his butt excitedly, looking at me with those big brown eyes. Poor guy, ever since Matthew's arrival, he hasn't had nearly the level of attention he used to get, though he is getting lots more food than he used to get. It's starting to show, too, in his expanding midsection. I hook him up to his leash and head out the front door.

It's a gorgeous summer night and the fireflies are out, sparkling twinkles of light all around us. Hoover is afraid of fireflies because he ate one once and apparently the stuff that makes them glow tastes awful. After eating it, he was scraping his glowing tongue on the grass, on his paws, on my leg . . . anything he could find, leaving a glowing streak of saliva in his wake. So tonight he dodges and avoids the fireflies, content to sniff out all the other wonders of the summer-night world. We do an eight-block circuit that I know is a little over a mile long from clocking it some time ago. As we walk, I look into the lit windows of the houses we pass, catching glimpses of the lives within, tiny slices of warmly lit life, cozy scenarios that seem bathed in a golden light like that of the fireflies. The people behind those windows and walls all look so happy, and satisfied, and *normal.*

Back home, I unleash Hoover and top off his food and water bowls. That's when I realize there are smudges on the floor from the door to the kitchen, and a foul smell hits me. I lift first my left foot, then my right, finding the culprit on the bottom of my right shoe. Somehow I've managed to step in dog poop and track it into the house.

As I kick off my shoes and grab some paper towels and spray cleaner, I realize this is the perfect metaphoric ending for a really crappy day.

CHAPTER 28

Once again, I have no idea when Hurley came home because I slept hard. I awaken to find a drool spot on my pillow and Hurley's arm draped over my waist. A glance at the clock tells me it's almost six, and even though every fiber of my being is telling me to snuggle in and go back to sleep, I know I need to get up.

We survive the usual morning chaos at home: Matthew snacking on the dry cat food when I turn my back on him for thirty seconds; Hoover stealing Emily's toast when she turns her back on him for thirty seconds; Hurley discovering, just as we're about to go out the door, that he's wearing two different-colored socks.

I leave the hearse at home and Hurley and I ride together to Desi's house to drop Matthew off. I made arrangements with Dom to give him and Izzy a week or two to recover before taking on Matthew again, and my sister is more than happy to have him. She wants to chat when I arrive, but we're running late and I have Hurley waiting in the car, so I brush her off.

With that out of the way, Hurley and I head for Chicago.

"I followed up on the name of that boat, *Court A'Sea,*" Hurley says. "Turns out it belongs to an attorney who lives on the lake. He reported it stolen the day after Hal and Tina were killed. Apparently, he was out of town and didn't realize the boat was missing until he got back. He kept the keys to it in a locked boathouse, but it was broken into. So that's basically a dead end."

I again bring up my visit to Lech Wyzinski. "I feel sorry for the guy," I say. "And I can't help but wonder if he's onto something. Tomas did pass a lie detector test."

"Beckwith explained that to you," Hurley says. "Those things can be beat."

"Then why did Tomas tell his lawyer to let it go? I wonder if she knows about that notebook Tomas kept. Do you think I should try to call her and ask her?"

Hurley frowns and casts me a look.

"What?" I say.

"You're such a softie," he says. "You feel sorry for Lech and want to help him. Do you think that might be coloring your logic? And also no, you can't call the defense attorney and discuss possible evidence with her. Do you want to jeopardize the whole case? Cause a mistrial? Besides, I heard the jury is already out. And if Tomas is innocent and thinks he's been framed, why hasn't he offered up a plausible alternate scenario?"

I can't answer that question. Maybe Hurley's right and I'm being too much of a bleeding heart.

After that, our drive is a mostly quiet one, both of us lost in our own thoughts. This comfortable silence has been a hallmark of my relationship with Hurley practically since day one. Given that my job entails plenty of awkward silences, such as when I have to inform someone a loved one has died, or question someone about a suspicious death, I highly value this aspect of our relationship.

We park in a structure and walk three blocks to the building that contains the U.S. Marshal's Office. A receptionist greets us, and after Hurley introduces himself, she informs us with one slightly raised eyebrow that Marshal Washington was expecting only one person.

"This is Mattie Winston," Hurley explains. "She's a medico-legal death investigator with the medical examiner's office in Sorenson and they have an interest in the same case." The receptionist asks for our IDs, and after checking and photographing them, she hands them back. "Please have a seat."

As we settle into wooden chairs with hard, uncomfortable cushions, the receptionist picks up her phone and has a sotto voce discussion with someone on the other end. I struggle to hear what she's saying, but I can't. When she hangs up, I half expect her to tell us we have to leave, but she doesn't so much as look at us. A few minutes later, a small-built, nattily dressed, well-manicured, African-American man emerges from the area behind the receptionist. He walks over to Hurley, his hand extended.

"Detective Hurley," he says. "I'm Greg Washington. Nice to meet you."

Hurley rises from his chair, towering over the other man. They shake, and then Washington turns his eyes toward me.

"This is Mattie Winston," Hurley says. "She's with the medical examiner's office in Sorenson."

I stand, too, and as Washington looks up at me with his extended hand, he smiles and says, "You grow them big up there in Wisconsin."

Neither Hurley nor I laugh. Hurley knows I'm occasionally sensitive about my size, and he's too smart to offer so much as a polite chuckle. Talk about awkward silences.

Washington clears his throat, sobers his expression, and says, "Come on back to our lair." He turns, heading back the way he came, and we follow him through a door the receptionist buzzes open into a large room with a conference table at the center and various offices around the perimeter. Washington steers us to the table and directs us to take seats. He settles into a chair at the end of the table behind a large stack of files. Before reaching for any of the files, he leans back in his seat, hands folded in his lap, and fixes his gaze on me.

"You are Mr. Novak's daughter, aren't you?"

"I am," I admit, disappointed the cat's been let out of the bag so soon.

Washington seems to sense this because he says, "We're very thorough here. We do our homework."

"My interest in this case is purely professional." I utter this in my best unemotional voice, which apparently isn't good enough.

Washington scoffs softly, looks away before shaking his head ever so slightly, and then looks back at me with the sort of tolerant expression a parent gives a child. "You might have convinced yourself of that," he says, "but I'm not buying it. Your father deserted you and your mother when you were young, and you grew up with no contact from, or knowledge of, him. That must have left some kind of mark."

I shrug noncommittally. "I'm curious about the man," I admit, "but I harbor no biases toward him one way or the other. His relationship to me will in no way impact what happens in this case, regardless of the level of his involvement."

Washington stares at me for a moment and I shift nervously in my seat beneath his intense scrutiny.

Seeing my discomfort, Hurley jumps in. "This case is more than professional for both of us," he says. "The victims in our homicide were people we knew and worked with, including one of the other investigators in the medical examiner's office. And it's my understanding that Cedric Novak is suspected of killing a cop named Roy Gilligan a few years ago. Roy happened to be an ex-partner of mine."

Washington nods knowingly and looks back at me. "I'm aware of that. Have you considered your office might be the target?"

"Let me clarify," Hurley says. "Only one of our three victims worked with the ME's office. One of the other two appears to be incidental—a case of being in the wrong place at the wrong time. We found some evidence on the third one that suggests it might be connected, but we haven't figured out how yet. We're looking for someone else who may be a suspect, but we haven't had any luck finding him so far. Our most solid lead outside of that person seems to be Mr. Novak."

"I see," Washington says. "If it helps, I know for a fact Mr. Novak didn't kill Roy Gilligan."

I have no idea if it will help our case, but hearing him say this floods me with such a sense of relief that I literally sag in my seat, sighing loudly. Washington looks at me, amused. "Right," he says, his sarcasm thick. "You're objective."

"How can you be sure?" Hurley asks.

"Because when Roy Gilligan was killed, Mr. Novak was in our office talking with a colleague of mine. Novak had opted out of the Witness Protection Program the year before and moved back here to Chicago." He gives me a pointed look. "He said he wanted to reestablish contact with his family and try to pick up some of the pieces from his old life. We tried to discourage him because the threat that led to him entering our program in the first place still existed. But he was adamant." Washington pauses and his face forms a half-grimace. "He wasn't reckless about it; he did keep up with his new identity. But he took a job at a mailbox store that turned out to be a front for a drug and money-laundering operation. Out of the frying pan, into the fire."

"What makes you think he didn't know about the illegalities?" I ask. "He grew up committing crimes, and he was still committing them when he met my mother. I'm sure his criminal contacts were extensive. It would have been easy for him to get back into it again."

"Actually, that's not true," Washington says. "At least, not most of it. It's true that your father came from a criminal background, but it was more of a family and cultural thing than any hard-core criminal instincts he had. He was raised by folks of Eastern European descent, a tribe that made their livings as thieves and con artists. They traveled in groups called 'families,' settling in areas long enough to work their cons, and then moving on when things started getting too hot for them. Your father's earlier crimes were of that nature. In fact, that's how he got into trouble. He conned the wrong person and got a hold of some sensitive information others were willing to kill for. I'll get to that in a minute."

"Anyway, with regard to the mailbox store, we believed him because the new identity we gave him when he entered our protection program involved a job working at a shipping-company hub, so finding a job at a mailbox store made sense. It was what he knew. Plus, as soon as he realized what was going on behind the scenes, he came to us. He thought about going to the local police initially, but because of his history— or lack thereof—he was afraid the cops either wouldn't believe him or would think he was involved somehow. And there was his ongoing need to keep a low profile."

"What name was he using at the time?" I ask.

"The name we gave him when we created his new identity. It was one he requested, Walter Scott."

"Interesting," I say. "Did you guys investigate this mailbox store?"

Washington shakes his head. "Not our jurisdiction or job. We dropped some hints to the local cops and to the FBI about the place and let them handle it."

"Given that Roy was already working undercover there by the time Novak came to you, I think it's safe to assume the local guys were already onto it," Hurley surmises.

Washington nods, but he looks distracted and lost in thought for a moment. And troubled.

"What aren't you telling us?" I ask him.

His eyes dart between Hurley and me, and I suspect he's vacillating about saying anything because of my presence. When his gaze settles on mine, I'm convinced he's about to lie to my face without so much as a flinch and deny there is anything more to tell. Turns out I'm wrong.

"Some things about that case bothered me. To start with, I'm not sure who killed Roy Gilligan, or why. And I don't know if anyone else ever learned the answers to those questions, either. Was Gilligan's real identity exposed? Did he piss off the wrong person? Or was it accidental? Of course, once Mr. Scott disappeared into thin air, everyone was more than eager to pin the killing on him. But one of the cops on the case, a guy I knew from high school, dropped a comment to me about how there seemed to be some worrisome leaks in the case. When I asked him what he meant, all he said was people knew things they shouldn't."

"Meaning what?" Hurley asks. "A dirty cop?" Both his tone and his expression make it clear the idea is repugnant to him.

"Maybe," Washington says with a grudging, sideways nod. Judging from his expression, he finds the idea equally distasteful, though not dismissible. "Somebody, somewhere, said something they shouldn't have. I know an internal investigation was started, but as far as I know, nothing ever came of it."

"Who received the lowdown on the mailbox store from you guys?" Hurley asks.

"Couldn't tell you. Our information was delivered anonymously in a computer-generated and printed letter Mr. Scott, or Novak, wrote and mailed. We helped him with it to make sure it couldn't be traced back to him in any way—in fact, that's what he and we were doing when Roy Gilligan was

killed—and then we offered to take him back into the program if he would testify against the culprits, assuming they
were busted. He refused, saying he didn't want to go back to
the lonely, constricting lifestyle he had to lead in the program, or complicate his life any more than it already was.
He felt he could do just as well on his own and have more
flexibility with fewer restrictions." Washington pauses and
gives us a grudging smile. "I have to admit he's done okay
so far. He's quite good at staying hidden."

"Not good enough," I say. "He was sighted on at least
two separate occasions lurking around the homes of our victims on the day they were killed. And the state troopers know
his real identity. When they were investigating me on a matter
a couple of years ago, it came out that I was Cedric Novak's
daughter. That caused some concern because Cedric Novak—
not Walter Scott—was thought to have been the hit man who
killed the cop during this mailbox store fiasco."

Washington frowns at this and gives a brief but frantic
shake of his head. "That information shouldn't have been
out there. That's what I mean about worrisome leaks. How
did anyone connect Walter Scott with Cedric Novak?"

"Maybe my father leaked something himself without realizing it," I suggest. "Or maybe someone recognized him."

Washington shrugs noncommittally. "Do you have any
solid evidence that suggests Novak killed someone?" he
asks. "Because I have to tell you, I don't think the guy's a
killer. A thief, liar, con man, incorrigible flirt . . . yes. Would
I trust him with my wife or daughter? Hell no. Would I trust
him with my money? Again, no. And I don't know if he'd
risk his own life to save someone else's, but I don't think
he's the killing kind."

"Anyone can be the killing kind under the right circumstances," Hurley says.

I look over at him and inwardly flinch, wondering if he is
thinking about me when he says this. While it's true I've

killed someone, it was accidental on my part and, in my defense, the other guy started it. Did I feel bad about it? Yeah, for a little while. But perhaps not for as long or as fervently as I should have. Maybe I had more of my father in me than I realized.

"What can you tell me about the case that led to Novak entering witness protection thirty years ago?" Hurley asks. I give him a look of gratitude. He has no real need to know these details so I suspect he's asking for my benefit.

Washington leans forward and removes the topmost folder from the pile on the table. He slides it over to Hurley, who opens it. "Novak pulled a con on a guy who worked for the Martin-Weiss pharmaceutical company."

Something in the back of my mind starts to niggle.

"Never heard of them," Hurley says.

"No, you wouldn't have. They were a startup at the time and they went out of business a short while later because of what Cedric Novak accidentally stole. Novak and another member of his 'family'"—Washington makes finger quotes with the word "family"—"a cousin named Petra Constantine pulled a con on a guy involving switched briefcases. It was a con they pulled a lot. Apparently, they scored money, wallets, car keys, credit cards, and such often enough to make it worth their while. This time, however, they came up empty, or so they thought at first. The only thing inside the stolen briefcase were documents. But among those papers were copies of some internal memos from Martin-Weiss detailing a kickback scheme that provided payments to physicians in exchange for the promotion of M-W's drugs to patients."

"That's nothing new," I say. "That sort of stuff has been going on for years. It still happens, except these days they typically disguise the kickbacks as speaker fees, or some other professional service fee that is actually a kickback in disguise. It's so rampant and so questionable in a lot of cases that a federal law was passed not long ago requiring physicians who receive more than ten dollars worth of money or gifts from any pharmacy company, for any reason, to be listed on the Internet."

"Apparently, this went beyond your basic kickback scheme," Washington explains. "Martin-Weiss had a weight-loss drug that caused catastrophic cardiac and liver problems leading to deaths in a number of the trial patients, but they convinced the physicians caring for those patients to alter the medical records so it would appear as if some other condition caused the deaths. And in exchange, those physicians received handsome speaking engagements in exotic, expensive places or, in some cases, simple cash payments under the table."

"Yikes," I say. "Sounds like it was a good thing they went out of business."

"Except they didn't. Martin-Weiss was a subsidiary of a larger company, and that was a subsidiary of a larger one yet, and there were several more layers on top of that. The owners, stockholders, and investors at the top were people with a lot of power, money, and strings. They simply divested themselves of the Martin-Weiss company, took their patents, their drugs, and their underhanded ways, and then divvied them up among some of their other holdings. Eventually they started new pharmaceutical companies, some of which were fly-by-night, and some of which are still around today."

"Did they arrest any of these people?"

Washington sighs and shakes his head. "These guys know how to armor themselves in Teflon, and make sure they're six *million* degrees of separation away from anything shady. They hide what they're doing well enough that no charges ever seem to stick. And while the companies might get the occasional slap on the hand in the form of a fine that is often in the millions, they have and make enough money to pay it and simply continue on as before."

"Big Pharma," I say, nodding knowingly.

"Unfortunately, your father and his cousin thought they could make up for the briefcase having nothing of obvious value by using those memos to blackmail the head honchos at Martin-Weiss. They spent a week or so negotiating, and during that time, unbeknownst to your father and Constantine, Martin-Weiss was rapidly being disassembled. The executives and supervisors—at least those who didn't simply disappear—were reassigned to positions in other firms overseas. Documents and files were destroyed. The participating physicians were warned and told to play dumb. And when it came time for your father and his cousin to swap the memos for the agreed-upon payment, things didn't go as planned."

I wince, sensing the ending to this story won't be a happy one.

"The people in charge at Martin-Weiss realized there was no way to guarantee copies of the memos hadn't been made, nor could they be sure the blackmailers wouldn't blab at some point, or try to blackmail them again. So they covered themselves by eliminating all the incriminating evidence—including the man your father conned . . . he showed up floating facedown in Lake Michigan—and then trying to eliminate the threat. The exchange was a setup designed to kill your father and Mr. Constantine. I'm sure the plan was simply for them to disappear, and I have no doubt these people had the resources to make that happen. But your father's gut told him something about the whole setup was wrong and he tried to convince Constantine to walk away from it. Constantine refused. This was more money than anyone in any family had made in a long time—maybe ever—and he had dollar signs in his eyes.

"In the end, Constantine went into the meeting alone, letting your father hang back with the memos as collateral in case things did go bad. Your father was close enough to hear what went on. When the thugs found out Constantine didn't have the memos, they killed him. Your father ran and went into hiding."

"And that's how you guys got involved?" I ask.

"Sort of. Your father went to the district attorney's office—he said he didn't trust the police because he was pretty sure one of the thugs who killed Constantine was a police officer—and told them what he knew. He told them about the memos, but he refused to hand them over until they could guarantee his safety.

"Shortly after the investigation was started, one of Novak's family encampments was visited by three men who kept asking for the whereabouts of 'Rick Novaceski,' which happens to be the name Cedric Novak used during his scams. It was also the name he gave to the district attorney's office. The family knew how to lie—they did it often enough—and even when they were threatened with guns by the visiting trio, they stuck to their story that no one had seen Rick for the past two weeks. The next day, there was no sign of the family. They had packed up and moved on, but not before your father had stopped by an hour after the visiting trio left and heard they were looking for him.

"Novak was understandably edgy about this visit to the family encampment, since his name hadn't been used in any of the negotiations with Martin-Weiss, and he had heard everything that went on with Constantine and the thugs. He knew his name hadn't come up then, either. It implied someone involved in the investigation had leaked the info about him, and that's when he came to us for help."

Washington pauses and looks at me. "Novak thought about going with the family, but he didn't want to leave you and your mother. He'd kept his marriage a secret because it was a big no-no to marry outside of the family. Good thing he did. That's what gave your mother the option of going into the program or staying put. Mr. Novak felt he needed to disappear, both for his own safety and that of you and your mother. But your mother didn't want any part of the program."

"I'm not surprised," I say. "She has some . . . issues, agoraphobia being one of them. She's also germophobic. I'm sure the idea of having to move and start over with a whole new identity was simply too overwhelming."

"Could be," Washington says. "According to Dan Kellerman's notes—Dan was the agent originally assigned to your father's case—your mother was angry and fed up with your father because he kept disappearing for long periods of time. When she learned about the double life he was leading, and the things he did to earn money, she'd had enough. So your father went into hiding and your mother stayed put. We altered the official marriage records and certificate in case anyone figured out your father's real name and traced it back to you and your mother. Your mother kept a copy of the original marriage certificate with the understanding it had to be kept absolutely secret. If the killers didn't know your father's real name, it was reasonable to think they wouldn't be able to find her or you."

"Did they catch any of the men who killed Constantine?" Hurley asks.

Washington shakes his head, looking troubled. "The investigation continued, but the culprits were never caught. There was enough hard and circumstantial evidence to corroborate Novak's story and convince the investigators. Unfortunately, being convinced and being convicted are two different animals. Martin-Weiss covered their tracks well."

"Did my father ever testify?"

Washington pushes out his lower lip and shakes his head. "The case never went to court, at least not the killing part of it. Your father did hand over copies of the memos, but the names had been removed. Your father said he destroyed the originals, but Dan Kellerman always thought he kept them as insurance against the future. There was a federal investigation, but by then the top layer of whoever owned Martin-Weiss had cleaned house. Nothing came of it."

"Any idea why or how Novak might be involved in our current case?" Hurley asks.

"None," Washington says with a diffident look.

Hurley frowns, and another of those awkward silences fills the room.

Washington looks at me and says, "There's something else you may or may not want to know about your father. It's in the notes Dan Kellerman had on file from his talks with your mother."

"My mother? She said she had no idea who this Dan person my father mentioned was, and that she never met or talked to him."

"That's not true," Washington says. "They did meet and talk once." He slides a folder across the table to me. "His notes are in there, if you decide you want to read them. I'll leave it up to you. But I should tell you, there is some very personal information in there you might find disturbing."

I finger the folder, looking from it to Hurley, and back to the folder. "Should I?" I ask Hurley. He shrugs and I push the folder over to him. "You look and tell me if I should read it."

He frowns and shakes his head. "Don't put the onus of that on me, Squatch."

Of course he was right. It wasn't fair. And I knew if I didn't look now, I'd regret it. I pull the folder back, take a deep breath, and open it.

CHAPTER 29

After thanking Marshal Washington, Hurley and I leave. On our walk to the car, Hurley broaches the topic uppermost on our minds.

"Are you going to tell me what was in that file?"

"Not yet. I need some time to think about it, to decide what, if anything, I should do about it."

I expect Hurley to argue, or at least try to cajole the information out of me, but he accepts my deferment without question.

For once, he lets me drive and our two-and-a-half-hour trip home is anything but silent. Hurley and I exchange thoughts and ideas about our case: speculating, wondering, and theorizing. But no matter how many ways we twist the facts, we keep coming to the same conclusion. Whether he's Walter Scott, Cedric Novak, or Rick Novaceski—my father is the key element. Until we can talk to him, all we have are suppositions and guesswork.

Just as we reach the edge of town, Hurley's cell phone rings. "It's Arnie," he says, and he puts the call on speaker so we can both listen in.

"What's up, Arnie?" Hurley says.

"Joey got into those files we found on Hal's thumb drive."

"And?"

"I think you need to come in and take a look."

"Okay, be there ASAP."

"Is Mattie with you?"

"She is."

"Have her come, too."

Ten minutes later, Hurley and I arrive in Arnie's second-floor lab in the medical examiner's office. Arnie is there, along with Joey. I haven't seen Joey in nearly a year and he greets me with an exuberant hug, which momentarily stifles my breathing.

"Mattie!" he says. "You look beautiful." I adore Joey, not only because he's a giant, sweet oaf, but because he always makes me feel good about myself.

"You look good, too, Joey," I say once he's released me. It's true; he does. His hair is slicked back with some sort of product, a definite change from his usual casual mop, and his clothes are a little more fashionable than the last time I saw him. I cock my head to the side and narrow my eyes at him. "Do you have a girlfriend?"

He smiles at me—a huge, brilliant smile—and his cheeks turn crimson. "Rhonda," he says, twisting his body, side to side, and looking at the floor. "She's very pretty, like you. Not as big as you, though."

Hurley stifles a snorting laugh, and Arnie rolls his eyes. Coming from anyone else, the comment might offend me, but I got used to Joey and his lack of filters a long time ago. His blatant honesty is kind of refreshing. "Good for you, Joey," I tell him. "I'm very happy for you."

"Thank you."

"And good work as usual, helping us with the computer stuff."

Joey adopts an aw-shucks attitude and beams his smile again.

I switch my attention to Arnie. "What did you guys find?"

Arnie directs us to the laptop sitting on his desk, and as he sits down in front of it, Hurley and I position ourselves over his shoulders "It's not much. We found a document that appears to be notes Hal wrote, but it looks like he used his own version of shorthand. It's peppered with abbreviations, initials, and symbols."

Hurley and I read what's on the screen:

CP off. JK.
ADA 1980 WK
Exp = 92
MW = KP
100.182
AKS – fed or state?
RO: France, Switzerland, New York
DW: Miami, Florence, London
PQ: London, Sydney, Belgium
TR: Edinburgh, Prague, Mykonos

"Any idea what any of that means?" I ask the room. No one answers, but Hurley is busy scribbling down what's on the screen into his notebook. "Is this the only thing you found on that thumb drive?"

"Nope," Arnie says. He nods at Joey, who clicks and brings something else up on the screen. This one is a handwritten letter that appears to have been scanned into the computer.

Dear Hal,
Hope you are having a great birthday! Hard to believe you're 45 already. Where did the years go? Have fun, but not too much. If you have too much fun, it will probably give Mom a stroke since you're her golden "good" child! Leave all the bad habits and behaviors to me.
Speaking of that, I thought I'd give you an update on how things are going here. I think I've finally found success with this new program I'm on. My blood sugars are stable and I've lost 78 pounds so far in just six months! There have been some issues with my liver enzymes that the doctor thinks are temporary and left over from all those diet milk shakes I was doing on the last program. I'm a little tired, but I guess that's to be expected when you don't eat much.
Sorry the birthday card is kind of lame. I couldn't find any good ones this time out. Maybe I'll have better luck next year. Come visit when you can.
Love you,
Liz

I give Arnie a questioning look. "I don't get it. Why would he save this particular letter and password protect it?"

"I was wondering the same thing," Arnie says. "So I did a little digging. It seems Hal had a sister named Liz who died a little over a year ago, right before he came here, in fact."

"Really?" I say, shocked. "He never said anything about it."

"No, he didn't," Arnie says. "Which is kind of odd, don't you think?"

"Well, he was kind of a quiet guy, a loner, but you'd think something like that would have come out in conversation at some point."

"And here's something interesting," Arnie says, tossing an evidence bag onto the desk. "This was among the stuff that was taken from Hal's house by the guys who searched it after he died. I didn't think much of it at first, but now I wonder."

Inside the clear plastic evidence bag is a prescription bottle for an Elizabeth Dawson. It was filled at a pharmacy in Madison a little over a year ago by a doctor named Richard Olsen. The drug is Leptosoma, one I've never heard of before.

"Did you look up this drug?" I ask Arnie, knowing that he, like a hound dog, typically finishes out a trail once he gets a scent.

"I did. It's some kind of new weight-loss drug that's being trialed. Clever name for it. It loosely translates from Latin as 'thin body.' There's a study that's been going on for the past four years. I e-mailed you and Hurley some links to websites with info about it."

"How did Hal's sister die?" Hurley asks.

Arnie smiles and points a finger at him. "Ah, I thought you'd never ask. I talked to an ME in Madison, a Dr. Canada. She's new there. The doctor who did Elizabeth's autopsy, Dr. Farmer, has retired and moved to South America, but Dr. Canada pulled the file and faxed me the pertinent info. According to the record, Elizabeth Dawson committed suicide."

"Suicide?" I say. "That seems odd after reading this letter she sent to Hal. She doesn't sound suicidal."

"But there's no date on that letter," Hurley says. "We don't know when it was sent."

"Yes, we do," Arnie says. "In the letter, Liz mentions it's Hal's forty-fifth birthday. And on April fourteenth of this year, he turned forty-six. So that letter was sent a year ago this past April, which coincidentally was a month before Liz died."

"Suicide," I say, shaking my head. "How?"

"She overdosed on painkillers that by themselves might

not have done her in, but they had large amounts of aceta-minophen in them and too much of that—"

"Destroys your liver," I complete for him. I look at Hur-ley. "We used to get acetaminophen overdoses in the ER, typically young women who were merely acting out, who took Tylenol thinking it was safe because it's an over-the-counter drug. But too much acetaminophen is deadly. If the patients got to us in time, we could usually save them. But if they waited too long, they were basically the walking dead. Without a liver transplant, they'd be dead in two to three days."

"Elizabeth Dawson was found in her apartment when po-lice went there to do a welfare check requested by her mother, who lived in Illinois. She'd been dead for several days by the time they found her."

"Did she leave a note?"

Arnie nods. "According to the file, she left a one-sentence note that said she was tired of being laughed at for being fat. She didn't sign it with her name, but did write a letter *L* at the bottom."

I shake my head. "I'm not buying it. According to the note she wrote to Hal, she'd lost a bunch of weight. It doesn't make sense."

"I agree," Hurley says. "I suspect Hal thought the same thing, and looking into his sister's death is what got him killed."

"We need to figure out what these notes mean," I say. "And I don't think it's a coincidence that Hal had this pre-scription in his house. Does a scandal involving a weight-loss drug sound familiar to you?" I say to Hurley, my eyebrows arched.

He nods slowly, thoughtfully. "That might be how our Mr. Novak got involved in the current case," he says.

I snap my fingers as I remember something, that little niggle that I had when we were talking to Marshal Washington. "Maybe I'm reaching again, but here's some food for thought. Tomas Wyzinski has a degree in chemistry and at one time worked for a pharmaceutical company."

Arnie looks confused, so I fill him in on my visit to Lech and his theory that his brother was framed. Of course a conspiracy theory is right down Arnie's alley, and he jumps on the bandwagon in a hurry.

"If there's a Big Pharma company involved in a cover-up, they could have easily framed Tomas." He sounds excited at the prospect.

"And what about Carolyn Abernathy?" I say. "How does she fit into all of this? Hal called her that one time a couple of months ago. Why?"

Arnie taps his fingers on the desktop, squinting off into space. "She worked for a clinic," he says. "Maybe the doctors she worked for are involved somehow." He sucks in his lower lip and stares into space for a few seconds. A smile splits his face. "Oh, man," he says gleefully. "This could be big!"

Hurley blows out a breath, shakes his head, and glances at his watch. "It's going on three-thirty. I think we need to pay a visit to the clinic where Ms. Abernathy worked and have a chat with some of the doctors there." He looks at me. "Care to come along, since you know them all?"

"Wouldn't miss it for the world."

After thanking Arnie and Joey for their great work, Hurley and I make a stop in the evidence room to pick up something that was collected from Carolyn Abernathy's house, and then we drive to the clinic building that sits on the hospital campus. The clinic houses offices for a number of the physicians in town, including my ex-husband, David Winston.

"The billing for all the groups is handled by one office located in the basement," I tell Hurley. "That's where Car-

olyn worked. If she had anything incriminating on any of
the doctors, it would be because she handled the billing on
the charts and picked up on something. We need to know
what she was working on before she died."

We enter the building and walk down a hallway past a
number of offices to the middle of the building. Here there is
an elevator that goes up to the second floor and, if you have
an employee badge, down to the basement level.

"Let's hope they haven't disabled Carolyn's ID card yet,"
I say to Hurley. Leaving Carolyn's badge inside the clear
plastic evidence envelope it's in, I wave it in front of the
card reader, hear a satisfying beep of success, and push the
button for the basement.

The elevator takes us down and opens onto a large area
studded with cubicles. There is a wide aisle in the center of
the room and we make it halfway down before someone—a
brown-haired woman in her forties or fifties wearing glasses
attached to one of those chains—sees and stops us.

"Excuse me, this is a private area. You can't be in here
without authorization."

"Does this give me authorization?" Hurley says, showing
her his badge.

"It does not," says the woman, who according to her
badge is named Deandra. "You need to leave."

"We're here because we're investigating the death of one
of your employees, Carolyn Abernathy," Hurley says.

"I don't care if you're here to investigate the death of the
president of the United States, you still have to leave."

We have attracted the attention of all the other cubicle
residents, and heads are peeking up over the sides of the
desk areas like rodents in a game of Whac-A-Mole.

"Lauren, please call security," Deandra says, and a young
woman off to the right turns around, picks up her phone, and
dials. "And how did you get in here?" Deandra demands.

Hurley ignores her question and fires back with one of

his own. "Does it make a difference to you if I tell you Ms. Abernathy was murdered?" Hurley says to Deandra.

Some of the heads jerk around to look at one another and there is an almost inaudible, collective gasp in the room.

"It does not," Deandra says. "That's all very sad, but I'm sure it has nothing to do with us or what we do down here."

"And just what is it you do down here that you think is so important and top secret?" Hurley fires back, clearly getting irritated.

"We handle billing, insurance claims, and medical records requests," Deandra says. "We handle sensitive and private medical information that is protected by law."

"I am the law," Hurley says, his lips tight.

"No, what you are is some cowboy cop who thinks because he carries a badge he can bypass the normal procedures and processes and bully his way into getting what he wants. But it ain't working here, cowboy. If you want something from us, get a warrant."

There is a *ding* behind us and I turn to see the elevator door open and a security guard enter the room. I can practically see the steam coming out of Hurley's ears so I take his arm and tug him back toward the elevator. "Come on, Hurley, this isn't working. I have a better idea."

The security guard puffs up his chest, puts his hands on his hips, and struts his way in front of Hurley. "Is there a problem here?" he asks.

"No," I say quickly before Hurley can respond. I tug on his arm a little harder. "We were just leaving."

Much to my relief, Hurley finally gives way to my urging and we get back on the elevator and take it up to the first floor. Hurley's angry stride gets him down the hall, out the door, and to the car a full thirty seconds ahead of me.

He's muttering something under his breath as I get in the car and shut my door. Instead of starting the engine, he sits there, staring out the windshield.

"Hurley, I have an idea," I say.

He turns to look at me and I can tell he has calmed some. "What is it?"

"I think it's time we involve Alison a little more with our case, let her have the spotlight."

Hurley looks at me like I've lost my mind. He may be right, but I tell him my idea anyway.

CHAPTER 30

We meet Alison Miller at the police station and fill her in on what we need her to do. She's more than happy to oblige our crazy plan, and twenty minutes after her arrival, she is off to put things into motion. Once she's gone, I glance at Hurley. His face looks haggard with a day's growth of unshaven beard, dark circles under his eyes, and a grim set to his mouth.

"Why don't you come home at a normal time tonight?" I say to him. "You look like you need a break. Let Alison do her thing and see where we end up. Get a good night's sleep and tackle it all with a fresh eye in the morning."

To my surprise, he agrees. "Some rest will do me good," he says. "My brain is having a hard time sorting out all the facts in this case. How about I run by the store and pick up some steaks to cook on the grill while you go get Matthew?"

"That sounds great," I say. "Grab some potatoes and I'll nuke them. We can have microwave baked potatoes, too."

"Right." He leans over, gives me a kiss, and then turns to leave. That's when I remember I don't have a car.

"Okay, revamp then," Hurley says, running a hand through his hair. "See, this is why I agree I need a little time off. I'm not thinking straight."

We drive together to the grocery store, wisely deciding to do that before picking up Matthew because my son and grocery stores always seem to be a recipe for disaster. He pulled down an entire display of canned goods a month ago, had a major screaming-and-kicking meltdown two weeks ago because I bought dog biscuits in a green box instead of a red one, and last week opened my wallet, took out my credit and debit cards, and handed them to some stranger, who, fortunately, was honest enough to give them back.

Once we're done at the store, we head for Desi's. Hurley opts to wait in the car while I go in to get Matthew.

"I've got some ideas for the wedding I want to run by you," Desi says as I start packing up Matthew's stuff.

"Can we do it tomorrow? I've got Hurley waiting in the car and he's exhausted."

"Oh, sure. No problem." She helps me pack up the stuff, and as I'm ready to leave, she says, "Did you talk to Mom about the trunk yet?"

"I did better than that," I tell her. "I busted the damned thing open."

Desi claps a hand over her mouth. "You didn't!"

"I did. And Mom is none too pleased about it."

"What was in it?"

"Some documents, and some letters between her and my father. I'll fill you in on the details later. Suffice to say, Mom is doing one of her cleaning-frenzy things and she has William all freaked out."

"Oh, poor William. Has she announced her terminal disease yet?"

"I don't know. I haven't talked to him today, but I warned

him about it. I told him to call me if he needed to talk and he hasn't, so I'm guessing he's getting through it."

"Maybe I'll give him a call," Desi says.

"Good idea. He could probably use the moral support. See you in the morning?" Desi nods in response. "Usual time. Love you."

Back at home, we unpack our groceries and divvy them up. Then, with Matthew at my feet "heppin" by dragging every pot and pan we own out of the pan cabinet, Emily and I wash and prick the potatoes to get them ready for the microwave. Hurley is out on the back deck grilling the steaks and some chopped squash medley we picked up in the produce section. He's also cooking a hamburger for Matthew, who isn't quite ready for steak yet.

Our meal is ready a few minutes before six, and after tossing a sheet over the coffee table, we carry our plates into the living room and eat there so we can watch TV. Hurley and I are sitting on the couch, and Emily, at one end of the coffee table, is sitting on a pillow on the floor. Matthew thinks this new adventure is great fun and he can't decide where he wants to sit, or even *if* he wants to sit. He alternates positions every minute or two, standing across the coffee table from us one minute, sitting on the couch between Hurley and me the next, plopping down in Emily's lap after that. At six o'clock, I flip the channel to a local station so we can catch the evening news. I can tell Emily knows something is up, but she hasn't asked, most likely because she knows we don't like to discuss work stuff in front of Matthew. Five minutes into the newscast, the part we're waiting for comes on. There is Alison in all her glory, being interviewed by one of the Madison newscasters, an adorable little blonde named Maureen.

"Yes, Maureen, it's true," Alison says. "I have it on good authority from Detective Steve Hurley at the Sorenson Police Department that the person believed to have killed three people there earlier this week is in custody and discussing a deal in exchange for the names of the people who hired him."

"So this was some sort of contract killing?" Maureen asks, assuming the perfect balance of horror and cuteness in her expression.

"It does appear that way," Alison says. "I can't say any more at this time because I don't want to jeopardize the larger investigation, but it looks like this is a much bigger case than originally thought. However, the police assure me there is no danger to the general public, that these killings were targeted. I'll let you know more as soon as I can."

Maureen thanks Alison, gives a quick recap of what was just said, and then hands off to the anchor desk. I pick up the remote and switch to the cartoon channel.

Emily looks over at us with one eyebrow arched. "Fishing expedition?" she asks.

I nod. The kid doesn't miss much. She gets up, grabs her plate and Matthew's, and says, "Come on, bro. Let's go do a picnic outside."

"Pick-ick!" Matthew says, and he gleefully follows his big sister out of the room.

"Do you really think this TV thing is going to work?" Hurley says once they're gone, raking a hand through his hair.

"It's worth a shot. We have good reason to believe all three of our victims were killed by the same person, and it looks as if that person is someone who was hired to do the killings. If that's the case, I'm betting someone who knows something about this case is going to contact you and try to work a deal before our supposed suspect does."

"We'll see," Hurley says, but he doesn't sound convinced.

We finish our meal, and while I do the dishes, Hurley goes out to the backyard to practice some Wiffle ball with

Matthew and Emily. I finish the cleanup and go sit out on the deck with a cup of coffee, watching my family play. Just before seven, Hurley's phone rings.

Hurley tosses the Wiffle ball to Emily and lopes toward the deck as he takes his phone out of his pocket. I get up and follow him as he heads inside, showing me the caller ID on the display. It's Bob Richmond.

Had our TV ploy worked already? Had someone called the station and reached Richmond instead of Hurley?

Hurley answers, putting the call on speaker. "Hey, Bob, what have you got?" He's a little breathless from his jog.

"I've got Mr. Novak."

My heart skips a beat—not what I thought the call would be, but almost as momentous. Maybe more so. The moment I've waited for, the moment I've dreaded, is at hand.

"He showed up at the library, just like we thought," Richmond says. "I've got him here at the station."

"We'll be there in ten," Hurley says, and then he disconnects the call. He looks over at me. "Are you ready for this?"

"I don't know," I tell him honestly. "But it's happening whether I am or not."

I head outside and ask Emily if she'd like to have her funny-money account augmented once again. "I'm happy to do it," she says. "But I've been thinking that on these occasions when I get such short notice, I should probably charge you double."

"Done."

The wry grin on her face morphs into a look of disappointment. "Crap, I should have gone for triple, right?"

I wink at her, give her a kiss on the forehead, and leave.

Hurley and I arrive at the station a short while later, and as we get out of the car, I'm tempted to get back in. Hurley is halfway to the door before he realizes I'm not with him. He walks back and puts an arm over my shoulders.

"You don't have to do this," he says. "Or if you want, you can just watch from the observation room."

"I'll be okay. I just need a minute."

To his credit, he stands there, holding me for several minutes, not saying anything. When I feel I have myself adequately steeled for what's to come, I look up at Hurley, kiss him on the cheek, and say, "Okay, let's do it."

Richmond is standing in the hallway when we enter. He says nothing, but he gives us an encouraging look. Then he nods toward the door to the conference/interrogation room.

My father is seated on the far side of the table in the room when I walk in. I look at him, and feel something in my gut slide. He is both familiar and a stranger to me. He looks less vigorous, less healthy than he's been in my memories, but that makes sense. It's been thirty years. His eyes, however, are exactly as I remember them: warm, loving, patient. They light up a little at the sight of me, and his lips form into a tentative smile.

"Hello, Mattie," he says, and the sound of his voice is like an arrow to my heart.

"Hello."

My father shifts his gaze to Hurley. "And you're Steve Hurley, the father of my grandson."

Hurley nods, but he says nothing. I want to stay standing so I can flee at a moment's notice, but I take the seat closest to me out of fear my legs will give way. I stare at the man across from me, wanting to ask him a million questions at once, unable to form a single word.

Hurley, thank goodness, takes the reins. "Mr. Novak . . . or are you going by a different name these days?"

"Novak will do."

"Fine. Mr. Novak, we have witnesses who say they saw you at the homes of two people who were recently killed, Harold Dawson and Tina Carson. Is that true?"

My father nods slowly, looking somber. "It is. I was trying to locate them, to warn them."

"Warn them? Of what?"

"Mr. Dawson was looking into something regarding an old case I was involved in years ago in Chicago. Unfortunately, the people involved in that case found him before I did."

"And Ms. Carson?"

"I knew she was seeing Mr. Dawson and hoped he might be with her, or she might be able to tell me where he was. But she wasn't at home." He pauses and sighs. "Apparently, I was too late."

"Was Ms. Carson involved as well?"

"I don't know," he says, and he looks and sounds believable. "I'm not sure if Mr. Dawson told her about it. I suspect her death may have been incidental—in the wrong place at the wrong time."

"What case is it and how do you know anything about it?"

My father's gaze briefly shifts to me, and then back to Hurley. "It's probably best if you don't know. There are some very powerful people involved, and they are extremely dangerous, as your recent murders prove."

"Oh, for Pete's sake," I say irritably, finally finding my voice. "Those people who were killed were friends of ours. How many more people have to die before you come clean?"

"It's your safety I'm concerned with," he says.

I'm momentarily taken aback. "*My* safety? What do I have to do with it?" But before he can answer, my anger takes over. "And I can take care of myself just fine, thank you. I've been doing it most of my life without your help, so I think I can manage for another decade or three."

My father flashes a toothy grin at me. "If you think you've been taking care of yourself all this time, you're wrong," he says. "I've had someone watching you for the past thirty years. How do you think I found out about that moron from Florida who wanted you dead?"

This shuts me up, and stymies me. I'm not sure I believe him, but if what he claims is true, I can't decide if I should be flattered, angry, or simply creeped out. Regardless, I can't deny that there is something to what he said. When the man he is referring to tried to kill me, someone killed him during a shoot-out with the police. Except according to ballistics, it wasn't any of the cops who shot him. And a man bearing a strong resemblance to my father was seen in the woods behind the cottage where I was living at the time.

"These people, they are very serious about keeping their secrets," my father continues. "And if they find out you're related to me, they won't hesitate to come after you in an attempt to draw me out. Your mother made her own choices—selfish choices that didn't take your welfare into consideration—but you never had a choice. So I felt it was, and still is, my duty to watch over and protect you."

His self-righteous speech plucks at my nerves. "At least my mother was there for me when I was growing up. Just because she didn't want to pull up roots, and start over somewhere with a new identity, doesn't mean she didn't care about my welfare. And since we survived just fine, it would seem her decision was a reasonable one."

"Was it?" my father asks. He opens his mouth to say something more, but then seems to think better of it.

"Look," Hurley says, holding a hand up to both of us. "I get that the two of you probably have a lot of history to cover and things to hash out, but I want to keep focused on our case for now." He drops his hands and leans toward my father. "Mr. Novak, is your involvement in the deaths of Harold Dawson and Tina Carson—whatever that involvement may be—related to the pharmaceutical case that landed you in the Witness Protection Program thirty years ago?"

My father's face pales. Clearly, he didn't think we knew

anything about that long-ago case, and discovering that we do has unnerved him. "What do you know about it?" he asks, his voice cracking slightly.

"We had a chat with someone at the U.S. Marshal's Office," Hurley says. "So pretty much everything."

"I see." My father looks back and forth between the two of us several times before dropping his gaze to the hands he has folded in front of him. He purses his lips and sighs heavily. When he looks back up at us, his expression is grim. "The one thing you don't know   because *I* don't know it, and neither do any of the investigators who looked into this case—is who exactly was behind it all. Sure, they have the names of some of the executives from back then who were properly punished with firings or relocations or worse, but no one knows who the real puppet masters were, the ones who contributed the big funds, the ones with the most to lose. They're well hidden behind a bevy of corporate curtains and business shenanigans that make it impossible to trace their involvement. I may not know all the players, but there are a few things I know for sure. They're still around, still determined to protect their dirty secrets, and not afraid to kill to do it. I wanted to warn Harold, but I was too late."

"How did Hal get involved in this in the first place?" I ask.

My father cocks his head to the side. "I think his sister was a victim of one of their latest disasters, a diet drug they're trying to bring to market. Hal started poking around and asking questions of certain people. When I heard about it, I knew he was sniffing up a dangerous tree."

Hurley nods slowly. "So you tried to talk to him, but you were never able to. Is that the case?"

"Correct. When I went by his house, he wasn't home. I went by the girlfriend's house, too, hoping to find him there, but it was empty."

"You're lying," I say, my voice filled with disgust. "Damn

it, don't play games with us on this. We're not one of your marks, waiting to be conned."

"I'm not lying," he says with eminent patience, scowling at me.

"Yes, you are," I insist. "We know you were in Harold Dawson's truck because we found something of yours in it on the day he was killed." I take out my cell phone, pull up the picture of the pendant, and show it to him. "Does this look familiar?"

His expression goes from wounded innocence to excitement in a split second. "You found it!" he exclaims, his eyes wide. "I thought it was gone for good. Can I get it back?"

His audacity stuns me. "Why don't you try telling me why you're lying to us first?"

"I am *not* lying," he insists. I give him my best cynic's face. "Okay, okay, maybe I did chat with Hal briefly, but it was only to feel him out and see what he knew, see if he intended to continue looking into it. I followed him to a restaurant parking lot and got into his truck to talk to him. I asked him if he was looking into something with the new weight-loss drug and told him he needed to leave it alone, that it was dangerous. He got angry with me, told me to get out of his truck. I tried to persuade him to listen to me, but he was too mad. He reached over, opened the door of his truck, and pushed me out into the parking lot. Then he drove off."

"And how did you know Harold was looking into it?" Hurley asks.

Novak aims his gaze down at the table, giving his eyes a hooded, almost menacing look. "I have a connection. It's the same person who's been keeping an eye on Jane and Mattie for me."

"And this person is . . . ," Hurley prompts.

Novak shakes his head slowly. "I promised I wouldn't

tell anyone about our . . . um . . . working relationship. And I'm known for keeping my word."

"And for conning innocent people," I toss out. "What about this Abernathy woman who was murdered this weekend?" Novak gives me a confused look, so I clarify. "Carolyn Abernathy? Twenty-eight-year-old nursing student?"

"I have no idea who she is," Novak says, looking genuinely puzzled. "What makes you think she's connected to Hal's death?"

"Trace evidence we found at both her murder site and Harold's," Hurley explains without going into detail about exactly what the trace evidence is. I wonder if my father will ask, but he doesn't.

"You said she's a nursing student?" Novak asks, and I can almost see the wheels turning inside his skull. Hurley and I both nod. "Does she . . . did she have a job?"

"Yeah, she worked at one of the clinics here in town, in billing and medical records. Why?"

Novak chews on his bottom lip, a habit I have. These glimpses into the parts of him that may be parts of me are both fascinating and annoying. "Let's just say the slap on the hands Martin-Weiss got thirty years ago wasn't enough to teach anyone any lessons. If you want answers, I suggest you start at that clinic."

"Why?" I ask. "Are you suggesting there are doctors at the clinic who are altering medical records for the benefit of drug research? Local doctors?" I'm hoping he'll say no—I still feel defensive about my prior field of work at times, and I've worked on some level with nearly every doctor in town—but I also won't be surprised if he says yes. Pharmaceutical research, development, and sales are hugely competitive, part of a multibillion-dollar business. And doctors, while they make decent money once they finish school and start their practices, typically have huge educational loans to pay off and a lot of overhead related to the day-to-day setup, functioning, and staffing of their practices. It's not hard to imagine some of them succumbing to the lure of easy money, and the drug companies know how to throw it around.

In fact, in the past, I enjoyed some of the fruits from that potentially poisonous tree when I was married to David. That trip we took to the Florida Keys the year my mother moved into her current house was bought and paid for by one of the drug companies. It wasn't obvious, though. They paid David to speak at a weeklong medical seminar in Miami, and it included first-class airfare for the two of us to get there and a nice hotel room once we arrived. We were responsible for our own meals, but the speaker fee was exorbitant enough to pay for us to eat all week long in the finest restaurants if we wanted. And there were also several company-sponsored activities offered during the week that often included meals, things like deep-sea fishing excursions, a seaplane trip to some island, and a daylong cruise around the Florida coast. We took advantage of a sponsored package that included diving lessons and a trip to the Keys for two dives. We had a great time and basically it was a weeklong vacation for the two of us that cost us nothing.

Or had it? Had David done a deal with the devil in exchange for that week? Had he started pushing some drug the sponsoring company produced? This thought naturally segues into another, more frightening one. Could David be involved in this somehow? There were other trips he'd made over the years: one to London, where I went along and spent the time visiting one of the stepfathers I had who lived over there now, and one to Italy, where I hadn't gone because I was sick with the flu. The realization stuns and sickens me. Had I been an unwitting accomplice in this scheme? Something else is bothering me, some niggling thought in the back of my head that I can't quite pull out because my father is talking again.

"Look," he says, "I know some of the doctors who were involved in this thirty years ago, and none of them are still practicing, at least not anywhere near here. As for who might be involved in it today, I couldn't say. I could speculate, but that would be irresponsible and dangerous. However, given your third victim in this case, I would imagine the clinic she worked for would be a logical place to start digging."

He and Hurley engage in a silent stare-down lasting a good thirty seconds or more. Then Hurley says, "Can you account for your whereabouts on Tuesday, after you went to Harold and Tina's houses?"

"Maybe," he says. "There might be some traffic cameras that tracked me. I drove around town here, running some errands, and then I drove to Poynette and spent the rest of the day there in my camper."

"At a campground?"

"No, in the parking lot of the Piggly Wiggly grocery store. I do hit up the RV parks once in a while, but for the most part, I just park wherever I want."

"Are you living in your camper?" Hurley asks.

"I am."

"Why do you borrow Peter Carmichael's car?"

My father flinches a tiny bit and I guess he didn't know we knew about that. "My camper is a little too conspicuous for some of the errands I need to run. So I drive it into town, park it somewhere, and walk to Mr. Carmichael's house to borrow his car. I pay him for it."

"Where do you get your money?" Hurley asks.

"I saved a fair amount of money during the years I was working under the ID the U.S. Marshals gave me, and I do odd jobs on the side to augment it. I don't have much in the way of expenses."

"'Odd jobs'?" I scoff. "Is that what you call it when you rip people off?"

Novak's mouth curls down with displeasure, making him look almost churlish. "I don't do that anymore, Mattie. Haven't for more than thirty years." He leans back in his chair and crosses his arms over his chest. "Look, I'm not proud of who I was back when I met your mother. It was a way of life, the only one I knew at the time. It was how I was raised. And the pressure the family puts on you to perform in certain ways, to marry within the family, and to keep things within the family unit . . . it messes with your head. When I met your mother, it was the first time in my life I started thinking about something different, about escaping from the family. As it was, I was living two lives, like one of those men who marries two different women and has two different families, neither one aware of the other. When I married your mother, I had to keep it a secret from the family and divide my time between the two. Then you came along and I became more determined than ever to break away and have a life with you and your mother."

"Why didn't you, then?" I ask, hating the whininess I hear in my voice. "Why didn't you just commit yourself to Mom and me right from the start?"

"I was working on it," he says, unfolding his arms and resting them on the table. He leans forward and pins me with his gaze. "You have to understand—the family doesn't let people just leave. Keeping everyone within the ranks is key to the success of their way of life and they can be quite adamant about it, to the point of physical violence. I tried to ease out of it, but it was a slow process. By the time I felt I was ready to make a move, things had changed."

"What changed?" I ask, my skepticism so solid it's almost a physical presence. "You were still conning people when you went into the protection program. That's what led to you needing it. So don't tell me you were ready to commit to my mother at that point."

He purses his lips again. "Actually, I was ready to commit to your mother *before* that happened. But . . . well . . . perhaps you should talk to her about what transpired at that point. Just know this. I loved you and your mother, and leaving you behind was the hardest thing I've ever done."

I stare at him, confused, angry, disillusioned . . . knowing there is more to this story of my past than either one of my parents is telling me. I have developed a throbbing headache; it feels like there is a tiny man with a pickax trying to escape from inside my skull through my forehead.

"Am I free to go?" my father asks.

"No," I say.

"Yes," Hurley says at the same time.

I turn and stare at Hurley. "You're going to let him just walk out of here?"

"I don't have anything to hold him on."

At that, my father pushes back from the table and stands. "I guess I'll be going then." He walks around to our side of the room and opens the door. I sit and stare straight ahead, refusing to look at him. "I wish it all could have been different, Mattie," he says. I want to turn around and ask him not to leave. I have a million more questions I want to ask. But I do nothing.

The quiet closing of the door behind me reverberates loudly in my chest.

CHAPTER 31

Hurley and I ride home in complete silence. I want to talk about what just happened; I want to dissect the meanings behind it. However, I don't even know where to begin or how to broach the subject without bursting into tears. And there's a burning lump in the middle of my throat, strangling me, making it impossible for me to talk.

It's dark as we pull into the driveway and I'm surprised I can't see any lights on inside the house. It's only a little after nine and Matthew is most likely in bed asleep by now, but I can't imagine Emily has gone to bed. Had she invited Johnny over for a little cuddling? If so, she was going to be in trouble because Johnny wasn't allowed in the house if we weren't home. Not just Johnny, but anybody. Hurley has guns in the house. They are locked up and kept where Matthew can't get to them, but teenagers are another story. All we needed was to have someone Emily invited over to the house steal one of the guns and hurt or kill someone with it. Plus, we have confidential files on our computers and we occasionally bring work home.

Emily understood the reasoning behind our request, but I know there have been times when Johnny has pressured her and tried to talk her into letting him come over when we weren't there because he has no privacy at his house. So far, Emily has stood her ground, but maybe tonight was the night she finally caved?

I pick up my pace and scurry past Hurley so I can be the first one through the front door. He seems so distracted I'm not sure he'd notice Johnny and Emily if they were making out naked on the couch.

But they aren't. There is no one in the living room or the kitchen. All the lights are out, which is unusual. Emily always leaves a light on downstairs somewhere if she goes up to bed before we get home.

"Why is it so dark in here?" I say to Hurley. The living-room drapes are closed, but there is a tiny amount of ambient light coming in through the front-door window from the streetlights outside. I can make out shadows, but not much more. I make my way through the living room into the kitchen and flip the wall light switch. Nothing happens. For a moment, I panic, thinking I must have forgotten to pay the electric bill this month and they turned off our power. I hear a muffled bark I recognize as Hoover's coming up through the floor. Then I realize a circuit breaker must have blown downstairs in the basement. Emily is probably down there now with Hoover, trying to fix it. I squint in the darkness and take a step toward the basement door, but then I hear a male voice I don't recognize.

"Stop where you are."

I freeze, and then I hear Hurley say, "What the hell?"

"Yes, that's a gun I'm holding to the back of your neck,"

the male voice says. "I don't want to shoot you, but I will if I have to."

"Oh, my God," I say in a panic. I hear Hoover barking again down in the basement. "Matthew? Emily?"

"They're both fine, for now. They're upstairs. And that's where we're going to go so we can have a room with full curtains on all the windows so we aren't visible to the outside. But first, Detective, I need you to take your gun out and set it on the table."

"Look," Hurley says, but the rest of his words are cut off.

"Do it!" the male voice says.

My eyes are struggling to see in the dark. I see Hurley's shadow reach forward, and hear the sound of his gun being laid on the table.

"Okay, good," the male voice says. "Now you go first, lady. Head upstairs and don't make any sudden or stupid moves because I've got a gun aimed at your husband's head."

Inanely, I start to correct him, to tell him Hurley isn't my husband. However, I wisely bite it back and walk slowly, carefully, past the two men's shadows and into the living room. I reach the foot of the stairs and start up. I'm desperate to get to Matthew and Emily, to make sure they're okay. At the top of the stairs, I see a trapezoid of light emanating from Emily's room and hurry toward it. When I reach the threshold, I see Emily sitting in her desk chair, her arms wrapped behind her and secured with a zip tie. Both of her ankles are zip-tied to the legs of the chair, and there is a piece of duct tape over her mouth.

Her eyes grow wide when she sees me, and they grow even wider when she sees her father and the other man behind me. I turn so I can move down the hall to Matthew's room and bump into Hurley right behind me.

I get my first glimpse of the man with the gun. "You're Jeremy Prince," I say, dread filling my gut. Hurley's eyes grow wide and his brow furrows.

Prince looks at me, blinking fast, his face contorting with emotion. "Yeah, I'm Jeremy Prince," he says. "I don't know how the hell you people figured that out, but you've made a huge mess of things. You're going to get my family killed."

"I don't give a crap about your family," I say, pushing past him and Hurley. "Where's my son?" I move down the hall, half expecting to feel a bullet in the back of my head, but I need to see Matthew. I need to know he's okay. I stop in the doorway to his room and breathe a sigh of relief. He's asleep in his big-boy bed, thumb firmly planted, cheeks moving in and out like a bellows. Tux and Rubbish are on his bed, the two of them situated at the foot of it like guard cats.

A surge of anger courses through me and I whirl around, confronting the man with the gun. "What the hell do you want? Are you here to kill us? Do you think that's going to solve your problems?"

"I'm here to turn myself in."

Our jaws drop and I look at Hurley, curious to see his reaction, wondering if he heard the same thing I did, or if I imagined the whole thing. Judging from the puzzled look on his face, he heard what I did.

"You what?" Hurley says.

"I'm here to turn myself in. I can't do this anymore. It's gone too far. I don't know why you put that bullshit on the news about having someone in custody, but you've totally screwed me by doing that. Me and my family."

"Your family?" Hurley says. He starts to turn around, but Prince jabs the gun in his neck.

"Hold on, Detective," Prince says. "I don't want you making any sudden moves. We need to talk and I want you to hear me out. Why don't you go over there and have a seat on the girl's bed?"

Hurley does as he's told and walks across Emily's room,

settling on the edge of her bed. Emily lets out a little whimper and wiggles in the chair, pulling her knees together.

"Undo her," I say to Prince. "We'll listen to what you have to say, but let her go. I think she has to pee."

Emily nods vigorously.

Prince nods toward Emily's desktop and says, "You can use those scissors to cut her ties. But don't get any wise ideas with the scissors or I'll shoot first and ask questions later."

I nod my understanding, walk into the room, find the scissors, and cut the zip ties around Emily's wrists. She pulls the tape off her mouth while I cut her ankles free and then she hops out of the chair and brushes past Prince with surprising bravado, heading down the hall to the bathroom.

"Don't try any funny stuff in there or I'll shoot your parents," Prince says.

"You're an asshole," Emily shoots back, and she shuts the door.

Prince motions to me with the gun. "Put the scissors down and go sit over there next to your husband."

"He's—" Again I was about to say he's not my husband, but I realize how stupid and irrelevant it would be, and once more bite it back. I put the scissors back in the pencil holder I took them from and go sit on the bed next to Hurley. From down the hall, we hear the toilet flush and water running. A moment later, the bathroom door creaks as it opens—I've been after Hurley to fix that stupid squeak—and Emily comes back into the room.

"Sit," Prince says, gesturing toward the chair she was tied to.

Emily does as she's told and we all sit there, hostage to this suspected killer who says he wants to turn himself in. I wonder if I'm asleep and dreaming, because this makes about as much sense as most of my dreams do, and they're typically *Alice in Wonderland* kind of stuff.

Prince sucks in a deep breath, squares his shoulders, and lets the breath out in a big sigh. "Here's the deal," he says, looking at Hurley. "I'm willing to confess to those killings . . . all of them, though I don't know how you connected Carolyn."

"The nicotine," Hurley says. "We found it in her skin cream, and in her work gloves. And we also found it on the lid of the cooler on Hal Dawson's boat."

Prince screws his face up in thought for a moment; then he bursts out laughing. "I had a soda," he says. "Done in by a frigging soda. I was wearing gloves, but they were the same gloves I'd used to mix the nicotine in Carolyn's cream."

"Why did you kill them?" I ask.

"Because that's what they paid me to do," Prince says.

"They who?"

Prince shakes his head. "No, that part's going to have to wait. I'm not giving up any names until I have a deal on the table. In writing. I want witness protection for me and my family."

"You killed three people," Hurley says. "They're not going to let you go free after that."

Prince looks confused for a moment, but then says, "We'll see. I didn't want to kill anyone. They sucked me in. They started paying me for little jobs—delivering packages and some bodyguard work—and they paid well. We needed the money. My wife, she's sick. She has multiple sclerosis and we have two daughters. I had to leave the military so I could be around to help take care of her and the kids. When they offered me work, I took it. I did some special ops stuff in the military and they said they needed someone with my skill set. And with the money they were paying me, I could afford to hire round-the-clock help for my wife."

He pauses and sighs, his expression pained. "They made me do some things that . . . things I'm not proud of. Then they asked me to get rid of someone. I told them I wasn't going to kill anyone, that's where I drew the line. But then they said if I didn't do it, they'd kill my wife and daughters." He pauses, running his free hand through his hair, and making a grim face. "They had it all planned out that first time and told me what to do. When I realized they wanted me to kill not one, but two people, I tried to back out again. But they kept threatening to hurt and kill my family, so I did what they wanted. Things didn't work out quite the way they planned, but in the end, they were satisfied with the outcome and I only had one death on my conscience. I thought that would be the end of it, but they didn't stop there."

I wonder if he's referring to Marla Weber and Tomas and start to ask him, thinking that's why he looked momentarily confused when Hurley said he had killed three people, but Hurley gets his question in first.

"Why did they want Hal, Tina, and Carolyn dead?"

"I don't know the 'why' part for Hal Dawson. I just did what they told me to do." He pauses, wincing. "I didn't like doing it the way I did, but I couldn't risk the sound of a gunshot out on the water. And I feel bad about the lady. I didn't realize she was going to be on the boat. She fainted after what I . . . after the guy went over the side, and for a moment, I thought about letting her be. But she'd seen me and would have been able to ID me later." He shrugs, indicating the conclusion from all this was obvious.

His dismissive attitude angers me and I struggle to stay focused and not rip his face off. "There were witnesses," I say. "They said the man on the boat had a beard."

Prince pulls at his clean-shaven chin. "A disguise," he says with another shrug.

"What about Carolyn Abernathy?" Hurley asks.

"That was different. Initially all they said they wanted me to do was to get close to her and search through her house and her computer to see if she was looking into anything related to drug research. I staked her out for a while, but she didn't go out much. So I created the false ID for Keith Lundberg, got a job at the mechanic shop, and followed her to the grocery store one Saturday. I flirted with her, told her I came there every Saturday at the same time and hoped to see her again the following week. Sure enough, she showed up. It was easy from there."

This last, cavalier phrase makes my blood boil.

"You dated her and then you killed her?" Emily says, looking aghast.

Prince shoots her a wounded look. "I didn't know they were going to ask me to kill her when I started seeing her."

Emily shakes her head at him and looks away in disgust. I do the same.

"And I thought the nicotine was a smart way to do it," Prince adds, seemingly oblivious to our reactions. "How did you happen onto it?"

"You got careless," Hurley says. "The invoice for the tobacco juice you ordered was in the Dumpster at the motel where you were staying."

"But I shredded everything," Prince says, looking confused.

"You should have burned it," Hurley says.

Prince shakes his head and again runs a hand through his hair. "Clearly, I'm not cut out for this kind of work." He gives Hurley an appealing look. "You have to help me get out of this. I figured I might as well turn myself in because they're going to believe that crap you put on the news tonight, and they're going to come after my family. I've got them hidden for the moment, but they'll find them eventually. They've got eyes and connections everywhere. That's why we need witness protection—if not for me, then for them. You get my family somewhere safe and I'll give you names."

"You should have come to us sooner," Hurley says.

"I know," Prince says, hanging his head. "I should have and didn't. But I'm here now." He walks over and hands his gun to Hurley. "Here. It's not loaded." Hurley takes the gun and checks it to make sure.

Prince takes a zip tie out of his pocket and hands it to Hurley. Then he turns around and puts his hands behind his back. "Take me in. But get me a meeting with whoever has the power to make a deal happen, and do it quick. *Please.* My family's life depends on it."

Hurley gives me a questioning look. I nod, and he goes ahead and zip-ties Prince's wrists together. He steers Prince out of the room toward the stairs as he takes out his cell phone and makes a call.

"Hey, Bob, I need your help," Hurley says as he follows Prince down the stairs. In my mind, I imagine darting forward and giving Prince a hefty shove. I squeeze my eyes closed to block it out. "I'm bringing a suspect to the station and I'm going to bring him in through the garage downstairs," Hurley continues. "I need you to make some calls and have the following people meet me there."

I tune out the conversation at that point and walk over to Emily. I bend down and wrap my arms around her, hugging her. "Are you okay?"

"I'm fine," she says with typical smart-ass, teenage bravado.

"You were very brave. I was so scared when that guy stopped us downstairs."

"He *was* a little scary," Emily admits. "He just walked in through the back door. He was going to shoot Hoover, but I convinced him to let me lock Hoover down in the basement. Then I tried to keep him downstairs in the kitchen so he wouldn't know Matthew was up here, but he insisted on going upstairs. And then he said if I didn't do everything he said, he'd shoot Matthew."

I release my hug on her and kneel down in front of her. "Thank you, Emily. Thank you for being such a good big sister."

Her eyes water up and she looks away from me. "I love that little guy," she says. "I don't know what I'd do if anything . . ." She can't finish the sentence, and a tear rolls down her cheek.

I reach up and hug her again, and her tears turn into sobs. I hold her for several minutes, hearing the distant murmur of voices from downstairs. Finally I let her go, brush her hair back from her face, and kiss her on the forehead. "Are you okay?"

She nods and sniffles.

"I'm going to go downstairs to check on Hurley and let Hoover out of the basement. Will you be okay up here?"

"I'll be fine."

I go downstairs and find Hurley standing in the living room with Prince, ready to walk out the front door. "I'm not sure how late I'll be," he says, giving me a kiss on the cheek.

"I know. We'll be here when you get back."

There is a knock on the door and we all freeze. "Is someone coming to meet you here?" I ask Hurley.

He shakes his head. Prince looks panicked and backs up several feet.

"Who is it?" I holler through the door.

"It's Alison," says a familiar voice. "I wanted to follow up with you guys on the news thing, see what's happening."

I look at Hurley and roll my eyes. "It's okay," I say to Prince. "She's a friend, a local reporter. She's the one who was on the news tonight."

Prince shakes his head. "No reporters."

Hurley sighs and says, "I'll take him out the back door and around the side of the house." With that, he nudges Prince toward the kitchen. I tell Alison to hold on a sec and wait until I hear the back door open and close. Then I unlock and open the front door.

"Hey, Mattie," Alison says with a smile. "I hope I'm not too late. I thought I might hear from you guys tonight, but when I didn't, I figured I'd stop by and—" She stops and cocks her head. Then she looks over toward the driveway. I have a pretty good idea what she's looking at, and she confirms my suspicion a second later.

"Who is that? Did you flush someone out?" she says, her eyes big as she stares into the dark. "You did, didn't you? It worked." She turns to step back off the front stoop and says, "Who is he? What does he know?"

I step outside and squint in the darkness. I see Hurley holding Prince by the arm and pushing him toward the door of his car.

Alison is off the stoop now, heading toward them. "Alison," I say in a sharp tone. "Wait!" But she's having none of it. She's hurrying toward Prince and Hurley. I make a mad dash after her.

From the corner of my eye, I see headlights coming down the street and my mind registers the fact that the vehicle is moving slowly. Something in my spine prickles, and when I look toward the headlights, a streetlamp briefly illuminates the dark SUV, the rolled-down window, the glint of something metallic. I open my mouth to yell, to warn Hurley, but I'm a split second too late.

Gunfire erupts, a staccato burst of bullets that seems to go on forever. I hear a scream, and a grunt, and then the squeal of wheels. From behind me, I hear another scream from upstairs, and the sound of Hoover's frantic barking from beneath me. I back up toward the door, ready to duck inside, but then realize the car is already gone. I look over toward Hurley's car and my heart leaps into my mouth. All three of them are on the ground. Prince is lying on his side in the driveway; Hurley is on his knees beside him; Alison is lying on her back on the sidewalk, her eyes staring straight up at the sky.

Emily hurtles down the stairs. "Mattie, what happened?"

"Go back upstairs, Em, and check on Matthew. Then stay there."

"But—"

"Now!"

She heads back upstairs and I shut the front door behind me. My legs are trembling and I take a tentative step toward the others. "Hurley, are you hit?"

"I'm okay," he says, the panic barely contained in his voice. "You?"

"I'm fine."

"Prince is hit. He's hurt bad. We need an ambulance." I take my cell phone out of my pocket and dial 911. By the time the operator answers, I'm kneeling beside Alison and see that she's been shot in the head and is beyond anyone's help. I fight back the tears and anger welling up inside me and focus on giving the operator the necessary instructions. In the process, I leave Alison and move over to Hurley and Prince.

Prince, perhaps ironically given what he did to Hal, has been hit in the neck and the bullet has nicked his carotid artery. Hurley has his hand over the wound, trying to stem the blood flow, but I can see it's coming too fast and furious. Prince is going to die any second, bleeding out the same way Hal did.

He seems to realize this and he beckons Hurley to lean down closer to him. Hurley does so, and Prince whispers something in his ear. I try to hear what it is, but sirens are closing in already and their sound drowns out the whispers.

I get up to my feet and walk toward the street to meet the cops and the ambulance. Just as they arrive, I glance back at Prince and Hurley. Prince's head is lolling to one side, his eyes staring up at the sky, sightless. I can tell he's gone. Hurley's expression is one of pure, red-hot anger.

I realize that in a strictly karmic way, justice has been served for Hal, Tina, and Carolyn. Their killer has been caught and is dead. But then it dawns on me that I never asked Prince about Tomas Wyzinski. Was he behind that, too? Had he framed the man? Was that what he'd meant when he'd said things hadn't worked out as planned, and he only had one death on his conscience? Had that death been Marla Weber's?

Though I can find some solace in knowing we solved the deaths of Hal, Tina, and Carolyn, I realize Prince was merely the tip of an iceberg that may be big enough to take all of us down. And judging from the look on Hurley's face, he knows this, too. We aren't even close to being done with this case. I wonder if we ever will be.

CHAPTER 32

Emily, Desi, Erika, and I head down the funeral home stairs and hit the buzzer on the wall. "Are you sure about this?" Desi asks me, looking back up the stairs longingly. I wouldn't be surprised if she made a mad dash in an attempt to escape.

"Trust me. I know the setting is a little unusual, but Barbara is one of the most talented stylists I know. You'll be amazed at what she can do."

"Well, duh," Emily says. "If she can make dead people look good, she has to be talented."

The door opens and Barbara smiles at the four of us. I make the introductions, and then Barbara says, "Please come in." She waves a hand toward the room behind her, which is hardly your typical salon interior. Here the walls are made of tile you can wash down with a hose, the chairs are actually stainless-steel tables with drain channels built in, and the primary smells are formaldehyde and something else sickly sweet and undefinable.

Desi looks pale and jittery, so I reach into my purse and dig out one of the mini bottles of vodka I stashed in there earlier. "Here," I tell her. "Drink this."

She eyes it skeptically for a moment, then unscrews the top and chugs it down in one gulp. I take out a second mini bottle and hand it to her. "Pace yourself," I warn.

She nods, but I can already see a glow in her cheeks. Barbara has put a mat down on one of the tables and she pats it and says to Desi, "Hop up here and lie down."

Desi looks at the table, then at me, then back to the table. "You get used to it after the first time," I tell her. "Trust me."

"What's the matter, Mom," Erika taunts. "Are you a scaredy-cat?"

This seems to stiffen Desi's spine. She squares her shoulders, walks over to the table, and hops up onto it. Then she opens her second mini bottle and chugs it. She blinks hard as she swallows, licks her lips, and says, "Let's do this." She flops down onto her back and Barbara hovers over her, studying her lines and colors.

"Ooh, you have beautiful high cheekbones," Barbara says. "And your skin tones are perfect."

Three hours later, Barbara has transformed all of us into chic, beautiful women. Everyone's makeup is done to perfection and we all have a sophisticated updo. I pay Barbara for her ministrations, invite her to attend the wedding, and then drive all of us to Desi's house in the hearse. It seems a fitting mode of transportation, considering.

"You weren't kidding," Desi says from the front passenger seat, looking in the mirror in her visor. "She is truly masterful with the makeup. I haven't looked this good in years."

"I've never looked this good ever," Erika says, staring at her face in a compact mirror.

Emily smiles, but says nothing.

We arrive at Desi's house with an hour to go before the wedding ceremony, which is scheduled for five. It seems like plenty of time, but I know it might take a lot of time to turn myself into something that looks marriage-worthy. Desi has taken care of the dress problem quite nicely, but I wish we could have found a better pair of shoes. I had hoped to find some heels we could dye to match the color of the dress, but they weren't available in Sasquatch sizes. I finally settled on a pair of silver pumps and had to choose between a twelve, which was a smidge too small, and a thirteen, which was a smidge too big, because I couldn't find anything in a twelve and a half. I opted for the thirteen, not wanting my feet to be cramped and painful. But it means the shoes slip on and off my heels when I walk.

"Come look at the backyard," Desi says, taking me by the hand. "Tell me what you think."

She leads me out through the back door and onto her covered patio. I stand there in awe, looking at what she's done. There are tiny white lights strung around the columns holding up the roof patio, and more white lights crisscrossing the ceiling with gentle arcs of blue gossamer fabric hanging below. A long white carpet path leads out into the yard, stopping at an arch decorated with blue and white flowers and more of the tiny white lights. White wooden folding chairs sit on either side of the carpeted path, and there are two white columns at the end of the path wrapped in the tiny white lights and bursting with blue flowers at the top.

"Desi, it's beautiful," I say, tears welling in my eyes.

"Don't start crying," she says. "You'll ruin Barbara's perfect makeup."

I sniff back my tears and take a moment to collect myself. "It almost seems wrong to feel so happy after everything that's happened."

Desi nods solemnly. "It's not your fault, Mattie. What happened to Alison is in no way your fault. You have to believe that."

I nod, but I don't believe it. My cell phone rings and I

take it out of my pocket. "It's the Realtor," I tell Desi, and then I answer the call. Desi stands by, watching me with an expectant expression until I'm done.

"Well?" she says when I disconnect the call.

"It's a done deal. The land is ours. We can start building as soon as our contractor is ready."

"That's great! The new place will be so much better for you guys."

It will, in many ways. After a long discussion, Hurley and I decided to go ahead with the wedding, even though it felt wrong to do it on the heels of Alison's death. And we also decided that Hurley's house was not going to work for us down the road.

"I've always felt like Hurley's house is . . . well . . . Hurley's house," I say. "It will be nice to have something that is uniquely ours."

"And the extra security will be welcome, too, I'm sure," Desi says.

She's right about that. Hurley and I looked at a number of different plans, eventually settling on a four-bedroom house that will be equipped with a state-of-the-art alarm system. In light of what happened with Alison and Prince, it seems like the logical thing to do. And it will be a better fit for all of us, leaving us with a bedroom we can use as an office. Or a family addition, if we decide to go that route.

Desi looks around to see if anyone is nearby; when she sees we are alone, she says, "Did Hurley take care of Prince's family?"

I nod. "He made all the necessary arrangements. It was the least we could do for the guy. He may have done some awful things, but he did them out of love for his family. At least this way his death won't be for naught."

When he realized he was dying, Prince had whispered the location of his family to Hurley and begged him to take care of them. Now that Prince was dead, we weren't sure the people who had hired him would have a reason to go after his family, but Hurley had promised the man he would take care of them, and he had. Prince had also told Hurley something else before he died, a name—just one, but it was a start—of one of the players in the drug scheme that had led to all this mayhem. Hurley hasn't told me whose name Prince gave him, but he has assured me the investigation will continue.

"Come on," Desi says, taking my arm and steering me back into the house. "Let's get dressed and get this show on the road before you change your mind."

"I'm not changing my mind," I say with a smile. "Hurley and I are meant to be together. I'm convinced of that."

We head for Desi's bedroom, where the girls are already parading around in the dresses they bought for the occasion. Desi helps me get my dress on, taking care not to mess my makeup and hair, and then I help her do the same. By the time we're done, the men come knocking on the bedroom door.

Desi opens it and Matthew comes running into the room. "Mama!" He stops a few feet from me and stares. "Mama booful," he says.

"And look at you," I say, happy tears welling in my eyes. He is dressed in a tiny suit in a pale shade of blue that has a jacket and shorts. He has white knee socks on, a white shirt, and shiny black shoes. "You look so handsome!" I pick him up and give him a big kiss, leaving a lipstick mark on his cheek.

Hurley is beaming. "You *are* beautiful," he says.

"Thank you. You're looking pretty good yourself, handsome," I say with a wink. Despite our conviction to keep things casual, Hurley eventually opted for a dark blue suit with a lighter blue shirt and a blue-and-silver–striped tie.

"I got you a little something," he says, walking over and handing me a small gift-wrapped box.

"What? Why?"

"It's just a little something I wanted to give you. Open it. I think it will be self-explanatory."

I tear off the paper, open the box, and look inside. It is filled with Little Debbie coffee cakes.

"I felt like I needed to give Tommy Smithson a run for his money," Hurley says.

Desi and the others all look at us with confused, inquiring expressions. "Inside joke," I tell them. And then I walk over and give my future husband a big kiss. "Thank you. It's the perfect gift."

"I have some news for you, too," he says. "I just heard that Tomas Wyzinski's sentencing hearing is over. He got life without the possibility for parole."

I frown at this. "Why can't I shake the idea that he was wrongly convicted? And that I helped do it?"

Hurley shakes his head. "To be fair, we don't know if Prince was involved with that particular situation. I talked to Beckwith, but the only argument I could put forth was your claim that Lech said the bad guy was driving a blue convertible and Prince owned a blue Mercedes convertible. We're going to have to come up with better evidence than that if we're going to get Tomas off. At least Beckwith was willing to forgo the death penalty."

"Well, that's something, I guess," I say. "I have some news for you, too. The Realtor called a little while ago and we got the land."

"That's great!" he says with a big grin. "With any luck, we can be in the new house by fall."

Lucien, who has been standing in the doorway the entire time, says, "The guests are arriving. I'm going to go make sure everyone gets seated." He glances at his watch. "T-minus twenty minutes."

Hurley gives me a kiss and then he and Lucien depart. I look over at Emily and Erika and say, "I need you guys to do me a favor. Can you take Matthew and go help the men get everyone seated? We'll meet you out on the patio in twenty. I need to have a private chat with my sister."

The girls look intrigued and I can tell they're curious about what I want to talk about, but they know better than to ask.

"Come on, Matthew," Emily says, taking her brother by the hand. She steers him out of the room, with Erika tagging along behind.

"Erika," Desi says, "check on Ethan please and make sure he's ready."

"Will do." The girls leave, shutting the bedroom door behind them.

I turn to Desi and tell her to sit down.

"Whoa," she says. "This sounds serious." She sits on the edge of her bed, her hands folded in her lap, her eyes on mine.

"I need to tell you something," I start. "I've been debating whether or not I should, but after giving it some thought, I decided you should know."

"Know what?"

"The truth about Mom's deception. She's not coming today, in part because of her phobias, but also because I spoke to her last night and told her I knew the truth and planned to tell you."

"Okay," Desi says hesitantly, trying to keep a smile on her face and failing miserably.

"I told you about my father and the trouble he got into thirty years ago and how he ended up in witness protection. I also told you that Mom decided she didn't want to go. She said it was because she didn't want to start over again, and because she was mad at my father for lying to her about his involvement with his family, but I discovered some things that made me think she had other reasons for her refusal."

"Such as?"

"I found some other stuff in that trunk in the basement,

stuff I didn't tell you about yet, like a marriage certificate for her and your father. They were married a full year later than what Mom has always led us to believe, and over a month after you were born."

Desi looks away, her face scrunched up in thought. "Are you saying I'm a bastard . . . that I was born out of wedlock?"

"Well, that's how it looked, yes."

She shrugs. "These are modern times, Mattie. It's no big deal. I'm sure Mom lied about the wedding date because it wasn't as accepted back then to have a child out of wedlock. But I'm fine with it."

I chew my lip, bracing myself for what I have to tell her next. "Except, as it turns out, you weren't born out of wedlock. Mom was still married to my father when you were born. Their divorce wasn't finalized until weeks before she married your father."

Desi looks confused.

"And your father . . . isn't . . . well . . . he isn't really your father."

Desi stares at me, her mouth hanging open. "What do you mean? Did Mom get pregnant by someone else?"

"In a manner of speaking, yes. When my father went into hiding and was trying to convince Mom to go with him, she discovered she was pregnant. With you."

"So . . . what?" she asks, her face scrunched up in confusion. "She was having an affair with someone at the time? Is that what you're saying?"

I shake my head. "No, she wasn't." I wait, and let it sink in. It doesn't take Desi long to figure it out.

"Oh, my God," she says. "You and I have the same father?"

I nod.

Desi lets out a huff of disbelief. She looks at me, then looks away, then looks at me again.

"And to make matters worse," I add, "he has a comb-over."

Desi lets out a near maniacal laugh. After a few seconds, she sobers. "Did my father know?" She winces and shakes her head. "I mean, the man who I thought was my father. Was he in on it?"

I nod again. "Mom admitted as much to me last night. He was someone she knew, someone who had flirted with her, and she went to him and told him everything and asked him if he'd be willing to stay with her, to marry her, and to go on record as being your father. She felt that if anything happened, if the people who were after my father . . . our father, figured out who she was, they wouldn't come after you. She and I would have been at risk, but you, at least, would have been safe."

Desi leans forward and stares at the floor.

"I'm sorry, Desi."

She huffs a laugh, but there is no humor to it. "Well, aren't we just a Jerry Springer show?" she says.

"I have some more of those little vodkas if you want one."

"No, not now anyway. Though I might take you up on it later. This is going to take a while for me to digest."

"You realize this means we're true sisters, not half sisters, but whole ones."

She looks up at me with a warm smile. "The blood connection never mattered," she says. She gets up, walks over to me, and gives me a big hug. "You've always been my best and only sister, and my best friend."

"I love you, Desi."

"I love you, too." We hold one another for a few more seconds and then Desi releases me and steps back. She glances at her watch. "I think we're on," she says. "Let's do this."

We leave the bedroom and make our way through the

house to the back patio. Emily and Erika are waiting there with Matthew. At the end of the white carpet, I see Hurley standing under the arch with Izzy at his side. The guests are all seated in the white wooden chairs; there aren't many of them. Several cops are here: Bob Richmond, Junior Feller, Brenda Joiner, and Patrick Devonshire, along with the day dispatcher, Heidi. Dom is sitting in the front row with Juliana in his lap, and behind him are Cass, Laura, Arnie, and Jonas, all of them seated together, with Laura sandwiched between Jonas and Arnie. Also present is Syph, my nursing buddy. Standing off to one side, camera in hand, is Charlotte "Charlie" Finnegan, the PD's videographer, who kindly offered to step in and manage the picture-taking duties Alison was supposed to handle.

Lucien is also standing off to one side by a podium that Desi informed me is rigged up to play music.

Noticeably absent are my mother and father—Desi's mother and father.

"Where's Ethan?" Desi asks the girls, zeroing in on another missing party.

"He's looking for Hissy," Erika says. "He got out of his cage."

Hissy is Ethan's three-inch-long Madagascar hissing cockroach, one of his prize bug possessions and, other than Fluffy, his tarantula, the only living specimen.

Desi shakes her head and rolls her eyes at me. "Ready?"

I nod, and Desi gives Lucien a nod. The "Wedding March" starts to play, the music emanating from speakers Lucien has set up around the yard.

"Go," Desi says, giving Erika a little push.

Erika and Emily take off down the aisle with Matthew, who is carrying a ring pillow, walking between them. Desi leans over, gives me a kiss on the cheek, and follows them, carrying a tiny nosegay made up of blue hydrangeas and white baby's breath. I grip my own bouquet, a slightly larger version of the same thing, take in a bracing breath, and set off down the aisle.

I've gone three steps when I see Matthew plop down on his butt. The procession halts as the girls try to pick him up and get him walking again, but he's having one of his little temper tantrums and he refuses to budge. He throws his ring pillow aside and lies down flat on his back, crying.

The girls look at me for help. I wave them on, and they leave Matthew where he is and continue down the aisle to the front row of seats. Desi reaches Matthew and tries to cajole him into getting up, but he kicks his feet and cries louder. She steps over him and walks up to the arch.

I reach my son and stop, squatting down beside him. "Matthew, can you please stop crying and get up off the ground? Mommy and Daddy want you to be up front with us."

Matthew gives me an exaggerated shake of his head and starts sucking his thumb in between angry sobs.

"Very well," I say, stepping over him. "Have it your way." I walk the rest of the aisle, stumbling once when one of my shoes slips off my heel, until I'm side by side with Hurley.

"Should I go get him?" Hurley whispers.

I shake my head. "Leave him be. I suspect he'll stop crying when he realizes it isn't getting him the attention he wants."

I shift my attention to Izzy, smile at him, and he winks and smiles back. He looks good, and it gives my heart a boost.

"Shall I go ahead?" the justice of the peace asks us.

"Please," Hurley says, and the ceremony begins.

We're only a few lines in when Matthew stops crying. I sneak a look over my shoulder and see him sitting in the middle of the aisle, sucking his thumb, watching us.

We get to the part where we are supposed to say our vows and I get to go first.

"Hurley, I knew from almost the first instant I saw you that you were going to be a significant part of my life, and not just because I was a suspect in the murder we were investigating." There is a ripple of laughter behind us. "It's been an interesting and rocky journey to get to where we are today, but I realized not long ago that every decision I made in my life, every fork in the road I took, and every action I've ever taken, they were designed to bring me to this moment. To you." I pause and look back at Matthew, and then at Emily. "To our family. Regardless of what the road ahead is like, regardless of how many more hurdles are tossed in front of us, I know I can handle it as long as I have you at my side. You are my strength, my happiness, my soul mate, my everything. You make me a better person and I can't imagine my life without you. I love you."

It's Hurley's turn and he stares at me, a wet sheen in his eyes. His Adam's apple bounces up and down, up and down, and he clears his throat. When he finally speaks, his voice cracks.

"Mattie, you are the most amazing woman I have ever met. You are strong, you are smart, you are kind, you are loving, and you are beautiful. I love your wit, your tenderness, your laugh, your sense of right and wrong, your devotion to those you love, and your determination to always see the glass as half full. I don't know what brand of insanity convinced you to hitch your wagon up to me, but I'm glad you did. You are my best friend and the one person I want to spend the rest of my life with. I love you with all my heart and soul."

I'm so glad Hurley didn't go first, because if I had to follow his speech, nothing would have happened. The lump in my throat aches and my eyes burn as I try to suppress my tears, but they're tears of joy. And as the JP declares us husband and wife, I swear my heart will burst with all the happiness inside it.

As Hurley and I kiss, I hear Matthew behind us say, "Mama, poo-poo." I laugh, breaking the kiss, and then Heidi, the day dispatcher, lets out a blood-curdling scream. She bolts from her chair and runs down the aisle.

Brenda Joiner, who was seated next to her, suddenly jumps up from her seat, knocking it over backward. She is staring at the ground as she sidles her way to the end of the row.

"What the hell?" Hurley says.

"It's okay," I say, heading down the aisle toward Matthew. "It's just Ethan's missing pet. And so our life journey together begins!"

Watch for Annelise Ryan's next book in the

Mattie Winston series,

DEAD CALM!

at

your local bookstore or at your favorite retailer.

Turn the page for a sneak peek of

DEAD CALM

CHAPTER 1

The chiming ringtone of a phone awakens me from a deep sleep, and out of habit, I roll over and grab my cell in an effort to silence it as fast as I can. My bleary eyes try to focus on the screen, but sleep's hold is too great; the whole thing is a blur. I blink hard, glance at the clock on my bedside table, and see that it's just after three in the morning. The ringing stops, and for a moment, I think the caller must have hung up because I haven't hit the answer icon yet. Then I hear a voice behind me say, "Hurley," and realize it wasn't my phone ringing.

Just as I'm thinking that my husband and I need to personalize our ringtones so we can distinguish whose phone is getting called, the chiming sound starts up again. This time I know it's my phone because I feel it vibrating in my hand. I finally see the answer icon and swipe at it, silencing the ring. I realize as I do so that if both my husband's phone and mine are going off in the middle of the night, it means someone is dead.

Annelise Ryan

My name is Mattie Winston, and I'm a medico-legal death investigator for the medical examiner's office in Sorenson, Wisconsin. My husband, Steve Hurley, is a homicide detective here in town. There are no regular hours to either of our jobs, though we try to maintain a façade of normalcy by getting up every weekday morning and heading into our offices. But people don't die on a Monday-through-Friday, nine-to-five schedule, and that means there are plenty of times when we put in a lot of long, extra hours.

"This is Mattie," I say into my phone. I sit up straighter in bed and look over at Hurley as I hear the voice of my boss, Izzy, emanate from my phone. I used to work at the local hospital; my original career was in nursing, and I spent six years in the ER and seven in the OR, good prep for the slicing and dicing I have to do in my current job. Now I'm an assistant to Dr. Izthak "Izzy" Rybarceski, the medical examiner in Sorenson, though for the past three weeks Izzy has been out on sick leave following a heart attack. I've been working with Izzy for almost three years now, and we work well together, in large part because we were friends—and, at one point, neighbors—before I started my current job.

"Mattie, we have a call," Izzy says. His voice sounds energized and excited, and that does my heart good because it means his heart is good. "It's a two-fer, so we should both go."

"A two-fer?" I echo, looking at Hurley with eyebrows raised. He nods, confirming that he has received the same info.

"The cops say it looks like a murder-suicide," Izzy says.

"Okay," I say, flinging back the covers. "Where?"

"It's out at the Grizzly Motel."

This gives me pause. "That's quite a way outside the city limits. Who's investigating?"

"The county guys pulled it, but they're terribly short-handed. They've got two men out on sick leave, another one out for paternity leave, and there are two accident scenes they're investigating right now in other areas of the county. And if the tentative IDs are correct, the victims are both Sorenson residents, so Hurley's probably going to get a call to assist."

"Yeah, I'm pretty sure he just did. Give us ten minutes to get going, and we'll meet you out there."

I disconnect my call and get out of bed, heading for the bathroom. Hurley is still on his phone, but he isn't saying anything at the moment; he's just listening. Our dog, Hoover, a yellow Lab mix—and, judging from the way he eats, I'm convinced there's a bit of vacuum cleaner in those genes—opens his eyes and watches me, his big head resting on his paws.

By the time I emerge from the bathroom with my bladder emptied, teeth brushed, and my hair partially tamed into a cowlicky mess of blond mayhem, Hurley is already dressed. We pass one another just outside the bathroom door.

"The Grizzly Motel?" I say.

"Yep. Murder-suicide?" he counters.

"Yep." I head for the dresser and grab a pair of jeans, a bra, and a T-shirt. "I'll go wake Emily," I say as I pull on my jeans beneath my nightgown. Then I peel the nightgown off, put on the bra and shirt, and shuffle my way down the hall to Emily's room, stepping over Hoover. Along the way I stop at our son Matthew's room and poke my head in.

He is sound asleep, and I utter a silent prayer of thanks that the ringing phones didn't wake him. His thick, dark hair—the color just like his father's—is sticking out on top of his head like a rooster's comb, the style surprisingly similar to mine even if the color is at the opposite end of the spectrum. He has his left thumb firmly planted in his mouth, but he is still, not sucking, not moving, no muscles twitching. A persistent internal alarm clamors, one I've had to quell hundreds of times in the twenty-two months of Matthew's existence, and I focus my gaze on his chest until I detect a slow rise and fall. Reassured, I resist an urge to tiptoe into the room and kiss him, knowing there's a good chance the action will wake him. And at this age, a just wakened Matthew is like the Tasmanian Devil cartoon character, a whirlwind of seemingly endless and frenzied energy with a penchant for creating crayon artwork on the walls and an apparent belief that any remotely wet form of food he eats is also a hair product.

I sense Hurley behind me—I can feel the heat of his body along my back—and his face appears over my right shoulder. We stand there that way for several seconds, both of us drinking in this most precious sight.

Finally, Hurley whispers in my ear. "I'll go nuke us a couple of cups of coffee. I think there's enough left in the pot."

I nod, and as he turns and heads downstairs, I make my way to the door of Emily's room and open it. The room is a mess, its normal state. Clothes are strewn about on the desk, the chair, the floor, and the bed, and two of the drawers in the dresser are open, with items hanging over the edges. The top of the desk is a chaotic riot of papers, as if a tornado had spun above it. There is half of a sandwich, the edges dry, brittle, and curling, on the bedside table. Out of habit, I head for the sandwich, intending to take it downstairs with me, but I change my mind. My seventeen-year-old stepdaughter and I reached a peace treaty some time back about the state of her room. We agreed that it is her space to do with as she wants, and that I won't nag her about the state it's in, nor will I venture into it and try to clean it up. Treaty or not, the mess still bothers me, but as long as there aren't any bugs in the room or mold growing on the walls, I'm determined to abide by our terms.

Emily is sound asleep in the bed amidst all this squalor, and I feel a twinge of guilt at having to wake her. But it's late July and summer vacation for her—no school to worry about, and she has no job other than the frequent babysitting she does for us—so I know she'll manage.

"Em?" I say in a low voice, giving her shoulder a gentle shake. This first effort does nothing, so I try a second time, speaking a little louder and shaking a little harder. I'm rewarded for my efforts with a grunt.

"A call?" she mumbles, not opening her eyes.

"Yes," I say. "Can you watch Matthew until we get back? I'm not sure how long we'll be gone, but I can get Desi to come and pick him up later this morning if need be."

She sits up and rubs her eyes. "I'm good for the day," she says. She drops her hands into her lap, glances at the alarm clock beside her bed, and smiles at me. "Of course, given the hour and the short notice, this job should probably be paid at triple time."

I smile back at her. "You got it." The girl excels at extortion, and her babysitting money goes into a fund she calls her funny money, money she is saving up to buy herself a car. Hurley and I have argued over this because I feel we should buy her a car, and frankly it would be nice to get rid of the chauffeuring duties I'm constantly having to do. But he is insistent that she earn the money and buy the car herself. So for now, I'm speeding up the process by caving in—willingly and happily—to Emily's attempts to pad her fund.

Emily's smile broadens at my capitulation. "I might get that car before school starts at this rate," she says.

"Indeed, you might," I say, giving her a kiss on the forehead. "Now go back to sleep."

She plops back down, fluffing her pillow beneath her head. I go downstairs, where I find Hurley nuking coffee that was left in the pot from earlier in the day. It won't be gourmet, by any means, but at this hour, just about any coffee will do.

Wordlessly, we fix our coffees in travel mugs and head out, slipping on shoes that are kept by the door. Hurley's car is parked in the driveway. Mine, a midnight-blue hearse, is parked in the street. Without any discussion, we both head for Hurley's car. While seeing a hearse at a death scene shouldn't be too shocking—in fact, it's ironically apropos—the car at times tends to attract attention that I can do without.

As soon as we're settled and underway, I say, "We probably should have iced these coffees instead of nuking them. It's still in the eighties out here."

Our weather for the past week or so has been a blast of furnace-quality heat and dripping humidity. The temps have been well into the nineties, and the humidity has been hovering in the 80th-percentile range. Though some people love this hot weather, it's not my favorite. I come with plenty of natural insulation, and my tolerance of heat is about as good as my tolerance of the tongue-in-cheek Wisconsin state bird: the mosquito. They've been out in force this past week, too, and I have the bites to prove it.

It's a Wednesday night—though technically it's now Thursday morning—and I spent the better part of the past weekend traveling to the land Hurley and I bought right before we tied the knot a few weeks ago, giving up our independence on Independence Day. The land is out in the country; the mosquitos were apparently having some sort of convention out there all weekend, and I was on the menu for every meal. As a result, I now look like I have the measles. It's a small price to pay, however, for moving along our building project. I'm desperate to get into our new home. The house we're living in now is Hurley's, one he bought and lived in for two years before I moved in. Now, with the two of us, two kids, two cats, and a dog in it, it's feeling kind of tight. It also feels like Hurley's house, and I'm eager to have a place to live that is not only roomier, but ours, with no prior history.

Emily and I have tried to fem up the place some, but our efforts have done little to eliminate the overall bachelor pad feel of the place. Apparently, it takes more than some curtains, throw rugs, and a box of tampons in every bathroom to lend a house a feminine air.

The only thing that truly felt like home to me before moving in with Hurley was a small cottage that Izzy had built behind his house. Back when I was married to a local surgeon named David Winston, Izzy was my neighbor. He built a cottage behind his house for his then-ailing mother, Sylvie, but Sylvie rallied after a year and then opted to move out and into senior housing. This happened right around the time my marriage to David went south, along with most of the local geese, after I caught him canoodling with an OR nurse at the local hospital where we both worked at the time. So I moved into Izzy's cottage until I could sort things out, a process complicated by my starting a whole new career, meeting Hurley, getting pregnant, and dealing with the discovery of Hurley's daughter, Emily, who he didn't know existed until two years ago. Her arrival, along with that of her mother, an ex that Hurley discovered wasn't really an ex because she never filed the divorce papers, coincided with me discovering I was pregnant.

For the better part of a year and a half, Izzy's cottage was my home. It was my fortress of solitude, the place where I acquired my fur family of one dog and two cats, the place where I launched my new career, the place where I learned how to be on my own again, the place where I gave birth to my son—literally, since it happened in the bathtub—and raised him on my own for most of his first year. It was small—what realtors euphemistically refer to as cozy—and I'm not, since I stand six feet tall and typically weigh in somewhere between one-seventy and none of your damned business. Considering that I moved into the cottage after living in a McMansion with David, one might think I found it to be a humbling, if not humiliating step down in life. But I never saw it that way. I grew to love the place, and it was one of the few things at that time that I could call my own. The facts that it was next to my old house—offering me ample spying opportunities—and only steps away from my two favorite therapists—Izzy and his life partner, Dom—were bonuses. To be totally honest, my favorite therapists are Ben & Jerry, but Izzy and Dom are a close second and kinder to my hips.

The house David and I once shared burned to the ground not long after I moved out—a whole other story in itself—though it has since been rebuilt. The new house is even bigger, and David still lives there, along with his new wife, Patty Volker, who at one time was our mutual insurance agent. Though the destruction of the house saddened me at first, it seemed fitting after a while. That fire gave me closure. It also gave me a decent little divorce settlement when the insurance check came.

Unfortunately, Sylvie's good health didn't last, requiring her to move back into the cottage. It was a move she didn't accept gracefully, given that it meant not only giving up some of her independence, but living in close proximity to Izzy and Dom. Sylvie doesn't approve of her son's sexual orientation, and having evidence of it in her face every day is something she hasn't taken to very well. She spent the first two months there without bathing, a curious quirk that almost led to Izzy putting her in a home. Then we learned that Sylvie knew I'd delivered Matthew in the bathtub, and in her mind that area was now like sacred ground. She wouldn't stand in it, sit in it, or run water in it. Izzy had to find a local priest to come in and do a special ceremony— one I suspect he made up—in which he "captured" the sacred essence Sylvie thought was in the tub and put it in a mason jar. Sylvie insisted on giving me the jar afterward, and I thought about tossing it out. But some superstitious vestigial corner of my brain wouldn't let me—that and a fear

of what Sylvie would do if she ever asked to see it and discovered I no longer had it.

Since I had to vacate the cottage for Sylvie, moving in
with Hurley was the logical option. But it wasn't an easy decision for three reasons. For starters, my relationship with
Emily was iffy at the time, iffy being a euphemism for a bar-
rel of TNT connected to a short, lit fuse. Her mother died not
long after the two of them showed up on Hurley's doorstep
unannounced, and while I understood Emily's emotional
turmoil—losing the only family she had known for more
than fourteen years, discovering she had a father she'd always thought was dead, and then learning that he was starting a new family with me—her behavior at one point
bordered on frightening. We eventually worked it out with
the help of time, patience, a lot of counseling, and a near-
death experience for Emily. I have grown to love Emily as if
she were my own daughter, but for a while there it was touch
and go.

Another thing that made moving in with Hurley an iffy
prospect was the state of our relationship. He'd asked me to
marry him—several times—and I wanted to. But I couldn't
shake the feeling that the only reason he was asking was because I was pregnant and he felt it was the right and proper
thing to do.

The final complication in our decision to cohabitate was
the four-legged baggage I brought with me. Hoover, who I
found hungry, skinny, and dirty, trying to eat out of a garbage
bin behind a local grocery store, wasn't really an issue. Hurley adores Hoover, and the feeling is mutual. But I also managed to rescue two cats: a gray-and-white kitten I found
abandoned in a Dumpster outside of a convenience store and
decided to name Rubbish, and a black-and-white cat named
Tux that had belonged to a murder victim on a case we investigated two years ago. And Hurley really, really doesn't

like cats. In fact, he's afraid of them, not that he'd admit to it. If I ever had any doubts about whether or not Hurley really loves me, they were eliminated when he agreed to let me move into his house with my cats. It hasn't been an easy adjustment for him, but over time we've managed to achieve a peaceful state of tolerance. This has been challenged of late, however, because Rubbish has started stalking and pouncing on all kinds of things: dust bunnies, shoes, Matthew and his toys, Hoover, Tux, and yes, Hurley. When Rubbish leapt at Hurley's feet from beneath Matthew's bed the other day, I heard my husband scream like a girl one second and swear like a salty sailor the next.

I'm not sure how I became a pet magnet, because I never had any pets before these. My mother is a germaphobe and hypochondriac of the highest order who considers animals of all kinds to be dirty, vermin-ridden sources of contagion. And David was allergic to pet hair, or so he claimed, though I came to doubt this as time went by.

While Hurley and I have managed to work through most of our issues over time, the housing arrangement remains uncomfortable. The solution we came up with was to buy a piece of land just outside of town and build a house on it that will be uniquely, and jointly, ours.

We drive past our new property on our way to the motel, and I gaze out the window longingly at it, imagining how nice the house will be. The property includes a slope of land that runs back from the road for several hundred feet, topping out on a rocky bluff with a forty-foot face. From the top of the bluff, one has a spectacular view of the surrounding countryside, and that's where we plan to build, taking advantage of that view as much as we can. If all goes according to plan, we hope to have it built and be in it in time for the holidays. But if there is one consistency in my life of late, it's that almost nothing goes according to plan.